NO FLAME BUT MINE

By the same author
(A selection from her seventy-eight books)

The Birthgrave Trilogy (The Birthgrave; Vazkor; Son of Vazkor;
Quest for the White Witch)

Novels of Vis (The Storm Lord; Anackire; The White Serpent)

The Flat Earth series (Night's Master; Death's Master;
Delusion's Master; Delirium's Mistress; Night's Sorceries)

Eva Fairdeath

Biting the Sun (Don't Bite the Sun; Drinking Sapphire Wine)

A Heroine of the World

The Paradys Quartet (The Book of the Damned; The Book of the
Beast; The Book of the Dead; The Book of the Mad)

The Venus Quartet (Faces Under Water; Saint Fire;
A Bed of Earth; Venus Preserved)

The Blood of Roses

The Scarabae Blood Opera (Dark Dance; Personal Darkness;
Darkness, I)

When the Lights Go Out

Heart-Beast

Elephantasm

Mortal Suns

White as Snow

Forests of the Night

Nightshades

Red as Blood

The Gorgon

The Unicorn Trilogy (Black Unicorn; Gold Unicorn; Red Unicorn)

The Claidi Journals (Law of the Wolf Tower; Wolf Star Rise;
Queen of the Wolves; Wolf Wing)

Piratica

The Gods Are Thirsty (historical novel)

The Lionwolf Trilogy (Cast a Bright Shadow; Here in Cold Hell)

TANITH LEE

NO FLAME BUT MINE

Book Three of the 'Lionwolf' Trilogy

TOR

First published 2007 by Tor
an imprint of Pan Macmillan Ltd
Pan Macmillan, 20 New Wharf Road, London N1 9RR
Basingstoke and Oxford
Associated companies throughout the world
www.panmacmillan.com

ISBN 978-1-4050-0636-1

1 3 5 7 9 8 6 4 2

A CIP catalogue record for this book is available from
the British Library.

Visit **www.panmacmillan.com** to read more about all our books
and to buy them. You will also find features, author interviews and
news of any author events, and you can sign up for e-newsletters
so that you're always first to hear about our new releases.

For Mavis Haut,
who so often sees to the roots of what I write
while I only swing through the branches

Acknowledgements

All my thanks to those who have contributed inspiration throughout, notably, as so often, my husband and partner John Kaiine.

And my gratitude and appreciation to my editor Peter Lavery and my copy-editor Nancy Webber, for their patience, tenacity and clear vision.

I would also like to acknowledge and extend thanks to the three ladies whose generosity permitted the names of *Lionwolf*'s foremost goddess:

Chilel (Chillel), Winsome, and Toyin (Toiyhin).

Translator's Note

This text has been translated not only into English, but into the English of recent times. It therefore includes, where appropriate, 'contemporary' words such as *downside*, or even 'foreign' words and phrases such as *doppelgänger* or *par excellence*. This method is employed in order to correspond with the syntax of the original scrolls, which themselves are written in a style of their own period, and include expressions and phrases from many areas and other tongues.

As with the main text, names, where they are exactly translatable, are rendered (often) in English, and sometimes both in English and the original vernacular – for example the name/title, *Lionwolf* (*Vashdran* in the Rukarian). Occasionally names are given in a combination of exactly equivalent English plus part of the existing name where it is basically *un*translatable, as with the Rukarian Phoenix, the *Firefex*. Note too perhaps the name *Jemhara*, which is a mix of Rukarian (*Jema*) and Latin (*hara*: hare), resorted to since in the original this second part of her name, which refers to her shape-changing, uses an obscure and ancient scholastic tongue of Ruk Kar Is.

A final point. Among Rukarians to abbreviate or alter the ending of a name may be a sign of affection. But to change or deform the first letter – as with *Pth* for *Zth* – is always a grave insult.

Note on Intervolumens

The three books of the trilogy make up, in the original format, *one* long book, composed of scrolls – here represented as Volumes. The *Intervolumens* are interpolated adventures and developments from other richer sources – since, in the scrolls of Lionwolf, many of these events are detailed sketchily, and in a sort of shorthand.

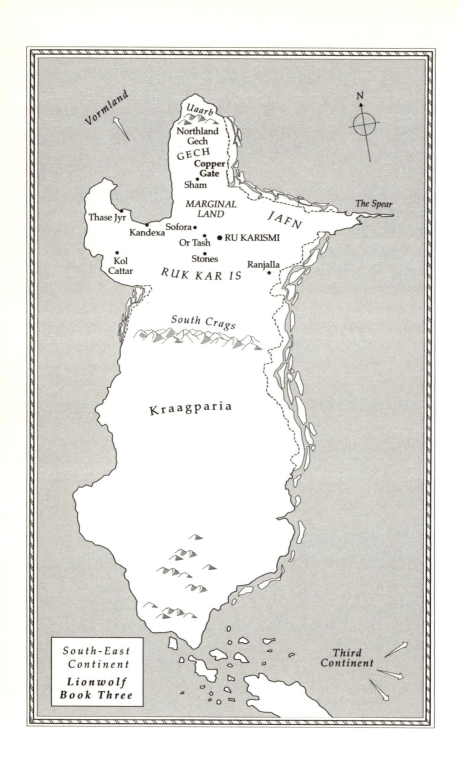

Vormland

Uaarb

Northland
Gech

GECH

Copper
Gate

Sham

MARGINAL
LAND

JAFN

The Spear

Thase Jyr

Kandexa   Sofora •

Or Tash   • RU KARISMI

Stones

Kol
Cattar

Ranjalla

RUK KAR IS

N

South Crags

Kraagparia

Third
Continent

South-East
Continent
Lionwolf
Book Three

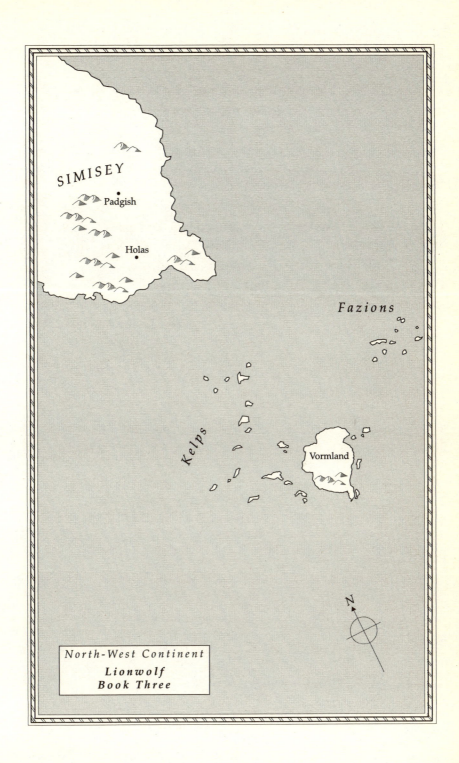

SIMISEY

Padgish

Holas

Fazions

Kelps

Vormland

N

North-West Continent
Lionwolf
Book Three

The One remains, the many change and pass;
Heaven's light forever shines, Earth's shadows fly;
Life, like a dome of many-coloured glass,
Stains the white radiance of Eternity . . .

Percy Bysshe Shelley
Adonais **LII**

Tenth Volume

ICE JEWEL AND HEART OF FIRE

Always are there enemies. Some at you run with knife, some smile at your side. Some you notice not till round your throat their two hands come.

> Inscription found on many male amulets;
> the warding spell is presumably carried
> by the stated facts: Vormlander

ONE

Gold moon sailed green sky. Beneath the two lay the world.

As she stood at her narrow window, the solid frigid sea to one side, and the wrecked city of Kandexa filling the rest of the view, the magician stared unblinking with her sombre eyes. The evening had a look it must often wear. The limpid and beautiful dusk alone seemed capable of change. The ice-imprisoned earth was *stuck*.

Of course there was always the chance of a savage fight. A pall of smoke hung on the city. The settlements of West Villagers and Clever Town had come to blows again.

Jemhara turned towards the door of her room. She sensed, as now she usually did, a human approach.

After a moment feet sounded on the attic stair and next the gentle rap of knuckles.

She did not move. The door opened at a twitch of her will.

A young man stood gaping. Yet all of them knew she could do such things. The people here had established for themselves she was one of the Magikoy, those mages that had been the most powerful, supposedly, in the world. Technically she was not Magikoy and she had never claimed the title for herself. But then too many of them said black-haired Jemhara was once a queen.

The young man cleared his throat.

'Someone has come to Paradise, Highness,' he announced.

She nodded gravely.

Inside herself the little involuntary leap of her heart was instantly squashed. Persons did arrive at the barricaded and stupidly named zones inside Kandexa. At first, on being told of

3

any newcomer she had frozen in expectancy. But it was never him.

The boy went on, 'The mageia says can you come and see to it?'

The lesser mageia was a sensible woman.

Following the boy down from the attic, showing the stair for them in the gathering dark with sorcerously lit glims, Jemhara heard the echo of words in her head.

A man is on the road to you. A man like a tower of ice with eagle's eyes.

Only one surely could be defined in that way: Thryfe, Magikoy mage of the Highest Order.

A dead god had given her the news in a kind of vision. But he was a god of wickedness and destruction.

Oh, she had still believed it. For a while. Most do when offered hope. And it sparkled before her like some image in a scrying mirror. Then, just as the dark now fell on the city, dark had fallen over her dream. She had asked herself simply how she could ever have credited a promise so obviously flawed. For though Thryfe was her only love, to him she was a despised and hated thing, causer of his guilt and utter despair.

The girl was seated cross-legged on the floor. She looked about eighteen or so, but *within* her face much older. A slender purple scar vividly marred her forehead; her skin otherwise was creamy. Ragged brown hair had been dyed green but the dye had now mostly grown out. A witch?

From her natural colouring she seemed to be from the Ruk. But the dye indicated the wild sorceresses of Gech in the far north.

Aglin, the older mageia of Paradise, was tending the fire-basket, lighting a couple of lamps by means of a nod and putting on water to boil.

Jemhara saw that the girl seated on the floor watched this with mild interest, calm but at odds with everything, as if she had given up either resisting or asking real questions.

4

'Here I am,' said Jemhara.

'Here you are, Jema. And here's this one.'

Jemhara looked again at the girl. 'How are you called?'

'Azulamni. But he called me Beebit. He said I'd have to answer to that or I'd be killed. And now I'm used to it.'

Jemhara raised her brows. She was familiar with strange coercions from her own youthful past.

'Why was that?'

'After the reivers came here, those years back.'

'You mean to Kandexa, in the time of Vashdran?' To speak the name of the dead god who had made war on the Ruk burned Jemhara's mouth, and left a bitter psychic taste. It was he too who had spoken to her in the vision.

'Kandexa surrendered to the reivers, the only city that did,' remarked Aglin to herself. 'Thought it'd save them but the buggers smashed the place anyway. Scum, like all the mixed armies of Vashdran the Lionwolf.' She stared at the water over the fire. 'Watched pot boil!' It boiled at once.

'I was hiding up in the roof,' said the girl now called Beebit. 'My father said go up, you'll be safe, and because I'm limber, I could. But they found him. I heard them murder him. Then I came down, so they caught me.' She was matter-of-fact. 'One of them, he was a Kelp, he stank of fish, he threw me down and raped me. The rest of them got bored and went off. There were other nicer things and women. But then the Kelp saw how I was, what I can do. He didn't hurt me much, he was only small. I'd served bigger.'

Aglin brought Jemhara wine and hot water with a stick of spice. The mageia murmured, 'Daddy had put her into the game. A cunning whore at twelve years.'

'So old?' said Jemhara.

Hearing this, the girl glanced at them and suddenly she laughed. The mageia and Jemhara were both surprised. Laughter was not what they expected.

'Look,' said Beebit.

Then she lay down on her back, not using her arms to help her, and slowly and evenly put up both her legs until her feet

5

rested flat on the floor either side of her head. Then she stood up once more, weight only on the soles of her feet, bringing her head and torso round and under and out in a sort of leisurely backward somersault. Still grinning she sat on the floor again and crossed her legs, this time with a foot on each of her shoulders.

'See, Highness?' she said to Jemhara.

'Honey bones,' said the mageia.

Jemhara nodded. 'And the Kelp liked that?'

'He *loved* it. So he hid me and fed me, and he brought me green dye. That sallow Rukar skin, he said, that'll pass for Gech, if you change your hair. He said he had met a Gech witch once. She was like that. Then I travelled with Vashdran's army. I soon learned the other languages, Kelp, Vorm, Jafn. I'm quick to learn.'

'The Gech mageias have magic,' said Jemhara. 'Were you never asked?'

'I said my magic was how I could do the things with my body I can do.'

They paused in silence then, each drinking the hot watered wine.

Outside somewhere in the ruin there was shouting, but far away. Dogs barked but left off.

Aglin sat in one chair and Jemhara in the other, and they gazed at Beebit sitting on the ground with her feet on her own shoulders.

'So then?' said the mageia. It seemed she hadn't heard all yet.

'Don't you want,' said Beebit, 'to know if I saw Vashdran?'

'Did you?' said the mageia.

'Now and then. Never close. He was very beautiful. He was golden, and his hair was red as sun-up and they said his eyes were blue – but in war they went the red of blood. He could do what I can – I mean he could *walk* straight up the sides of walls and trees, up the hard ice. He'd ridden into a battle standing on the back of a chariot-lion.' Her face was dull again and she said all this impassively. 'But I never liked men, even gods. Only my father. He was always kind.'

6

'He made you a harlot,' said Aglin flatly.

'Oh, that. He was a harlot too. Since nine years. It's a profession. I'm not ashamed and nor was he.'

'And the Kelp who saved your life?' asked Jemhara.

Without any expression the girl replied, 'I swore to myself I'd kill him first chance Fate gave me. But it didn't find me, that happy day. Never mind it. The Magikoy saw to him and all the rest at Ru Karismi, City of Kings. They unleashed the great magic weapons of power and the White Death came. The whole enemy horde – gone to dust and powder. Even the Lionwolf, I think, for no one saw him since.'

'Someone told you this?' said Jemhara. Her flesh prickled with silver quills under the skin. 'Because you had got away from the Kelp and so avoided the White Death, which none present escaped.'

'No, lady,' said Beebit. A tiny and impertinent smile crinkled her mouth. 'I was *there*. I saw it *happen*. It was like noise without noise and a lightning flash that went on and on. And then – just powder and dust, and me standing in the midst, by the baggage carts where the women were. Only no carts left, no women or beasts. Even the chain he'd put on my ankle and the peg in the ground – not even those. My clothes were all lightninged off me too – but not my hair.'

Jemhara spoke very softly.

'And the scar on your face?'

'That? A man threw a knife at me when I was fifteen. The dad killed him. That's all *that* is.'

A second moon rose, but only a thin crescent. The third did not rise and the first was already down. On the nights of strongest triple moonrise – two moons at least at or nearly full and the third not less than half – Kandexa bleakly resembled a scorched skull smouldering fires, where people came and went with rapid unease, like lizards darting over stones. But tonight was not so violently lighted. A lot could go on in the dark.

Beyond the city, the humped old orchards of frozen fruit had been burned down during the war, along with anything else potentially useful to the enemy. Years' snows had covered these places. Now the approach was a sheet of white. Anything which moved *there* even on a night of thin moons showed at once.

It must then be a tall man, tall and lean, casting a lean long shadow.

Behind him his footsteps were imprinted in the softer snow. They stretched off for a vast distance, hours off, before different terrain hid them. Apparently he had walked a great way, which for a man alone was not so usual. Sometimes one noted a slight discrepancy to the left side of the prints – an intermittent halting in the left leg.

Kandexa had no gates. That was, she had no external ones. All her fortifications and barriers were inside. They ringed in the rival zones of the city.

The man who walked passed into the city.

Most of the thoroughfares now wound between the settlements, for most of the larger roads had been blocked off two or three years before.

As he moved through a narrow alley then, that once had been part of Kandexa's Royal Road, he was spied from two storeys above.

'Who's *he*?'

'Some fool.'

'His garments are good; look at that cloak.'

'He strides as if proud of himself.'

'Too big for his boots to carry.'

The low voices sizzled like ice-snakes.

Certainly the stranger could not have heard them . . .

Nor the sudden twang of a dart-bow.

The dart, of ice-hardened black flint, speared down and caught the stranger between his shoulder blades. The three men rose to their feet on the roof, waiting for the idiot to topple over.

But he did not.

'You mucked your shot.'

'Never – *never*! You saw – it hit him square—'

'Well, he's seen us now – Hey!' one of them shouted over into

8

the alley. 'Fancy us, do you? Then we'll come down and join you.'

They swarmed along a rope kept ready and landed in the compressed space. The stranger had not moved. He stood there, and the dart lay on the street. It had struck him – yet missed?

The biggest man, first to reach the ground, slung his knife with all his weight behind it. It too struck the tall man, this time in the heart. Then like the flint it shivered and let go, dropping back to earth with a *thunk*. Bloodless.

'He's mage-spelled.'

Yes, it seemed he must be. There had been the faintest gilded quiver over the air as the blade touched him. Except, sensibly, they had put that down to a trick of the limited moonlight.

'What do you want?' he said. The voice was compact, and primed with power.

They faltered. Only the big one said, 'Don't try to lord it over *us*. No lords *here*. They died when the scum-horde came.'

'I know.'

'Then know *this*: whatever you are, we can take you.'

The stranger turned and walked away from them.

That was all.

Each of the three men stood dumbfounded. Then the big one threw the paralysis off. He charged after the tall stranger and, from a few feet behind him, lion-like leapt up on his back.

It was as if he had jumped on to a disc of cold fire that spun him and whirled him down, and as he met the hard ice of the street it seemed softer and far sweeter than the wide shoulders of the one he had attacked. Through a pair of just-broken teeth the big man mourned, 'He is a mage.'

The other two faltered – then ran away.

The mage, if so he was, walked on. No limp was obvious now. He turned out of the alley that had been part of Royal Road, and moved between crushed buildings. Here and there a stray cat, by now adapted to the outdoor cold, its fur long and abrasive as wire, glared with glacial eyes. They had been beloved, silk-coated pets only three years before. But the walking man knew very well how quickly all things were by now educated to adapt. Five centuries of Winter had seen to it.

Beyond a kind of tunnel of collapsed masonry he found himself at the gate of one of the several zones of Kandexa. Inside the ill-formed walls, lamps showed in darkness much as the eyes of the cats had done.

Five men now came out from a house and frowned at him. They wore the mail of Ru Karismi, the deceased capital of the Ruk. And over the gate drooped a stained banner once the crimson and silver of Ru Karismi's colours.

'This is Wise-Home,' said one of the men. 'We don't welcome aliens.'

They had been drinking, something never brewed in a still. The walker looked at them, and through the muffle of his hooded garment they glimpsed a pair of eyes.

'Shush,' said one of the five to the other four. 'Can't you see?'

'What's to see?'

'Highness,' said the fifth man, 'my father was from the capital. I believe—' The stranger did not speak. The fifth man asked in crumbled tones, 'You are Magikoy?'

'No.'

'But sir – *sir* – I've heard of you – my father, he sent me away just before the Vashdran horde besieged Ru Karismi, before the White Death brought down plague into the city— But I'd heard him talk of you, though never myself had I seen you— He would say, If Thryfe had been here none of this—'

'I am not Thryfe,' said the stranger at the gate of Wise-Home to the refugee from Ru Karismi.

'Forgive me, sir.'

'My forgiveness is only a question.'

The men muttered. The fifth man said, 'Ask it.'

'You mistook me for one of the Magikoy. Perhaps others of the order are here in Kandexa?'

All five stared at him.

Another of them said, '*Here*? Do you think we'd live like this, like frozen rats, if we had Magikoy to help us? They're dead.

They died too in the White Death. Serve them right. It was their fault, their filthy weapons— *Curse them.*'

The stranger appeared unimpressed. He said, 'You know of none, then.'

The fifth man, he who had been tender almost with admiring love, spat on the snow. 'Get on your way, whoever – whatever – in Hell you are.'

Shadows moved, refolded.

The stranger was gone.

Jemhara had been for a moment distracted. She had felt something like a bird's great wing brush coldly over her hair, the shoulders of her cloak.

She did not turn to see. The sensation might indicate several events, perhaps ominous, but none of them occurred inside the room. Instead the scene there had turned to stone, the contortionist girl seated on the floor, Aglin sitting forward, eyes wide.

To Beebit Jemhara said, 'Do you know then how it was you survived at Ru Karismi?'

'No, Highness.'

'Had you had some dealings with the Magikoy beforehand?'

'No. How would I? I was the Kelp's slave and trech, and chained up otherwise. Even when I had to walk behind the army – their precious Gullahammer – I was on a chain with one or two others. Not every woman wanted to keep the army company.'

'A mystery then,' said Jemhara silkenly. 'Or else you're lying.'

Beebit did not react.

'Or *else*,' said Aglin, 'something proofed her against death. I heard a story that some of the men survived too – a handful compared to the whole huge horde of them – thirty, fifty, sixty men. Some witch had done it. That's all I ever heard.'

Beebit finished her drink and put the cup down. She swung her feet careless from her shoulders, stood up on her hands and walked round the fire-basket. From this position she said, 'I came back to Kandexa to find my father's bones, if I can. Bury them nicely. Then I'll work at my trade.'

'Your whoring,' nodded the mageia.

'Just so. All places need a good whore.'

Jemhara, despite herself, gave a low laugh. Aglin joined her. 'She's got the right of it there.'

Jemhara said, 'But why then did you seek my friend the mageia?'

'Because of my daughter,' said Beebit, lilting over to her feet. 'You see, ladies, I thought she might have the magic power.'

'Oh, why's that?' crisply asked Aglin. 'What can she do?'

'Nothing, yet.'

'I suppose she is still young,' said Jemhara.

'About two years.'

'Two years,' snapped Aglin. 'What can they do at that age but squeak and shriek and fall over?'

Beebit smiled her impertinent smile. 'Shall I call her in? I left her in the street—'

'You unfeeling cow!' yelled Aglin, darting up. 'A kitty of two years left in the cold alley – the gods know what'll have happened—'

'Oh, it's fine as sunlight, lady. Just you see.'

Beebit flowed to the window, lifted aside the heavy leather hanging, and sent out a fluting whistle.

'Calls her like a dog too—'

'Gently, Aglin. Wait and see.' Jemhara had also got to her feet.

The three women stood, once more in silence, and there came the light patter of feet running along the passage beyond the room. The door opened and through it stepped another young girl, about the same age as Beebit, although her colouring was, or had been made to be, rather different. Her skin was a light smoky fawn, while from a central parting her long thick curling hair was, on her left side, pale brown, on the right side black as coal. Jemhara noted that her eyes too were unalike, which must surely be natural. Her *left* eye however was the dark one, shining black, the right eye a pale clear hazel.

'This isn't any daughter of yours,' said Aglin. 'Unless you're a great deal older than you look.'

'It's that *she* is a great deal *younger* than *she* looks,' said Beebit.

12

Aglin fizzled on the boil and Jemhara held up her hand to quieten her.

'What is your name, little girl?' said Jemhara to the newcomer.

'Azulamni,' she said. She had a very beautiful voice. Indeed, apart from her weird colours, she was strikingly beautiful.

'Your mother's previous name.'

'She named me for her past,' said the girl.

Jemhara said, 'And who was your father? Was it the Kelpish man?'

Beebit threw back her head and wailed with laughter.

'*Him*? He fired his bow without arrows. Most of them do. Or, to be fair, maybe I have no target.'

'This one time you did. And you do *know* the father,' Jemhara said.

Beebit stopped laughing.

'Her *father*, lady, was a *woman*.'

He had travelled for a vast while, so it seemed to him. And yet his intellect knew it had not been so extended a journey.

That night he went away, he had seen the Stones, those immeasurable, indecipherable obelisks, looming at the stars. Two half-moons stood over them like guardian spirits. And the Stones, which had always taken colour after dark, flooding with blue, grey, silver, rose and white – at the last with brilliant green – were unlit and empty. He left them behind him yet felt for a space a kind of leash around his ribs, paying out from their core. It was not detaining him, rather going with him. Then he forgot it for it was only an illusion. It was she, the woman he had loved, then hated, then come to love again, it was *she* who had cured him of his despair and woken him back into the pragmatic agony of life.

Thryfe, magus of the Highest Order of the Magikoy, had stridden over the lambent desolation of the snows.

He had turned his back on almost everything that upheld his former existence. Rigorously trained in the occult Insularia at Ru

Karismi, he had become the warden of the royal court, disliking his post, wanting to serve mankind not the engoldened hollowness of kings. At the final test, when the horde of the Lionwolf's Gullahammer swept in to destroy the Ruk, Thryfe had been unaware, knotted with Jemhara in the throes of oblivious lust. For this mistake of his he had not forgiven himself, or her. The self-dealt torture he subsequently underwent she had freed him from. Only after he had once more driven her away did he grasp her innocence of all wrong in his affairs. And – more terribly – her genuine *power*. For she was as much a Magikoy as any that the Ruk had trained, her natural gifts polished by adversity – the trite truth of the School of Life. And, of love.

Ru Karismi, the Ruk, were lost by then. The Lionwolf too, and all his legions.

The steel-white snows Thryfe had trodden had covered huddles of ruins, abandoned villages and little towns, steads where wild elephant fed among the neglected runnels of dormant grain.

The mage mirror, the oculum, which Thryfe had rebuilt in his house at Stones, had been able to show him all Jemhara's past, but nothing of her present. Armed with her own new-minted powers, had she veiled herself from him deliberately? At first he thought that must be so, or that her pain at leaving him – for she had surely proved she loved him more than her life – had wiped the superior scrying glass with ink.

Now he began to think that some other mad force perhaps abroad on the ice-locked earth had got between them.

He could therefore only use deduction to seek her.

At first he went towards the small city-town of Sofora.

Jemhara had grown to her twelfth or thirteenth year in some impoverished village not far from there. But of the village he could find no trace. He entered the town compelled by aversion more than will.

Sofora it was which had, on viewing the advance of Lionwolf's horde, sent word to the capital. *They are too many.* And later the perilous warning: *There is ONE among them . . .*

14

Not much remained after the attentions of those that were *too many*, or that One.

A single magical cannon of Magikoy design lay smashed below the walls. Neither landscape nor weather had been able to absorb it. Instead it had become like those curiosities of the Jafn coasts, their Thing meeting places, where some object was frozen in ice – a mammoth, a pylon or a bizarre ship. The dragon head of the cannon's mouth snarled its verdigris jaws. It had never been fired. He had learned, those psychic cannon which had been used at Thase Jyr had blown up and helped obliterate the city.

Further off a parcel of bones were inside the snow. He could not see but only sense them. Some strong mage then had died there.

After Sofora he wandered back and forth, searching.

As she had done if he had known, and in some manner he did, Thryfe came to settlements where men remained, and where needed he helped them. He rebuilt by sorcery their walls and homes, healed them, secured their husbandry and assisted their beasts. Perhaps curiously they took him only for a talented mage, some minor intelligent magician with no one else left to care for. In Jemhara's case as he had learned, she had been instantly taken for a Magikoy. This amused him. He was both glad and sorry, paternally proud of her, and ashamed of his own descent – not from pride but because it showed him, he thought, he had been too sure of himself in the past.

There were nights seated in the open against some scarp or rock, protected from the cold only by his craft, when he dreamed of her. These dreams were never sexual. Sexuality, now he had again accepted it as inherent in him, lashed him with its thorns and fires during his conscious hours. Asleep Jemhara was his mother, the young woman he had as a boy seen torn apart and eaten by a wolf. Or else she was his daughter. A little child, he led her by the hand, astonished by that hand's smallness, while she looked up at him with shining, happy eyes.

She is what I missed. All that I missed. Or never allowed myself to have.

The Magikoy had no stricture against the sexual act. Even union was possible, providing it never clashed with the role of magus. Celibacy had been Thryfe's choice. He had fought ferociously with his own self to achieve it. Letting celibacy go he was bereft. He no longer knew himself or what he was. He had never been, he supposed, what he reckoned.

Aside from that the Magikoy were mostly gone. The White Death had proved impartial in its sentence.

Only his idea that he, had he returned to Ru Karismi at the proper time as he had meant to, might have prevented use of the pan-destructive weapons – only this still nagged at him. Yet even there he was no longer certain. For who *was* he to assume he alone might have altered destiny? If the weapons had remained unleashed, instead Vashdran, that demonic bi-bred of god and mortal, would have sacked the city and razed it, exactly like Sofora and the rest.

Thryfe's physical search continued. Which way then to seek?

North lay the Marginal Land; within and beyond that the lairs of the Olchibe nation, what was left of it. Further north Gech opened, long spoiled from ancient wars. Ice swamps, mountains and ice desert tumbled eventually back into an ice-plated sea. East was Jafn territory. But again Jafn was depopulated after the Death. All north and east had joined with the Lionwolf to consume the Ruk, and so perished.

Thryfe had on his travels nevertheless heard some talk of a new Ruk capital in the far west. Kl Ctaar it seemed to be called: *Phoenix Risen from Ash*. He was ignorant of where it lay precisely. He tended to think it a legend quickly invented to salve the horror of aftermath. One of the royal line too was said to be in charge there, and that also convinced Thryfe it was a fable. All the kings of Ru Karismi, one way or another, were *unrisen* ashes.

He wondered now and then if Jemhara had made her way southward towards the unknown country of Kraagparia. There every man, woman and child had thaumaturgic ability . . . it was said. Elder writings spoke of the Kraag but no one from the northern end of the continent, reportedly, had met with them for centuries. The Kraag dictum was that reality was unreal, unreality real. Maybe such a thought would have tempted Jemhara as she had come to be.

One night there was a blizzard. The wind raced by visible as silver lances. Thryfe strode through this wind, which widely parted either side of him.

His power was yet very mighty. Reminded, he sat humbly on the ground with the torrent searing past, smoothed the ice beneath the snow to a primitive mirror and gazed into it. 'Show me her and where she is.'

Where the oculum, Magikoy master-glass, had failed him, after an hour the ice sheet obeyed.

It had needed only something simple.

Almost a year back Thryfe had dreamed of the Lionwolf. The creature was a beautiful and couth young man, a sun god. Yes, a god of the sun, for Thryfe himself saw as much, and in the dream told Vashdran so. This delusion Thryfe had since filed far off in his mind. It was illustrative of illusory things, and irrational. And yet in moments of inspiration it returned to him.

Now too it had done so. And for a second a golden-red flicker stirred in the ice-glass.

Only for a second even so. And the picture of Jemhara standing at the centre of a small dark orb had faded. Yet he knew by then where he could find her. The blizzard flagged as he turned due west, towards the coastal junk-heap of Kandexa.

'No two human female things can make a baby.'

'Lady mageia, they can, and they did.'

'It was your crap of a Kelp,' grated Aglin.

'Never. He'd lost his interest in me long before, gone off with some other girl. He kindly told me he kept me alive as he might have a use for me after the war was won – and he didn't want to see me killed after all the joy I'd given him.'

'Maybe he didn't,' said Jemhara.

'Am I to care? He still kept me fettered too. Except . . . one evening, as the army drew near the capital Ru Karismi . . . that was odd. He went off to his other bint, gods help her, and he forgot to chain me up. I pretended the chain was locked tight, of course. I was thinking I might get away. But then, she came by.'

'She?' Even the exasperated Aglin had lowered her voice.

'Well, I'd seen her in the distance. Half the men in the war camp had fucked her. That was sure. Well, they said so, you know what men are like. But they said that Vashdran wanted her as well. Just wanted and went without. He'd ride into a battle without armour, laughing. They said the only time any man saw him tremble was if she was by.'

'*She.*'

'She drifted over the ground like a black unfrozen leaf. I saw one once, in old Kandexa before. It fell from a richman's hot-house door. A black leaf off a fig tree. Like that. I *had* seen her in the distance, the way I'd seen the Lionwolf. At first I thought she painted herself all over to seem so dark. But – it was real.'

'The Kraag say,' Jemhara murmured, 'what is unreal *is* real.'

'She was *black*,' said Beebit. She shut her eyes for the fraction of a second. 'Only not – inside.'

'The Jafn peoples have a god or hero who was black,' said the mageia surprisingly. 'Only the inside of his mouth was red like a man's. And the balls of his eyes were white – and his teeth.'

'And she was like that. But inside her – I mean, in *there*. Like a dark pink rose.'

Hushed, the women now. This silence was unlike the others.

Beebit's daughter-if-she-was seemed unworried by Beebit's words. She had, the girl, a smooth and almost emotionless face. There was truly a look of something not wholly ordinary about her; even if her hair and eyes had been normal and her skin pale, this look would remain.

Beebit was remembering, and now she told only a little of it. The black woman was called Chillel, and she came walking quietly through the huge camp, where men turned always to stare at her. Beebit saw her draw nearer and nearer, until she was crossing among the carts. If a man had stepped out and spoken to Chillel of wanting her, she would have gone away with him at once. This was what she did. She had apparently told a kind of parable about herself. She said she was a cup the gods had made and filled. Whoever wanted might drink from the cup. But tonight no man approached her. Their minds perhaps were all on the important battle soon to come, the jewelled capital bursting with riches. If they went with any woman tonight it would have to be a more average one. Nobody else was near the place where Beebit had been tethered or rather left *un*tethered. Suddenly Beebit, not knowing she would, had got up.

'It was never that she was looking at me,' said Beebit in the mageia's room; 'she wasn't aware of me at all. Her eyes were far away. But I looked at *her*. You couldn't *not* look at *her*.'

Beebit's life, she said, had made her discount all men but her father – the only one who had not molested, bought or raped her. But now and then she had made love with women, usually her fellow harlots.

Chillel drew level with Beebit, and only then she turned, as if Beebit had called out to her, which the girl would never have dared to do. 'Perhaps,' Beebit observed, 'my *look* called out to her. Her beautiful eyes fixed on my face. They were like the night sky, blackness and stars. She said, Is it that you want me? What could I say? I shook all over and stammered, Yes. Then I am yours, she said. And held out her hand to me.' Stunned by memory Beebit paused again. She thought of the texture of the hand of Chillel – silken, slender, not soft, more like a wonderful weapon of some sort, sheathed in costly material. Beebit finished, 'We went into one of the little tents. Two Gech girls had put it up then gone off with some Jafn. I didn't think they might come back. They didn't until later. It was over by then.'

She lowered her eyes.

This censored account left out the amazing act which had taken place between herself and the goddess – she could be nothing else – Chillel.

And the act was made amazing not only by its extreme delight, its sensual gentleness and ultimate orgasmic delirium, but by the fact that Chillel too proved to be herself able to manipulate her own limbs as Beebit could. Of course, to a goddess, such a knack must always be available.

Afterwards Beebit had seen their joining over and over in her mind. Yet from the strangest vantage, as if she had left her flesh in the seizure of pleasure and watched from the tent's low ceiling. They had lain forward on their ribs and forearms, heads held upright, almost in the pose of lions, but hands clasped and mouths fused. The rest of their bodies had risen like the tails of two snakes. Above them their torsos and their limbs arched, met and twined, until their loins could also meet in a perfect and irresistible momentum.

'My spirit,' said Beebit in a whisper, 'came out of me. When I came back to myself, she was gone.'

The fire flickered. The mageia spoke to it and it steadied.

Beebit did not speak. Instead it was Azulamni who matter-of-factly said, 'My mother screwed no one else. Not long after, the Lionwolf's Gullahammer reached the big city. The Death happened. Eight months on I was born.'

Beebit brightened. 'I was in a village by then miles to the west. I was already wending home here, but I got too large. The villagers took me in; there were only a handful of them. I had two days and a night over her. They wondered, as I could do such clever things with my joints and spine, why I had such a time birthing, but I did. And she came out already with two-colour hair and her eyes unlike, and then they were frightened. Rather than drive me off *they* ran away from their village. I could see them up on a snow-hill, hunkering there, moaning. So as soon as I could I tied the baby on my back and went away. The journey took about two months. By then she was already walking, and talking to me. In a pair of years she's got to be what she is. I'm not bothered. What can you expect if a female god gets a baby on a woman? She'd have to be special. She can do all my contortions too, but that's nothing to what maybe she *can* do. And so I thought the mageia here might train her for magic, or you, Highness, since you were kind enough to look in.'

In Jemhara's vacant attic room, the moon-skimped darkness showed little. A cat might have seen: a mattress animal with rough furs; a table of intricate mosaic found in the ruins and brought to her, on which lay a piece of mirror for scrying, a goblet, some sticks and a tiny knife. A small hearth was blackened from fires. A peg jutted out of the wall near the window. Here hung another gown, this one of darned wool. Something else hung down by a ribbon. It was a twig formed disconcertingly like a hand of too many fingers.

A temple of Ranjal, the Rukarian goddess of wood, had given Jemhara the twig when she had been going to Ru Karismi. Although she finished the journey in her shape-shift of a black hare, the twig had remained with her. It had its own peculiar power, and helped her find Thryfe in his cell of self-torture below the city. She had kept the twig, naturally.

Nevertheless, can a twig be a hand? Can a hand listen?

The hand of Ranjal listened.

A faint pollen-like glow settled on its western edges.

Slowly the twig rotated on its ribbon. The many fingers pointed.

About half a mile off at the west end of Kandexa, the Magician Thryfe was standing by another barricade. *This* ramshackle haunt of the West Villagers was licking its wounds after today's defeat by Clever Town. Half the sheep had been stolen and seventeen men were hurt, six more dead. Soot and burning lingered on the night air.

The man with the badly splinted broken arm spat at Thryfe, but the spit bounced off which gave them pause.

'He's some mage.'

'Hey you, can you mend bones?'

'Yes,' said Thryfe. 'But I charge a fee.'

'Then you're no true mage. How much do you want, you bastard?'

'Tell me which settlement here has the Magikoy woman.'

Sly and uncomfortable they started away and grunted among themselves like badgers.

It had been plain enough everywhere here that most of them knew such a woman was in their minced city of zones. Envious of the group which had her, the rest refused to tell.

Thryfe mused on the eccentricity of the *non*-human thing that also masked her whereabouts from him. Even though he had been able to fathom she was at Kandexa, once arrived some type of uncanny tangle hid her again and more completely. He now sensed, he thought, an intelligence withdrawn and scheming, yet primal, nearly instinctual.

The fellow with the broken bone stepped forward again. 'Here's my arm. See to it, and I'll take you over there myself.'

Perhaps it was a bluff; the man was chuckling scornfully when Thryfe put both his hands on the mess of the arm. The chuckle became a scream. The break had been bad, a shattering. Thryfe pushed energy through the splinters of bone, realigned them, adjusted the splint, caught the man as he pitched forward in a dead faint. Thryfe handed him back to his mates.

They remarked bemusedly on the heat the arm gave off, admired the splint and leered at Thryfe, deciding to be friends.

'Well?' he said.

'She's with that herd at Paradise. Across the city eastward, the lower section. Black-haired piece – er, lady. They say she was a queen once. They say she can change into a hare.'

Thryfe had gone.

The east had been clearly marked, another moon risen there, this one thin as a child's nail.

He had noted in several spots before the fading of either fear of or respect for mages, even the Magikoy. Those few years in the past it would have been unthinkable. The world had been altered. Only the endless snows were changeless.

The endless snows—

It was at that moment, passing beneath the ruin of a tumbled tower, that Thryfe heard the ominous groan of shifting ice. The noise was overtaken instantly by a deathly crunch, as if some more enormous bone had broken in the crooked arm of the tower.

He flung up the shield of his power with less than a second to spare. From above him blocks of snow and stone cascaded to the street. He watched the avalanche, a falling wall of white that missed only the hollow space which surrounded him with its shimmering bubble. The falling wall hit the earth and began once again to build itself upward.

Within a single minute, Thryfe found himself inside a cold chimney. The snow had imprisoned him – yes and totally, for now one extra gush of white slammed down to shut the chimney's upper opening.

Thryfe stood immobile. He heard, dully now through the chimney's sides, the rumble of some other subsidence along the street.

All settled.

The Magikoy Master gathered himself. He would speak certain words of release, and send a surge of might against the incarcerating snow.

He spoke the words, and the pale prison shone; he sent the surge, and saw the snow-wall crack to the pattern of a spider-web. But that was all.

Again he uttered the mantra. Again he thrust the spear of mental strength into the snow. Now not even a crack resulted. The first webbed crack was healing with a skin of ice. The pallid luminosity went out. He could hear the slow hard beating of his heart. No other thing.

TWO

Far north of Kandexa, beyond the northern head of the southern continent, over the sea now black, now green, plated with scales like pearl, past the lands of reiving Vorms and Kelps and Fazions, westward and northward still: the new continent lay behind its aprons of ice. The landscape rose there to tall hills and mountains, columned with forests like black glass chiming with cryotites, and albino birds that piped but never sang. Some days gosands flew over, long necks stretched, chanting in their unearthly language to the sky. Across the frozen plains below tigers sprinted, shadow-striped white pelts hiding them, but at a certain angle the fur flushing pastel amber – so they seemed to vanish, reappear, vanish again. The Jafn pioneers had never learned their name. They called then lionets, the nearest creature to them being, perhaps, Jafn lions.

Despite the magicality of the pelts, obviously they were also invaluable as covering.

Today, even before the sun had risen, Arok went out with ten of his men to hunt lionet.

Arok's men had initially been composed of the five warriors who remained with the Holasan-garth, and those fishermen and whalers who joined them on the chancy voyage north.

In the time since landfall, the younger ones had grown up and some of the older ones died. Compared with the numbers the Jafn Holas had boasted in the past they were a meagre crew, but Arok did not carp about it.

Directly behind Arok's chariot rode one of the more recent warriors. He was unlike the rest. Fenzi, son to a Holas fisher and his woman, was black as the hero Star Black. He had grown up too in these three years to be a man with the physique and mind of seventeen or eighteen. His father, who like Arok had cutched the fabulous Chillel in the Lionwolf's war camp, and so survived the White Death, seemed happy enough for Arok to favour Fenzi.

That Arok's own black son had been stolen by Vormish raiders was Arok's reason for making this unconscionable voyage at all. Then, virtually in the hour they sighted the second continent, Nirri, Arok's wife, informed him she was again with child. He had acted great surprise and elation. The elation was real but not the surprise. A Jafn ghost who had travelled some way with them on the ship had already foretold the pregnancy. The ghost had warned too this second child would not be made like ebony. Nor had he been. Birthed, he was a fair-skinned boy with white hair like Arok's own, and many other Jafn. He was well formed, the usual kind of offspring any Jafn father would celebrate. And Arok did so, and Nirri loved the boy. He was an infant still, not much more than a year in age, and maturing normally, that was *slowly*.

In a moment of strange inspiration Arok had named him for the helpful ghost: Athluan.

Reaching this new country all of them deemed it enough like their own sloughed southern continent. The terraced mountains and frozen forests were only like an extravagant reinterpretation.

Probably some of them mourned the land they had left. This replacement was interesting and good enough, but incapable of matching up.

Just as Arok, admit it though he never must, found his second son.

Did she think like that too, Nirri? He was unsure. Women kept their secrets. Best let them. They were more foolish yet also more wise than men.

Leaving their ship they went inland, away from the bleak shores which, in the other country, they had never much avoided. They entered this upland of high plains between hills and mountains. At that season Nirri was very big with the child and another couple of women the same. Everyone was tired, the success of having got here making them lax. Deer and edible rodents abounded. Having made a camp they stayed. After the children were born, they did not move on.

A garth rose on the slope, constructed with wood from the surrounding forests. They made too a Holas House, and set the traditional sword over the high door, horizontal for peace.

The land was empty of other people, and benign to them, as if pleased to receive visitors. God they thought had assisted, rewarding courage and persistence.

Frequently they said, the males of the garth, that when the hour was right they would set out again to explore and to search.

And Nirri? She who if truth were told had brought them all to this place through her determination to find her first lost son? The vision had been hers of a black woman riding over the sky on a sled drawn by a black sheep, while the woman's hair was fire-red – Nirri had declared this an omen. They would locate black Dayadin if only they would sail after his abductors. Nirri had then once or twice looked up at Arok, the new, pale, ordinary child at her breast, when exploration of the new land was mooted. She said, 'When he's grown a little. He isn't like our other one – this boy can't become a man in only three or four years. May we wait, sir,' – for always she was respectful, save in moments of lust or supreme stress – 'until then?'

The chariots ploughed through the softer top snow.

Tiger-lionets had been sighted north of the garth, two of them, or so the Holas scout reported.

The true lions of the chariots, elder beasts but vital, leapt along the slopes and up the hillocks. They never objected to cornering their lionet cousins. Nor did the lionets ever seem inclined to be charming to the lions. Some months ago on a similar hunt a tiger had sprung and grabbed one of the chariot-lions, killed it.

Lionet meat was foul to human taste; it was that of a meat-eater, too strong and acidic. It was the white-amber coats that were the prize. Already half the warriors, Arok the first, had mantles of such pelt. Nirri as well. Even the little white son Athluan had a wrapping of tiger fur.

Over the petrified fields of the sea the lion-drawn chariots came flying, winged with ice-spume. Torches spat green against a night long emptied of its moons. Far out . . . liquid waves moved with a sullen sound . . . The grey, densely furred lions, their black manes plaited with coloured beads and metal . . .

The Thing place. An area of truce. The Thing appeared. Ancient, curious and huge, a seventeen-masted ship, frozen.

Athluan knew it well. He had been brought to Thing meetings since the age of nine; the Chaiord of the Jafn Klow had been his father.

But why tonight? No longer nine or twelve but thirty years, he recalled he had come to ask leave of his allies, the Jafn Shaiy, to pass over their land while seeking his lost betrothed. She was a girl of the Ruk, with yellow hair, said to have died on the journey to meet him. He knew instead he would find her inside a pyramid of ice. She would be alive, beautiful, his heart already held inside her own. Saphay . . .

He opened his eyes.

He lay in the cot in the corner of the upper room. A colourful rug sprawled over him, and his lionet-pelt.

It was still mostly dark but by the warm light of a lamp Nirri his mother leaned towards him.

'Was dream,' he said. And for an instant a flash of irritation rattled through him at his lack of language, his inability to grasp strength or autonomy. Never mind; this stage would pass. He would grow up. Everyone promised him this. But Great God, how long? Twelve years? Fifteen? *Twenty*?

'Were you dreaming?' she asked.

How could she be so tirelessly patient with him, when he was so self-*im*patient—

The mood, which had run directly out from the fragment of dream, melted and left him only bemused. Slumber always bored him on waking. Though all the Jafn kept sleep to a minimum the very young were indulged. They needed to sleep often, to grow. Should he then sleep *more*?

'Morning?' he asked. *'Good.'*

'Yes. I'll blow out the lamp.'

She did so. The deep grey light in the window blinked white behind the shutter of membrane.

'I dreamed a ship,' he said, 'all ice. Ten and seven masts.'

Nirri said, 'That was the ship we came here in. I've told you about it. Were we at sea in your dream?'

'No. Was long off – long ago. Stuck in ice.'

'I told you about that too. How your father and his men and the werloka and wise-women released it. I pulled on the ropes too.'

'My father is Klow Chaiord,' murmured Athluan to himself. 'I have two brothers. Conas who is good. And Rothger who is stink.'

He saw Nirri's face. The returning dawn was carving it from the shadow. She seemed disturbed. She said nothing.

'But long off,' he repeated, apologizing.

'Do you say your father was another man? He never was.' Her voice sounded hushed and flat. 'Your father is Arok, the *Holas* Chaiord. You have only one brother – he who was stolen.'

'Yes, Conas died. Roth died after. The Lionwolf killed Roth. That was after *I* was dead in any case.'

He heard Nirri catch her breath sharply, as women did when sewing and the needle pierced their fingers.

He thought, less in words than in pictures, *What did I say?*

His mind cleared to its general infantile opalescence. He was left solely with a faint sense of having been cheated, and drummed his heels angrily on the cot.

'There,' she said, and stood him up. 'Now tell me—'

'Want pot,' said Athluan. 'Quick! Quick!' Between childish amusement and alarm.

So Nirri brought him the chamberpot.

The two lionet were a male and female. They were fighting, perhaps as a prelude to sex. As a rule these were solitary animals and to come on two full-grown ones together was a bonus.

Not until the five men had left their chariots and slunk forward did either animal register encroachment. The male it was who spun immediately away. A flung spear did not even graze his flank. They were so difficult to pick out when moving.

The female though stood her ground, snarling. Her teeth were already daubed by contact with the male – if the hunters had not been able to scratch him, she certainly had.

Arok sprang forward, Fenzi to his left and Khursp just behind and to the right.

The female cat also sprang: she came in like a living bolt at Arok, and landed heavy and entirely dead in the snow at his boots, Fenzi's spear through her brain.

'I marked the pelt. My regrets, Chaiord.' Fenzi was always self-controlled.

'Well, the furry fellow marked her worse – look at this gash along her side,' said Khursp. He bent to her admiringly. 'Forgive us, fair lady. We need your skin to keep us snug and your meat for the dogs. Her holed skull, if painted,' he added, 'will make a lovely lamp with oil and a wick inside. Do her honour.' Khursp was the poet among them. He had been a whaler before and always, he said, begged pardon of the whales and fish he slew. 'God allows it,' he said, 'providing it's for food or cover, or to defend.'

The tigress's fur was lush. They combed it with their fingers.

'She's one of the best we've taken – so glossy and full.'

Khursp straightened. 'Now we see why. Ah, shit.'

Turning her they had found her primed with milk, her dugs rosy from use.

Black luck to kill a nursing mother.

'No wonder the male was here and she so tetchy. Over there,' said Arok, 'that hole through the ice under the trees.'

They went to see, and there was a single cub about six days old, pretty with its youth, blue-eyed and whining on a bed of ice-moss and bones.

'Let's take the poor boy home,' said Khursp.

'We could raise him,' said Fenzi. 'Perhaps for the chariots when he's grown.'

A sound behind made them draw their heads out of the ice-cave so fast necks were ricked.

Holas were shouting.

'Arok – a band of men is coming!'

Arok's brows contracted. 'This country's empty.'

Through all their trek inland, all their sojourn during which they had put up the garth and the House, none of them had seen even in the distance another human being than their own.

'What sort of men?'

'About a hundred, warrior-looking, all mounted on a kind of beast – like great sheep—'

Arok scrambled up the slope where the look-out was. Standing there under two or three crystallized palms, he too saw. A hundred, a hundred and fifty men riding tall sheep that galloped with the rhythmic, sickening lurch of a ship. They were heading straight towards the area of the hunt. Decidedly any activity here was what had brought them.

Too near to flee, too many to fight.

Arok directed his warriors. They mounted their chariots, and into Arok's vehicle was lugged the female lionet's body. Fenzi ran out from the cave, the lionet baby squalling and clawing in his arms. Leaping back into his car Fenzi held the struggling cub in one arm, the reins round his waist. One hand was free now for sword or dagger. He seemed not to care. 'Hush,' he said to the lionet. 'Hush, baba.' And the lionet grew still.

Extravagant clouds of snow and rime spurled up from the advancing band.

Unpleasantly Arok was reminded of the Lionwolf's legions on the march. Then of the reiver raid that had dispossessed him of his first son Dayadin.

He drew his sword with a crisp abrasive noise.

He began to see yellow and red cloth, with silver and brass winking on the fitments of the peculiar sheep-like riding animals. They had long necks like serpents beneath sheep's heads, and behind on their backs rose a pair of hills which seemed a part of their bodies. Between the hills their riders perched. In colour the beasts were various browns, some almost black, and one almost white as dirty cream. When the mass was about seventy feet from the Holas a group of the animals separated and came lolloping forward, the white one to the front.

Arok indicated to his men that they should wait. He flicked the reins of his chariot and drove forward alone.

He rode into the space between the Holas and the unknown riders. By the Eye of God, though, the sheep-brutes were big – bigger than lamasceps.

We have no language in common. He thought this almost idly. Then, *They're angry.* Then: *Is Chillel's magic still on me? I think not. I was hurt in the last fight. I can die, now.*

He offered the Jafn salute, fist to shoulder, head unbowed. A politeness. He conserved himself. The other side was now mostly static, drawn up in jostling lines. Just the pale animal picked forward.

The man on the animal was dark-skinned – not dark like Fenzi, but more as if he had been seethed in honey and smoke. His hair was black, with scarlet wool woven into its plaits.

He stared down at Arok with contempt and animosity. He said no word, only pointed with a gold-ringed finger at the dead lionet.

'Who gave you leave to slay our tigers? Only our royals may do so, or their servants for them.'

Arok found he could understand. That then had remained to him if invulnerability had not, one more fringe benefit from lying with Chillel. But would this other understand *him*?

'We're strangers in your land and didn't know.'

The man on the tall sheep widened his eyes.

The tall sheep burped with a disgusting sound that filled the air with the odours of fermenting grain, rotten wood and decaying vegetables. This did not disconcert the rider, only Arok, who coughed.

'You speak Simese?'

Arok cleared his throat and risked the throw. 'I speak all tongues.'

'I see you are an outlander. You're snow-coloured and have the hair of an elderly man.'

'I'm young enough. What reparation do you want for killing your beast?'

'Probably your death.'

'Then sing for it.'

'No. My king will sing for it and we'll skin you and hang your pelt by the tiger's.'

'You think so.'

'Come,' said the rider, almost gracious with scorn, 'you have about twenty men. We are ninety.'

I misjudged the number. Ninety? Can we do for them? No.

'Take *me*,' said Arok. 'I killed the animal – your *tiger*.'

'And you've thieved the cub. All of you will go with us. The king will like to know how you reached our country. Before he skins you *all* with a blunt knife.'

Athluan was a child again, a toddler with strong legs that, once grown, would be long and muscular. He was paying visits in the garth, ambling up and down the man-made slopes and terraces.

People were always pleased enough to see him. He did not know yet clearly sensed they gave him their approval and kindliness in lieu of something else. Although he had been told of the stolen first son, Dayadin the Hawk, no one had ever made Athluan miserable or jealous. No comparisons were ever voiced. It would be unlucky, disregardful of God's second gift. In any event Athluan's was not a jealous nature, He was a serious boy, already bright and generally reasonable.

Behind him walked the nurse of fourteen who acted as his guardian on such excursions. She was always careful of him, yet here he was safe enough. So she had paused to linger with one of the younger men by the hothouse. A few kisses and fondles and she would pluck an orange for Athluan and catch him up.

Arok's lionet hunt would be gone for some days. The garth was usually a little more relaxed in his absence. More than a year without sight or sniff of an enemy had lulled them after the brittle last days in the former country.

Athluan had also paused. He had been going to the blacksmith's, to watch the hammering of metal and the sparks fly. But in a small yard between there and the houses, an interesting whirling went on in mid-air. What was it? Almost it was like the smithy sparks, only wilder.

Or was it bees? He had seen bees somewhere, the hive-bees that must always live indoors – the Holasan-garth did not have such hives, but Athluan did not recall this.

Soon he went towards the bee-sparks, fascinated, unafraid. At that moment they coalesced in an unlikely upright formation. Athluan stopped still again. Something was about to happen.

It did. The glinting nothing of the shape drew itself swiftly into lines and curves and put on washes of colour.

To a young child magic is everywhere, startling but seldom unbelievable.

He looked up at the pale young woman in her silvery dress and fall of saffron hair. Her eyes were black. They looked right into his grey ones.

Somewhere inside the boy's brain a thought skipped. *It* – but not he – *knew* this apparition, this lovely young female who had emerged from thin air. He knew her frown too, the flinch of bad temper, and then the two tears that spilled like stars out of her eyes.

'What is your name?' said the woman.

She spoke in a language Athluan had never heard, at least not recently. Jafn did have some affinity with it but this was not why he knew what she said. But then a curtain closed and anyway he did *not* know it. And so he stared. Then she said, in perfect Jafn, 'How are you called?'

'Athluan,' said he. He added, to be helpful, 'My daddy named me for ghost that have guided his ship to land.'

The woman in the air clenched her fists.

He was not afraid of her. He laughed.

'Oh, *you* can laugh!' she exclaimed. 'Look at this mess! What a fix to get in. Don't you remember?'

Really startling himself the child heard his own child's voice reply, 'No. Cheer up though, my darling. Here I am.'

Then they both lowered their eyes and gaped at the ground, as if the words had been printed on the snowy yard.

'I should smack you,' she whispered.

'My mother would smack *you*,' staunchly the boy answered.

'Yes, like *life* – always a smack for *me*. You heartless – no, no,' she wailed. 'Poor boy! How handsome you are – just as you must have been in childhood before. Do you remember me?'

Guileless, sombre, the child said, 'Love you.'

She put her hand over her face.

How golden her hair was. He had never seen such hair – or had he? He thought perhaps she was a gler, or a corrit – worse, a sort of sihpp – but Nirri had told him most of those Jafn demon-sprites had been left behind in the old country.

He tried to make amends for thinking her a gler.

'Love you almost as much as Mother.'

'Shush,' she said. She was crying.

He went up to her then and attempted to take her other hand, very white and graceful. But when he touched her, there was nothing of her at all.

Was *she* a ghost?

She dried her eyes and he saw that, unlike ordinary physical people, her tears had left no mark on her. She said, 'I'll return soon. Then you'll be able to hold my hand. It's only that I'm not yet here.'

He nodded. 'Where then?'

She pointed. 'Across those mountains. The great upland forest. I've had to look for you a long time, and you're to blame for that.'

'Oh.'

'Yes. You are. But men – always it *is* their blame.'

'You won't be here long time,' he said, 'if all over across there.'

'Silly,' she said fondly. Her frame of mind seemed to alter nearly with every breath. 'I can fly. Don't you see? I'm a goddess.'

Ah, a goddess. Yes, that might explain a lot. Except there was only God. Other gods were inventions.

He nodded again, judiciously not protesting.

34

'Sunfall,' she said. 'I think I'll come back then. Oh, just look at that House up the slope. What a sty! I suppose it's no one's fault, building in this wilderness—'

Athluan glowered now, furious at her insult to his father Arok and the men of the Jafn Holas. But in that instant she winked out into nothingness.

He stood there now actually *un*believing, until his nurse came with her smiling kissed mouth, and the orange.

Around ten hours after, as the garth prepared its suppers, and in the joyhall of the Holas House women hurried from the cook-fire to the long tables with meat and bread and beer, the watchman at the west gate heard a faint knocking. Looking over from the height he saw a thin old woman lurking on the plat-form outside. The last of a dull sunset was behind her. She resembled nothing so much as a dilapidated crow.

'Where have you come from, Mother?'

He was *genuinely* startled and disbelieving, for she did not belong among the Holas and no other human thing lived in these parts, as they knew very well. Despite leaving your own local demons behind, you often admitted there might still be demons native to the new place.

'Miles I've trudged, over hill and mountain, through ice-wood and ice-jungle,' grumbled the reedy old voice below. Oddly he could hear every syllable – in Jafn, too.

'How have you survived then, Gran?'

'Wise-woman I am,' she snapped. 'How the cutch else, you gobbler!'

The watchman recoiled. Perhaps though she was? But the Holas had five such women in all, plus the grouchy male wer-loka. Let them see to her then. If left outside she might, as some of them were said to do in legends, fly in over the wall and cause havoc.

THREE

What came along the alleys, around the outcrops of Kandexa, was a sight to cause sore eyes not cure them. If any *did* see they made off, banged the shutters, told themselves it was a fluke of the shadow and the last useless bit of moon.

For a kind of fast-growing vine crawled through the dark, over the snow and the stone.

Up a wall, across a roof, down an old mashed stair, on through another alley.

At the end of the wriggling, leafless, woody vine was a thing like a clawing hand, running spiderish on its far-too-many fingers.

Thryfe, standing in his chimney prison of ice, detected the scratching outside. A rat?

He had been unable to pierce the confine, let alone thrust it apart. For an hour therefore he had waited, aware of the horror of a gathering cold which seeped even through the psychic bubble that protected him. He had been trying to learn the nature of this sudden sorcery. For sorcery it must be. No every-day avalanche could contain such a magician as Thryfe. Even in his recent humility he knew it.

The cold laid its own claws on his body, invading blood and muscles, vision, thought; questing. He ignored it. He must find out the motive force of this foe, for only in that way—

The scrabbling above turned to a mad skittering.

A tribe of rats were about to burst through the lid of ice above. Could they also break the bubble of defence? Formerly he would never have believed so.

36

But formerly he would by now have freed himself. Every-thing had therefore become doubtful.

The ice above split. It fell in a cloud of powder. After that another thing fell.

He saw it dive straight down at him, a spiralling black spider already clutching for his face.

Like a man ungifted in magic Thryfe, as best he could in the narrow space, stooped quickly away, slinging the edge of his cloak across his head—

A voice spoke in the air.

'Greeting, man-mage. It right you bow me.' *Bow*? He had *ducked*. 'Ask now, be I get you out?'

Thryfe pushed off the cloak, then straightened. He had rec-ognized, he thought, the dialect and syntax of the rural eastern Ruk, but with some other essence in it far more sophisticated. Yet as he expected no figure was visible. Only the spider hung dangling, which now he identified as a carved wooden hand, with other hands sprung from it and at least twenty-one fingers. Something tickled in the back of memory.

'Yes, I should like you to get me out. Is it possible to you?'

'Why I offer if not?'

'Reasonable. In exchange, what do you require?'

'Nothing. Give now.'

Thryfe acquiesced. 'You are part of Ranjal then, goddess of wood.' He had heard of her, seen her temples in the eastern vil-lages. Nothing was what she was always ceremoniously offered.

Thryfe did not believe in gods. At least, his attitude towards them was ambivalent. Everywhere they reportedly abounded, or if not then one omni-ruling and all-purposeful God. These things to Thryfe were merely magic focuses, or the power surges either of men or of the earth, both entirely misunderstood.

Nevertheless here this being was. The recollection of his dream of the Lionwolf as sun god sparkled across Thryfe's inner eye. He dismissed it.

Some antagonist was at work against him: this unknown element, felt when Jemhara had been hidden, felt again in the attacking snow, might have stirred up, inadvertently, the arrival of a rogue helper symbolized as the primitive Ranjal. Benign energy to balance the malignant one.

Thryfe offered Ranjal several elegant palmfuls of nothing. He had seen this done in her rough little temples. Though unreal she was presently alive and not to be offended.

The hand seemed satisfied. It gave him a playful tap on the shoulder.

Without any other preliminary the wiry vine that coiled behind it paid out like twirling whipcord. It roped him harsh and hard. The hand hooked companionably about his neck.

The force of Ranjal, whatever motivated it, was conclusive. Lifted without effort, Thryfe was rushed up through the chimney, out of its top, and deposited neatly if ungently in the alley.

A muffled rumble and further cloud of ice crystals signalled disintegration of the chimney.

The hand unhooked. It lay down on its vine on the street.

He might as well ask.

'What caused my imprisonment?'

'How I know? Some enemy cause it to you.'

'Surely. Then why help me?'

A pause. He sensed a shaggy divine puzzlement.

'How I know? Is to do.' The hand bounced and administered a sisterly slap on the arm. 'Go us now.'

'Where?'

'Where you want go, where you as were going.'

'You know Jemhara's house here?'

'This one of me,' the hand flapped, 'live there.'

Then it gripped him, not quite by the scruff of the neck. He was reminded of a mother cat dragging her young to shelter, although Ranjal of course was more the mustelid type, a badger. By means of her merciless clasp they flew up walls, scraped rather against them, over roofs and sheets of ice.

They landed among a bundle of dwellings, some marked by old fire. A door gave on a stair. The hand let go again, retracted its vine and leap-crawled away ahead. 'Attic,' was the last word the goddess vouchsafed to him.

When he reached the top of the stairs the hand had vanished.

He read that the door was firmly secured by magecraft. He read too Jemhara was not at the moment here. She had been. A faint non-physical perfume lingered.

Thryfe leaned to the door and spoke an inaudible word.

Unlike the ice-prison, the door reacted at once and in the anticipated fashion, opening without fuss.

Something terrifying happened.

A flood of joy sang through him. Twenty years – no, a hundred – dropped from his shoulders. He thought, No, not terrifying. *Am I still such a fool?*

He saw the narrow bed with its pelts, and the pillow where her head had rested. He saw the objects on the inlaid Rukarian table. On the wall was a peg with a worn, darned dress that seemed to turn his heart to butter, then harden it to a fierceness that burned. A twig hung there too, rather like an uncanny hand. Thryfe saluted it. He crossed the room and stood over the empty hearth and brought fire to it from nowhere in a single splash.

Soon she would return. Soon she would enter this room. It occurred to him she might be afraid to discover him there, or think him some illusion, even a trick played by a talented malevolent rival witch.

He put one goblet, made apparently from clearest ice, ready on her table, filled by dark red wine. And beside that an apple with a pure green skin that he had found on his travels and kept for her. A case of ice still swathed it, but the warmth of the conjured fire would deftly thaw that through. By the apple he laid an ancient ring of tarnished silver.

Outside, the now moonless city crept unknowing towards morning.

Thryfe opened the shutter.

Whether he stepped out, or simply disappeared into the shadows there, was uncertain, but where he had stood nothing visible of him remained.

On the peg the twig-hand twitched. It seemed Thryfe the Magikoy Master would not often need Ranjal's assistance.

*

39

The journey was a bumpy one.

Up hill, down dale – snow slide, treacherous crevasse, bear-fur forests, mountains poking like dagger behind dagger. They had been told to leave their chariots. That was to get out of them, give them up, for the seventy-nine men who had been one hundred and fifty, and themselves lied about being ninety, had captured Arok's hunting band and decided they would keep the chariots for themselves. Instead the prisoners were hauled aloft the hills of the giant riding-sheep.

Dromazi the mounts were called. Most had two humps, between which the Jafn men were each obliged horrifiedly to perch behind the original cavalier. Some other beasts had only one hump, and there the rider sat forward on the creature's neck. None of the captured were offered a seat on these. They were entirely grateful.

The position and motion of the ride anyway were agony. Arok expected to become seasick but did not. Only marvellous Fenzi took it all in his or the dromazi's stride. He had mastered the knack in a couple of hours. But his reward for this was to have his hands tied to the saddle in case he also mastered his jailer, unseated the man and escaped. Meanwhile the Jafn chariot-lions padded behind the party snarling, in custody.

Once or twice you could spot a heap of buildings high above amid rocks and trees. Farms? Strongholds? No one said.

Up and down their procession went over the terrain. Then up and up.

Only Arok and presently Fenzi understood the new language, Simese. Their conquerors called the land Simisey. They were ferocious and loud, bellowing songs and curses, their hair woven and beaded like the manes of Jafn lions.

The little lionet-tiger cub had first been cradled lovingly by their leader. But after it bit him repeatedly, he was urged at last to have Fenzi's hands untied and to give the cat back to him. 'There, baba,' said Fenzi, now in Simese, 'come to your elder brother who loves you.'

'No brother of *yours*, barbarian!' roared the red-wool-braided leader, whose name was Sombrec.

'There, there,' repeated Fenzi sweetly to the tiger, just managing to say it also to Sombrec, who seemed on the road to exploding from rage. His mount however did so instead, letting off a colossal fart. That quenched even Fenzi's flirtatious sarcasm.

They finally reached the Simese city. Arok registered a crows' nest of a town up a mountain. This tip was known as Padgish. It was the capital.

To Arok only a garth could have any worth as either town or fortress; only a Jafn clan House had any credence as a palace. Sullenly he scowled at Padgish as they entered, until at length, reluctantly, he changed his mind.

For Padgish was impressive.

One long straight paved road, worthy of Ruk cities, led all through. On either side were edifices of two or occasionally three storeys. Some windows had glass. The palace had an excess with colours stained in them. Gardens boasted vast trees, and tree-trunk columns upheld the frontage of the palace house, then marched away in ranks inside.

Next something went tearing by, a man riding an animal that was not tiger or lion, not even a humped and huffing dromaz.

'Horsaz?'

'No – no scales. No pong of fish either.'

The horsazin of such reivers as Kelps and Faz did bear some vague resemblance. But the Simese variety were made of warm-tinted hide, the flying mane and tail of hair. They had no horn jutting from the forehead.

In depressed wonder the Jafn captives were herded into a yard of the Padgish palace.

'This one can speak our tongue. And the black one, he too.'

Arok, and Fenzi still with the cub in his arms, feeding from a vessel of milk the captors gave him, stood in the throne hall. Sombrec, a warrior aristocrat born from a long line of farming royalty, scathingly listed the captives' only worth.

Trunk columns forested the edges of the hall. A king sat on

a carved seat. Before him lay a knife with a blade of shattering brilliance. 'Diamond cut by diamond,' Sombrec had loftily remarked. The king was like his men, dark-haired, dark-eyed, brown of skin. His clothes were rich and his demeanour frankly grim. He had asked questions of Sombrec and his men as to who, or what, the strangers were. He had already been told it seemed the strangers had killed a tiger, and freely confessed slaughtering others in the past year.

'Well, if you can speak our language, step forward.'

Arok did so.

Fenzi walked just behind him, with the cub.

Khursp and several more attempted to follow.

'Two are enough. Keep the rest of them back.'

A brief kerfuffle. Arok did not turn to see. He could guess.

He faced the savage king with bleak dignity, well aware the king thought *him* the savage.

'What,' said the king, 'is your outland name?'

'Arok, Chaiord of the Jafn Holas.'

'*Ch*— What does he say? Their *king* is it?' Murmurs. Yes, this chalky barbarian was the other nineteen barbarians' 'king'. Ha ha. What a ripe jest! 'Is he old? His hair is white.'

Arok interposed. 'Among my people, young men and women too have such hair.'

'*Women*, you say?' The king was intrigued. Disgusting. 'Do you have any with you? Women, I mean.'

Arok's glower eclipsed his features.

'None.'

'I think you fib, Whitehair.'

Arok said, 'We came to your God-forsaken country on a great ship. Do you think we'd risk our women over the seas?'

'A pity. Why did you come?'

Arok decided on truth. 'An omen. My son was stolen and, the omen said, brought here. I came to find my son.'

'Ah,' said the king. For the half of one half-second a glint of slinking sympathy lit his eyes. 'This I understand. To lose a son – to have lost him – what can compare with such a loss? Have you found him?'

Arok did not credit the sympathy. It had a weird colour to it for him, like wine that was too dark.

'Not yet.' It was still the truth.

'Meanwhile you poach the tiger-kind. Know this. They're only for us, for our royal families among the farmers or hunters or herders. Or of course for me, and mine.'

'How could we know?'

'If you speak our language, how could you not know?'

'We met none of your folk to tell us,' barked Arok.

'Then you lie in all things. For how can you speak Simese if you came sea-over and till now met none here to teach you?' Crafty, the king, twiddling the diamond-bladed knife.

Arok said, 'I can speak many languages because I'm witch-gifted.'

'Are you, by mighty Attajos, may his fire burn bright? Where's your proof?'

Arok stalled. He had none. None at least he could trust.

Fenzi spoke carryingly yet quietly behind him. 'I am his proof, sir. The witch that spelled him was my mother.'

Another murmuring ran around. Already, the Jafn had heard no black-skinned man or woman was known in Simisey.

'Yes, you are bizarre. What are you made of, velvet?'

Fenzi smiled in a disarming way, not insulted. 'Of skin and flesh and bone and hair. Sir. As are you. But my mother was made of snow and at the touch of God grew living and black. Arok, my Chaiord, lay with my mother.'

'Then Arok is your father too.'

'No. He is the father of my half-brother, Dayadin, who is also black . . . as velvet. It was Dayadin who was stolen, and brought into these distant lands.'

The king gave a dangerous laugh. 'I'm confused. Enlighten me.'

'My witch-mother, in fact a goddess, carried seed like a man. Any man she lay with took in this seed and then passed it to his own woman. Both my second mother, and Dayad's second mother, Arok's wife, received this seed. And so each woman bore a black son.'

'I commend your story teller's skill. We like it. That alone may save you from death. But otherwise your tale is like the air that comes from the back gate of a dromaz. It stinks.'

Fenzi shrugged. It was the tiger cub, gazing at the Simese king, that lifted its lip and gave a miniature growl, which plainly offended the king. He rose, the diamond knife still in his hand.

At that very instant a woman walked into the hall, and by her side a tall boy about twelve years of age.

Every head turned. Even that of the incensed king.

Arok swore very low, and behind him, held firm by warriors among the pillars, the remainder of the Jafn. Not all of them so decorously.

For the woman, who was herself tall, and voluptuous, had long hair of a red-bronze shade. Exactly as black skin was unknown in Simisey, red hair had been unknown among the Jafn or elsewhere on their continent. Save in one instance only: Lionwolf, red-haired hero and genocide.

The woman seemed to take all this mixed attention as her right, used to scrutiny. Mixed ethnicity seemed equally unchallenging. She inclined her head to the Simese king. Gold and silver jewels swung in her rufous tresses.

The boy though, he looked round at Arok and the Jafn and he too laughed – but not as the king had.

'Curjai,' said the king, 'Curjai, we are—'

'You are making something of a mistake, sir,' said the boy called Curjai.

He was utterly confident yet completely without arrogance. He looked at his king with fearless *kindness*. Yet no king could allow such an affront even from a beloved son. No king could make a public *mistake*.

Nevertheless the king failed to lose his temper. He put down the knife and nodded at the boy. 'We listen, my son.'

He *was* a son then. Even so—

The boy was extraordinary. Yes handsome certainly, and well made, long of leg, strong, wide-shouldered, his brown-black hair streaming to his waist with jasper clips winking in it. He was brown-skinned like the others. His eyes were rather lighter.

But none of that was what caught you. No. This boy – this son – even supernatural Fenzi was gaping at him in recognizing astonishment – this boy was perhaps more than merely unhuman. This boy just conceivably was—

The boy said, 'Everything the newcomers say, Father, is true. Oh, except that they brought no women. They have fine women at their garth. Excuse me, sir,' he added mildly to the staggered and threatened Arok, 'but we're to be confided in, when once you accept us. Friends don't keep secrets from one another.'

Arok opened his mouth. Before he could let out something sure to spoil the party, Fenzi placed his hand on Arok's arm. Crazily Arok was aware the cub had started purring. 'Wait, Chaiord. Don't you see?'

'The boy? He's a mage – he's an enemy mage.'

'No, Arok. This one is fully a god.'

Jemhara had halted in the street. Her way was blocked by something that, initially, she had taken for a natural subsidence of snow or rubble. Now and then walls, whole houses, being largely unmaintained, might collapse.

But she had made light to see. The lit globe hung in the air and showed her an astounding heap of what she took for gemstones. Icy pale, yet they were, every one, cut into glittering facets which shot off tiny rays of prismatic colour.

Nevertheless such an enormous hoard seemed unlikely. They filled all the alley, and piled high up against the sides of dwellings, ending in one huge barricade against the house where she kept her attic. She could see nothing of it save the top of the roof, and there her window too was almost covered over. The depth of the barricade meanwhile could be, she judged, far deeper than the width of the house itself.

Had some witchling from another zone done this to spite her? It seemed feasible, but on the other hand were any of them canny enough?

Jemhara approached the stack of gems. They glinted prettily. She touched one with her finger's end. The cold scathed her and examining her hand, she saw a blister form at once on her fingertip. An effect of cold so intense was also unusual, for the people of this five-century Ice Age had adapted to it long ago. Only extended exposure could burn, never such a brief touch.

Jemhara stepped back and threw a psychic blow at the pile of gemmy ice. It would have been crucial enough to fell a man. The ice never moved.

Someone uttered a low sound behind her then.

Jemhara did not turn.

Every hair on her head and body had risen. She spoke softly, civilly. 'How may I serve you, most mighty one?'

But no answer came.

Instead a sensual caress slipped over her neck and shoulders – light as nothing, perhaps no more than the lilt of a night breeze. Before she could prevent herself she had veered to face it. She caught the slightest glimpse.

She had seen him before, she thought, or had she? For the god who had once visited her in her misspent youth, the Rukarian god who had fathered Lionwolf – Zeth Zezeth, the Sun Wolf – he had not looked as this one did. And yet, yet for an inexplicable moment he *was* Zeth. And then—

Then he took on another masculine image. That was of a man in a mail of rime, his black hair spun and chipped with frost. And *this* Rukarian god's name was Yyrot, Winter's Lover.

Her own hair smoothed down on her head. Whichever – whatever – it had been was gone.

What had the double image said to her? Was 'said' too precise? It was more a noise, like that some large sombre animal might make, vocal, untranslatable. Jemhara calmed her breathing.

The night had stayed otherwise very still. Or was it only that this part of Kandexa seemed closed in by heavy curtains?

She looked again at the barricade.

She remembered how she and Thryfe, lost in their lovemaking in the house at Stones, had also been shut within walls of timeless ice. But that had not been like this . . .

Except probably that now, as then, there was involved a kind of occult magery, a thoughtless obdurate thing that did, could, would, obey few other magical laws.

Jemhara's earliest ability had been to thaw ice. She was a small child when first she did it. With her, it was less talent than intrinsic knack as, say, she had learned to walk.

After a little while the edge of the barricade began to steam, or smoke. Rivulets like molten crystal snakes ran down into the street. Here and there flashing jewels tumbled from the pile.

But then that too ceased. Though she had damaged the appearance of the gemstone wall the rest of it would not give.

Jemhara saw she could not break through. And as she was she could not climb over, however swiftly or sorcerously aided.

She had sensed an adversary all instinct. Thoughtless itself, could it read her thoughts? She brushed them away.

Quietly she turned and went back along the alley and on, into another.

How well did the faceless intelligence know her? If it came from a god, no matter which one, it might know all. But if it could not *think*—

Jemhara wiped clean the whole surface of her mind.

She crouched down in the pre-dawn dark – and was gone.

A few minutes later another night-walker, a slender jet-black hare, loped into the eastern alley, reached the faceted cut-glass blockade, and sniffed it disdainfully.

Then it bolted straight up the ice, its powerful hind limbs propelling it forward at breathless speed. Gaining the head of the heap it launched itself directly at the just visible window. A shutter slapped inward with a bang. Down into Jemhara's attic room hurtled the hare, to land as if well practised on the bed of pelts.

One instant more and Jemhara rose up from her shape-shift, a woman black of hair, fair of face, naked as cloudless morning.

Outside, with an aggrieved rasp and crackling, the diamanté wall gave way, showering the alley with sparklers that quickly dimmed and melted, then again froze over in the ordinary manner.

Inside the room Jemhara saw a fire burning, a glass goblet of wine, a green apple dewed with snow, a silver ring, a tall man made of shadow but with the eyes of an eagle.

For an old woman in rags she was haughty enough, so they all thought in the Holasan-garth. Brought to the Holas House by one of the night watch, she clacketed through the joyhall uninvited and unabashed, and stood there by the table, where this evening Arok's wife was sitting among her women. Arok was away of course on his hunt. But the garth looked fine, decked with lamps and hangings, a couple of lions and a dozen dogs there, and some hawks on the rafters, and plenty of tough young men and weapons.

'Pardon, Nirri-lady, she just—'

'Hold your squeaks,' yapped the old crone the watch had let in, he said, from sheer compassion. 'It's her I'll talk to.'

Nirri, who everyone knew had been a fishwife before Arok got her with child and wed her, was now an excellent Chaiord's lady. She sat with dignity, and only a slight smile whisked over her mouth.

'Speak then, Mother.'

'I'm no mother. I renounce any mother I was. I've come a long distance. I have mage powers.'

'You're a wise-woman?'

'Better. Behold!'

There had been a cooked bird on the table. The old beldame pointed at it and it leapt, whole and live, covered all over in its original feathers, flailing its wings and knocking items about, honking through its angry beak before taking off into the rafters. The hawks fled.

The whole hall danced to its feet. Children shrilled, women yelled, men bellowed. The lions and dogs got up rumbling. Nirri's girls were upset, but Nirri only said, 'Very clever.'

'*Clever*?' Granny did not like that evidently. 'Can *you* do it?'

'No, I can only *cook* it. Which is more useful, do you think?'

Some laughed. Others held their breath. After all this wise-woman *was* wise. Be careful.

48

But then the witch too broke into a cackle.

'What shall I do with it? Make it into a roast again?'

'No, poor thing. Let it live now. We'll eat something else.'

The old witch flumped herself down among the unsettled Jafn waiting ladies, and reached for a pie.

'You must be hungry, madam,' said Nirri.

'Not unless I feel I'd like to be.' The witch ate the pie. Something odd there. She had pedantically good table manners.

Nirri, who had brazened it out till now, began to experience a curious tug in her recollection. She stared at the witch. Where before had Nirri seen this raddled mop of yellow-grey-white hair, these creased yet once delicate features, hands and frame?

'Do you tell any your name, lady?' she asked the witch abruptly.

'I'll tell you. Not here. Who d'you think me to be?'

'There was an old – lady once, when I lived by the shore in the other country. Fishers found her and brought her to me. A great while she lay in my hut. She was a foreigner. I called her Saffi.'

The witch's face broke like a plate in shards of bitterness.

'That, that. You would have to recall *that* to me, wouldn't you? That was never me, fishwife. Just some bit of me that sloughed off. My real old age I shall never have. And so maybe I had to have it somewhere then. And besides, do you think I don't recall how you left the old bat in your hut, left her to her fate, didn't you, when the whale-demon poured up the vast wave? She must have died, must she not? Let me tell you, I met her after. *Saffi*. She taught me how to act this out, this crone I am, but she is never me. But for all that now she's dead as a nail in your door.'

Nirri had recoiled. The witch craned limberly forward. Nirri was nonplussed yet again by the unlikely freshness and fragrance of the crone's breath. There was a subtle perfume on her too emanating from her rags of hair or garb, her sackcloth skin.

The witch said, 'Where's your son?'

'*My son*? Do you mean *Dayadin* – my lost best boy—'

Now the old crone's mouth dropped open. Did she go white?

'Dayadin . . .' she said. The voice had changed. 'Oh God – oh gods – was he *yours*?'

'*You have seen him?*'

'Don't ask – don't ask me—'

With no warning both women were in floods of tears. They leaned together, sobbing, finally clinging to each other weeping. The already anxious joyhall palled with trepidation.

It was a fact Arok had rescued Nirri from the tidal wave the whale-leviathan Brightshade had raised, and the old mad Saffi was left behind, turning up later on the whale's nightmare back-country of mud, monsters, stench and bones. There Saffi and her inadvertent originator Saphay had perished together. But when Saphay rose from death a goddess, and ruled a while over the Vormish, Dayadin had been brought to her as their captive. As she was taking her new people across the ocean to this second continent, Brightshade, on the orders of his father Zeth Zezeth, had attacked her. In the fracas the bloody whale had swallowed Dayadin whole.

Nirri wept for her lost son, not asking, fearing the worst.

Saphay, goddess in guise of crone, wept for all of it: lost Dayadin, Lionwolf her own lost son, Athluan her lost lover now born back into the witless world as Nirri's second child.

How tangled the lives of men and gods.

When the tumult of grief drained off, Saphay in her crone form straightened and patted Nirri on the arm. Nirri was cinder-eyed from tears. The crone naturally was fresh as a shrivelled hothouse peach.

'I meant your *other* son. Athluan.'

At this one of the waiting-girls jumped up and shrieked, doubtless unsensibly, 'Don't let the old bitch near him! Kill her! Kill her! She's a gler!'

'Oh, sit yourself and shut up,' snapped Saphay. 'I'm unkillable. Don't waste all our time with such stuff.'

Upstairs in the Chaiord's apartment, Athluan had woken up and asked his young nurse what the noise was for below in hall. The nurse had been unnerved by some of the cries. She said if he would be good and not stir from his bed, she would go down and inquire.

Athluan sat there, wondering who he was. He had had another bad dream, the recurrent one about Rothger, his brother who had slain him in the previous life. At the moment the child could not put any of it together. Asleep he was someone else, or, more troubling, who he *really* was or should be. Waking was often a trial.

His nurse did not come back.

Then he heard his mother's step on the ladder-stair.

She appeared in the room and he saw she had been crying. He held out his arms mutely, full of sadness that something had made her unhappy. Was it his father? No, for Arok was away. Had something happened then *to* his father?

'No, hush, nothing like that. But a wise-woman has arrived. She spoke of your – your lost brother.'

'Rothger . . .'

Nirri was growing used to these discrepancies. They were upsetting but would surely fade out of him with age. She said, 'Dayadin.'

The wise-woman now stepped off into the room. She was very agile for one so elderly. Athluan stared.

'It's you,' said Athluan. Suddenly he was all smiles.

Saphay the crone poised in the upper room, still fazed a little by her refound lover so unsuitably young – as indeed he had told her he would have to be, when last they met. But her eyes strayed from him. The room was extremely familiar, very like the upper room of the Klow House. There a bed with coloured quilts and furs, there the Chaiord's weapons and a lamp that might be turned to give a darker light. In such a room years past they had first made love, and in the phantom of such a room that ultimate time, Athluan a ghost and she a god, they had again made love. What else terrible and tiresome and soul-destructive would occur before he grew up and once more they might couple?

To Nirri Saphay spoke solemnly. 'I have bad news, lady. Your beautiful black son was swallowed by a giant whale.'

Nirri turned, clutching Athluan. The toddler was all that kept her from falling on the floor.

Tact had never been Saphay's strong point.

'I saw a vision – an omen—' said Nirri, stumblingly. 'A black girl with fiery hair on a sled drawn by a black sheep, riding over the sky— And then the ghost promised my husband the Chaiord that Dayadin would be here – or somehow found here. And then Fenzi dreamed Dayad *was* here, in a *nice place*, Fenzi said.'

'There are always these things,' Saphay replied with a wretched dismissiveness. 'They mean little. Or else something *gives* us hope to torture us more. A nice place . . . probably that's death. At least death would be restful. I'm sorry.'

'My son.' Nirri buried her face in Athluan's small body. Her 'son' did not mean him, he knew.

Athluan sighed. It came from deep within him, from the former one he had been. He said the words the former one had said: 'Nothing can divide us, death least of all.'

Then the one he now was began to sob, not knowing what he said or why.

Sombrec glared at Fenzi. Fenzi shrugged, and, extending his hand, helped Sombrec to his feet. Both young men were stripped to loin-guards. They had been wrestling, a favourite warrior sport at Padgish. Fenzi, wrestling Jafn fashion, had seemed an easy target. Not so.

Risen, Sombrec went on glaring, now at a pillar. Risen, he was struggling with a physical reaction to Fenzi that was more than martial.

Fenzi apparently missed this. 'I hear the tiger cub is doing well,' he suggested generously, as they strolled towards the communal hot tub.

'How not, with Curjai to tame it.'

Arok and his men had been at Padgish ten days. Everyone was friends, as Prince Curjai had predicted – or had ordered.

The Jafn men, picking up the new language, were quickly told the story, taken for flat fact by the Simese, all of them, one heard.

Arok, despite his own interesting adventures with goddesses, giant whales, and invulnerability, reserved doubts. Two women, one supernatural, and a man might perhaps create a child between them. But *this*?

The king was said to reckon it true. And if a god *had* seen to the business, any king would be cracked if he objected.

Riadis, the red-haired queen, was one of many regal wives but had borne no children. Then she did bear one, which she claimed to have got from the Simese fire god Attajos; she had, they said, the burns to prove it. This first boy however was crippled, missing limbs or something of the sort. He had died young of a fever. Not so long after, the shaman attached to the queen's suite beheld a vision of the dead lad, who had been named Curjai, returning, this time equipped not only fully to live as a man, but as much more. At which another sparky smacker burst out from the heart of the fire, scarred Riadis again and again made her pregnant. When the second boy was born there could be no doubt of a resemblance to the earlier child, though this time nothing was awry, and next thing he began to grow at a prodigious rate, one year for every two or three months, they said. A couple of years now under his belt and he was twelve or thirteen – as certainly he did look to be. Moreover he could work magic as elegantly as any mage or shaman. He healed, he drove off dangerously bad weather, he summoned fire. He could even, for a joke if it were wanted, turn water to beer, iron to silver and silver to gold and – best of all – snow to fire. Well, if the dad was Attajos, how not?

Arok, saved from the White Death by Chillel's charms, Arok who had watched Dayadin grow faster than any other child he had known, and likewise Fenzi – Arok sat on the fence between the two courts of belief and doubt.

'We never saw the lad before. Maybe a sorcerer got him on her—'

'The Simese king says the god, and that the god asked his, the king's, agreement first.'

'A likely idea. Please may I beg to borrow the sweetmeat of your wife. What damn barbarian god ever thought to do that?'

Fenzi did not argue. He had known Curjai for a god instantly. That was that; why scramble about?

'There *are* no gods.' Arok was irritable. 'There is *God*. Aside from Him there are sprites and demons.'

'Did God not make all things?' had asked Fenzi equably.

'So you were taught. At least I trust you were.'

'So I was. Thus, if God created all, men and demons and the rest, why not create gods too?'

'*Gods*? Why?'

'To save Himself a little of the work.'

Despite this Arok and the Simese king made themselves sociable with each other, as did the Jafn and Simese warriors and definitely some of the Jafn and the Simese court maidens.

Arok had meant to despatch a messenger to inform the garth of his whereabouts.

The Simese king declared he would send some of his own men to do it, save Arok the bother. No doubt the king wished to note the virility of the garth, while keeping the rest of its warriors busy in Padgish. Arok worried. His men seemed only glad to go on roistering in the jolly palace, which had underfloor heating from braziers and pipes and several other luxuries. Not to mention exotic horses and girls.

'Why must we stay, why do they want us,' Arok said to Khursp and Fenzi, 'save to try us out and subdue us?'

'Their young prince seems to like us.'

Khursp said darkly, 'I asked this prince how his mother came by her copper hair. The boy says to me, Oh, are there none in your continent with red hair? I answer. Only one: he's dead. I've heard of something like that, says the prince. He meant that scourge, that gler-get fiend the Lionwolf. And Curjai does know of him, I *swear* he does, but not from us. There was a sort of laughter in his eyes.'

Back in the exercise court and reaching the tub, Sombrec plunged in. Then Fenzi.

Presently Sombrec gave in, and asked a question.

Fenzi smiled. 'Among the Jafn too, with warriors who like

each other that way, it's not uncommon. Why don't you swim a little nearer?'

Riadis was combing her hair, that talking-point. Curjai, Escurjai among his friends and intimates, stood watching her, so far unseen.

All at once a flurry of purple jewels formed in a garland round her brow.

She laughed with delight, and saw her son then in her second mirror of real glass.

'How long will this diadem last?'

'As long as you want, Mother. As long as love lasts.'

He was especially *himself* today, she saw: he glowed – like the fire.

'Love,' she said, playful. 'Does that then last?'

'Though the world's cold,' he said, 'living hearts are warm as flame.'

Riadis thought abruptly of how, those years ago, she had gone to her private interview with the king her husband, proud and sure, telling him straight out the god of fire again demanded use of her. The latest burn raved rawly on her leg; she knew that already her womb was filled. 'I have heard of your mad dreamings,' said the king. 'You said the *last* one was the fruit of Attajos. Another than I would have killed you outright for fornication.'

'Another,' had said Riadis, 'would not then have been so prudent or pious as you.' She knew the king was afraid to harm her. Yes, even though her first child had not been his, and malformed so *they* said. Her family was important and influential. And now if she had twice betrayed the king he would besides look such a fool.

The king said acidly, 'If you birth another monster—'

Riadis turned and left the chamber.

She had been utterly certain of vindication. And when Curjai was born, swiftly and with little pain, she had it. Since then the king could do nothing but revel and boast of her choosing by a god.

'Stay,' she said to her son now. But before the word had left her mouth the glass rippled. Curjai had simply vanished. Only the glory of the amethysts, only the glory of pride, remained.

They were motionless, frozen. As if ice had clustered over them, a chimney of it, a barricade of icy prisms.

Jemhara: This, the third time he had beheld her naked. There might have been a fourth. But that time she assumed he never saw her at all – her entry to the wreck of Ru Karismi, searching for him—

On that occasion, and one other, it was the shape-shift that laid her bare, as now. But once he himself had undressed her body, laid bare heart and soul.

What had she been before that conflagration?

What was she now?

Had he come here to kill her after all? She had dared to save his life and his sanity – surely when undesired a capital crime.

Thryfe: What was she then beyond that blaze of white flesh? The hair – lips – eyes— Little black creature of the order of lepus, that lilted in at the window when the shutter banged. Something was in the alley. He had been about to look and see what it was – a snowfall. Was he thinking now like a man? No, no mage, no man. A boy.

Did he want her? What did he want? He must reject the evidence of his lust, perhaps his human need. It must be more than either of those.

What then? She frightened him.

Jemhara too was afraid. Not of any violent act, even though with Thryfe she could not, she believed, protect herself. She had dreamed how he wrung her neck, or meant to.

He had despised her.

Hated her.

Thryfe drank her in through eyes and nostrils, through every pore of his skin. The room brimmed with her.

I loathed her. The touch of her like thorns – worse, because I have been lacerated by thorns and borne it easily. Her eyes are full of something, maybe love, maybe only my reflection . . .

'You are an illusion,' crisply said Jemhara. 'I will banish you.'

'You are *not* an illusion,' steadily said Thryfe. 'I will keep you here.'

Between them was the inlaid table, gleaming in firelight, or from another source. The wine and apple and ring shone, three tinted moons, ruby, emerald, silver. On a wall a twig glimmered too, unnoted.

Jemhara drew back. She sat on the edge of the bed. 'Please sit, Highness,' she said.

Thryfe ignored the single chair. 'I'll remain as I am, Highness.'

'How can you address me as a Magikoy?' Her voice was very thin.

'I think others have done so.'

'They were wrong.'

'*I* was wrong, in so much, until now. What shall I do, Jema, to put it right?'

'Leave me,' she said. 'Go hurriedly away. That's best.'

'Then,' he said.

'Then nothing. I was foretold you'd come. By a devilish god. By Vashdran—'

'A sun god, if his foretelling to *me* was real. I've never been sure. We can discuss it.'

'Go away,' she said.

He sighed. 'I'd suppose you took your revenge on me, but I don't think you so petty. What is it? Have I ruined it all, wounded you so deeply that all you feel now is the wound?'

A whisper. 'All I feel is love.'

'Oh, love. Love is always fearful. It sees its first object torn in shreds under a tree of ice by a black wolf. It sees the people it must protect dissolved to sand. It says, hang yourself, atone, suffer. That's what love does. Is there nothing else?'

Her voice now was even less, a flake of tinsel dropped inside a cup. 'Why did you leave the wine and fruit, the ring?'

'I found the apple on my way here. In a derelict hothouse, the last single apple, all the rest black and rotten, but this one pristine and preserved in ice. The wine was frozen too in a goblet which had itself become ice. I lit your fire and let them thaw.'

'And the ring . . .'

'The ring. That was mine, when I was young. When I had a little money, in a city – then. Then I left it off. The display of Rukarian kings made me sick. So no adornment for proud Thryfe. I found it recently at my house near Stones, after you'd gone away. I was – drawn to it again, to my earlier self – innocent, unembarrassed to be happy. But I found too I can't wear it now. My left hand's turned partly to stone.' He saw her start, glancing up with a firework of concern in her gaze. Oh, women. Women. He said, 'You have my ring. I'll go away now.'

'Your hand—'

'It's nothing, and serves me right. It happened from the punishment I gave myself in the Insularia. That jail from which you rescued me at such cost to yourself.'

'Perhaps,' she said.

'Perhaps,' he said. 'Perhaps come here, Jemhara. Perhaps come here and make certain I'm an illusion. Or a liar. Or a ghost. Or a lover. Could I be that? Come here, Jemhara.'

Exquisite, clad only in her body – bizarre to him as any garment from another earth – Jemhara rose. She crossed the room with slow, even steps. A few feet from him she halted. Thryfe, astonished, amused, aroused, *reassured*, felt his own clothing peel from him at the action of her will. He, now, naked as she. Jemhara laughed, her head tilted to one side.

'Yes, my lord,' she said, 'this is you.'

I touch – I burn—

I burn – I touch—

FOUR

Distant by much more than miles, lands or seas: the Southern Continent again, but up under the handgrip of the hilt which forms the north extremity of its mass. Here is a terrain of snow and ice-jungle one day to be known as the Marginal Land. But not yet. Now it is a territory named Ol y'Chibe, which means *We, the People.*

Rather further north stands the golden city of Sham – whose name too has a meaning: *None Greater.*

Few are.

At Sham the terraces tower, the huge metallic gates lift the sky on their backs, idly holding it up to be helpful. There is the Silver Gate, the Golden Gate, the Iron and the Bronze and the Copper Gates. Great plazas lie inside Sham, linked by squirrelling roads made of hammered coal, where dazzling markets display the cunning of the Ol y'Chibe and their affiliate people the Ol y'Gech – *We, the Cousins.*

Beyond the Copper Gate of Sham-None-Greater spread icy lakes and swamps that frequently unfreeze, and home savage beasts used in the contests of Sham's arenas.

The y'Gech are sallow-skinned like mature ivory. The y'Chibe are yellow as creamed gold.

Neither people has gods. They have never needed them, they say. They believe that always everything of theirs, once down, will rise up again unaided, just as the beautiful white ourths they rear and ride kneel down at a command, and stand up at another. The dead drop too, but the spirits of the dead stand up and come back in new flesh. What business is this of any god? Let gods go worship themselves.

South of Sham in what will, centuries on, become the Marginal, Ol y'Chibe forms its al fresco towns of sluhtins.

The cold surrounds all this in pallid blankets.

There have been two or three centuries of Winter so far. But what have the Chibe and the Gech to fear? The witches of their kind are well versed in magic. Crarrowin they call the women of this type, though in Gech they are known as Cruin. Both names are basically the same. Both mean *four*. This number is the most important among either people for it signifies Brain, Heart, Loins and Life-force, the four ruling features of a human body. The brain and heart and loins are of course physical, but dominated by the life-force – that which always stands up and returns. Every Crarrow or Cru coven comprises a girl child, an older girl who is a virgin, a woman who has had sex and borne a child or children, and a Crax or crone, their leader, who has been and done all these things and now, past child-bearing, knows too another deeper state.

In godless Ol y'Chibe then, among the crystal woods, a Crarrow girl is trotting to her sluhtin in the dusk, seeing a snowstorm brewing to the north. And having seen also something more curious, miraged there on the snow.

Amid the tented cave-town of the sluhtin Yedki sat before the Crax of her coven.

Of the four witches Yedki was yet the virgin member, though fifteen years of age. If not a Crarrow she might long ago have been wedded, and doubtless childed. *As* a Crarrow, with more autonomy than other women, she might have chosen a man for herself, either to marry or merely to bed. But Yedki preferred to hold her place in this particular coven, and so stayed sealed. The Crax was her favourite grandmother.

'What then did you see in the snow?' the Crax now asked her.

Yedki was not astonished the older woman read her mind. Such matters among their sort were regular enough.

'I saw a kind of cart – but not quite that. It had great wheels. There was a crowd, perhaps – and men riding in the cart-thing, which was drawn by big, cat-like animals with long hair round their faces.'

The Crax looked down into the little fire-pot, at the charcoals. In the enclosure of the sluhts and sluht-towns, the y'Chibe always contained their fires; it saved on smoke pollution.

'What kind of men were they? Gech or Chibe?'

'Neither, Mother. They *shone* – one rather darker than the other. I couldn't make out their faces – one too dark and one too bright. But there was a boy there too, and he was one of our own, yellow of skin, comely and bold. *Too* bold. He gave me such a look: impertinent – yet surprised.'

'You say?' Again the Crax paused. Then she bowed forward and breathed lightly on the fire-pot. A single thin flame rose out of it, became detached and hovered in the air.

Slowly the loose flame formed the symbolic shape of a female womb. Evident inside it something peacefully curled. A foetus.

'You've foreseen your first son.'

'But Gran – I'm not even undone yet!'

'By this we behold you will be, and soon.' The Crax saw fit to overlook the incorrect use of her house title.

Yedki stared sullenly at nothing. 'Even when I was tempted I *refused*. I wanted to stay with *you*.'

'So you shall, my girl. You're gifted and sit well with this coven. Tibtin has finished her nubility and must leave us to make her own foursome as their Crax, or to retire from our work if she wants. So you will take Tibtin's place. Ennuat is twelve now and may take the virgin's place. And there are girls enough with skill to fill the child place Ennuat has had. So, you stay with me, coupled and seeded.'

'Thank you, Mother,' said Yedki, formal again with relief.

A man walked through the shadows by the door of the Crax's cave. Yedki's eyes inevitably followed him. Was *he* to be the father? Or that warrior she had looked at last year? Who would he *be*?

*

Yedki woke in the night.

Someone was sitting at the foot of her bed-place, a fine man of the y'Chibe.

Startled, Yedki sat up – remembering even as she did so what she had seen pictured on the snow, and what the Crax had told her.

This man seemed familiar, yet she knew she had never met him before. Did she like him? It was surely not proper he had crept in on her like this.

Yedki noticed his gleaming dark hair with its elegant long braids tastefully knotted through by bird and rodent skulls. He was tying a complex knot at his belt, impressively.

'Good evening, lady,' said the unknown warrior. He looked slightly bashful after all. But too he spoke not quite in the accent or with the phrases she would have expected. His teeth had been painted exquisitely, as only the Chibe leaders or their most heroic fighters were permitted to do. So many contrary elements.

'Who are you?' Yedki asked briskly.

'You saw me earlier.'

'Saw you where? I'm Crarrow,' she prudently added. 'Keep this fixed in mind.'

'I assure you I do.'

'You talk like a foreigner – yet in the language of the People.'

'Always that,' he said. 'Olchibe always. It's woven through my bones, even these bones now.'

'*Now*? What are you meaning, rebirth?'

'I lived,' he said broodingly. 'Now I live another way.'

'You are some spell-fetch of the northern swamps beyond mighty Sham.'

'*I*?' He looked upset more than riled. 'No, I'm not so bad. I'm no ghost. Not any more.'

The Crarrow girl hissed an incantation.

Wild waves of light went over the space. She and he watched them, she rather angrily, he with respectful interest. They clustered round him in the end, then melted off. He seemed untouched. He said, wistfully, 'A long while since I lay down with a woman of my own kind. No women so lovely as the

women of Olchibe. No wise-women so wise as the Crarrowin.'
The tied knot also said something like this.

'Flattery will get you nowhere save out of the door.'

'Ah?' He shrugged. 'I'll only come back. Come on, don't you like me a little? I'm just as I was. Twenty-eight – or is it nine? – or so. And fierce as a wolverine. You should see me ride the mammoths.'

Yedki understood herself sufficiently to know that, though disturbed and perplexed by many aspects of this confrontation, she was excited. And when she looked at him she, like her magic, swirled to him and melted. She had felt nothing like this with any man before, even those she had liked.

'What's your name?' she said.

'You'll know it – later. When the hour comes.'

Then, almost piteously, he leaned forward and put his hand on her knee.

At the connection, which was physical and, somehow, *not*, every tension and doubt ebbed from Yedki. She *knew* him. Had *always* known him. But too he was new as every dawn.

They stopped talking, save in sly, low, persuasive murmurs. Presently they stretched out side by side. He let her untie and then rebraid some of his beautiful hair. When she inquired, he spoke of battles he had fought, and she believed him, despite a continuing oddness in all he described. He mentioned living and dying, and *re*living, in the gentlest and most ordinary terms. But y'Chibe accepted reincarnation. Such things were not outlandish.

In the end he covered her and she dragged him closer. Within a rushing tangling of pleasure she let him achieve in her the wound of her undoing, and nipped his shoulder hard at the pain.

After the climax of this amazing act she fell asleep, thinking he must only have drawn away so his weight did not inconvenience her.

Half waking near sunrise she recalled everything, and looked for him, but he was gone. She slept again. Then, at her second wakening, Yedki, the bed otherwise empty, thought she must have dreamed of mating with a charismatic stranger. As she got up and daylight filled the tent however, various twinges, and the shocking traces of her virginal blood, showed her this had been no dream.

A thrill coursed through her. A man had truly lain with her. He would be somewhere in the sluhtin now. She would soon see him again.

In that, of course, she was both right – and wrong.

Guri, former warrior of a vandal band and adopted uncle to the god Lionwolf, hunkered down on a snow-hill.

The camp-town below was much smaller than the last sluhtin of Guri's former leader, Peb Yuve, had been – or rather would be. Guri shook his head, mournful and slightly irked. He had seduced a Crarrow, poured himself into her, *left* himself there, or that physical fleck of himself which was needed for a rebirth in flesh. For some reason which eluded him it was apparently necessary that he return in fleshly form, even if it was to be the fleshly form of a god.

Lionwolf had understood these things. Or, if not, irresponsibly cared nothing about them. *Lionwolf* had already got himself born once in flesh, died in flesh, come to in the cold blue Hell of his own personal punishment, died *there* etherically and so been *reborn* etherically, *there*. After which a kind of different death had expelled him from Hell and back towards the waiting world. Lionwolf's third, earthly birth would finalize his processing.

To Guri, bewildered, nearly exasperated, the whole method seemed excessive. Especially since he himself had been born and died in the world, then persisted as a sort of ghost in it, then died *again* and landed in his own punishment cell of Hell. Eventually released from Hell he had been tossed back here.

With one major alteration. This now was the *past*.

It had stunned him when first he figured it out, hanging over the glamorous city of Sham.

Sham had been only a bitter remnant in Guri's former earthly life. Long ago sacked and wrecked by conquerors from the southerly Ruk, Sham then was a jumble of debris and mud and ersatz slave-markets. Of all the legends of glorious gates just one, a Copper Gate, had partly stood. Here and now however there were five, and each of these in excellent repair. This Sham too had towers and terraced blocks and decorated squares and superb fighting-grounds.

Ambling through the air and over the landscape of the past for some while, Guri had observed the peoples of Olchibe and Gech, and incidentally discovered their lack of gods. In Guri's original life the Great Gods of Olchibe were an accepted fact.

Knowing the inevitable format of his own return to flesh, a dire suspicion welled up in Guri then.

As for last night, no other way to put it: he had fathered himself.

Oh, he had never *meant* to. But he had seen the girl before he left the purlieus of Hell, a vision. The moment he was here and spotted her therefore, as she trotted back towards her sluhtin, an unavoidable attraction had enmeshed him. He had had to accost her.

What he had actually done certainly offended him. If he considered it, he had copulated with his own mother, although naturally at that point she was *not* his mother. One coming myth to hush up then, probably.

Irresistibly now Guri squinted through the early morning, through snow-mist and ice and the legs of frozen trees and rocks, and saw the girl whose name was Yedki examining her blood-stippled blanket. How complacent she looked. Women!

Guri braced himself and peered on, right through the slender curve of her belly. Within, a shape balanced among the branches of her inner organs, like a rosy pear. Yedki's healthy youthful womb. And yes, deeply fastened was a tiny sequin, wiggling just a little; frightening, miraculous atomy, already flexing its amorphous muscles—

'Me,' said Guri.

Resigned, he closed the book of his potentially god-like brain and leapt instead straight up into the cloudless height above the mist. He might as well enjoy himself for the few mortal months of freedom he had left. For after that who knew what fresh horror and muddle would ensue?

FIVE

There was an eye in the sky. Visible only to a mage or a highly gifted psychic, it might have belonged to any number of deities. To vicious Zeth Zezeth whose name essentially rendered was Zzth, or to mild Ddir the artisan god, who rearranged the patterns of the stars. The eye might even have belonged to the yet unreborn floating godsoul of the Lionwolf.

The eye belonged to none of them.

It had more the ambience of an opaque window, something blind which was yet somehow *watching*.

Around the window too, gradually, a type of activity gathered. Ultimately this would come to be seen quite readily by anyone as weather.

Beneath sprawled the sweep of the Southern Continent, and there the shamble of Kandexa, fenced off in sectors by the hem of the frozen sea.

Streamers crossed the sky now. The hour was early but the light was deadening. A storm must be imminent. But there, storms happened. Nothing new in that.

He had been dreaming. He was two years old and his mother was going out to break ice for the water jars. He had had a premonition. He ran to her and begged her not to leave the house. Her face became serious and she nodded, and sat down by his side. A little later both of them saw a black wolf steal from the shadow by the tree. They shut the house door and were safe.

Thryfe had always hated wolves, even the less terrible white wolves of the south and east.

How different would his life have been if his mother had heeded his inarticulate screaming, and not died under the village ice-tree?

He opened his eyes and saw in front of him the sweet sleeping face of Jemhara . . .

Had she cured him at last of the nightmare?

She stirred. The smooth petals of her lids lifted. She gazed deeply into his face.

During the twenty-three days and nights they had been together here in Kandexa, she had quickly lost the look of fear and of perilous search which her first awakenings beside him had engendered.

The first few times he had taken her back into his arms at once, kissing her hair. 'All's well, beautiful. *Now* all's well.'

She had been recalling he knew that previous first time, there in his mansion at Stones, when he woke at last from the trance of their gorgeous mutual lust to remember his chastity, and Ru Karismi's fatal error that he had been determined to prevent.

He could never have saved the city from itself. He was sure now. He would have died, that was all.

And so – missed this.

She roped his neck with her arms, her breasts pressed against him, all the slender curving warmth of her body.

For a while then once more all the dialogue between them was made of sex.

Spent, he held her closely. Over on the wall, he noted that the twig-hand of the bucolic goddess Ranjal seemed ridiculously wooden and over-motionless, as if clumsily concealing its alert involvement. A voyeur goddess?

'Let me go,' demanded Jemhara. 'Let me heat some beer. Let me see if the apple's grown back again.'

'It always does.'

'Perhaps,' she murmured, 'we shouldn't eat it. It's thaumaturgic. How do we know if it does us good?'

'Highness Jema,' he said with profound gravity, 'don't you think you would know if you were poisoned?'

He watched her as she went about the attic room, setting the buckled pan of beer over the brazier, placing the bread neatly on a platter. The green apple he had brought here always regrew when they had eaten it, providing they left it hidden under a bowl, as if to reform from its own core in plain sight was indecent. Why the apple *did* regrow he was unsure. But it was nourishingly wholesome and tasted always clean and fragrant – as this woman did, this beautiful woman made of alabaster skin and crow-wing hair.

Besotted fool, he thought, amused. Let him be one, then. He must learn these human ways.

They ate and drank and devoured half the apple each. Back under the bowl went the core.

'What a canny village wife you are.'

'And you a bad, lazy husband. Get up, Lord Thryfe, or shall I come and bite you?'

'Bite me.' *Is this* myself *saying that?*

'No. I will bite you only if you leave the bed.'

'Here I am.'

'Perhaps not a bite. Will this do . . .'

'You called on God,' she said afterwards. 'Which?'

'There are none. No, not even that live twig over there. I called on something as men always have in joy or anguish. We're taught these things. They live in us like mice in walls, and mean nothing.'

Soon they would go out and walk through the zone named Paradise. There would be persons to see to, and tasks to accomplish. Paradise was bursting with mad hubris that now it had *two* Magikoy, and one of them, as most suspected, the famous magus Thryfe. Who always denied he was, as Jemhara always denied herself too. Other sections of Kandexa had grasped the idea jealously. But then they skulked to the gate begging for this or that assistance, and willing to trade sheep, cattle, wine and treasures looted from under the city's hearthstones. Mage help was never refused but tricks – there had been one or two – were crushed, their authors chastened.

The sky from the attic window looked odd to him. Ribbons of shadow streamed from a dot of glassy emptiness itself like a window of grey sugar. Thryfe stared at it, and for a moment was on the verge of divining something vile.

A faint low cry distracted him.

He sprang back to her across the room. 'What is it?'

'Nothing at all. I was dizzy.'

'Sit. Now, look up at me. Yes.' He gauged her acutely, for a second merciless in his scrutiny. She had gone very pale but her natural colour was returning and she smiled, still fearless before his stern mask, that of a Magikoy healer in mid-diagnosis.

'You see. It wasn't anything.' The eyes of the eagle clouded. Jemhara stiffened. 'What have you seen?'

'You,' he said quietly. 'And one other.'

'Which other?'

Thryfe felt a pang, a sort of horror, unjustified maybe, or not. For certainly neither of them had inclined to predict let alone want this. Though it was the one thing any other man or woman might have wanted or predicted.

'You're carrying. And by me.' Her mouth dropped open. He wanted to kiss it and held back. 'Have I wronged you, doing that to you?'

'You speak – as if you'd harmed me . . . a *child*?'

'Yes, a child. It's firmly lodged and has the aura of a male. Do you *want* this, Jema?'

'Do I want—'

'Don't fog your thoughts with village superstition. There's no life-force there as yet. That will come later. It's a seed smaller than a pin's tip. If you truly desire to bear this thing, we can secure it. But if not—'

'Wait,' she said in a very little voice. Suddenly she dipped her face into her hands.

Instantly he knelt beside her. 'My fault,' he said. 'Whatever you decide, blame me for it.'

'*Your* fault? Do you think I can't protect myself in that way?'

'Yes, yes. But neither you nor I – we took no precaution.'

'It's never that, my love. Oh,' she said, 'oh, what's been done?'

He held her, waiting. He felt a huge current like a turning tide far out beyond the ice-locked shore, which shouldered roughly through the room. Dread after all sank its claws in him. Must everything of his be spoiled or *spoil*? Coldly he thrust off the thought. Here was one lesson he must *not* relearn, the petty recrimination at an act of mindless fate.

Jemhara sat lost in memory. She saw a treacherous red-haired god who came to her and told her, even if she had denied it to herself, that Thryfe would find her. And Thryfe and she between them would create—

She said, 'What do you hate most in the world?'

'Hate?'

'Say without thinking.'

'Useless cruelty – wolves—' Checked, he glanced back at his own words.

She said, 'I am to bear the reborn Vashdran. Lionwolf. Look into me again and see.'

'No, Jema. He's gone, burned away for ever by the White Death. This is some fancy—'

'Some fancy I was given and made to memorize. *I foresaw.* He told me you'd come to me. He told me, in obscure ways now made clear, *he* would be the result. A god, a demon god. Inside me.'

'Never. This isn't—'

'Look into me again.'

'Jema—'

'I will look too.'

They looked.

Each saw something other, and the same.

To Jemhara it was a citadel, rose-red, holding in it a sapphire that was an embryo. She felt nothing she could analyse let alone comprehend.

To Thryfe came the image of a fiery crimson heart. And inside that a tiny second heart, flaming.

A womb of fire that held – a son. A *sun*.

When he blinked he saw her eyes were cold with tears and he caught her hands.

'This means *nothing* to us. You, or I, can rid you of it.'

She said simply, 'My love, I doubt even the god you called to can rid me of *this*.'

Outside snow blurred across the window. But the man and the woman did not see.

'It's snowing,' said Beebit. 'What a filthy sky. Are you off to Aglin today?'

'Yes. She said to go back this morning.'

'Azula,' said Beebit, 'it doesn't matter any if you can't learn. Aglin's a fine mageia, but perhaps not so clever a teacher. Now if Lady Jemhara had taken you on—'

The daughter of Beebit and the goddess Chillel continued calmly tying indigo beads into the dark right side of her hair and pale ones into the brown side.

'I don't mind, Ma. It'll come right.'

Beebit sighed. She had had high hopes of her daughter's latent sorcery. But really it was *extremely* latent, was it not? Though grown to full womanhood in so short a time, bright, intelligent, lovely, and fast to master the contortionist's art, Azulamni had never manifested any other magical flair.

And though Aglin was trying every handful of days, as her own duties in Paradise allowed, to teach Azula the basics of witchcraft, it seemed this novice had no talent. The fire, called to light, stayed unlit; the water told to thaw stayed adamant. The small stone that should have scuttled along the ground sat as if glued in place.

Yet how could that be? Azula was herself a wonder. Some great power must be there in her.

While Beebit fretted, and revealed as much by telling Azula *not* to fret, the girl herself seemed merely vaguely sorry to disappoint.

Her hairdressing complete Azula got up. 'Where will *you* go, Ma?'

'As mostly,' said Beebit grimly, 'back into the western ruins. The old house is down, as you've seen for yourself, like everything else for a mile around. But people still dig. So do I. My daddy your granda's there, under the bricks and snow.'

Perhaps with unconscious unkindness Azula said, 'But will you know him, Mother? Won't he be a skeleton?'

'I shall know him. I *must* know my own.'

'Shall I come too?'

'Not today, Azulamni. Off you go to Aglin and have your lesson.' They had had this conversation many times. The phrases were almost ritual now. 'After all, when your magic breaks out of you, you'll be able to help me with more than physical strength.'

'Wouldn't Aglin help you?'

'Shift bricks? Don't you think she's got enough to do already? Off now, girlie. Off to school.'

They embraced at the doorway of the hovel, under the roof hole pegged over with an ancient sealskin, mother and daughter who appeared to be sisters, not an inch or an ounce or a year between them.

No sooner was Azula out on the street, however, than she began to pick up on some other element. This was most like dully hearing something, or mistily seeing it at the back of her brain. Now and then the effect had occurred before. Azula never referred to it, or took much notice. Perhaps she had assumed others experienced similar moments. And perhaps they did, some of them.

Skimming along the alleys, Azula hurried to Aglin's room. The snowfall grew thicker as she went. It turned both colours of her hair to white. In the background, hundreds of miles away, something jangled dimly above in the sky, and Azula, who had no magic, listened with half her inner ear. Generally she did not think a vast amount. She acted as events happened. When they were over she filed them tidily behind some mental cupboard door.

Running along the passage to Aglin's apartment, Azula found the mageia awaiting her with a suppressed look of impatience.

What could be worse, said the suppressed look, than trying to get blood out of a snowball? Fond mothers, said the look, always reckoned *their* kidlet was a genius. And if the other parent was a god – well.

This did not distress Azula. She bowed to the mageia and closed the door. Turning, she listened with her own patience for the umpteenth time to the proper rules and chants, and watched Aglin bring fire from the air. 'Now you try, Azula.' And hey presto! Nothing.

Dressed for the outdoors, Thryfe and Jemhara had remained in the attic. She had put on more beer to heat, and poured it for them, but the two cups stood untasted.

Peculiarly, and both noted and thought this, they had begun to reminisce aloud over their pasts, as if they had grown very elderly and had nowhere now to go save backward. She had confessed to him her sins, which he knew of and had already witnessed replayed in the oculum at Stones, when he began to search for her. He talked of his training, of his journey to the Insularia at Ru Karismi, of the eagle familiars of his boyhood – stories already told to her.

Then, step by step, they brought their two histories together. To the capital, to the death of the king Jemhara had murdered at the will of the king's brother Vuldir, to Thryfe's tenure of office and his riding away, and the last mission imposed on Jemhara by Vuldir, which had been to pursue Thryfe and somehow ensnare and destroy him.

She had done it too, although she had not meant to. She had never suspected she could.

It was their love they would have spoken of next, and sex and possession, and how time or their grasp of it had frozen the mansion over and caged them, willing and unknowing prisoners, inside an endless night of concupiscence.

Something then suddenly interrupted the mutual narrative. Before they could reach the nostalgic peak of their idyll, a fearful revelation interfered.

Speaking of his sleekar ride from the city to his house, and how the windows had been white with warning, and his gargolem servants out on the snow standing guard against some sorcerous invasion, and how the invasion had been Jemhara's shape-shift to a hare, Thryfe abruptly grew silent. He was staring at an anomaly never before seen.

Recalling how Vuldir had sent her to Stones and her own comfortless ride to the village, an hour's journey at least from Thryfe's mansion; her sulky sojourn there – she too beheld abruptly the *same* anomaly. It lay like a boulder on their path to meeting.

They sat in the attic, halted by discrepancy.

After some minutes he said to her, 'You see it too.'

'I see it. How can it be?'

'I had left the capital some days before you.'

'It was *because* you had gone that Vuldir read such danger in your attitude and forced me to follow.'

'But that very night I reached the house the windows shone to warn me – and that night too I went out across the snow and found you at the Stones, in your shape of the little hare.'

'And I had been already at Stones two days and a night. How can I have arrived there *days after* you yourself, yet been there two days before you, and still you met me, I you, on the first day of your return?

Unlike this discrepancy of a mysterious and awful glitch in time, before them years and spotted only now, neither was aware of the world or the sky outside.

The daylight had flattened and smoked over. For a long while only the brazier had given either light or dimension to the room.

It was as if some perfect scene-stealing effect took place, and no one paid any attention. Of course, whatever had expended such effort out there, *up* there, might be affronted that the audience ignored it.

Without prelude the *bang* sounded high above. It shook the house, the built streets beyond. From walls and roofs solid slabs of snow dislodged and crashed in the alleys of Kandexa.

Jemhara and Thryfe, along with some thousands of others, were on their feet.

The noise had been as if the sky itself had blown up, split right across, and might now give way like a damaged ceiling.

There came an immediate gushing rattle.

Past the window flared a sparkling, straight-dropping hail of what seemed tiny embittered glittering stars. As they hit the walls and ground in turn, a million sharp and metallic impacts resounded. Below, out in the alley, a man screamed unpleasantly. Next moment the pane of glass in Jemhara's window, closed still for the night, was smashed. A cascade of diamonds shot through into the attic.

Thryfe spoke. Another pane, this one of energy, dashed up to fill the window-frame.

Like maddened wasps hatched from some defrosting orchard, colourless gems flew and smacked against the barrier. Splintering appeared in air—

Jemhara flung the wooden shutter closed and fastened it.

In near total darkness – the brazier fire had sunk down like a frightened dog – they stood listening to the arrows of ice striking on every outer surface over and over. There was distant shouting too and wailing cries.

Another roaring bang bisected the sky overhead. It had seemed impossible the concussion could be repeated. The house shook again. In one wall a hair-fine crack undid itself and powder sprayed across the room.

Jemhara smote the brazier. The fire regained its courage, jumped up. Across the floor white wasps of ice sizzled malignly, not melting.

In the alley outside a man, arms and back broken, was calling, his howl weakening, lost too in the rattle of the hail. He had attempted to crawl to shelter. His track had been like that of a snake, but was already obliterated, and his body half covered by prisms of ice. Jemhara had seen this in the instant she slammed the shutter. She had not been able to help the man. She said nothing.

Above, a low grunting complaint stirred from the roof.

A beam twisted a little, over their heads.

The shutter too had been dislodged. They watched as it slid sideways like a turning page and thudded in on the floor.

'We must go down,' he said.

She snatched her cloak, a handful of things from the table and Ranjal's twig off the peg. They went towards the door.

A new note sounded – a whistling tearing screech—

Everything flamed white.

Jemhara saw something like a gigantic blazing spear cast from the sky, parting the jewelry hail – it fell to earth perhaps half a mile away. Where it hit home white fire and blue detonated outward from whatever it had struck. A barking explosion followed, unlike the vast noises of the sky.

Despite the danger, Jemhara had looked back at the window, transfixed, staring. Now a second blazing shaft lit the gloom – now another – and another— Scores of these things tore through the hail, rushing from the sky each with its shrilling note and blank white flash of light. Wherever any struck anything below there was the yap of explosion and blast of harsh iced fire.

'Jema—' He pulled her from the room and out on to the stair beyond. The stairwell was very dark but neither of them conjured a lamp.

The stair kept creaking, swaying a little.

Thunder-stones – these were the things that fell, a sort of lightning. He had read of them in old manuscripts, never entirely assured of their nature.

Visible through a freshly made aperture in the wall by the stair, another shaft shrieked by. It had a broken and terrible shape, all angles. Now the strike was only a street or two away. Their own building recoiled at the blast, and he heard some other neighbouring architecture sharply snap, the crush and push of stones plummeting.

Down the shuddering stair they eased. This house could offer no refuge. But where they went to next he had no idea. He had cast a cordon of force about them, which to some extent held, but loose plaster and chips of brick pierced it nevertheless. As with the ice-avalanche that had encased him here something in this weather shorted out other powers, considerable though they might be. In all his life he had never witnessed a storm of this character, and only the sheet lightning of a brief thaw, or the flicker of northland lights reported to him, at all resembled thunder-stones.

Reaching the house doorway they lingered. A curtain of vicious hail deterred them from any further step.

The other occupants of the house he supposed were out. In the alley Thryfe detected a dead man under the glistening heaps of hail, a dead animal and a smashed cart.

A woman was leaning from a window across the alley, waving her arms and whimpering in panic. It was this property they had heard crumble; part of the lower storey had collapsed, only a stair and wall holding up the higher rooms.

Jemhara called to the woman above the drizzling spat of the hail. 'Come down. Throw yourself out – I can guide you to the ground. You won't be harmed—'

'I'm afraid—'

'Do you know me? I'm Jemhara the mageia, Aglin's friend. Trust me – I will guide you down.'

Thryfe thought perhaps she could not. Her powers too might be impaired. He put his hand on her shoulder to warn her of this, but in that instant the sky directly over them opened a violet seam. He saw it descend then, a solitary thunderbolt, its evil zigzag of frozen brilliance and the blind white revelation thrown out all about it. It dropped towards them single-purposed on a tail of frayed splitting silver.

Thryfe hurled Jemhara back into the well of the stair, and from his guts drove out a shield of energy that seemed to rip his bones and blood out with it. The doorway and frontage of their shelter turned opaque – but exactly then the lightning bolt met the street.

Curiously mellow, this near explosion, and dim . . .

Far off the muted flutter of fire.

Jemhara. Her cool hand, healing flowing from it like wine through glass, and he the glass.

He pulled himself up. Jemhara supported him. Strange, how

78

strange. He had felt the pressure of the ring he gave her, there on her middle finger, pressed into his forehead.

Despite the thaumaturgic shield all the façade of the house was down and lay across the alley. The hail, quieter and almost delicate now, was pattering like white rice over it. The opposite house where the woman had cried had mostly tumbled and was burning with a blue flame.

His hearing came back with a shock, and he could see.

He held her and Jemhara lay against him.

They seemed to be beneath a bowl of nothingness, but it was neither temporary deafness nor their own protective power. Arrows and pins of lightning still howled earthwards, but no more landed here. Their trajectory had changed.

An irrepressible notion seized him. The bolt had *looked* precisely at them, studying them both with some implausible and non-existent eye. It had indeed come searching for them; or – it had come searching for *her*. He had used his magic as a rank beginner would, unkempt, injuring himself – his solar plexus, the inner core of his brain, felt stung. But there had been no space for sophistry. And they had lived. Wildly it crossed his mind that this primal thing, whatever it might be, which hated them, was perhaps handled better by brute force than by wisdom and cunning.

'Are you unhurt?' he asked her.

'Are *you*?'

'Of course.'

The rubble of the other house over the way grumbled and gouted bilious sparks. Both of them considered the trapped woman who had not escaped in time.

'The hail's less,' Jemhara said.

'Yet the lightning bolts—' He pointed. 'They're running all one way.'

They stared. The galvanic missiles streamed by overhead. Each ran horizontal now before diving downward somewhere to the northern west.

He thought of the weapons of Ru Karismi. He had never seen their flight, save with his inner eye. They would not, he believed, have looked like this. Even the lightning 'flash' he had heard described by those from the city who had been aware of it and still survived had not been the same, let alone the detonation.

New explosions racked north-west, echoing against the ice-shelved sea. Something else had drawn off the bolts of heaven it seemed, something more attracting than Jemhara.

They moved forward from the house. When they were twenty paces off, picking over the bright shale and debris, the stairwell they had so carefully negotiated plunged inward behind them with a cloud of brown dust.

Beyond the alleys they found many corpses lying in the road. The gemmy hail was finally disintegrating, showing all the clever things it and the lightning had done.

The concussions of the bolts were fewer now, he was certain of it. A count of thirty or seventy could be made between them, and now a hundred.

He glanced at her again, assaying her as he had before in the attic room, wanting to be sure all was well. But everything of her had remained in perfect connection, beautiful as some magical mechanism. And what else was the human body after all? At the centre of her too the flame-heart of the second life lay tucked safe, *immutable*.

The house had been two streets from the shore. It was not in Paradise either, but among West Villagers, and Beebit had had to buy her way into the zone with her body. But that was easy and reasonable. Made of petrified wood and stones the dwelling had not held out under the onslaught either of Lionwolf's rampaging invaders, or of subsequent weather.

It took Beebit many days to locate it, for everything was down. But, just as she had at last identified the jumble of her former home, so she was convinced she would know the bones of her father.

Yes, she had loved him. She knew of others of their kind, their profession, who *broke in* their daughters and sons personally to the trade. The dad had not been one of these. He had brought to her a young good-looking minor noble of the city, who had a little cash and was grateful to find a tasty virgin, particularly one who could do such tricks with her 'honey bones'. 'Don't fall in love with him,' her father warned her. 'He's from the idle class, and we belong among the proper aristocracy, the working class who are creative and useful.' She had listened seriously, absorbing his advice. And although her first experience of a man was acceptable she felt more pleasure in her own abilities.

All these years after, day by day she grubbed through the layers of rubble. She had got down to the foundations of their house that morning and was singing softly, thinking of her own wonderful daughter, hoping that this moment, or this, Azulamni would achieve the release of her inevitable powers.

When the astounding sky-crashing bang sounded above, almost every one of those who dug in the ruins leapt up and stared. Beebit herself had not got to her feet. She was holding apart two slabs of broken stuff; she had just got a glimpse of cadaverous white. She did glance at the sky.

The sparkling hail began seconds later.

Skittish and separated it only needled and pricked the skin. Beebit pulled the hood of her cloak over her head, and bent again to her task.

A cloven skull and heap of bones lay in the cavity. She knew it was him. She leaned nearer, ignoring the scrambling and calling and shouts of the others round her, and the hail's increasing thrash.

Then the hail altered. This was between one breath and another. It passed from insectile venom to whips and mallets.

A hundred prismatic assassins broke Beebit's neck in half a blow and stove in her cranium with the other half.

Did she realize what had happened?

Pain beyond pain. Then none.

'Daddy—' she said.

For her father was stepping out of his grave under the house, all done up in wholesome flesh and not much older than when she had been twelve.

'It's all right, flower.' He took her hands.

81

'But I thought you were dead—'

'Hmm,' he said.

Beebit, who had herself been Azulamni, looked about and saw the world becoming very small while something else lavishly opened all around.

She *knew* and flung out one fist to clutch back her life, screaming, 'My girl – my daughter—'

But a cool liquid wave moved over her, what now she was. It was like waking from a dream where everything had been entirely real and involving, but it *was* a dream . . .

At the start of the storm the second Azulamni, daughter of Beebit and Chillel, ran out of the mageia's room despite Aglin's protest. She sprinted through the alleys, going northerly and west towards West Villagers. People dashed past her, groping for shelter, some yelling and many offering prayers to various Rukarian gods.

Azula ducked and wove through the hail. When the second thunder came she paid it no heed. At no time did she have any fear for herself, though the hail sometimes grazed or slashed her. When the spearing lightnings began to drop she did not know they were lightnings, or thunderbolts. A group of standing houses was struck not ten feet ahead of her, all of them exploding, fires unreeling and bricks flying round her head, and still Azula had no dread – for *herself*.

It was her mother she was frightened for.

Because she had grown up so swiftly, all memories of her time with Beebit were condensed to a shining acuity. With adult commitment Azula ran to aid her mother, but also with the leftover need of a child.

At the barricade of West Villagers dead burned guards lay on the ground, smothered by hail, only a crisped hand, a bloody foot, stuck out. The gate itself had taken a direct hit and burst.

Azula raced over hail and bodies and walls.

She had visited the site of the house before. No one, that was no one alive, remained in the vicinity.

The girl flew up the escarpment of cast-out stones.

Beebit lay face-down on the other side.

Thoughtless, Azula crouched and pulled her over.

Ah.

Beebit's face, unmarked save by the tiniest scratch on the cheek and a faint flushing from the coldness of the ground, ended just above her eyebrows. Her forehead and her greened brown hair had vanished. Her opened head was filled like a cup by the glittering hail-jewels, while the old scar, there since she was fifteen, had been removed along with the top of her skull.

There was nobody else left out on the street. Either they had crawled to some dubious refuge or they were corpses.

Azula bent low over her mother.

The hail broke round Azula, smarting, doing nothing more.

Strong as most young men, Azula lifted her mother in her arms and stood up. She slung back her head so the hail-beads tinkled in her two-tone hair. Her own face, exposed to the sky, received no serious wounds.

Like a wolf she howled. On and on.

In the howling was the death of love.

The storm seemed to pause at it. Perhaps this was a delusion.

Then high overhead in the black-white parasol of cloud a sort of eye appeared, tracking the howling and the thing which uttered it.

A purple vein ruptured.

Out of the vein the levinbolt came down, straight for the howl, to silence it for ever.

Azula saw it come. She bared her teeth and bellowed into the core of it.

If anyone near could have been watching, and none could but the dead, the bolt would have been seen to strike the earth directly *through* Azula.

A cannonade erupted at the place. A ball of ice and white fire surged skywards sidelong – and caught in the midst was the fragmented, exploded body of lifeless Beebit. But no sooner had the flames sprung out than they failed. Like fire meeting water they were distilled, losing their light and all velocity. Smoke and a low rumbling were the only evidence of the strike. One object stood upright where the bolt had landed: Azula.

She had ceased her lament. Her brown skin bore a faint silvery tarnish, and in her hair all the coloured ornaments were dust. Aside from that there was no sign on her. She was yet alive, and turning her head slowly like a snake, her teeth still bared and her eyes gleaming with rage.

The next bolt coursed in moments later and struck home. It too boomed out with a brief incandescence, fading almost instantly to spume and smoke. Then the others knifed down after it. They came one on another, now and then two or three together. Each cut into the spot where Azula stood, head back and feet planted wide, her arms and hands stiffly stretched as if still supporting her mother's shattered body.

What does she feel now, the goddess's child, Beebit's daughter?

Nothing unique. Only fury and a sort of furious drunken gladness as the potence of this enemy reaches and is destroyed by her.

This then is her magic? She does not think of that. There is no truly unusual sensation as the bolts disintegrate around and within her. A kind of fizzy fieriness, not nasty, let alone epic. Nothing much.

Across the decimated city any living spectators behold the spears of the storm flying all one way, zooming to the ground somewhere in West Villagers sector, detonating more feebly, defused.

Azula, as she earths each lightning, stays fixed in one endless loop of approach, impact, dissolution.

The storm however wilts. The hail sprinkles to a stop. The lightnings are growing fewer, thinner, nearly flimsy. Some perish in mid-sky.

One last bolt stumbles towards Azula and triggers itself midway down, filling the upper air with a long, spreading blue ripple and the metallic reek of ozone.

Quiet returns. There is only some crying and calling that hovers, like an afterthought.

Azula kneels and sees a bone. That is all she *can* see of her human mother, now. There are bones everywhere, naturally, but she knows whose this was. Of course she does.

Saphay the crone was sitting in a corner of the joyhall of the Holasan-garth.

She spied under her seamed lids, watching Nirri talking to the four men who had ridden out to search for Arok and his hunting party. They had found no trace. Snow had fallen in the night, they said, as if Nirri might not know. No doubt the men of the hunt had taken shelter, but any tracks were wiped away.

Nirri was worried, Saphay could see that much, but she behaved well and steadily, and now had the men sit. She herself brought them heated ale.

When I was a garth queen, Saphay ruminated sarcastically, *I was never any good at it. It takes the low-born*, she mentally decided, *to do such things well.*

She asked herself if she should go personally to search for Arok. It would be nothing to her. She could fly, or more properly levitate, over the snows. Had he died? As a god she ought to know such things. She did not seem to. Perhaps she was afraid to find out. The tumult here resulting from his demise would interrupt her own concerns.

Arok's son was having a nap upstairs. True Jafn, he already resisted the enforced periods of sleep given small children.

Arok's son.

Saphay scowled. One of the women going by with food for the searchers skipped round a pillar to avoid the crone's eye.

All these days and nights Saphay had haunted the garth. She was bored beyond patience with it all and angry with Athluan. How dare he try her in this way, reborn an *infant*. Every time she saw him she felt a rush, not of love, but of confusion. She must wait at least sixteen years for him to become a man again; she would have no lover's feeling for what he was until then. She thought even had she been a child herself and he as young, she would not have liked him till he had grown. In her own youth the only males who ever caught her eye were always three or four years older. Athluan had been thirty when first she met him, she seventeen. His ghost had since informed her she had loved him then and he her. But she had never been sure; was not now. The little white-haired boy she regarded, in gentler moments, with nervous, wary tenderness. Lionwolf had been wrenched from her twice. Other surrogate sons too. One of those had died. Athluan, a sort of son-figure mingled with a perhaps-lover due to meet her later, might also, once more, be snatched away.

He was mortal. Therefore he could die, again.

Saphay swept to her feet at the very instant Nirri walked up to her.

'No news of my lord,' said Nirri in a calm way. Unease was held firm behind her eyes.

'Well, he's off hunting.'

'They've been gone eleven days. An Endhlefon.'

'Thoughtless,' said Saphay. 'Men. Hunts, wars.'

'Can you help me, lady? To learn if he's safe. All our house mages left us. We've only the wise-women and the werloka, who have—'

'Less ability than scrats,' Saphay observed.

Nirri said, 'Their talents vary.'

In another corner the old werloka was playing a noisy board game with two of the older men. Respectful, they always let him win. The wise-women were out in the garth at a birthing. Which meant, Saphay thought, their eating and drinking, and sometimes chiding the groaning or shrieking woman in labour for her laziness.

'Finding spells are not my province,' said Saphay.

Nirri nodded and looked away. 'I should have thought they might be. You knew what had become of Dayadin.'

Saphay flinched. She had not, did not, admit why and how she had known, having been there and unable to save him. The glimpse of her past cowardice did not improve her mood.

'You have your other son,' ironically she said.

'Yes. But I'd wished to ask you – is there some way in which you might *secure* my son?' Saphay stared. Nirri said slowly, 'This is an unknown land to us. My husband the Chaiord is long gone from home. Men are lost, as well as children. My other boy, all I have, is here. Witches can make charms, protect human things.'

She had spoken without desperation, and carefully. She saw, through the crone's withered exterior, continual strange hints of other elements – youth for one, and eccentric irresolute powers. When Saphay was with Athluan Nirri also saw what she took for a latent or foiled maternal instinct. *Is she too searching for a lost child?* But there was more. *Perhaps,* Nirri concluded now, *this one has been widowed of her husband.*

Saphay though turned on her sprightly old heel and marched down the joyhall and out through the door.

In the yard a man was hoisting oranges along from the hot-house, poor wizened objects but even so reminding her . . . of the Klowan-garth. Where she had lived with Athluan, then.

She heard his steps behind her.

Without looking round she knew them, as she seldom knew another step of either adult or child, even of god.

'You were laid down to sleep.'

'Only the dead can't avoid sleeping.'

She gazed at him and there he was, standing beside her on the snow.

'That is a cliché of the Jafn,' she said. 'Why use it?'

But, 'I dreamed of another brother,' he told her, pleased. 'He was called Like-a-Lion. He was nice.'

'Conas,' said Saphay.

'That's it. You never met him.' His face clouded. He would lapse into the other life, then falter. It was terrible for him. He had reached for her hand and held it, and led her to the yard gate. Together they looked at the winding ways of the garth. 'I remember a pear tree, all knotted over, and you broke the ice and got out the pears. But it doesn't grow here. Oh, look,' he added.

She looked. Where her gnarled claws clasped his small hand, an ember of light had formed. It was warm; even she could feel it now. It seemed protection of him seeped from her automatic-ally.

'What do you want most?' she asked.

He gazed at her now. 'To grow up. If I could grow up, I'd marry you.'

'I'm an old woman,' she said. She felt it, or thought she did.

'Not so much,' he said. 'I saw you. You were in the air and you were young. Well,' he amended justly, 'young *enough.*'

She laughed. 'Ungallant.'

He only smirked at the Rukarian word and concept, and rubbed his face on her hand, and the amber ember of light curled round his head like radiance freed from a lamp.

Saphay doused it. Someone else might see.

He gave a mutter of disappointment.

She sensed then the *energy* of the light, the protection, swirling and pushing inside her to get out. By all the gods she could now never call on – it was like a sort of birth.

'Come along,' she sternly said, 'you must go in and sleep.'

'Saffi – no—'

'Perhaps if you do, I can find a gift for you when you wake.'

So adult, his sceptical glance. 'Oh?'

But he let her lead him back inside the House.

She and Nirri both conducted him up the ladder-stair, and various unliking and suspicious eyes oversaw their progress. The werloka alone voiced the discontent. 'Too much allowed that outland female. Arok needs telling.' But Arok was not at home.

'There, he's asleep at once. At that age such a fuss. Only my Dayadin – only he never had to put up with it. He grew so fast. He was almost beyond the sleeping age in a month.'

Saphay sat the other side of the cot-bed. 'I've been pondering, Nirri.'

'Yes?'

'What you asked me.'

'Yes . . .'

'To protect him. There is something – but you will have to trust me.' *And I must trust myself.*

Nirri stared into Saphay's eyes, her face. She said, 'I don't really, lady. But I trust the world less.'

'I have known your son before. *This* son, Athluan.'

Nirri bowed her head. She understood none of this yet something in her had opened to receive it. After all, almost from the first, she had thought she also knew the old woman.

'Do what you can, lady. I'll be responsible for your act. If you harm him I'll kill you. And then my husband will kill me. Those two results are sure.'

Saphay shook back her hair. A wild glint of gold lit somewhere in the strands, and from her floated the always present perfume that attended her.

'You can't kill me. I shan't harm him. Now go out and let no one enter. Is that clear? I'll call you when you may come back in.'

It speaks inside me, Saphay thought. *But it is me.*

When Nirri was gone Saphay leaned over the boy and breathed on him. From her mouth issued a soft scented flame that burned nothing. And then from all her body the flame issued. The release of it was to her very sweet. It covered the child like bloom. In wonder Saphay did as her own power drove her to do, inaugurator and bystander both.

Outside, the sounds of the House and garth were far away.

She could not see herself in those minutes as she was, a golden figure with the head of a lioness, maned in dawn, whose eyes wept tiny suns.

Despite the blood in her hair and her snapped left wrist, Aglin bent over the girl lying on the blackened snow. With her right hand the mageia stroked back Azulamni's bi-colour hair. 'Time to get up, my girl. We'll go to Highness Thryfe. And you'll be needed, now you've found your magic.'

'I won't get up. I'll stay here with my ma.'

She did not shed tears. At least not out of her eyes. Azula was all crying. She was like a vessel full of water.

'Because she died?'

'I've got her bone. I'll keep her bone.'

'You keep it, that's good. She'd want you to. Now up you get.'

'I'll stay here.'

'You never will. Come on, make her proud, your mother.'
One-armed, Aglin, shockingly tough, dragged Azula to her feet.
'Make her proud, Azula. You're more than a mageia. I ran after
you, though I was too slow. I saw some of what you did from
that little rise, you see? You're a warrior and you're a goddess.'
Azula leaned on Aglin's healthy arm. They walked together
away across Kandexa, through the smoking, twice-powdered
rubble, and the dead.

When Nirri first re-entered the chamber she turned only once
to Saphay. The old witch, who had just summoned her, was
blushed by the rich glow that filled the whole room like red-gold
wine.

The pivot of the glow was Athluan's cot.

Nirri paused, her hands caught under her chin.

She could see her boy, but in an unexpected way, because he
slept there right in the middle of a ball of flamy brilliance. And
he too glowed, palely, like snow held safe in the heart of a fire.

Nirri took a step.

'No,' said the crone, 'no further. You mustn't break the web
of sorcery.'

'Is he – does he – does it *hurt* him?'

Scornful: 'Does he *seem* to be hurt?'

'Excuse me, lady.'

Lofty: 'You have a right to ask. But there's no discomfort. He's
asleep. Yes, that thing the Jafn despise so, *slumber*. And he'll
sleep some while.'

'How long? An hour?'

'More than an hour.'

'A whole night?' Nirri shot Saphay another astonished stare.

'More than a night. More than many nights and many days.'

Nirri said in tones of cold wood, 'What have you done?'

Saphay rose up. She rose up tall as the room until her lion's mane brushed the roof timbers. Nirri stared after her and saw Saphay in her aspect of goddess, and dropped on her knees in the prudent loosening of her joints.

'He will sleep,' said Saphay the goddess, 'until the fire has cleansed him of mortality and childhood both. He will sleep until he remembers what he has been, and his promise. Then never again will he be taken away from me.'

'From *you?*' whispered Nirri.

But this time the goddess, in the customary manner of her kind, did not reply.

Eighth Intervolumen

Man salvages: Fate ruins. Man ruins: Fate salvages.

Bardic Lay of the Hero Kind Heart: Jafn

Thryfe scanned the sky, horizon to horizon. Seen from high above it the cumulus was itself a world. Clouds had formed a dark blue ice plain pierced by cobalt mountains. Westward spread an apricot lake of light. The seventh day aftermath of the hail and thunderbolts had left this tropospheric landscape consistently placid – unlike the carnage of Kandexa.

The magician, in his shape-shift of eagle, soared in steep wide combings, searching out any pocket of threat. But there was none. Since the storm had been uncharged, that oblique intelligence which must have crafted it seemed also to have withdrawn. For now. Thryfe glided downward, riding the winds of the air, entering the topaz eye of the sky-lake.

From here he could detect a caravan a mile and a half below. It crept so sluggishly over the ice, a colony of abstract dark more like a toy snake than a train of wagons, carts, slees and sleds; it crawled between the vast tracts and runnels of packed snow. The earth too was now turning bruise-blue with ended sunset. Night was out hunting. Night's first arrow burst on the shadow – one star, another and another.

Furling his wings the eagle dropped.

In his man's brain something said to him: *You see far better as a bird of prey. That was always so. But since your self-damage in the Insularia, even as an eagle Thryfe is not quite, any more, the eagle-eyed.*

Neither of them, though they meant to leave together, intended to take with them any further companions. In the stunned limbo after the storm both Thryfe and Jemhara had acknowledged, unspeaking, that she had been its target. The obscure adversary had originally tried to prevent conception. Now its aim was to nullify it; the child Jemhara carried was to be negated. For this reason therefore they must exit the city alone. Once stripped of them, Kandexa would be safe, ironically, as houses.

But like iron filings pulled to a magnet, of course the fearful and distressed survivors immediately rushed at them from every side. In an hour a huge crowd pressed round them, sobbing and shouting for help and reassurance, and for the shield, and the bandage, of Magikoy sorcery.

He drew her aside. 'Once free of us their peril ends. We're its focus.'

To his dismay she checked him quite harshly. 'No. You are not. I am the one it wants.' Perhaps he had hoped she was not completely aware of her plight. Which had been foolish of him, he thought.

But the crowd called and entreated. Up pushed a woman with two infants and several others all with injuries and grey faces, tales of horror. There was no space to discuss alternatives.

Thryfe and Jemhara resumed their role of healer and mage. Only when all was done could they slink away, under cover of darkness.

The maleficence of the occult enemy seemed spent for now. That was in their favour. Each time the dedication and vigour of it had been limited. They outwitted or eluded and it seemed to give up.

Methodically they did their work. The crowds surged and went and came. Others had naturally arrived from most of the zones. Sometimes pleading people led the two mages to different spots. Here they discovered more injured, and many dead. A thousand varieties of human woe.

Both of them noted that their attempts to repair those buildings not totally destroyed were met with indifference or hostility. Constantly the shaken heads, even words flung out at them: But we can't stay here! Twice-cursed Kandexa – the gods must hate it. Vashdran's devils razed it, now the wrath of the heavens smites it – we must go away, far away. Soon the nearly mythic name of the new Rukarian capital Kl Ctaar was offered. It was said to lie west and south of here. Surely it must exist? There would be security there.

In the afternoon, by which time anyway Thryfe and Jemhara had been separated by those begging their assistance, Thryfe met the mageia Aglin, Jema's friend, as she surfaced from the throng.

'These are only scratches. It's just my wrist. Cleanly broken. I've made it not hurt, Jema taught me that trick, but it needs fixing. Do you see, Lordship?'

Thryfe looked where she pointed with her sound right hand. There were camp fires everywhere, burning for warmth among the often still-smoking re-ruined ruins, and in the glow of one of these he beheld the contortionist's daughter, Azula.

'She's on her own. Is Beebit dead?'

'Yes, dead. It was quick, I think. But by the time I found Azula—' The mageia swiftly told her tale, keeping her voice very low so no other should hear it. The low voice painted in flat bright strokes the girl like a silver spear on the mound of rubble, the lightning bolts pulled down to her, flying at her, through her, exploding *in* her, dying, doing no other harm.

Thryfe and Aglin stood in silence a moment, as if to allow the roaring echo of the quiet words time to fade.

He watched Azula at the fire. She was smutty from smoke and her face and hands were covered in little grazes, her clothes torn. Her two-colour hair had bits of beads sugared in it.

'*That* is her gift, then.'

'They called them fire-takers, where I came from, Lordship. We had a legend of one, a man. But that was hundreds of years ago, and it was only the sheet lightning he used to suck off the sky. Not great zinging bolts like she did.'

Thryfe asked himself then if after all the girl should be brought away with Jemhara. She might prove protective in areas he was not. Besides, Jemhara might need Aglin too. Aglin was a fair midwife. He had not decided where they could go, yet he too had considered Kl Ctaar. The murmurs of the Kandexans had not deterred him.

He saw to Aglin's wrist; she was a spry witch and felt no pain as he slapped the bone together again and internally soldered it, matter-of-factly binding it up herself afterwards and tying the knot in the cloth with her right hand and her teeth. That seen to, Thryfe walked over to Azula.

'How are you doing?'

She looked up. Her eyes were empty. 'I'm well.'

'Your mother was killed, I hear,' he said bluntly, to try to fathom the depth of her state.

Azula emptily said, 'Skull crushed off then blown apart. But I've got her bone.'

'That's good.'

He touched her head. Under his fingers he felt the after-throb and pulse of dead lightning. Had it seared her out? Not her brain, but her heart and spirit? It was impossible to tell. She was bereaved. And she was uncanny too, if Beebit's history of her was a fact, and why should it not be in this age of mad foul wonders?

Near midnight, sky currently lucid, soft cloud reflecting two veiled half-moons, he located Jema over at Happy To Live zone. Happy To Live was flat as a stepped-on cake. Jemhara held two weeping women in her arms while a weeping man leaned against them.

Thryfe waited until Jemhara had done all she could, seeing he thought the healing seethe out of her, iridescent and not quite there, like the moonlight in the clouds.

In the name of any gods, how had he ever doubted her, this woman coined in the non-existent heavenly Paradise?

They stole off eventually in darkness, clandestine as two adolescent lovers.

'I can't leave them yet,' she said. 'Can you?'

'No, not yet.'

'I think the entity that pursues me has gone to ground. It expends such passion – and then gives up. Besides, Azula *hurt* it.'

'Perhaps she did. Let's hope so. She must come with us when we go away. And Aglin too.'

She rested her head on his chest. For a few seconds she dropped asleep, exhausted. He held her. Above them the moon unveiled, veiled, seeming to sail for ever to some gentle shore. If one refused to see the mess of the earth, all might have been well.

He knew already if these people, all of them, wished to leave the ruin accompanied by both their Magikoy, neither he nor she would deny them. Maybe Jema and he could go elsewhere at some later date and so ensure the general preservation. And yet, without mages, other problems might arise for them.

His thoughts moved sidelong. Holding her, he gazed for a moment deeply into his mind. *What do I feel?* It was so extraordinary that despite all resolve it seemed he must question, must challenge it. For whatever spark of Hell or flame would come to possess the physical budding in Jemhara, also it was – his. His *son*. Against this unseen radiance every dilemma abruptly meant little. He stood there with her, silent, holding her under the sky.

Some people elected to remain.

They were defiant, adamant, and in a minority.

About twelve hundred persons said they would travel west of south, to Kl Ctaar. There was a new king there, perhaps one of the King Paramount's lesser sons who had somehow not died after the White Death.

Factious zone-wars were forgotten. They were again a single nation: Rukarian.

The best slee was brought for the female Magikoy. It even had its silk carriage-shell and furs. For Thryfe they brought an aristocratic lashdeer chariot, a sleekar. The runners were oiled; the deer had been cared for and were well fed.

Separated again, he and she rode away from the city, out into the snow waste, among the throng of evacuees.

Jemhara and Thryfe performed their mage duties for the

travellers. About the caravan they folded sheaths of weather-protection and semi-invisibility.

But the skies were swathed in blissful clarity, rouged dawns and gilded sunsets, pale, mild, blue days with strands of feathered cloud, or banks of cloud always smooth and white. No snow fell, only light winds blew. By night the stars were sharp as spikes.

'Look, d'you see that? That eagle flying up there – it's him, his Highness the male Magikoy. He flies over the cloud to scout for us.'

Thryfe and Jemhara sat by night in a small tent.

'Where has it gone, our faceless enemy?'

She said, 'It's everywhere. Don't you feel that, Thryfe?'

'Yes, in its very *absence*.'

It was waiting for them. Avoiding the young girl Azula, who might again be able to deflect its mindless, *focused* venom?

'What can it be? What is it?' Jemhara murmured. 'I'm afraid to know.'

'Remember that what it hates,' he said quietly, 'is not yourself but the child inside you.'

She lifted her head. 'Then it must go on hating. I've no choice.'

'Should we reconsider this? Perhaps I should attempt—'

'No, Thryfe. Even you – what can you do? It is *set* in me, like a *stone*.'

He said with an acted coolness, 'But there's grave danger even if you get to term. How can you birth such a creature?'

'I shall have to. It will want to live and may guard me from harm to help itself. Besides, another woman gave birth to it – to *him*, before. Saphay.'

'He was partly mortal then. Now . . . the gods know what he is.'

'Gods again. Are you coming to believe in them?'

'I believe in that one. The one who has claimed what's in your body. Either a god, or something that can only go by such a *title* as god.'

'The Lionwolf. Should I therefore . . .' She lowered her eyes.

100

She had been about to suggest that Lionwolf, if a god, might be the very one to pray to now. He had a vested interest after all.

But she did not finish her sentence and Thryfe did not ask her to continue.

Jemhara thought, with a glitter of her old slyness, *Vashdran won't let anything damage it, this embryo he wants. He is selfish and terrible and golden. So, I must live, and Thryfe surely must live too, so he can assist me. At least until the hour of birth.*

Would Vashdran then simply kill both no-longer-needed parents – she first, torn wide, like wrapping from some long-wanted gift?

Chilled, she kept her eyes on the earth. Not knowing she did so, she turned Thryfe's ring round and round on her finger.

Thryfe, whose thoughts had been similar, also did not look at Jemhara.

Outside a naive weary singing rose from the travellers' fires.

Occasionally Aglin and Azula rode with Jemhara by day in the slee. The two older women were not inclined to chatter. The girl was almost always dumb. Virtually unblinking she watched the snowscape pass. When Aglin pointed out oddly shaped ice-hills or rafts of frigid forest, obediently Azula looked at them. Now and then, if seldom, they went by old villages. Most of them were deserted and snowed under, but at one spot a host of bellowing men came bounding from some group of hovels, brandishing farming tools and rusty weapons, intent to rob or just to slaughter any passers-by. The Kandexans, trained to fast reaction and fighting mostly from formerly attacking each other, beat them off. A couple of dozen village corpses littered the ground; the defeated living hurried away. After this moronic battle, Azula spoke a sentence: 'Ma told me most men were idiots.'

Later, at the evening halt when they were alone – Azula had gone to fetch a hot drink for them – Aglin recalled these words. 'Is it good she spoke out? I don't know. Whenever she says anything of any substance it's to do with her mother.' The mageia grunted. 'Beebit had a premonition she was due to be off, or so I think. Just a day before she said to me, It's a chancy life, whoring, but now Azula's with you, lady, she'll learn better.'

Jemhara saw she had let fall her scarf in the snow and bent to retrieve it. Aglin tapped her on the arm. 'Don't you go bending like that, Jema. Oh, I know you're in the family way. Have a care.'

'You've grown too clever, Aggy.'

'And who taught me *that*?'

At which they smiled and Aglin picked up the scarf. But no more was said, for Azula came from the cook-fire with the hot beer.

It would be a long journey. None could have doubted that. The smooth milky days progressed, and the star-sparkle nights, during some of which the caravan forged on.

Ten days further south white woodland came down the land to meet and envelop them. The trees, though stretching every way for miles, were widely spaced. Glacial spires of pine and balconies of glassy cedar, damson and fig in knotted rings like petrified dancers, the stems and roots making hurdles between, forced the caravan from its serpentine formation. Vehicles, riders and trudgers alike were scattered out. Here stabs of ice tall as towers dripped moisture at the persistent sunlight. A faint musical tinkling filled the air even by night, a song of water drops let fall on the thin white tin of centuries-frozen leaves.

This would be a bad place for an ambush or other assault. Nothing like that occurred, but they pressed forward as quickly as they could. Men riding ahead presently returned and told how the woodland lasted for many more miles.

Thryfe the eagle, too, quartered the sky and pored over the terrain below. The woodland did indeed go on and on, breaking only at last on a bleak plateau that hung above a craggy mass of snow fields. Nothing was there either. Far away and away the land ran, melting into distances the too-gentle blue of the sky.

Even if Kl Ctaar existed, this would be a quest of months. Though the people had brought food and other stores with them, and the men hunted where they could, even the woods were unusually sparse in the matter of game. A strange impression fastened on Thryfe. A giant broom seemed to have swept the country bare of anything more useful than wood, ice and snow. Perhaps *not* strange. Perhaps *something* had.

Jemhara saw, across the woody vista of dark glass and white tin, a figure walking steadily towards her.

The trickling tinkling sound of the melting water drops was very shrill. No one else was near by – and abruptly she noticed that the six dogs who had been harnessed to the slee standing just to one side were not there. This did not seem particularly notable. She sensed huge thaumaturgic pressure in the air. She was here to meet the one who strode towards her.

He was clad in a mail of ice. His dark hair blew back behind him. *The god Yyrot*, she thought. *Winter's Lover.*

The god spoke. 'A beautiful Winter's day, Jemhara.'

Jemhara bowed.

When she looked up again, Yyrot had altered. Now he was another god. This had happened before, she believed, this sudden metamorphosis.

Now the god was Lionwolf – yet—

'Surely you remember me better than that, Jemhara?'

Golden this god, with laval hair like molten silver. And *not* Lionwolf, but the one who had first fathered him on Saphay.

'So I did, or was made to. But *now*,' said Zeth Zezeth the Sun Wolf, 'his father is mortal and his mother mortal. And even though they are of that wise little sect the Magikoy they are made only of dust and cold human mud. What a shame. How far he has sunk, my former *son*.'

Jemhara knelt down on the snow and this time bowed her head very low. Inside her body her heart hammered, like a fist in her brain, like a drum in her womb. Did the foetus hear too?

'I doubt he hears. As yet he is not in the flesh. He was in Hell a long while. So currently he will play about incorporeally on the earth, refinding it. *Do you see this?*' Without preface Zeth turned his back to her. She beheld, through the layers of whatever cosmic fabric clothed him, and perhaps also through layers of etheric skin, a scar that jagged like one of the death-storm's lightnings along his spine. 'Oh, it is nothing,' said Zeth, terrifyingly resentful and frivolous. 'But I have shown you. Something flung me against the sky. I will admit it hurt me. I have been hurt. I do not like to be hurt. Not that any save great powers could ever do it. One like you, little Jema, or like your paramour that *cripple* Thryfe, neither of such as you could touch me even if you ripped your souls apart with trying. Do you see? Answer now.'

'I see, perfect lord.'

'Yes, such good manners. You learn all your lessons swiftly and superlatively well – magic, whoring, excessive *virtue*. Now learn *this*. I am quite fond of you, Jema. Never disillusion me in my fondness. I have many scores to settle and you will be my handmaid. Then I may spare you much that others will have to endure.' Jemhara knelt on the snow. The aura of his gold and silverness vibrated in rhythm with the drums that clanged in her body. 'You are, in this at least, modest, and inquire of yourself how it could be likely that you might ever aid a god such as I am. But I shall find for you a way. An honour and delight for you, is that not so?'

'Yes, perfect lord.'

He laughed then. The wonderful quality of the laugh seemed to squeeze her inside out – and, worse than that, inside out of the *world*—

Jemhara woke as if breaking free through thick ice. A violent nausea convulsed her. As she vomited, she felt the strong hand of her human lover supporting her forehead.

'The child,' Thryfe said, as bonelessly she slumped back against him.

Jemhara whispered, 'Yes, that. And a dream.'

'What dream?'

'I don't recall.'

The caravan crawled on through the woods, a dislocated snake. At last the white plateau, balanced on its shafts of cliff ice, gaped in front of them. It was unwelcoming and apparently featureless. However, it made a change.

As night descended, long before any moonrise the brilliancy of the daggerish stars shined the plateau up. The travellers became aware that the starlight was exceptional.

From about the camp fires they gazed at the heavens.

Gradually a mutter began, then a calling. The noise was excited yet without any hint of alarm.

Thryfe left the tent where he had been doctoring a feverish old man. He stood on the snow, gazing up as did countless others. Even the animals seemed to take in the picture in the sky and had raised their heads to stare.

A city blazed up there, made of stars, picked out in piercing splashes of turquoise, reddish and yellow fire. It had walls and roofs, high terraces and towers, a reminiscence for many of Ru Karismi herself in the era of her glory.

The incredible sight covered so much space that even a man's two hands held up against it did not obscure more than half the image.

Across the camp the voices were exclaiming now that Ddir had done this, the god who placed the stars. He must have drawn in millions of them to create this fabulous artwork. A Rukarian deity, he could only mean it for them or their kind. A lustrous omen. It was his guarantee to them: they would soon reach the new metropolis.

Behind him Thryfe heard the old man's two grandsons carrying him out to witness as well. 'Look, Great-da. D'you see it? Isn't that fine?' Thryfe thought they should not have moved him just yet. Nevertheless the stars burning in the old man's eyes were probably excellent medicine.

Thryfe wondered if Jemhara too had left whatever she was at to look at the phenomenon. Probably she had.

There were gods, then.

It seemed to him he had always, secretly, feared as much.

Some hours after, when the city of stars had moved further to the west, one vaporous dim breath of cloud blew over them and covered them for a minute or so. They blazed on through the cloud, then all at once their unique fire deserted them. They became only stars again, vanished back into the void, making no special pattern. Only three narrow moons gave light.

The next day virtually every person in the caravan was imbued with vigour and hope. Jokes were shouted to and fro as they urged their transports on. Song carolled. The snake, again in flawless formation, hurried.

During the afternoon the clear sky showed a sheet of purity, the air motionless. Seen from above, as Thryfe this time did not see them, they had moved about one-third of the way across the plateau. Perhaps some forty miles lay behind, eighty or ninety ahead.

There are forecasts in most situations. The hammerhead cloud closes before the storm, the glare burns on the face of one about to strike you. Now nothing, no clue.

Those behind saw the head of the caravan serpent suddenly dip – as if it had found something intriguing in the ruffled thick-packed snow.

Then the serpent's head was all gone. Instead there was a black hollow about a fifth of a mile in radius, full of a loud rushing gasp.

Into the pure air sprayed ice crystals – tiny stars – shimmering. And on the edge of the hollow there was a peculiar writhing upheaval and commotion – which was wagons, carts and animals and human things attempting to save themselves, each other – yet pulled forward and away by some invisible horror which sang, *Now, now, why bother with that? See, this is so much easier – why trouble to resist?*

Slipping, tumbling, the shambles poured down into the vortex – struggles at a further edge here and there anchored, hauled back, stragglers and their property – or struggling, anchored, hauled and then still prised loose, losing everything, everything— *Down*—

A liquid wave of shrieking and cries, the crack and groan and smash of wooden things, sloughed wheels bowling merrily along the snow – uproar bleached to a dull moaning boom. A sort of stasis after, in which to attempt understanding of something never to be understood.

Even in this stasis, however, one major flaw. There was to be no margin to attempt anything of consequence. The drama is not done.

Another hollow opens.

It is a huge throat, yawning, swallowing.

Repetitive the awful action – living things and vehicular things – slipping, tumbling – the gush and crackle, ring and thud, the screaming – the lovely lacy sprays of ice and snow—

Thryfe, standing in the sleekar, blinds himself deliberately to any thought of Jemhara in her slee, and where she may be positioned, or if already she has gone into the abyss. He dredges from the ravaged gulf inside himself, the core from which he wrested raw power to save her from the lightning bolt, and slings with gargantuan force a kind of armour round and over the piece of plateau where the caravan reels, round and over and under, down into the shuddering fault lines beneath.

For a moment he thinks the cordon holds.

Then comes another black gulping, another plunge – so close now that Thryfe can perceive, exact as a printed scene on a bowl, the arching bodies as they spin and dash away – the dogs tangled in harness, the woman with her flying curly hair—

Snow spray mantles him. His power is rubbed out.

To the sky he roars in silence, utter silence: Take me. If I'm useless that way, use me another. *Use* me. Seal up the snow with *me*—

And he feels the blow slam down on him as if the sky fell. His last thought is a wordless, hating *arrogant* thanks.

Unconscious in the sleekar he does not get another view of the next subsidence. He had believed in himself, he had reckoned his power might transmute, through sacrifice. An ultimate hubris? If so Thryfe is unaware of his punishment, the humiliation of redundancy.

The whole of the plateau is going, streaming inward on itself, down, down into the gut of the ice-cliff, the outer walls of which, eighty, ninety miles away, now rock and spit at the shock.

Jemhara had been with Aglin and the girl Azula.

After the first and second catastrophes Jemhara had seen Aglin glance urgently at Azula, and then give up. Azula only stared, sallow under her brown skin – frightened?

Then Jemhara saw the crack in the snow that came ribboning towards them like dark ink spilled. She pushed both women out of the slee. 'Get away! It's only me it wants. *Run!*'

But Aglin at that instant, all across the chaos and the plumes of upthrown spray, saw Thryfe had fallen. And how the area about him settled – grew *solid*.

Aglin jumped back at Jemhara. 'Sorry, my pet.' She had herself learned a few methods of survival, this mageia of the backlands. She punched Jemhara full on the jaw with her sound right hand.

As Jemhara collapsed Aglin caught her awkwardly. 'Help out, you!' she snapped to Azula. Like an embarrassed child the girl sprang in the slee and took Jemhara's weight.

'Why did you?' Azula asked.

'Can't you see?' All around, crinkling and griping, the plateau was now insanely stabilizing. 'She said, it was her it wanted. Her – and *him*.'

'But—'

'Enough. Look, the crack's sealed over. The ground's all right now. I've got her. There, she's resting on the floor. Run and fetch my herbal bag. There are plenty to tend. Gods grant I haven't harmed the kidlet.'

Westward, where the city of stars had dissolved or sunk, Bhorth, King Paramount, descendant of the royal line of Ru Karismi, paused just outside the wooden doors of his palace in the physical city of Kol Cataar, *Phoenix from Ashes*.

Inside the hall, now stolidly built of rock-hard wood, the after-supper poet was whinging away to his harp. Strains of the poem seeped out.

All are selfish. Even the savage
Have their own concerns.
The house-dove sees darkness fall
With such regretful petulance
She longs to fan with her wings the fires
Of sunset,
And keep them aflame;
The hunting wolf regards the sun
As thief of night's pleasures,
And would tear out the throat of day.

Bhorth had never had much patience with poetry. Years ago at Ru Karismi he had tended to nod off when the poets started, or else had absented himself with a woman. In this new-built and rough-hewn conurbation, the sophistry of such stuff had for him a false note. The poet's harp, for example, shaped like a great copper and gilt butterfly, strings stretched over the pin-shaped body; did that have any excuse for being here?

A guard on the door saluted over-solemnly. '*He*'s in right good voice tonight, sir.'

Bhorth pulled a face. 'Probably eaten too many ginger leaves.'

They laughed. Poets? Keep them. Soldiers were better, soldiers and sensible artisans. You knew where you were with those.

Bhorth moved off along the terrace which, only a year back, had still been fashioned of crammed ice-brick, but was now of finished stones. Much of the palace had been constructed of stone or wood. The areas of packed ice remaining stood out. As for the town – the city – whatever it was – the majority of the buildings were hardwood, some of stone, at the worst sheathed in something less finite than hide or snow. The two successful hothouses had been expanded. The third one which nobody had been able to make work, it was cursed the architect declared, had at last been remade on the barbarian plan – and since went on not badly.

And who are we to argue
With our savage inmost hearts—

Bhorth glanced indoors through a high narrow window with a disordered curtain, now bottled in glass. He saw his queen, Tireh, seated with her women and her aunts, listening to the poem and the music.

Neither of the city's two Magikoy women were there. They tended to keep apart as had been proper earlier in the true city, when Magikoy were plenteous. As for the ancient male Magikoy here, he had died five months before sitting peacefully at the iron-clad hearth of the hall, smiling as if amused at running out on them like that.

Deeper into the palace the pair of infant princesses, Bhorth and Tireh's latest children, slept in the care of nurses.

Bhorth realized he was making an itinerary of facts and persons, achievements, weaknesses, precisely where everyone *was*. As if he would soon be reporting on it all. Why was that? Did he sense something?

After the White Death, after he had passed on the black pearl seed of Chillel, some other awareness had sometimes stirred in him. Not too often, and he was glad of that. A mage or sensitive he had *never* wished to be.

Turning the palace's stone corner Bhorth beheld his son, his son by Tireh via the peerless loins of Chillel. The young man was standing on the terrace's edge, gazing up into the steel-blue icicle of the moonlight.

Sallusdon was named for the former King Paramount, to remind Kol Cataar that he would be a king. But how could there anyway be any doubt of that? Such beings *must* be kings – or something higher.

Getting on for four years of age, Sallus was a man and already taller than his father. You would put him at nineteen or twenty years. He had too a maturity behind his look that signified unusual intelligence and spirit.

Women sighed when Sallus went by. Men stared. But this was not a beauty to woo or be envious of. Black Sallus was a hero, a god maybe, at least partly.

Bhorth bulked there, watching his son. If he was honest the awe had never quite left him, though generally it was subsumed by some other emotion. The ever-present love and pride were perhaps more unwise. How could you pride yourself on father-ing – *this*? It was like patting yourself on the back for dropping, accidentally, an apple pip – and four years later there soared a miraculous tree growing from snow, its arms burning with golden fruit.

'Come and see, Father.'

Bhorth pulled himself together. He walked over beside his son.

'What's up? Are you star-gazing?'

'I am. About an hour ago something like a city, picked out in stars, appeared through the cloud in the west. It went down before I could be sure.'

'A city. That's old Ddir Star-Placer then, pottering about up there.'

'Now he's made something else.'

Sallus pointed. Even the flex and stretch of his arm, ebony with a single gold wristlet, was a marvel.

Bhorth forced himself to regard not the arm but the sky. The three quarter-moons were in a row, and bright.

'I can't quite—'

'*He* knows,' said Sallus, with a grin.

Bhorth noticed the chaze, the snake which should have slain Sallus about two years before when it bit him in childhood. It lay coiled under Sallus's cloak, but the flat head had come poking out, weaving a little, one quartz eye on the heavens.

Bhorth was accustomed to the snake by now. He recalled how he had sucked the poison out, and how his son, less than two years old, had himself already killed the snake. Bhorth had feared Sallus would die too – but neither did. Sallus survived; the snake came back to life, and was his son's pet.

'Well, he can see, and so can you. I can't.'

'Follow my finger, sir.'

Bhorth did so. Instantly and unerringly the finger described for him up high, in the blue circle of moons, a faint, lit scribble.

'I *do* see. It's like a snake too. One that seems to move for-ward—'

'Westward, after the star city,' said Sallus. 'Or towards this one.'

'Here? A snake? As you say, he'd know.'

The chaze swung its head, darting Bhorth a glance. Had it learned human speech? That was not inconceivable, seeing whom it belonged to.

Sallus said, 'I don't think the stars really show a snake. The snake symbolizes some other thing.'

'I'll send to the Magikoy women. Get them to toil over it. That's their job.'

Sallus looked across. His face was calm yet alive with interest. 'Father, I think it's a caravan of people. Suppose instead of looking up at it one looked down from the air – then the shape might resemble something of that kind.'

Bhorth was musing. *No Rukarian, apart from ourselves, has journeyed here before. I always thought others would come. Splendid and rotten, the canny and the indigent and the useful, the useless. Why now?*

In the long street recently named Rose Walk, which led across the city to the so-called Great Market of Kol Cataar, the priesthood were abroad and gathering alms.

It was about an hour after sunrise. The carts from Second Hothouse and the farmed ice-fields beyond Eastgate had mostly trundled through. People were about, to sniff the air, or here and there they had stopped a vendor to buy. When the priests shifted into view, swinging their brass censers of incense, several doors slammed. It had never been like this in the old capital. For a start Ru Karismi's high-nosed priesthood had never begged. But this fellowship, revived from the dregs left living by the Death, was slight in number and needy. It was a fact too their temple-town here was very small, a handful of buildings on the north side of Kol Cataar and not one of these yet rendered in anything more durable than ice-brick.

Then, at the head of the column a boy began to sing.

Dressed in deepest blue, their hair impoverishedly greased

with candlewax into long stiff tails, the priests advanced, each holding out his left or right palm for coins or other presents. The boy was dressed in the same way. He was about eleven. His face was almost boneless with youth, his fair hair only slicked back with water. His voice however was sheer and faultless, less like that of anything human than some instrument of the old city, a flute perhaps. It peeled effortless as a golden wire off the side of the morning.

After all hands delved in pouches and pockets. 'Here—' 'Take this—' 'All I can spare – religion is familiar with you. Bless us with a lucky day.'

The grabs of the priests shut like the mouths of certain sub-oceanic beasts found only far off in moveable water. The boy himself did not even seem to see. Eyes glazed he sang on, praising the kindness of divine otherlings, gods no one could recognize. Yet something had given him a wondrous voice. For an instant faith in gods seemed credible.

Only as the priests flowed away into the market did those loitering on Rose Walk grow aware of another noise to the east.

'It'll be some feud. Like before. The dilf-cutters fighting with the vinery wagons.'

Presently five or six men bolted down the road, pushing off onlookers eager to gossip.

'What are they saying? Strangers? What strangers? Is it enemies again?'

Fearful, the refugees of old war huddled on the street. Soon another group trotted by, going more slowly and more ready to talk.

'About five hundred of them there are, a big caravan. Rukarians—'

'What are they running from?'

'Have they drawn it after them?'

'*Will it now fall on us?*'

'We've borne enough.'

Not long after, hurrying soldiery from the palace of the King Paramount clattered the other way along the thoroughfare. In passing they urged citizens back into their homes. The road must be cleared to allow representatives of the caravan to enter. The king wanted to interview them.

Again doors slammed.

All through the new city by now the tidings flooded, and either the barricades went up or else the crowds stepped out to see.

'And your name?' Bhorth asked.

'Svurnar, lord king. I'm leader of this caravan, under the authority of our Magikoy.'

'And who is that?'

Svurnar, a metalsmith of Paradise-in-Kandexa, looked glum.

'Probably more was than is, lord king.'

Bhorth was seated on a gold chair from the former capital. He glowered direly back. 'Why, what's happened to your Magikoy?' The palace hall was choked with people, the ten allowed in from the stranger caravan, many more from the royal household, all ears and eyes.

'We had two maguses, lordliest. Very fortunate for us – till recently.'

'Both of them are dead,' Bhorth pronounced with leaden disfavour.

Svurnar bowed his head. 'As good as. It was when the terror-weather attacked us again.'

'*Attacked* you?'

'So it seemed. First thunderbolts – that's why we left Kandexa. But then when we'd begun our journey, the other calamity. The plateau opened in huge fissures. A multitude were swallowed down.'

'A storm,' barked Bhorth. 'Then a crevasse which had partly thawed—'

'Oh no, lord king,' said Svurnar with abrupt composed assurance, meeting Bhorth's frowning eyes. 'The maguses themselves were certain it was an attack. Something personal.'

Bhorth marshalled his ideas. 'Then you'd offended some god.'

'Perhaps Yyrot, Lover of Winter, maybe.'

'And your Magikoy are dead.'

'Entranced, lordliest. Not to be woken. Shut in cold sleep.'

'This is a bizarre tale, metalsmith. It *sounds* like a tale, something for the evenings by the fire.'

Svurnar hooded his eyes again.

At his shoulder the middle-aged woman clicked her tongue,
so Bhorth noted her for the first time. She was a mageia apparently; vestiges of fresh blue streaked her greying mop.

'You, mistress. You stand forward. Are you their witch?'

'Yes.'

Like all her kind she was not overly polite to kings. She must
have credentials then. Bhorth gave her after all a deferent nod.
He said, 'This story seems a funny one. Can you explain it better,
lady?'

'In private I will,' she said.

Bhorth shot a look now at his two resident Magikoy. Both
women were staring at the mageia, alert as hunting dogs. *They*
judged her valuable, it seemed.

'Very well then,' said Bhorth, getting up. 'You and I and the
Magikoy of Kol Cataar will discuss this.'

His court grumbled and surged about, but with the assistance
of the guards he chaperoned the mageia through into a side
room. Handy, this little chamber had only been added on ten
months back. The two Magikoy women entered last. Left out in
the crowd Bhorth saw his queen Tireh, seated as if only gravely
attending to everyday matters. Her presence of mind never
failed to please him.

Bhorth himself shut the door with a thump.

'Well then.'

'See,' said the mageia.

Her eyes turned *white* and appeared to fragment – crooked
shafts of boiling lightning clove the ceiling and lanced into the
floor. Screams and shatterings splintered the air. Bhorth beheld
and smelled acrid smoke. Blue fire expanded and for a moment
he glimpsed crashing brickwork and dead bodies cast about as
if in battle.

Somehow he kept his own self-control.

This was a show, a demonstration from the near past. And the ability of the mageia who gave it must be extremely potent.

A gust of dark swept the awful mirage away.

It was replaced at once by its partner in horror.

Bhorth watched as, amid a crack and roar, constituents of the Kandexan caravan plunged miles down into the guts of the hellish fissuring plateau, women and children, men and animals and wagons, a facsimile of the world toppling like shards of a brightly painted bowl.

Then the shadow stirred again and brushed the chamber entirely free of the sights, sounds and odours of calamity.

Bhorth glanced about.

The Magikoy had remained firm, of course. The solitary guard Bhorth had kept by him seemed likely to lose his wits. Bhorth turned to him and said very low, 'Brace up, or I'll tell you in detail what your wife did with the butcher's best goat.' And observed the man's face alter – ash, red, normal, and the shaky laugh. 'Yes, she only fed the brute, since the butcher is her uncle and the goat so fine. You're steady again. Well done.' Outside there was no beating on the door, no yells. The scenes and sounds of mayhem had been contained in here.

The mageia herself stood quietly. She seemed ordinary enough now.

'Where did you get such a prodigious talent, madam?'

'I was taught it by one of our Magikoy.'

'One of the two now in sleep-death.'

'They're not,' said the woman, cheeky, almost irritable. 'But it was all I could do to stop it. What attacked us wanted *them*. They needed to *seem* dead.'

'And you managed that.'

'I, king. I told you, she trained me.'

'Give me,' he said, 'the names of both your Magikoy.'

'Very well. Her name's Jemhara. She was lesser queen to your brother Sallusdon, when he ruled in the capital. You may recollect her.'

'By the—'

'*He* is Thryfe.'

'*What?*'

'Thryfe, Magikoy Master, Warden of Ru Karismi.'

Bhorth's tongue stuck to the roof of his mouth. His throat shut then undid in a brief fit of coughing.

When he finished, Kol Cataar's younger female Magikoy, Lalath, said softly, 'She speaks truth. Everything said and shown is fact. This woman has vast powers. Thryfe meanwhile lies at Eastgate.'

'And the other one, Jemhara, that bitch—'

'A bitch no longer, Bhorth. She is Magikoy too,' said Lalath icily. 'Redeem your temper. My kind don't make such mistakes as bitchery.'

Less than twenty minutes later Bhorth, paced by a phalanx of eight guards, was himself belting down Rose Walk making for Eastgate.

The caravan was a sorry draggled sight. But, like Kol Cataar, it flew, if raggedly, the crimson and silver banners of the lost capital.

A great number of the people waiting there recognized Bhorth instantly. A wild response between anger and relief gurned through the mass of carts, slederies and slees. Half of them would suppose he had run away from the final battle and only so escaped the White Death. Oh, he had heard all that. In fact he had ridden against the Lionwolf and his horde with every man he could muster, while that villain Vuldir, then Paramount King, sat on his arse and provided nothing. Bhorth had been captured. And then the Death tore out the whole page and burned it to white cinders.

But there was no time today for any of that.

An unguessable threat hung all around. An enemy without a face but equipped with the fangs and claws of natural disaster – those acts of gods.

'Take me to him,' Bhorth commanded the first man he reached. There was no need to translate. The man took Bhorth to Thryfe.

Despite the rest Bhorth could not quite hold off the memory

assembling itself in his mind. The figure of Thryfe, imposing, haughty and absolute, standing so tall and faultless before himself and Vuldir. Both of them had then been only Accessorate monarchs. It was thirteen, fifteen years ago – more. In retrospect time seemed pleated.

'I'll tell you plainly,' said the impressive Thryfe of memory, 'you will be accommodating some force which will eventually destroy you.'

'*I*?' Vuldir had been amazed.

'You,' said Thryfe, 'and all your line. All the line of the Ruk. The land, the people. It will set the world on its ear.'

And Bhorth, that fat fool, had grumbled, 'Unending Winter has done that . . .'

And Thryfe replied: 'To this, Unending Winter will be *Summer-time.*'

'Good morning, Highness,' said Bhorth to the pale gaunt man lying in the wagon's back.

'Good morning,' said Thryfe. He smiled. He – *Thryfe* – smiling. 'How are you?'

'I do well enough. I was – improved, shall I say. By a brief dalliance.' In Thryfe's eagle eyes, ringed by dark shadow, a flicker of alertness. But it sank. 'I see you, Highness, don't do so well.'

'No. I was injured. This thing – has the woman Aglin told you?'

'The mageia? She has. An elemental foe.'

'These people are in extreme danger. Let me be frank, you also and your brave little city, if you take us in.'

'My brave little city has had to be strong before. Not quite our first test.'

'No. But this—'

'The mageia says you're attacked by crazed natural forces.'

'It seems so. She, I mean Jemhara, carries a child. The child is the focus of its rage, whatever it is that rages.'

'*Whose* child?'

'Ostensibly mine.'

'Oh? Some other was before you?'

'Not exactly. Listen to me, Bhorth. Do you believe in the gods?'

Bhorth hesitated, gave up. 'Sometimes.'

'That's sane. Why not *sometimes*? Try to believe in them now. Jemhara's baby is to be a god.'

Bhorth scowled. 'Your get. My, my, sir. How proud you must be.'

'I, and she – our getting is only the carapace of what this – *thing* – is to become. He was here before. *Vashdran*. Saphay bore him the first time.'

Bhorth, who had been standing bent over under the wagon's roof of stretched skin, decided to seat himself on the stool by Thryfe's improvised couch. Incorrigible faith clouded his thoughts. Although this was absurd, he had known the second it was spoken that it was real and disgustingly immediate.

'I don't want some dramatic argument,' said Thryfe. Indeed, he looked as though he could not sustain the mildest squabble. 'Remember what I was. Trust me.'

'Very well, Highness, I do. You and she have coupled and now she carries some sort of third party's seed. I can reckon to know *that* gambit. What do you want me to do?'

'Whatever searches after us means to destroy the child. In doing that it's quite sanguine on the matter of killing in random vast quantity. Therefore we try to hide. I shall go down again into a kind of sleeping death. For me that's now quite simple. I may even truly die there. I apologize if you had other plans for me. It can't be helped. But she—' A sudden violence blazed in Thryfe. He raised himself off the cushions and caught Bhorth's forearm in a grip like granite. '*She must live.*'

'Because of this obscure supernatural child in her.'

'Fuck the child. *For her.* For her. She must live.'

'*Jemhara*?'

Thryfe lapsed. He let go Bhorth's arm and absently, muscular resilient Bhorth massaged the aching bruise Thryfe's grasp had given him. 'She isn't what she was. She has become what perhaps she always should have been, if in the beginning people had left her alone.'

'Very well. If you tell me so.'

'I *do* tell you. Forget her as you knew her. She's been reborn.'

'And you say the accursed Vashdran is to be reborn too?' Bhorth anxiously leaned forward.

Thryfe's vision had blurred over. He was glad of Bhorth's uncluttered acceptance; it saved much time.

'Yes. Maybe somebody can smother it in the moments after birth. But be quick. It – will mature fast, and to colossal vitality.'

'I'm used to that. I have a son like that.'

But Thryfe's face had slurred away into the pillow as if every bone in his neck were water. He was unconscious. Already this mighty magus of whom, those years back, Bhorth had been if he were honest in extreme awe, appeared more than two-thirds a corpse.

Bhorth sat there. He considered the predicament. He considered how, after his capture, he had *met* Vashdran in his war camp of the barbarian Gullahammer. The golden creature which had talked to him in such a courteous and friendly, winning way. 'Won't you accept my hand?'

'I will not,' Bhorth had said.

'Oh, then,' said the Lionwolf, 'I must take yours.'

'By all gods,' Bhorth now murmured. Bewildered, blank, he gaped at nothing.

But something else darkened the entry to the wagon. This dark was warm, and shone.

'Father?' said a caring voice. And then, 'I've been looking for you.'

When she opened her eyes she saw the three women, two unknown, watching her intently, each in a different way.

Jemhara drew herself upright. She was weak still from the last six days of induced sleep, which had followed after Aglin had punched out her lights. No mark showed of the blow except in Aglin's concerned physician's gaze every time they met.

That was Aglin's look now. Aglin had acted intelligently and ruthlessly and saved many lives, Jemhara's – as she herself was quite sure – among them.

The other two women were Magikoy, Jemhara assumed. They had that special concentration in their look all of their ilk came to have. Even Thryfe had it. She, Jemhara, did not. She had not been Insularia trained. She would never consider herself a member of this elite.

Even so the Magikoy women nodded at her. The younger, who was the more thin and stern of the two, remarked, 'Anyone can see at once.'

The elder then declared, 'One of ours. Greetings, Jemhara.'

'You've recounted everything?' Jemhara asked of Aglin.

'Everything. The city's thrown open the gates to us. The king here – it's Bhorth – has been told the facts by Highness Thryfe.'

Jemhara forbore to pose the one question she craved to, *How is my lord?* Someone would have mentioned, or in some manner given it away, if Thryfe were worse.

'I'm ready then,' Jemhara said. 'Do what you must.'

Aglin shook her head.

The younger Magikoy Lalath said, 'It isn't to be more sleep for you, Jemhara. That would harm you probably, and no doubt the baby you carry.'

'Is to harm it possible?' Jemhara was scornful.

'Who knows? It's a god, or what will pass for a god. So we were given to understand. Whichever he is, few Magikoy would risk the health of such a foetus. Besides, my code is always, save in rare extremity, to protect the unborn. I know you weren't lessoned quite as we—'

'No, madam, I wasn't. I now put the lives of a few thousand persons before the hypothetical well-being of this – *lodger* inside me. And it can protect itself, I'm sure.'

The older Magikoy spoke. 'There's no leisure for a debate. What we propose is this. By your own powers, Jemhara, you will change your appearance, not superficially but *intrinsically*. You will be given another name. You'll live out in the city, unknown, and be treated there as any common woman heavy with a bastard got lying with gods know whom. Aside from your disguise, you'll use no magic, either for yourself or any other. In secret you'll be cared for and kept safe. We've no notion what is hunting you, but this manoeuvre will perhaps defend us all.'

Jemhara lightly laughed. She said, 'Yes, why not? That makes some sense. And I would rather move about than sleep. Will Thryfe—'

'No. He *must* sleep. His waking power attracts this element much as you do.'

Jemhara flared. 'Only through me. Therefore *I* will sleep. Let *him* be awake. He is so weakened, further hibernation might kill him—'

'Thryfe himself has decided. Do you wish to go against him?'

'And do you tell the truth?'

'The Magikoy don't lie in such matters. You must learn that, Jemhara, now you belong among us.'

'*I am no Magikoy.*'

Lalath said, 'How vehemently you spurn us. Do you dislike yourself so much?'

Jemhara turned her face as if at a slap.

'And was it Thryfe who decided on the manner of my disguise?'

The older woman said, 'We have done that. Does it displease you? It is the best course.'

Jemhara said, 'Perhaps. I wished to know only if the idea was yours. And now I do. I will of course accept all of it. Now I should like to see Thryfe.'

Lalath looked at Jemhara. Lalath's eyes said clearly, You remember you were a queen then, do you? Aloud, 'No,' said Lalath. 'Already Thryfe sleeps again.'

Jemhara gazed far away into an inner bleakness and darkness. Her face was that of a girl of about five, sent from home to live with a human monster.

'Very well. Let my lord sleep. And I shall be a pregnant refugee. What's my name? Have you decided that too?'

'Apple.'

Jemhara looked sidelong at Lalath.

Did she know that also? The apple he had brought that always grew back after they had eaten it? What had become of it when the house fell? Fool, she thought, to grieve for an apple—

She thought, *Perhaps all things grow again after death devours them. One way or another.*

She thought, *I still have his ring.*

'Apple, then,' she said.

Azula sat on a low wall, running one hand over and over her shaven skull. She had herself chopped off all her hair and burned it, an offering to her mother's memory. Aglin had then suggested that the residue be shaved that it might grow back more evenly.

Azula's other hand held Beebit's lightning-blanched bone. She spoke to the bone, as sometimes she did.

'I miss you. Where are you? You're all I know. You loved me. I wish you'd come back to me. Can you hear?'

Then she stayed quiet, her head bowed and both hands on the bone. It had come from Beebit's right forearm. It was healthy, though broken at its upper and lower ends.

At the beginning of the narrow alley, one of an assortment lying just above Kol Cataar's smallish Great Market, there was a sound of marching mailed feet. An example of King Bhorth's city patrols must be going by.

Azula paid no heed.

She held the bone.

Her tears, very slow, glycerine, almost emotionless, spotted its ivory. She studied them through the next group of tears that formed and fell.

At the alley's mouth came the slight scrape and scuffle of a military halt.

Next, individual steps. These were masculine, a man well built, young, and without any impediment; also nicely shod.

No shadow covered Azula. And yet she sensed a type of darkening which had nothing to do with shade or loss of light.

Reluctantly she raised her eyes.

Night was in the alley, elegantly cut into a perfect human form. Through her demobilized brain flew the picture Beebit had so often painted, Chillel, goddess and beloved, Azula's second mother. But this was a male. He was youthful. He was dressed as a prince. Gold and silver hinted. They were nothing to his own intense lucency – like that of a dark star.

'Is your name Azulamni?' he asked. The question was a commonplace. As if he often inquired the names of those he met, straight out, nothing to it.

'So my mother called me.'

'That was Beebit?'

'My mother.' Holding the bone, the girl got to her feet. He was weightier and taller than she, and a man and royal. She said, 'What's that to you?'

'Everything. I'm Sallus – King Bhorth's son by Queen Tireh, and by Chillel the goddess.'

'Chillel . . . ?'

He held out his hand.

One gold wristlet clothed it and a ring that was a silver snake. There was a live snake, she now noticed, coiled over his shoulder. It too looked at her but with a sideways eye.

'I am your brother,' Sallus said.

Azula stared.

She could not move, it seemed. From tactful reserve at her shock, neither would he.

So the chaze, the serpent, unroped itself like flexible cord. It swayed forward, its tail still cinched round Sallus's arm, and lowered its head on to Azula's breast, gazing up at her from that one fixed eye she could see.

Azula was not frightened of the snake. She should have been: they were poisonous usually and she had been told of them. But it seemed a prince of its species, as he was, the man who had brought it. The feel of the snake too, contrary to all she had heard, was heavy and tepid and dry. The sinuous life in it was like a conduit that joined them now, he and she – like an artery running heart to heart.

'You're not afraid of him,' said Sallusdon presently.

124

Azula, the bone now returned to her other hand, stroked the flat head of the chaze. 'No.'

'Then,' he said, 'why be afraid of me?'

Seen from above, the city of Kol Cataar, unfinished in its determined and valiant 'finishes', like a model created by amateur artisans experimenting – but now the more clever workers have been called away.

Does Thryfe see that? Has the eagle of his magician's psyche got out from his trance? Has it quartered the sky, searching, watching, keeping guard? If so it leaves no evidence for other lesser mages to decipher. And he himself is unaware of it.

The chamber of his unconsciousness lies under the palace. Here Lalath and the older Magikoy woman check on him at strict intervals. Servants creep to him nervously and tend his sleep, turning him regularly, bathing and rubbing his body to keep it supple. Water is drizzled through his lips, and in the trance he swallows it. Even Bhorth uneasily visits the couch, frowns and departs. Black Sallus also has come here, although his reactions to Thryfe's coma are unreadable. When Bhorth frets, Sallus is reassuring: 'But look, sir, he is one of the greatest among the mages. We must trust his judgement.'

Only one person is always absent from the room. If she had gone in there what might have happened? The electric passion in her heart, roused only by seeing him – would that too be like a lure to the thing which pursues? Doubtless. She had better keep away.

Otherwise the city goes on much as it had. The newcomers from Kandexa have been absorbed. Some have even found long-lost relatives, who generally have taken them in and made them, gladly or grudgingly, welcome. Others have started their own straggly estate where, with the permission and indirect help of the king, they are transforming wagons, huts and tents into wood and ice-brick houses. A fourth hothouse has gone up. It is so well made by those Kandexans who erected it that Kol Cataar's architect has approached them to learn their secret.

Months pass.

Two or three thick snows come. Nothing malign or unusual in them, simply an everyday ingredient of the five-centuries-old Ice Age, the ice-jewel of the earth.

Months pass too that bring various festivals of Ru Karismi. There are the hanging of wreaths of frozen leaves and hothouse or paper flowers, and processions of candles to and from the small temple-town, where the blue priests crouch over their altars largely neglected.

After the last of the thick snows the sky stays pallid and dense. A filmy cloud, a kind of icy fog, covers the city. Through this the sun can only be spotted when very bright. Only a triple moonrise is visible by night, when the city is flushed with a rare antimony sheen.

And all the months of time and festivals and moons pass on, and on, and on.

For some they hurry too fast. This house and that is not yet ready. This heart and that is not yet calmed, or revved up to eagerness. And for some the months shift like dragging, enormous boulders. One month is like seven, one *day* is a month . . .

'Get along, you dirty whore! We don't want your sort here. You'll earn nothing from us.' And a flung chunk of snow, striking sharply, left its track on her cloak, an invitation to others.

'Doesn't even guess its father.'

'For shame – in times like these. A known murderess.'

'Ugly bitch!' screamed voices, and next a battery of hard bits of snow, some of which contained pieces of flint or pottery, stung down.

She knew to shield her breasts, face and head with her arms.

Her belly, engorged with the hugeness of the child, was neither to be hidden nor preserved. Let it preserve itself. By this hour she often dreamed it and she might die. But that was a silly premise. How could *it*? Therefore how could she?

A handful of times a man had caught and raped her, once standing at a fence with, behind it, some lashdeer grazing on dormant grass, paying no attention. On another occasion she was pushed flat on her face, which in the early days was still just possible. That assault tore her; she bled. But such treatment meant nothing to the thing inside her. And if it meant anything to *her* she never said.

She remembered the two Magikoy women. Months before the younger one, lofty and contemptuous, had commended her. 'You've cast an able illusion on yourself. I shouldn't have known you.'

'She's done wonders,' Aglin had agreed.

There had been an edge to her tone. She resented the change on Jemhara's behalf, for Jema had been so beautiful. But now, her hair hacked short and bleached to a tawdry rusty blonde, her face and body, even her skin and features, altered by both mage-craft and make-up, Jema was a puffy-faced and warty woman, slit-eyed and pig-nosed, with sloppy breasts and splayed fingers. She stank too. She, who had smelled always of some perfume, her breath clean as cool water. Jemhara had been nearly amused when Aglin had stepped back in revulsion. 'Have I done that well?'

'You will live,' Lalath had gone on with her dictum, 'in the slum quarter. Kol Cataar inevitably already has one. It lies behind the temple-town. Significant perhaps. Our gods have been debased. In trouble men either cling to them the harder or throw them out with the trash.'

'Another identity has been arranged for you,' said the older Magikoy. She looked less implacable, more vindictive. This would be against the Magikoy creed. 'Word will go about that you, now called Apple, are not merely a prostitute but one who tricked a man into marriage, then murdered him in cold blood. His sons had cast you on the streets a few days before Lionwolf reached the capital and the White Death was unleashed.'

'If that had been the case, would said sons not have put her up for trial?' barked Aglin.

The woman refused to take affront at Aglin's directness. 'There was no proof.'

Jemhara said nothing. Infallibly she had recognized her punishment.

In cold blood she had murdered a king. She had been cast out.

'Such notoriety,' said Lalath, 'will cause others to avoid you, which is in their interest as well as in yours. As for your remarkable pregnancy, Apple does not know who got her with child. An unfussy and unhygienic customer, obviously.'

The older one interpolated priggishly, 'This too is necessary. We don't mean to sully the reputation of Thryfe, former Warden of Ru Karismi.'

'Despite the fact,' added Lalath, 'some have wondered where he was when Ru Karismi fell.'

'With me,' Jemhara said.

Only her voice had stayed the same, musical, lovely.

Lalath said nothing. She looked away.

The older woman let out a truly chilling hiss. 'Then it is good you should now pay some small price, Jemhara.'

At that Aglin had startlingly shouted. 'What do you know of prices paid? Did you ever live in the real world? You shot up from the Insularia like weeds round a rose-bush. What *can* you know of how women – and men – have to live out here on the snow? Magikoy,' she concluded. In the word was a contempt to which their own was nothing. '*Magikoy.*'

'You will be silent,' Lalath suggested.

Jemhara had turned to Aglin. 'All's well, Aggy. It is nothing to me.'

Aglin quietened. Without another syllable, the two mages left the room.

Jemhara had been afraid from the beginning, the instant Thryfe told her what had happened to her. She had seen at once that her own compliance with the vision of the Lionwolf had put this upon her. She had longed for Thryfe. The rest must follow. And from that hour she had no defence, would expect none. She too, as before, could only live as one did out here, on the snow.

Not long after, in the persona of Apple, the slut and murderess, she was living in one of the alleys in her allotted shack.

When she was three months gone with child she was not very

big, but seemed larger due to illusion and padding. That had not deterred the first rapist, he who had thrust her over on her face.

She sat up in the towery of her brain, mind and soul. As he left her she found she had automatically sheathed herself against his parting kick. She reminded herself then that she must forgo all self-protection. That alone, despite disguise, might call back to her the hunting foe, the demon of the storm. The god in her womb would have to look after her. She could not.

There was she learned a terrible release in giving up. She had never essentially done that before she met Thryfe. Any surrender had been pretence. *With* Thryfe her surrender had been total; it was only love. Her fate in Kol Cataar however was itself a sort of death, and thus a sort of laziness. But it too must be.

So Apple existed in her shack. A man had died of fever there not long before. Everyone else kept clear of the place. It lay behind a refuse tip which, as the boulders of the months piled up, seemed to symbolize them under its weight of snow and muck.

When she went abroad Apple was spat on, insulted verbally, a quantity of times hailed with garbage and rocks. During those last adventures Bhorth's soldiers had miraculously eventually appeared. The militants were told Bhorth did not like such goings-on in the slum.

At night secret slinkers arrived at Apple's shack. They brought her packets of decent food and flasks of wine. Even unpolluted water was brought, for now Jemhara was not allowed to employ her most basic talent of thawing. She had also a burning coal that could not go out. Aglin had given it to her in a pot. After the fever-fear left the surrounding slum-dwellers, several times men or women came to extinguish the fire. When it would not perish, 'It's mageified,' they snarled. 'The rotten bitch has stolen it.' Wary, they would not steal it in turn.

So slow, so heavy, month on month.

Jemhara puzzled. Of those few humans who did know what she carried, would none seek to kill her after all? They could not suffer the return of Vashdran. Yet it must be impossible. They too would have no choice. She realized her thoughts had become confused a little, circular. Meaningless.

And slow . . . heavy . . . month on month on month . . .

Four months. Eight months.

Now it must be soon.

She felt no spark of him in her womb – of neither of them, the vile god Vashdran or her beloved Thryfe. It was only a *lump*.

Which weighed her to the earth.

Her back split with pain. She sweated and shuddered through the nights, still often vomited on rising.

Soon. *Soon.*

Nine months.

Ten months.

With a woman who had never borne before, an initial child might well be late.

Aglin crept in at midnight, swathed as a dirty old hag and guarded by a single brawny soldier, himself disguised as the most revolting of sexual customers. A sensible lad, he played his role with gusto outside, and became a model of decorum in the shack, turning his back as Aglin examined Jemhara.

'You're sound,' said Aglin. 'It's there and in the right position, and alive.'

Jemhara who could have learned this for herself had had to ignore her diagnostic skill. 'Then when shall I give birth, Aggy?'

'Oh, sweetheart. The gods know. The thing lies there like a balnakalf – big and solid. Two years you might port it about.'

'Don't say so.' Apple took a breath. Her squinting eyes were pulled earthward at the corners, her unkissable mouth was a crescent moon upside down.

'No, no, it won't take so long, sweetheart. How could it? But it's comfortably lodged. It's biding its damned moment.'

Ten months. Eleven months.

Now was the festival of the Rose Star.

No star was visible over Kol Cataar, only the antimony night sky of triple moonrise.

Bonfires on the streets, and firecrackers let off in emerald and magenta flights, which descended over-suddenly, starting one or two small house fires, so illuminating a corner of the rancid shack.

Now?

The arson nights of the Rose Star passed.

Twelve months.

It was a year.

Then more. Thirteen months.

Apple stared into a tiny slice of glass, careful not to scry.

She was a mountain of flesh, her eyes two lines scratched deep inside the blubber. No longer was any padding needed, and not much of an illusion. As well. This lonely magery of concealment was becoming too much for her to perform. She could not wear his ring. It hung on a string about her neck.

Confused and circling her thoughts. Even her constant trepidation over Thryfe had muddied and grown vague. She had been condemned at last, as before, to care only about herself.

That morning she did not bother to drag her body from the mattress. The previous night someone had come with food, and a salve for the blistered inflammation of her hands and legs that would not heal.

She had not eaten the food but thought of eating the salve to poison herself. Then of simply reiterating her own power, blasting herself to bits and, if she could, the fiend inside her too. She did not upbraid fate, demanding why this had happened to her. She wanted only release.

About noon, when the slum market bell rang, Apple heard the boy priest, the one who sang so well, fluting some hymn tune as he walked through the area. Eventually he stopped by her door, having presumably discovered it behind the refuse tip. She glimpsed him through an unmended slat. By himself the boy begged only with the song. He did not knock let alone hold out his palm as the blue priests of Kol Cataar always did.

'I've nothing,' Apple panted. 'Go away.'

The boy turned and as he did so Apple – or Jemhara – felt something break inside her, as if a goblet of white glass took the full crack of a hammer.

She expected immediate agony. There was none.

An abstract energy flew her up into the high tower of her mind, and there again she sat and saw, astonished and appalled and ultimately dismally uninterested, a tunnel opening in her physical core. Out of it flowed a swimming creature most like a smooth silken flame.

I'll die now. That's good.

Beautiful again, and herself, though only in the surreal mind-tower, she was aware something bent over her and touched her forehead lightly with one finger. She saw him. His red hair lay around them like a cloud of fire. She heard him speak. *'Forgive me,'* he said.

The words, the voice, went on echoing over and over, through and through. He did not sound sorry, only kind.

Her body thrummed like harp strings, that harp someone had mentioned in the palace, shaped like a butterfly and brought from Ru Karismi where once she must have heard and seen it played.

The god, so like Zeth Zezeth, so unlike, stood above her, perfect, distant, near, kind and regretful, yet smiling. A smile of cruelty? Or some promise—

He shook his head.

Then came a falling flutter of butterflies, ruby and golden, bronze and pearl and opal. Their exquisite otherness settled over her, sank through her. She was crystal and filled by a dance of wings.

If this is death then death – is wonderful.

She remembered Thryfe and her tears poured inward, themselves turning to winged insects, these made of mirror.

Long distances away a door which had opened was closing. Miles off a baby lamented shrilly. The last she saw was the crying of the newborn child, which crying had also turned to butterflies, blue as lapis lazuli, silver as clean knives.

Going out after supper Bhorth found his son once again on the terrace, staring up at the sky. Nearby the very young woman from Kandexa also stood, circumspect perhaps, her shaven head covered by a fur hood and the pet snake round her waist. She was a liaison that one should not instantly try to detach. If one did probably it would only grow more intense. A sister, Sallus had declared. Bhorth was not happy with that. But then he was scarcely happy with anything. Jemhara had incredibly not yet given birth to the abomination Vashdran. Bhorth's spies watched her, by now reporting hourly. He had just heard the latest report. She was sick. Perhaps then she might die, crushing the monstrosity inside her? Why had he never tried to have her seen off? Fear of her power, or of Thryfe's? He thought distractedly it was as if, in some cell of his reason, he had wished to protect her and what she carried. But that could not be so.

'No stars tonight,' said Bhorth. He felt now he wanted to discuss with Sallus, alone, the problem of the impending devil child, its removal.

'The stars can't be seen,' said Sallusdon.

'Nor for months,' acknowledged Bhorth. As yet he was not at a loss. He parted his lips to suggest privacy, nicely, so as not to annoy his gallant son.

But Sallus spoke again. 'Let me show you, Father.'

Bhorth saw Sallus had a small hunting bow from the more primitive Ruk. The young man fitted an arrow. The arrow seemed gilded with some luminous stuff. What joke was this, then?

Quirkily Sallus leaned back and fired straight up into the night sky.

Sallus seldom acted randomly, did not clown about. Bhorth therefore patiently watched the arrow's shining ascent, waiting for it to reach its apex and so prove the point, whatever that might be. All that could happen of course was that it would arc over and drop back to earth.

But it did not.

Instead the arrow raced into the vault of foggy heaven, which one isolated full moon had barely lit, reached the peak of its flight and struck the upper air. Struck it and *stayed*. Quivering and minuscule, three hundred feet overhead, the arrow trembled but did not return. Very clearly it had pierced the roof of the sky, and stuck.

Eleventh Volume
THE WOLF REGARDS THE SUN

This place I have returned to is unfamiliar to me. Before I came here I lay in a grave. That grave, though unremembered, was better known and greatly more comfortable.

Part of an untitled tract woven in cloth:
Antique Ol y'Chibe and y'Gech (translation approximate)

ONE

His dream had been horrible. Waking, he moved to seize and destroy it, as he would have done a physical enemy. But already the nightmare wavered, subsided.

He could not recall detail, only the dread and anguish that spread over him like a mountain of black stone.

Yet its colour had not been black. It had been smoulder-red, *warm*, like fire beneath the sea.

In itself even so the colour was not favourable.

Thought-*shapes* bubbled through the psychic blowhole of Brightshade's exquisitely hamfisted inner mind.

Even unremembering he *knew* what this input meant.

Lionwolf.

Ah, since the first awareness of that unique other being, his *half-brother*, the whale Brightshade had floundered. His ideal and virtually brainless path of unmitigated living and enjoyment had been *soiled*. But striking out, made into an assassin by their father, Zeth, Brightshade had ultimately failed at murder more than once. Thereafter the vicious insane assaults of Zzth had slung the whale to the floor of this north-eastern ocean. Here beneath an element frozen and un, someone now forgotten had come unheralded to *comfort* him.

Brightshade laboured to recapture the strange sense of gentleness. What had it been? Two different things happened. His eyes opened and a sore itching physical pain made itself known. All the other hurts the god-dad had inflicted seemed cured. Not a trace of them remained. Only this thin and intruding strand of – less pain than honed *feeling*.

Something had pierced Brightshade, right through from outer hide to within the inner left wall of his stupendous gut.

Muddled, he flexed his vast form. Nothing worse occurred. No dangerous twangs of crippled tissue alerted him. He was healed. Yet had been *penetrated*.

He did not need to consider why.

Brightshade's back was always to some extent landscaped by a terrain of wreckage, marine flora and bones. But his most creative, or destructive, principle was the ingesting of things. Even now a swift sweep of his belly-contents consoled him with the knowledge of hundreds of interesting bits still stored there. They included ships, antique and modern, treasure of various sorts, freakish plant life resultant from all the above. Nevertheless, one unidentified item he could not even picture had been removed. Though he had mislaid its nature, obviously it had been most valuable. Of this he had been robbed.

Brightshade lay in the neverness of ocean. His waking eyes followed the flights of blind black fish that found their way by other senses.

Dainty as the undoing of a small door the whale's endless jaws cracked. The black fish were whirled inside.

Brightshade swallowed.

Better?

Was he safe here in all this utter dark? Zzth his persecutor was a sun god, albeit a defunct one. Zzth could still burn under the sea when the mood took him. It was down here after all he had begotten both sons, Brightshade, unarguably on a female whale, and Lionwolf on a drowning woman.

Deep depression lowered itself over Brightshade.

A great deal had happened he did not understand but two awful thought-*shapes* stayed staring in his not-mind. First the worldly rebirth of the loathed half-brother whom he had failed to eradicate. Secondly the fact of Zeth Zezeth who inevitably must return to harm and mutilate.

The human thoughts *I am in despair – where shall I turn – there is nowhere* blew inside the leviathan's intellect.

Poor child sang memory in another voice. Once it had been dulcet. Now it was spiteful, mocking, taunting.

Brightshade realized. It was the former comforter, now this taunter, who had operated the penetrative stab of robbery and hurt in his side.

Brightshade on the ocean floor wept. His tears were white iron. The streamers of blind fish goggled at them with their sightless optics. Indifferent, the submarine ice floes snored.

And the watcher watches.

Large eyes, not even open perhaps, see everything.

If the giant whale has been aware of scrutiny he fails consciously to know it. He is busy with himself and his own grief.

In any event the condition of Brightshade is soon logged, and the watcher turns from him. The eyes open or closed move like two midnight lamps, away. And then – far off into the unformed past.

Though Crarrow, the young girl was not as experienced as others of her calling. She had carried her offspring for three months only, her belly swelling up like a loaf in an oven. At two months she had seemed six months gone, and at three it was obvious she was ready. Yedki was outraged by this, and even her grandmother the Crax's reassurances had not done much good. The grandmother anyway was still plainly troubled, conceal it from non-officiates though she did. She had guessed from the first something bizarre was going on.

Now Yedki shrieked. She did not have the knowledge to detach her spirit from her body and spare herself the excruciation of childbirth. Her labour had lasted three hours. Already Yedki shouted that she could not bear it. When the pains came she kicked and wailed, begging to be killed.

The other members of the coven exchanged glances.

Apart from the grandmother Crax, Ennuat the virgin was thirteen, and the child member eight. All had witnessed and all in some form assisted at a birthing act earlier. Never had any heard a woman carry on like this. Doubtless they had been lucky.

'There, there, Yedki,' Ennuat soothed, frowning, 'it will soon be over.'

'You – told me that – a day ago—' Yedki screechingly exaggerated.

'I never! You've only been in the throes this past hour or so.'

'Quiet,' said the Crax. 'Yedki, all's well. Bear up.'

But another surge enveloped Yedki who screamed, punching the ground as if to knock it out.

'*I will never,*' she grated in the aftermath, 'endure this hell again. Gran – kill me – kill me!'

But 'Your baby!' squeaked the little girl Crarrow.

'Befuck the baby! No more of *this*!'

The Crax now frowned. She leaned suddenly over Yedki and tapped her on the forehead.

Yedki gave a yelp and her head lolled. She was senseless.

'Stand away,' said the Crax. She stood up straight as a black tree in her mantle, locking her feet to the earth, releasing her own inner life-force.

Swirling outward this incorporeal element nearly collided with a non-corporeal young man of the Ol y'Chibe, who was abruptly present, buzzing round the prone Yedki like a worried insect.

The Crax deduced instantly what he must be: the reincarnating soul that claimed the baby and would become it, once it was delivered; that is, the expectant son.

'Out of the way, boy,' the Crax cried. 'Leave this to me.'

The man respectfully fell back. 'Yes, Mother.'

As she darted forward the Crax became aware also of a curious rupture in the air. She thought she glimpsed something watching her and believed it might be female. It did not seem malign but apart from that she could tell nothing about it. She had no time to waste.

Guri, transfixed by dismay, saw the Crax seat herself on the writhing belly of his unconscious mother.

Squeamishly he crept away.

The baby-body was leaving the womb. He felt now no connection to it. It was like a symbol, a corpse even, something modelled on or redeemed from a living entity, and really quite unusable.

Did he honestly wish to reoccupy a fleshly form? To lie helpless, dumb and half blind, at the mercy of all?

Like Yedki Guri contemplated the possible escape route, even if only temporary, of another death.

But he had delayed too long.

Out squeezed the newborn child in a veil of crimson, anchored briefly by a starry umbilical cord.

Released to breathe, the baby sucked in air to sneeze. And in that fatal second Guri too was sucked right in. What thereafter sneezed *was* Guri. His follow-up yodel of regret and rage was taken for a healthy kiddling's bellow.

Only Ennuat, holding him fondly, staring down into his eyes, noted for a moment something else that glared up at her – something alien and annoyed – but sinking, already overpowered. The Guri-baby loudly grizzled.

Yekdi awoke also in that instant and began to sob. Upset, the child Crarrow broke down too. Ennuat and the Crax balanced, grimly cheerful, amid the uproar of howling, hiccuping misery that welcomed to life a new god.

The other child did not appear to have faced such a bold dilemma. He was a mature infant, and lay inside an upper room, in a house of wood and stone with a horizontal sword hung over the main entrance, and a formless unvisited statue of God in the cellar.

The upper room had a large bed in it, but the child did not lie there. He was in a cot, or had been. The vague outline of it persisted, but mostly it seemed to have burned away, as had presumably any clothing the child might have worn. Now the child slept suspended inside a ball of flickering flame. Washes of red and gold passed continually over him, shading his whiteness, for he was a very white child, complexion and hair light as snow. In fact, if one observed *closely* – one did, but also many already had – the fire washes might be thought to be running about *under* his skin as well as across its surface.

A woman of the Jafn, a queen called Nirri, poised in the doorway at the top of the ladder-stair. Her face was a study in strain. She did not enter the room.

The great bed was unslept in too. For almost a month Nirri had instead been lying down on a mattress in a specially constructed room of screens below.

She was not allowed, she had been told, to break the sorcerous web of fire.

'Athluan,' Nirri murmured.

The child did not respond.

Nor did the shining thing that sat there on a chair. The shining thing – the goddess Saphay also known as Saftri – merely stared at the child. And shone.

'Lady,' said Nirri with toneless formality, 'can I or my women bring you anything?'

'Nothing,' said the shiner.

'And he . . . ?'

Nirri asked herself, blinking at the fluctuation of the fire, if her son was much bigger, far older – six years, seven?

'Go away, queen,' the shiner said. Her musical voice was not even ungracious, certainly not maleficent. Simply remote, shiny.

Nirri went back down the stair. In the hall below the warriors still present, the women and other children averted their gaze from her face. Outside a filthy snow-thatched gale was blowing. Arok the Chaiord had not returned. By now it seemed fairly sure he and the other men who had gone hunting must be lost. The goddess upstairs doubtless could have settled the question, but she never did. No man either had been elected to take Arok's place. The coronation of a makeshift king was pointless probably, given the rest of this scenario.

Nirri walked out of the hall and into the room of screens. She sat by her brazier, whose firelight was not anything like the fireball upstairs.

Carefully breathing she slowed the beat of her heart. She

thought, *Arok lives. I would know if he didn't. I knew in my own way with the other one I wed. And the child's well. The child will grow and be a hero – a god – as* She *seemed to promise.*

Nirri thought, *Or I am wrong.*

Very bad weather had started almost as soon as they left the capital.

As they descended to the snow plain, winds had come at the party from north and east, lashing and driving the top-snow before them. The dromaz mounts that every man rode made not so much of this. They lowered their heads, snake-like, and the riders too bowed forward, turning each compendium of beast and man into one humpy arrow on four racing legs.

They had offered to Obac Tramaz before leaving; even the visiting Jafn men did so. Obac Tramaz was the god of the dromazi, a fawn gentleman with a dromaz head, dromaz pad feet and hands, and two little humps on his back. The queen at Padgish, Riadis, venerated Obac above all others, even her occasional mate Attajos. 'Obac sent her a sign I was coming back,' Curjai had told them, with an offhand familiarity over gods that was, Fenzi said, only to be expected.

Curjai rode at the front of the eight men, with Fenzi and Sombrec.

Arok had privately remarked to Fenzi that Curjai had grown older even in the short space they had been at Padgish. 'I took him for twelve. Now he's what? Fifteen?'

Fenzi had shrugged. 'What else?'

To which Arok, as if playing a clever move in a board game, added, 'But so did you grow – quickly.'

Curjai had volunteered to take news of Arok and the other Jafn back to the Holasan-garth. This it seemed was permissible, also that Fenzi go too.

Eventually a lull came in the winds. They made a bivouac in a slight valley among fat blades of mountains. Sombrec tried to curb his jealousy as his Jafn lover Fenzi, and his prince Curjai, spoke intently by the second fire.

'I feel it tug on me,' Fenzi said. 'I'm sure I know what it is. But how to put it to them that I'm going soon. Especially to my father. And Arok. He lost his son Dayadin, and all this comes from that. I, inevitably, remind him of Dayadin. He has always been kind to me, favoured me. Unspoken between us, but I try to measure for him as – a son. Where I can.'

'But you haven't a choice,' said Curjai. 'Well,' he added reminiscently, 'I saw your mother, of course. I mean *that* mother.'

'Chillel. Did you? I understand she's very beautiful.'

'More than beautiful. There's no word here for her beauty. Nor, really, any word there.'

Fenzi nodded. One god naturally could soundly evaluate another.

Aware of what Fenzi thought Curjai said, 'I was only half god then. It was in the blue Hell with Lionwolf. Chillel ruled there as Hell's queen. She was called Winsome.'

'I . . . seem to know this.'

'Yes, very likely. Perhaps you can see her for yourself too, if you look *inward*. Like scrying but without smoke or a glass.'

'I think my sister does that. At least, one of my sisters. I thought there was only one. But now – again I seem to think there are two. It's unclear to me and I don't know what the second one looks like. The first is black.'

'When will you leave?'

'I could leave now. Exactly now. Just get up and stride off towards Chillel. A magnet draws me, that's what it's like, even though I don't know the direction, let alone the country. Is she here – no – where then? But I could set off: somehow I should reach her. I dream of it, journeying towards her. I've felt this almost half a year, on and off. Now it's solid as a steel rope. It isn't,' he gravely added, 'that Chillel is *forcing* me towards her.'

'It must be mutual attraction. Maybe she doesn't even know she exerts such influence.'

There was silence.

Then Fenzi said, 'Stars are attracted towards the heart of the earth. They crash on the surface. All you see is a golden scar left for a moment on the night sky.'

'It won't be like that.'

'She is *Chillel*. A god made her from dark and snow. I may walk into her presence and burn up in a sudden self-combustion.' Fenzi was calm, perhaps sad. 'She is Chillel.'

'And you're her son. Come on, man. *You* can't be consumed. Half god is good enough to survive meeting a mother. Attajos knows, he's pure flame, but I never even got singed. And now, look.' Curjai put his hand into the fire. He did it surreptitiously however, hiding the action from those around so as not to alarm them. He knew they were awed enough already. He constantly had to work at it, jest and chaff them back into partial easiness.

Fenzi and Curjai observed Curjai's hand in the fire, burning, burning and completely at home. Curjai removed his hand and laid it quietly on Fenzi's own. 'There. Not even very warm.'

Fenzi grinned. 'I couldn't do that.'

'How do you know? Think of what you are. What you *may* be. Well, but maybe don't try it just yet.'

'Nice advice. The Lionwolf was half god too. He died, though you say he's coming back.'

'He's already back, my friend.'

Sombrec had stopped himself jealously peering at the two young men and so, fortunately, missed the hand clasp. Less fortunately he now also missed the glorious look on Curjai's face which was obviously not for Fenzi. Curjai, like Fenzi very well among men though he might, clearly *loved* among men elsewhere.

Behind one of the mountains a great panorama of cloud abruptly shouldered high. The sky bubbled. The lull in the winds had ended.

Men turned apprehensively, seeing the whole north sky shift into a tumble of masonry cumulus, black-white, from which icy shafts of hail had already begun to clatter.

Ten minutes later the men and the dromazi were once more heading south towards Arok's garth.

They had propitiated the Simese god of winter too but it

seemed to little effect. You could never be sure of gods. Not even *gods* could be sure of them.

And the watcher watches. Now the eyes – open, closed – move neither geographically nor into the past, nor even that past's future. The eyes move towards some indecipherable elsewhere which, once seen, at once *becomes* decipherable, although doubtless always a different cipher depending on who looks.

Called for dawn, Ushah walked along a wide paved road, and dawn itself, pastel and lily-like, lustred before her in a limpid sky. Nothing and no one was otherwise visible. No birds untidied the polished atmosphere. In the misty grasslands or fields of growing grain that ran beside the road, nobody toiled, no jolly peasant rejoicing in the non-cold abundance of the corn. Ushah recalled just such a road and such a walk from some while before, but that time everything had kept altering to please her. If she thought *Bird* at the sky presently there was one. On the other hand the country she had now recently come from, Vashdran's Hell, had been changed by him into a heaven of crops and flowers, sunlight and soft rain. It seemed to Ushah she had got up and walked off across the Hell plain where for a year or more she had lived. The Lionwolf, whom she had meant to kill, had died and been born again, and she had had no more purpose. Curjai, whom she had fallen in love with, also went away. She had sat mourning for aeons, and then simply risen and started off across the plain, thinking nothing, least of all if she were going somewhere.

The sun today was lifting higher quite properly. It was like an earthly sun, mundanely normal and bright, and now the sky was blue and if the feathery fields were extremely pale they did not appear unreal.

Ushah stopped. She had sensed she was no longer alone. She turned and looked behind her.

What was it?

Something bounded along the paving.

Ideas of dangerous animals – wild barbarian lions, black wolves, even some ghastly wolverine like the creature the witch Taeb had slaughtered – stiffened Ushah for fight or flight.

Then the thing that rushed after called out to her.

It was barking. It was a dog. It was the blind jatcha dog from Hell which had become a proper dog with brown eyes – Vashdran's dog. He had named it.

'Star-Dog!' she shouted. 'Starry! Here! Here!'

As Curjai had deserted her so too Lionwolf had deserted Star-Dog. She and the dog, fellows in misuse.

At the last second, the dog nearly there, she thought he would leap and knock her flat on her back. Ushah braced herself, but he did not leap. He brought himself to such a sudden standstill he nearly toppled over, and then anyway threw himself at her feet, rolling and panting in a delight of refinding.

Ushah knelt down and embraced the dog. She had always liked animals, when she was alive or dead.

After a while girl and dog stood up and they ran a race on up the road. Both sped as if on winged feet. Next at one or two points both left the ground. She had forgotten she could now fly – or levitate. Star-Dog had taken up the habit too.

They soared, laughing and barking, and galloped round each other about a quarter-mile above the vista of the never-changing fields and never-finishing road.

'We must find a way out of this dull place.'

Star-Dog agreed in whuffling mutters. Then he looked off along the sky to what, judging from the sun's position, was the south. He emitted a low growl.

Ushah stared where he was staring.

'What is *that*?'

Neither of them liked it. His blue-grey coat bristled and his muzzle wrinkled. Her skin pricked and the fine down rose on her neck.

Even in an unworldly condition animal responses seemed always to be happening.

The things in the sky were darting along almost as the dog

had on the road. A type of sewing light attended them, thinnest silver, getting all the time nearer and leaving behind it scintillant stitches that faded slowly.

Ushah breathed, 'Is it *him*?' She meant Vashdran.

In her much metamorphosed universe there were still really only two significant *he*s – Curjai, Lionwolf.

The other she had forgotten.

Never forget gods. It is their way to remind you.

The silver thread split. Its first needle went piercingly blue and exploded into proximity and shape, unmistakably male, glamorous and awful. As it roared by in a vitriolic scorch of velocity, the head turned. Two golden eyes glared contemptuously upon the girl and her dog. A voice, unspeaking, spoke. 'You have failed me. Goddess you may have become, but I have destroyed goddesses before and shall again. In passing for now I warn you. Later we shall meet more intimately. Anticipate the dread and terror until we do.'

Ushah recalled. Her Rukarian name was Ruxendra. She was an apprentice Magikoy of Maxamitan Level. And he – he was Zeth Zezeth in his malignant aspect, blue-faced. He had bound her at death to slay Lionwolf. She had slipped up.

In a splurge of agonizingly electric indigo the god thundered from view.

Ruxendra-Ushah reeled, Star-Dog cowering and slavering and snarling beside her.

The second being arrived in their airspace.

'Oh, a Rukarian,' said the second god.

Actually this advent was not of one being but of four. The main protagonist was the god Yyrot, Winter's Lover. He was in his malign aspect as well, but in the case of Yyrot that meant heat and a sort of seeming good-humour. He beamed on Ruxendra, but the second being, travelling in his arm, spat and hissed. This might have been caused only by her having noted the dog. For this being was a cat-woman covered in silken ginger fur, with a cat's head, a woman's body, a tail, two human hands, and two pawed feet.

'Hush, Shimmawyn my paramour of ecstasy,' Yyrot placated her.

Shimmawyn slapped him hard across the backside with her lashing tail.

The two other smaller beings were sitting, one on each of her pawed feet. They were *very* small and had perhaps reduced their size in order to accompany their grand- or great-grandparents. The dog-cat drajjerchach had a dog's head, cat's ears, cat's front paws on dog's legs, dog paws on cat back legs, and three tails two of which were canine and wagged, making the middle cat tail also wag – was it pleased or angry? Hard therefore to tell. The chachadraj cat-dog was all cat but for a dog's nose and jaw from which a huge dog tongue draped, running with spangly spit. This beast had no tail at all, but something issued from the chest that was either a low growl or a loud purring.

'My dear Ruxendra-Ushah of the dark brown hair and worried eyes,' said Yyrot, 'take no notice of the psychopath Zzth. Did he not mention you are a deity yourself by now? Minor but not unimportant.'

Ruxendra mastered herself. Despite all else a wisp of Magi-koy control remained to her.

'Yes, Mighty One? Why? How?'

'We live in interesting times,' said Yyrot unhelpfully. Shimmawyn bit him on the shoulder. He turned absently and kissed her furry head. 'There is fresh power abroad in the world. Or two powers. They are very great, though one greater, far greater, now. One is an enemy and one a friend. But the friend may be more volatile and dangerous by far than the foe. As for us, and I include yourself, as we are gods we have only to put up with eternity. Never fear. Even eternity will one day conclude.'

Ruxendra said prudently, 'It is kind of you to speak to me, Mighty Ethereality. May I compliment you on your beauteous companions?'

Shimmawyn looked haughtily away. But she had ceased to sizzle. Was she displaying her best profile?

The draj and chach had now slipped off their ancestrix's paws. Star-Dog, an opportunist, had begun playing a chase game with both creatures. About twenty feet away they bounced and sprang. Mostly it was the dog being chased.

'Children.' Yyrot, fondly exasperated. 'But you, maiden, should return to the world.'

'Great One, I don't know how.'

Yyrot chuckled. Ruxendra was reminded of a middle-aged uncle she had had in Ru Karismi. Next instant he was not like her uncle at all. Yyrot too had changed into a sleek grey hound.

He chased Shimmawyn away over the sky, their sparkly stitchings of holy light attending them. The 'children' left off the game with Star-Dog and followed. Star-Dog followed *them*.

Ruxendra shouted to him to come back.

Star-Dog reversed. Regretful but loyal he bounded to her side.

They stood in the morning sky as all the illuminated extended family grew smaller and eventually vanished. Below, the fields reached two of the horizons, while the road went either way to the other pair.

Ruxendra seized her dog by one ear. He allowed this. He had been Lionwolf's but was now hers. She shut her eyes.

The watcher, eyes shut or *open*, beheld a pucker in the sky. Something gleamed cold and white beyond it. Ruxendra was visualizing the world of mortality. A mild flash lit everything. Fields, road and morning were gone. The watcher saw that Ruxendra stood now with Star-Dog on a bleached mountain of cut-glass ice.

Below them here the country of Simisey folded up and down and up. Miles lower a party of eight men, two of whom were more than that, (Fenzi, Curjai), was riding dromazi in the teeth of a white gale. And over another mountain or three lay a Jafn garth with a ball of fire in it.

The watcher's eyes move on.

Skimming southward down the length of the northern continent, towards the cliffs of ice and the icy shore . . .

They had been used to live by the edges of ocean. To them,

still, an upland and a long foreshore represented memories of islands, *home*lands.

Fazion, Kelp, Vormlander – what had been left of their pioneering fleet, after every ship was sunk by the storm and the militant icebergs that had greeted them? Not so many. And now the brief extra years had passed, their number was further reduced. Less than a hundred persons occupied the village built above the littoral.

It was in the style of their joint peoples, wooden houses, for they had found ice-forest inland and enough of their weapons and tools had been salvaged. Even the roofs had the old boat-shaped look, though they had not been made from boats for none had been recovered. The villagers were accustomed to working at survival. And they were too a proud race, these sea reivers hated and despised over half the southern continent they had left. Who else but they would have dared send their goddess packing, saying she had failed them? This they had done. The name Saftri, once their guiding star, had been refashioned as a swear-word in the village under the cliffs. *By the stench of Saftri* they would exclaim, to insult her delicious scent. *Saftri-ugly* described they, to slap her loveliness. *Saff off* they added to those they disliked.

What was to be seen today was the usual village activity. Men were at work in the village street on repairs; a woman or two was milking the deer they had also come on inland and managed to capture and breed – all the cows were lost to the bergs. A shaman's longhouse, which held by now but two shamans, let go greenish lights through its smoke-hole. Only the shoreline looked empty in a peculiar way. The village had constructed no new fleet, just a handful of small botched boats put together for fishing. Sometimes the fishers had great luck, as ten days back. A pack of seals had veered across the bows. The village still ate well. They had made a hothouse too. There were things to be thankful for, but they thanked each other, no god, for these.

They had met no other people on or near the shore, nor in their narrow hunting grounds. This alien land, so vaunted by accursed Saftri, was barren. They had not even seen one of the white tigers, for they were uncommon so close to the sea.

Nor had there ever been any thought of, let alone attempt of, a return across that sea. The inertia of fatalism and low-banked resentment perhaps prevented it. Conceivably with forest wood and determined labour they might have replaced sufficient of their ships to bear them home. But it was as if 'home' had become already a myth among them. They spoke of it as if of a golden age, or a *Summer* garden from which silliness or sin had seen them driven out. Go back? No. This otherland was their punishment, their cold Hell. For surely the isles had been better, more fruitful, more . . . warm.

A quartet of young men had left the village. They were strolling along the icy shore.

Easily spotted due to their pure blackness, they did not often exchange words. They looked away across the ice of the sea.

The Children of Chillel. Two had been born each of a Kelpish man and woman, one from a Fazion couple, one from a Vormlander pair. These last parents, as with one of the two Kelpish unions, had perished in the saffing berg attack.

By now all the Chillelings were full grown, men of twenty or twenty-two years, despite the fact none of them, even in Kelpish calendar years, was more than five.

A mound of ice weirdly formed like a slightly over-large whale bulged from the beach. They paused beside it.

'Then, we should go away from Fazkelvor?' This was the man born of Faz parents.

'Yes. Is there any choice? We have lived in Kelfazvor long enough.' This the first Kelp-born.

The second Kelp-born said softly, 'Ah, Kelfazvor. Don't we also love *them*, a little?'

The Vormlander man spoke last.

'Vorkelfaz will do well enough. And love them a *little*? My birth mother died in the green liquid outer sea. She is my mother, and always in my heart. But *She*—'

'*She*,' '*She*,' '*She*,' said the others, low as the distant hint of surf beyond the ice.

'*She* is *Mother*. She is a god.'

'Not like poor saff-off Saftri.'

'Chillel is like—'

'The earth—'

'The sky—'

'The snow—'

'The night—'

'And—'

'Like—'

'The—'

'Moon.'

Alas came the reverberation of the distant surf. *Alas*.

In the village of Kelfazvor-Fazkelvor-Vorkelfaz, certain women, men, children, *deer*, lifted their heads as if at an unheard sound, a flutter of invisible wings.

While watching, the watcher sees the shore is entirely empty. There are no ships or boats, and no young men in the black of heroes or gods. Only the eerie lambency on the horizon, a dark brilliancy, a cloudy shadow which is – bright.

Brinnajni opens her eyes.

Or possibly, if they had *been* open, closes them.

She was, is, the watcher.

She, daughter of Chillel and Lionwolf, conceived during their congress in Hell itself, brought forth on earth painless and divine. A young woman. Her skin is black, her hair red fire, her eyes midnight.

Behind her Dayadin, her half-brother whom she rescued from the interior of the appalling Brightshade, looks and sees what his sister has seen.

He too is full grown now. He is twenty-four. His face is self-contained and pensive. His tight-curled hair pours down his back, a black like dusk smoke for his sister's fire. And sometimes his hair moves too at the whim of a tame wind, a hovor, a Jafn spirit that stays with him.

Where are they? Oh, one more Ice Age region of snow. Who can tell where they are?

Dayadin says, 'Every one of her sons is drawn towards her now.'

Brinnajni says, 'And you? Do you wish to go there?'

He looks at her, whether her eyes are open or shut, with his own eyes that have no tears in them, only sometimes behind them.

'*Nirri* is my mother. *Arok* is my father. You are my only other kin.'

What does Brinnajni do? Her name means Flame That Burns. She goes to pet the black sheep that grazes by the door, and the red curtain of her hair obscures her face.

No longer a watcher watching. Therefore does the next episode of this collection pass *unseen*?

Maybe Brinnajni has already noted it. Or others watch instead.

The path was a sheet of white beneath two white moons at the full. Anything which moved there showed at once.

A tall man then, tall and lean, casting a lean, long shadow . . .

But it is not any image from before.

What moves across the snow fields, approximately from the east, is neither man nor woman. Nor mortal, nor god.

The Gargolem was mechanical. Its metallic body, delicately frosted now and patched in places with rime, was that of a human male, though far greater in height and somewhat in girth. Its head was a beast's, a beast unknown, maned and fanged.

It strode across the snow, unimpeded by garments or footwear, or flesh or nerves or any ordinary incapacity. Eyes indescribable yet glowing were fixed on an edifice that dominated the horizon.

This was a sort of enormous mound, smooth in contour, a

kind of dome. The densest ice seemed to have formed it, yet it had no appearance of random naturalness. Surely it was far too regular and *finished* to be natural. But then again a brain such as that of the Gargolem, former custodian of Ru Karismi's kings, would be aware of such natural artefacts as ammonites, the crystalline veins of tiny leaves, the patterned structures of plasma and atoms. Perhaps the dome was, in its extraordinary manner, a creation of nature.

The two strong moons bloomed on it. But inside it had lights as well. These dimly reflected out, making the dome translucent as a lamp of frozen milk.

Steely tails of winds lashed round about, and as the Gargolem went on it was enveloped by this localized weather.

Unquestionably the Gargolem was able to shift itself through dimensions. It had had a method of vanishing and reappearing that with the recent years of turmoil had grown more noticeable. Yet it seemed it had stridden all this way from the old city, and now it reached the dome on foot and paused there.

Kol Cataar was inside the dome. Since the ice had formed no one would have left it and none – if any tried – had entered.

The Gargolem did not batter on the wall, did not politely knock. Instead the consciousness of the Gargolem separated and delved deep into the ice, deep and deep and out again on the inner side.

The Gargolem's thought drifted like a brazen shadow through that barrier known as Eastgate, along that street called Rose Walk. The awareness of the Gargolem reached the edge of the Great Market. A misnomer of course to any who had known the markets of Ru Karismi.

Torches burned on poles. People were at their late buying and selling. A pretty whore went by. A dog nosed among some cheese rinds. Now and then people lifted heads or eyes to the sky which was not sky. They knew but did not, would not admit, their city was imprisoned. No, no, the ice had piled up by the gates, they said. It would give way some time, or have to be cleared, but the king's guard were busy. Anyway, why want to go out during such a big freeze? The exterior fields and fruit trees would hibernate as ever. There was still sufficient food in here. King Bhorth had opened the palace stores. That fog stayed so bad though, did it not, smoking heaven up. Not a star. How long since anyone had seen a star? *You* did? You never did. And only when the moons were two or three and this big could you see your hand in front of your face when you put out your lights. Some muttered that ice had formed high up in the air. None spoke of a *lid*. Hell had such lidded kingdoms, like boxes, in ancient poetry. But that was Hell.

Unwitnessed the brazen shadow glided on.

It crossed areas of commerce and habitat and came to a refuse tip. A shack lay behind. Something – everything – in the shack was not normal. That was to an everyday eye unapparent. To a seeing one, a psychic earthquake had clearly occurred. The environ was in rubble, smeared with ichors and blood, and maybe torn bits of souls smouldered and decayed on the ground. This the Gargolem examined for a while. For there was no immediate hurry. It was already too late.

TWO

After she had died among the veils of butterflies, Jemhara spent some while in nothingness. She was partly aware of this, despite its contradiction in terms. It was comfortable, nullity, in fact restorative. Then in the end she decided the time had come to wake. And so she did, and there she was, despite the rest, still lying on the filthy floor of the shack in Kol Cataar, while the child she had borne wailed in a corner. Jemhara felt in that moment grossly cheated.

She did not know quite why, except perhaps she had glimpsed the balm of death, but now the life struggle was here again, like some exhausting task she could not evade. Nor for a few minutes did she fully recall who she was, either her false identity or her true one. Nor even Thryfe, nor even love.

But it all came back. Bad and good together.

Then she sat up at once, mislaying what her body had endured. Yet her body was intact. It was whole as if it had not, only hours before, expelled a child after thirteen months of misshapen servitude. Already she could dimly see in the semi-dark her flesh was returning to its original dimensions and young firmness. Her belly had shrunk, tautened.

There was nowhere any other sign that parturition had taken place. Not a spot of blood. No odour. Nothing. Apart from the crying baby.

Presently she went and stood staring down at it – at *him*.

Vashdran's words in the former trance made a kind of sense at last: *When you see me next, I'll be a fool again for a while, a type of fool.*

Was he helpless, a *fool*, as any tiny child had no choice but to be?

The newborn god was magenta in the face, bald and mottled with arrival, not comely, *not* god-like. She would have foretold, if she had thought to, even at nativity he must be astonishing and fair.

Jemhara leaned towards him, to pick him up, or only to ask something.

And this was when the universe parted to let through a roaring elemental force that could only be another god, quite grown up and bent on adult violence.

Instinctually, barely realizing what she did, Jemhara in straightening dragged the hem of her rags over the being on the floor – which must itself have had some comprehension, for it stopped its noise.

The manifestation of Zeth Zezeth filled the humble hovel.

He was the blue of Hell. His malign side. His golden eyes blazed out of it as if his godly brain were on fire.

A backhander of light hit Jemhara away across the shack. It was a glancing blow, a mild slap. Scorched and gasping she crouched on the earth.

'Why hide it? I could see it shining through the wall of the world, through the ice-lid of this midden called city, let alone your dirty dress. Do not say you were not hiding it.'

Jemhara hardly needed his instruction. She lowered her head. Logically she expected, again, to be killed. Yet guessed wildly execution was not the penalty.

'Well. There it is,' said Zzth.

The internal dimensions of the shack were changed. It had become very high and shambled away for miles all around. Zzth towered upward in it like a violet pillar. Below, the baby stretched small and motionless and dumb. Was Lionwolf already dead?

Two drops of a blue to rival Zzth's panoply seared suddenly through the eyelids of the baby. *His* brain it seemed was also on fire. Without preface, as babies will, he vomited.

A smell of tinders and fireworks flavoured the air. The vomit was a fountain glittering like liquid gold. It sprayed from the child in a jet, falling back only to cover and enclose him. The golden stuff immediately shaped itself to an egg, which hardened visibly. *He* was inside.

Gouging tides of rage, worse than any projectile sick, erupted from the pores of Zzth. He kicked at the eggshell. Panes of air shattered. The egg did not. It *disappeared.*

The events that then happened in the shack were soundless, not really visual. The mutilated space shrieked and rocked and exploded and collapsed upon itself. *Nothing* physical fell, but everything else had come down.

Outside, the city Zzth had called a midden heard, felt, saw nothing untoward. Only certain occurrences going on amid mankind. A healing wound which virulently burst, a bone that broke without cause, deaths that were expected coming too abruptly, untouched platters smashing on a shelf, a fire going out, blindness striking an old woman, fresh fruit rotting. Only such things. The things that do occur, that are bad luck or coincidence or inevitable and dismissed as such, and that maybe always *are* the side effects of the invisible and unrecognized and insane wrath of something evil and petty and powerful, near at hand but beyond justice.

Jemhara felt the thunderclaps of horror rake her through. She gave up and was rolled about the tilting electric floor. Once Zzth's seizures even cast her across the spot where the eggshell of golden vomit had been. There the ground was fiery hot.

Then Zzth grasped her. He was vast and towering still, with eyes like topaz windows. She was to be the only prize he could wrest from this débâcle. He had told her in a dream, too, she was to serve him.

Wavering in her mind came the image of her Magikoy lover. She saw Thryfe dead and she turned to dust.

Jemhara closed the shutter of her heart and the blue fiend spun her away. He had not even had to pass in or out of the ice-prison that enwrapped the city. Such was the magnitude of Zzth. But an eggshell had defeated him.

From the outside however the shack had stayed as always, or so it looked. None of the 'minor' unpleasantnesses in the city had registered as evidence of anything.

Near sunfall the priests went wandering through the market. The one who sang would not do so, which meant their takings were poor. Night dropped its conjuror's black cloth.

Later, the brazen shadow of the Gargolem gazed into the shack.

But this too went away.

A brace of drunks had a fight with knives not thirty paces from the door. Neither was slain though both were rather cut about. One recollected in after hours, 'There was a temper to that spot. Bad cess.'

Near midnight the noise of mailed men on the march thumped and jingled along Royal Way from the palace end.

A man of the spy troops Bhorth had set to watch Jemhara-Apple had met the king on the terrace. Bhorth had still been gaping at the gilded arrow his son had fired heavenward, and which had stuck in the sky as if in a ceiling beam. Nearby was Sallusdon, and the girl with a shaved head Sallus claimed was his sister. And the damned snake, of course.

Bhorth drew the spy aside. The man was dressed as something shabby and unclean from the alleys, and adorned with the appropriate pong.

'Well?'

'Sir, pardon me – I'd have been here sooner, but a wagon of bread caught fire, blocked half the city – no one would take the blame, said it just happened—'

'Is the fire out?' Bhorth ever on guard for his capital.

'Yes, sir, only she—'

'The bitch Jema?'

'*Yes.* She's shat it out.'

'*At last.* Does it live?'

'No one knows. It's peaceful as a grave in there now.'

'Then how *do* you know anything at all?'

'It was one of the priests, lord king. The boy that sings. He'd stopped by the shack for alms; he begs anywhere, they all do.

My man Catnose – you know Catnose?' Bhorth's face suggested a renewed acquaintance was superfluous and the spy hurried on. 'He often oils the priests, money and that. He found the boy priest all huddled up so he says, What's on, my pilchard? And the boy said he'd asked alms at the shack and been turned off, but as he went he heard a cry, so turned round and went back and looked through a gap at the door. It seems the cry wasn't like anything – average.'

'*What did he see?*'

'All sorts of nonsense, if you believe him. But he's crazy, the sing-priest. Lights and stars and butterflies – what are *they*? Well, but in the middle she drops the brat. Oh yes, he was sure of this one thing. A baby. Dark red as a ripe plum.'

'Did it live?'

'It seems so. It's got a lusty yell, Catnose says – he heard it. Though the shack's quiet now.'

'And when was this?'

The spy was uneasy. 'Forgive me, I said, my lord, that fire—'

As Bhorth swung round to leave the terrace Sallus came up to him. For the first time in their lives together Bhorth raised his hand to ward off his son. 'Not now. I must do this. I meant to have spoken with you about it. We never have. And you'd prevent me.'

'Her child's born and you'll kill it.'

'If I can. It's a god from Hell.'

'The Lionwolf. Father—'

'*No.*'

Sallusdon, stationed on the terrace, watched Bhorth pound, shouting for his men, into the palace.

A midnight bell had struck by the time Bhorth and his ten soldiers reached the refuse tip.

There had been no pretence at secrecy on this occasion. Curtailment was imperative. Concealment could wait – that was, if any of them survived.

Having broken in the door, as Zzth's tantrum had already broken it in all but a physical way, the Rukarian soldiers clustered, dejected.

'Fled, my lord.'

'How hot it is in here,' Bhorth pointlessly remarked.

Thryfe emerged from the blank tunnel of coma, but not into awakening or the real world.

He was in flight. An eagle, his vitality unimpaired, the huge wings spread, speeded by the thermals over a map of cold mountains, and above zircon stars grouped in constellations like question marks.

The eyrie resembled a dish of wires and sinews. The starlight slid along its arteries. Inside, she had plucked out her own feathers to provide a lining. They were thick as fur. She—

He did not know where she had gone to, his mate. All that remained was the egg. It too was englamoured by starlight.

Like a winged sword the eagle set down on the nest's wide rim. Instantly he saw the cracks that patterned the eggshell.

He craned forward the predatory length of his neck, and with a measured blacksmith hammering began to tap on the undoing shell.

Thryfe, high up in the chamber of the eagle's brain, stared out impassively.

I have lost her. I shall never see her again. Only this shall I see. This – which has used us.

As one, like a chord of music, all the particles of the shell gave way. Star-like, jewel-like, they rained upward into the sky.

And it emerged, the eagle's child.

'Snow! Hard snow—'

'It's hail – great chunks – beware – look out!'

Look out, look out, the sky is falling—

Over Kol Cataar, Phoenix from Ashes, the lid of ice, disintegrating, spiralled and sprinkled and rumbled down.

Pieces of ice big as house storeys dashed on Rose Walk, but they were thin too, and hitting home did little damage. Other lesser fragments were more harsh and stabbed like pins. A couple of chimneys crashed behind on the market. A man who had not taken cover was knocked senseless but revived after half an hour.

Even as the sky plummeted the city began to make out behind the drizzle and bustle of the jettisoned ice the proper sky of night, with one full moon and two skinny lunar attendants, and stars everywhere like unstrung necklaces.

Five centuries of Winter, and it could still play tricks. Ice in the sky. Who would have thought it?

Tireh the queen and her ladies were spectators behind the relative safety of palace windows. The two little princess daughters had been allowed up to see.

Sallusdon, roped by the snake, had drawn his sister Azula to shelter under an overhang. There he said to her, 'Our mother is calling to me. Chillel. I must go to find her. Do you feel that?'

But Azula only looked at him and replied, '*My* mother is dead.'

Deep in the grey architecture of the labyrinth lies motionless colour. The labyrinth knows it, has grown used to it. It lives here.

That is, if it does live.

How long then has the child, the newborn, sprawled on the weighing slab of stone against which sacks of milled flour had reposed? A month. At that age, they grow so quickly. One moment the floppy babe-in-arms, and then, and then—

Rats that exist in the underpalace have sometimes come and stared at this motionless yet undead thing. Their eyes are sequined with rubies. So would the child's eyes be if ever they moved, to catch the light.

For there is some light here.

An old man, tall, gaunt and stooping, goes about the storeroom, always slowly. There is an aura to him of great presence, but it *wobbles*, as if he had become displaced from it, as if all that was ever anything in him has entered the aura, and inside he is just a memory, something left over.

The eyes of the baby are even so phenomenally blue.

The magician looks into them.

'What do you want? You have crushed the world in your hands. I should destroy you. But I don't, do I? Is it because she bore you? I doubt that. Even the rats won't have you. You'd choke them, probably.'

The baby does not stir. On the floor around the slab where the flour once was are pieces of what look like broken eggshells.

The baby itself is *vivid*. He is mottled with rings of dark tan and the red of a banner. He is less like a child than like a fabled insect.

Thryfe the magician seats himself in the chair Bhorth's men have brought him.

Since the miraculous child appeared here in the chamber where Thryfe had lain in his trance, no one will enter. Thryfe is well aware the king expects him to throttle or smother the child, as the magus himself had advised.

'In the dream,' Thryfe says, 'you emerged as an eagle, fully fledged. And you are a sun god. So too you told me some while ago, there in the oculum which never lies, wish it would as one might. Not even in a dream.'

Thryfe has tried, without undue cruelty, to be rid of the perilous creature on the slab. For it is *not* a child. He laid a pillow over it and pressed down. There was no struggle. After what seemed an hour of personal torment he straightened and beheld the child exactly the same, mottled, bald, breathing, serene, eyes wide. There have been other methods since. After each assault Thryfe fell back shaking in the chair. It must be his fault. His ability and knowledge have bled out of him.

The stories told how the Lionwolf, Vashdran, had grown in ten years to be a man of twenty-one. Other legends had wafted about that it had asked only ten days for the god to grow to manhood. The god now has been on earth a month. He does not seem to require sustenance, not even a mother's milk. He does not move or cry or show any even quasi-natural reaction. His eyes do not follow anything. Yet when you stand above him, they gaze deeply into yours.

For the hundredth, thousandth, time Thryfe nerves himself to stare into the blue eyes of Vashdran.

'*What do you want?*'

Minutes pass.

Thryfe leaves the monstrosity where it lies and goes back to his seat. On his instructions they have walled up this chamber. The air at least is dying. The mage thinks of his lover, and how he has no power to help her.

In a sort of dream again, Thryfe is viewing Bhorth in an inner room. No one is with him.

Bhorth's beloved son, the witch-seed of Chillel, has gone from the city. Whatever scenes attended Sallusdon's quittal leave no mark, except in furrows between the king's eyebrows, and below his eyes. He has put on weight again and looks older.

Thryfe recalls Bhorth's heavy portentous steps finally descending to this area of the underpalace, and how Bhorth had demanded to come in and free the city, and Thryfe himself, of the burden of Vashdran.

Thryfe's own weariness and disgusted boredom by then perhaps had exceeded Bhorth's panic and ruthlessness.

'Wall up the entry here,' had said Thryfe. 'I told your man that when I told him the child was here.'

'Don't be a numbskull, mage! Already it's shifted itself from one solid place into another. It can pass through stone.'

'Not any more. Perhaps it's exhausted. It doesn't move, perhaps can't. And too I shall watch that it doesn't.'

'How can you prevent it?'

Thryfe had smiled unseen and drearily. 'I am its physical father. I believe that has tethered it. And I am, even now, one of the Magikoy.'

They had argued then, and for some days after off and on. Or Bhorth had done so. Thryfe did not speak again, nor did the king enter the chamber.

The child lay throughout motionless, and iridescent with its unnerving, insectile colours.

165

At length Bhorth went away for good, and then his men came and there was the noise of the walling up.

It is true Thryfe has also spoken words to anchor the god-thing where it is. But really Thryfe believes it will not be able to leave him. Ironically, while the heroic demi-god Sallus has removed himself from the care of a loving father, the fiendly Vashdran has come psychically running to his hating progenitor – who thereafter has attempted many times to destroy this son.

What binds Vashdran to Thryfe is not really any mantra. Presumably it is habit. The first father, Zzth, had also hated his son, and attempted wherever possible to kill him. The rubbed place in the heart most often attracts the blow. Men are caught by this snare. How can gods be immune?

The magician pushes off his meditation. He drinks from the crock of water on the floor. There is nothing else. He sits in silence until the rats steal out again and watch, then steal again away.

Something in the air.

The rats are dazzled.

They have stars in their eyes now, not rubies.

A starry filtered flicker and glister ensues, a circular unravelling, that swarms through the storerooms over and around jars of oil and preserves and closets of frigid meat, eddying always inward to one goal.

Like snowflakes the stars infiltrate the walled-up room.

Is anyone here aware enough to note them? The magus has again sunk in deathly sleep. But does the uncanny baby see? The eyes of it still do not move, yet the stars obligingly dance about the child's head before prancing on and amalgamating high up in the chamber's darkest corner.

And there the stars form something. If stars do this the something will be spectacular.

Nondescript in his garments coloured like biscuit crumbs,

Ddir descended, walking down the wall as if it were a flight of stairs.

Ddir, the third of the trio of gods active in, or somehow swept up in, this supernatural tragi-comedy from the start, was the artisan, the maker. His arrangements of stars and their subsequent portents had brought him much attention. Ddir himself seemed never to be aware of that.

Now the genius of his unmind was already working. He had forgotten – if he had ever known – what had attracted him to this storeroom. Nothing was of consequence to him apart from the creative process, in this case represented by the child on the slab.

There had been something like this before. Years ago, or minutes. Or centuries.

The gaudy baby was not a blank canvas. More a spoiled one.

He stood looking at it.

Then he began.

The fleshly bundle became instantly formless. It was a lump of dough or wet cement, the colours swirled in it. Only two blue dabs of light hovered now here, now there, under its surface. The eyes, perturbingly able at last to move, were swimming about through its mass like busy fish.

Then the doughy mixture parted in the middle. Two halves slicked back. Inside, a light like a dawn sun rayed upward. Although of such intensity this light *lit* nothing and cast not a single shadow.

Ddir gazed into the ray, causing and monitoring its realignment.

The two halves of mass fell off on the floor. They shrivelled to husks and went to crumbs. *More* crumbs. The light however spread and now it swiftly assumed a shape. That of a tall and full-grown man.

The body was of perfect proportion – what else could one expect from an artisan such as Ddir, no doubt obsessed by flawless maths? Lean, and long of leg, wide at the shoulders, hair streaming out behind a mask of face that quickly accumulated features. In seconds every correct anatomical element was present. The closed eyes were lashed, the brows drawn, the lips sculpted and the mouth equipped with faultless teeth. Male nipples gemmed the flat muscles of the strong chest. At the groin the phallic weapon lay impressively sleeping. The hands and feet took on their nails. Even this time a navel formed, not having been forgotten. Whether it might have been extant anyway was debatable.

Ddir looked on intently. But the blue eyes, those independent fish, hovered about, watching too. Did they approve?

Apparently. As the fiery substance of the madeover god began to cool to a golden opacity, fire now only in the hair, the eyelids lifted. Into the sockets dropped the vagrant eyes like two blue spoonfuls of water.

Something shuddered in the stonework. An unphysical quake.

The atmosphere settled.

Ddir closed his hands and put them away in his sleeves like valuable tools.

And on the slab the god sat up. He was a young and beautiful man of about twenty-five years of age, his nakedness resplendent as any new suit of clothes.

'My thanks,' he said to Ddir. 'That saved some time.'

Ddir did not speak. He was losing interest. The project was complete. He levitated upward. When his head brushed the room's ceiling he simply continued on and ebbed through and away. His bare feet went the last, already transparent, and the toes not well manicured.

Lionwolf stretched himself, and rose.

He crossed the room as a man would have done. He had been a man in life, and death. Humanness remained comfortable and appropriate for him, despite so many talents.

Thryfe lay crookedly sleeping in the chair. Lionwolf set one hand quietly on the magician's head. Thryfe, though starved of air, was not yet dead.

Lionwolf nodded to the doorway that had been walled up. Stones and mortar mellifluously crumbled and powdered down. Outside ran a dim corridor of the labyrinth, empty of anything except a dead torch. But when the eyes of the god touched the torch with their glance it sprang into hot flower.

If he could do so much, why had he needed so much help to break from the matrix? Zzth had interrupted his arrival: was it that? The ritual, once begun, must be concluded in good order. If that, then now for sure it was.

The wall having given way fresh air was soaking through. Curiously ordinary once more Lionwolf picked up Thryfe's mantle, discarded on the floor. Lionwolf dressed himself, and belted the garment with a length of cord drawn from a nearby sack.

Thryfe moved. He drew in a long, clicking breath.

His eyes opened and fixed on what stood in front of him.

Saying nothing, pulling again only on enormous reserves of will, the magician dragged himself to his feet.

His sole and total plan raved in his glare. He must once more assault the creature, whatever it was, whatever it might do. He must somehow impair it.

But the boy – boy? – this beast-thing from some Hell – the boy held out his hand. 'You'll feel better in a moment, sir.'

'What?' said Thryfe, arrested by absurdity where terror and horror and despair had not stopped him.

'You've suffered, but you heal. Give it a chance. That's best.'

Thryfe sealed his lips. He came at Lionwolf in a lurching leap.

Lionwolf caught him. Held him.

Something . . . The touch of the god was wonderful, like fiery wine which – yes – healed.

'I can't call you *Father*, can I?' the god asked with a certain tactful inanity. 'Physically of course. But there.' He put Thryfe down gently on the slab.

Ashamed by a dreadful wash of compliance, Thryfe felt how life flared in him now. It ran like lions through his veins.

He forced out words. 'What happened to the woman who bore you?'

'Jemhara lives.'

'*Where?*'

'She has been taken, but the one who has her thinks her valuable.'

'*Who?*'

'The god Zeth Zezeth.'

'Are all of you *real* then?' Thryfe blurted scornfully.

'Some of us are.' Lionwolf had now, it seemed, the grave authority of a great earthly king. Surprisingly again, he knelt by Thryfe, looking into his face. 'But Thryfe, a destiny may sometimes be immovable. The parts we play, gods and men, may be written out for us before we are born. And in that writing we too may have colluded.'

Thryfe sat stunned, stupefied. He felt vigorous, healthy, young. He was hungry and thirsty in sane and eager ways. He was *greedy* for his existence that, less than five hundred heartbeats before, he had meant to sacrifice. It *was* like becoming drunk on wine, he thought. As the drunk believed, it should despite anything be possible to move the world in the desired direction.

I must wait to regain my right mind. Until then there is no use in questioning, even in thinking. He had touched a god. God help him.

Somewhere above the room and corridor there was the sound of general disturbance. Men were coming, Bhorth's guards no doubt.

Thryfe became aware of the rats then. They were emerging from all points of the room, crowding in like a thrilled audience. They stared at the Lionwolf.

And the god rose, turned abruptly and saw them, and his face lit with laughter. He shook his head at the rats and the scarlet hair shook too like a wild wing. But the rats only kept their ground, chittering, tweeting like strange birds. Some held on to others, as people did sometimes when amazed or delighted.

'Oh, then,' said the god. A kind of pale, soft fan of light flew off from him. It covered the room, the dank dark walls of which shone out like honey. The rats jumped and sported in the wave of light, washing themselves and each other.

When it sank they scurried off. They were gone and the room was dark again and empty but for the magician, and the god he had fathered.

'What did you do,' Thryfe said, 'to the rats?'

Down to such a ridiculous and irrelevant query had this vast event driven him.

But the god only laughed aloud and did not answer.

Above came the noise of mailed, running feet. Below rang the bird-like song of rodents doused in beams of supernature.

'He is a fool. Yes, as he foretold, a fool. Does he have no idea of what constrained him – what can still *unmake* him?'

The voice was melodious. The place, glorious.

Jemhara took in the scene with a deadly rapture.

She sat in a grove where trees in heavily gilded leaf gave on a view of distant mountains, russet and vermilion, some of which mistily fumed into an amber sky.

The warmth was rich but not oppressive. A fountain of liquid water spouted through twists of copper.

'No, not quite what you see, Jemhara,' he said. 'None of you ever can see it, or report it, quite as it is. Perhaps nor do I.'

His malign side was shut off. The god Zeth was attractive and delicious in all ways. He looked not only unsurpassably hand-some but *good*, wholly benign, as if no unjust or spiteful action could ever be possible to him.

She thought, *I am in his paradise, where the Rukarian priests and poets say he goes for recreation. It's true they all describe it differently.*

She looked down and saw she was clad in orichalc tissue. Her hair was clean and perfumed with an attar of some unknown and matchless plant probably foreign to earth. She was young again, not even young as she had been before Apple, but about seventeen. She did not need the flitter of little glass mirrors hung in trees to tell her her loveliness had returned repaired, in fact improved.

Her first actual thought had been one of fear – she could not find, either on her hand or lying where it had about her throat, the silver ring. Fear subsided to a small grey ache, the familiar bruise of loss. But then she had wondered if the ring too, magical and representing so very much, were still a part of her, had *become* a part of her. She imagined it grown into the marrow of her bone above the heart. *Let that be so. Let me think that.* And the ache melted away.

By then beside her stood Zeth Zezeth, the Sun Wolf.

'Don't bow to me,' he said. He did not mean it. It radiated from him that she must always bow no matter what he said. He caressed her cheek with one finger. The sensual pleasure of this was nearly unbearable. Rapture – deadly, deadly.

'Please pardon me, lordly one. I can hardly bear to see—' she attempted as he led her towards a prism drifting between the leaves and the water.

'But you must.'

So she must.

It was the world naturally that was to be scried in the prism. She expected to be shown Vashdran there, the Vashdran baby crying, frightful yet vulnerable and pathetic. Or the sudden egg. But what was revealed was a snow-high street and over it, between house walls, a stream of rats scampering. Each was very large and seemed to have been dipped in gold leaf.

'Playful,' said Zeth. He smiled. 'He plays about like a little boy even now. Imparting energies to rats. But can he know, or does he not, why Thryfe could both draw him in and hold him put? Only that roaming moron Ddir, who had nothing better to do today, was able to release the simpleton called Lionwolf from his stasis. Well, Jema, you have been a Rukarian scholar. What do you think?'

'How can I know, lord?'

'Even you, my Jema, trammelled and trapped Lionwolf. Thirteen months. Poor *boy*. Poor *Jema*.' The jeer in Zeth's sublime voice was enchanting. Nothing foul or vicious could be involved with it at all.

'Did I, lord? I had thought the delay was—'

'No, Jemhara. It was you. The two of you.'

Jemhara wanted only to listen. She did not want to listen. She wanted anything, even pain and degradation, all but this. Irresistibly she gazed into his face. Her spirit seemed sucked right out of her. But then he had made a slave of her spirit already. Without thought she knew even the silver ring within her breastbone could not anchor her soul against this flood. She drooped with desire for Zeth, and love, and in her heart a little knife began to turn slowly on and on, coring her like the apple she had been named for.

'If—' she said.

He paid no attention. He told her: 'He is a god now created using only mortal material. Before, he was made of myself – of *me*, my very *essence*. Now he is common clay. Oh, he transcends it utterly, and with all human others he will meet it has little bearing on him. But Thryfe, though not able to kill him, has been like a magnet to him. One which, if properly manipulated, might weigh him to the ground. You however, my Jema, are better. Lionwolf has grown in you, and you have brought him out. *You* will be able to sink the fool lower yet, into the very pit, back to his hells. You are to assist me in this task.'

Jemhara knelt on the gilt turf. Little hot fruits grew in it, and blossoms. She wished only to serve Zeth.

Again he touched her, one finger, on the crown of her head. The other had done that, her – *son*. Sweet flame trickled through her body and bones, her very hair. By now her heart was a hollow pip.

'Jema, I would take joy in lying with you,' said Zeth. How prim his terms. She knew, her hollow heart knew. She languished, knowing he would *not* be 'lying' with her. 'One kiss from me would blast you apart. My congress with the other doy was different – I mean with his first earthly mother, Saphay.' Something bluish evolved, a skitter of malevolence; it was smoothed at once back into satin beneficence. 'Even I have never known, would you credit me, what Saphay possessed to claim me, and to survive me, let alone to bring out Vashdran with my brightness locked inside. There have been women elsewhere, you understand, taken by me and so destroyed. And beasts now and then; they seem immune, perhaps protected by the beast form I must assume in order to dight them. Nor have any of them been able to steal from me, as Saphay did, and *he*. But then,' mused Zeth, moving from Jemhara, crossing like a flight of sunlight into the avenue among the trees, 'does there have to be a reason for everything?'

THREE

Embedded in the court of Padgish, Arok knew himself reckoned a barbarian, but recollected plainly he was a king.

He believed he had been retained as a hostage against the threat of the warlike intent of his people. Their number was not known here, and doubtless their fighting ethic had been noted. That the Simese kept the Jafn rather as interesting zoo animals was beyond the bounds of consideration.

Arok stood now with a group of his warriors, ostensibly watching a peculiar game that the Simese conducted, on a court cleared of snow, with long, flat-bladed sticks and a ball. The ball must reach and strike a gong, of which there were two, one either end of the court. Each team of men had a colour, black or red, stitched to their sleeves. Some attempted to prevent the ball from striking the gong, throwing themselves flat, rolling and kicking; others tried to whack it home. Unluckily both sides constantly managed to score, and the continual clang of the gongs had by now given Arok a headache. This whole stupidity was it seemed to honour the god of Winter. He presided on the side. It was an ugly statue with pointed teeth.

Under the noise the Jafn spoke in their own tongue.

'But how's it to be done?' said Khursp.

'Simply.'

'Yes?' The others crowded close. All around the game-enthused Simese ignored them. The ball, of goatskin over split rope, bounded once more to a gong. *Clunggg*.

'Tell me who among us still finds himself a Jafn?' demanded Arok, clenching his brows with pain rather than anger.

They named themselves. There were others – 'So-and-so, he's besotted by a fellow here, who treats him like a scrat.' 'So-and-so, but he's gone crazy on a girl, some bitch, I think she's poisoning him.' 'And *he* and *he* have taken up Simese manners, in the bath all day, even worship these outland gods – I don't mean as I have, to be on the safe side of things. No, it's real with them. You say, But what of God, and they say, Ah, that.'

'Us alone then,' said Arok. He had already counted them in his mind. There were five men beside himself here in the court. Fenzi had been sent with the Simese princelet to the Holasangarth.

'Can we leave them behind,' asked Khursp, 'those others of us?'

Arok clenched his forehead more tightly.

He did not want to. It was not the Jafn code. To comrade and subject you stayed true. If you could, if he deserved it.

'Khursp,' he said, 'try to speak to them.'

Khursp winced. 'If you want, Chaiord. But they're stuck on Simisey.'

The gong went off again. There was a definitive uproar of cheering and yells in which the Jafn sensibly joined. The ball contest had ended.

Arok felt the oddest thing. Without warning a cold finger seemed to have tapped against his brain. It cleared the headache instantly but left a fractured echo, as if his mind had divided in two or three segments.

Across the ball-court he sensed impulsively the grim presiding statue. Arok looked over. What an object. It was not humorous and logical like the dromaz god Obac, nor pretty and frivolous like Obac's tiny wife, the naughty mouse goddess Vedis. This was a staring face of bleached stone with slitted eyes and fangs. Winter was unpleasant. Perhaps that was logical too but Arok, raised to have faith in something much larger and far more enigmatic, automatically took against the Simese god of snow and ice and cold.

'What's that idol's name?' he asked Khursp as they left the court.

Aware of Simese all around, Khursp muttered, 'That fellow is the Lord Tirthen.'

'We'll go out then come back. We'll make an offering to the filthy thing. Tell the others. The mages will come up to oversee it, shoving in their beaks. Let them.'

'Why do we offer then, Arok?'

'There are things that have – power. They're never gods. But one treads with care.' He did not add that, of all the Simese in the court, that one with the teeth had seemed to overhear his thoughts. To *want* something from him.

There was to be a hunt tomorrow. The Simese king had invited Arok and his men, as if to honour and reward them during a happy visit. Arok's 'simple' plan involved going along with that, then spurring the sheep-mounts they would be riding and most of them had mastered, and getting away.

Now Khursp murmured, 'And at the hunt when we run, will none of them try to shoot us down?'

'We'll risk it. They don't spend much time refining their bowmanship. They prefer to bat balls at gongs.'

'But still we make an offering to their Winter god?'

'Still we do. While we're there we can ask for rotten weather to cover our retreat. Winter hates us all, regardless of race or creed. He won't mind.' And Arok thought of the true God in that moment, His neglected statue brought from the first Holas House. How faith now failed yet persisted, persisted, failed, never being resolved.

Below the hill of the capital lay a sort of ice-wooded deer park, maintained for hunting. Certain exits led from it out into the country beyond, but also there were lines of enclosure to keep the bulk of the wildlife in.

The Simese king led the way, his favourites around him, on this occasion mounted on choice brown horses from the royal stables.

At these the Jafn men looked sidelong. They were snagged

between enamoured covetousness and allergy, because of the established resemblance to horsazin.

The Jafn themselves all rode dromazi. They were no longer inept at handling these beasts; nevertheless their hosts slyly mocked them. Many of the Simese rode dromazi on the jaunt too. They showed off, to put the Jafn in an unflattering light.

The light of the sky however was very flattering, unclouded and blue.

Game was started.

Everyone rocked and jounced between the aisles of the frozen forest, pyramidal conifers of silver spines and spreading marble plantain trees, to the brink of a river identified from the muscles stranded in its ice. It must have entirely thawed and refrozen quite recently. Curjai, somebody said, had undone the river months ago to provide a display for the hunting king and his men. Arok had seen Curjai often make magic after dinner in hall, rousing flames from the hearth to wing about like birds, or turning water to ale.

No deer were cornered at the river. The quarry was a pair of enormous furred pig, ruffed and tusked, the white swipes on their foreheads like paths of ice.

The hunters swung from horses and dromazi. They would not risk their mounts against sharp tusks.

Arok ran forward with the rest. The overcast or snowfall he had wanted to cover escape seemed unlikely. But the hunt would not be satisfied with just two pigs. It would go on most of the day, even to sunfall. After dark their chances would be better. No Jafn would move until he gave the signal. There were still only six of them anyway. No others had been judged viable.

Khursp, Elbar and the other three joined the cluster of Simese hunters. Arok pushed quickly forward. He was ahead of all of them. He raised the long spear. Simultaneously the larger of the pigs shook itself and came heavily cantering at him. Elbar broke suddenly across the animal's path. Its lethal snout swerved after him only a handspan away, but Elbar had dived into a somersault. The tusks missed him and the running pig stumbled.

Arok flung his spear. It caught the beast under the breastbone.

Then Khursp's spear thunked home. Both shafts were stuck close together and well in. Their iron blades had met the heart. Staggering and squealing the bloody barrel slumped over into a snowbank and Arok's spear snapped. Noise ended. The pig was dead.

Certainly the Simese had ceased sneering. Perhaps they had not realized incomers might have hunted such pig before. If one needed proof of Simese contempt, ironically now their applause furnished it.

The other pig abruptly lumbered off into a thicket of thorn trees.

Khursp lifted his brows. 'No, no,' said Arok graciously in Simese. 'Let our friends of Padgish have that one. It's the smaller too.'

Something began to happen in the thicket.

'What is that pig doing?' Elbar asked.

One of the Simese shouted. 'Look – the thorns are burning.'

Thick white clouds went pouring up from the embrangle of glacial trees. A sinister gleaming colourless light was wound in them. They made a pillar that rose into the sky; far overhead yellowish lightnings crackled. The cloud-smoke did not disperse, nor did it spread. There was no smell of fire, only of unusual cold.

'Stand away,' said Arok firmly in Simese, as if he had forgotten the Jafn tongue. 'Something sorcerous is at work.'

He and his five warriors stepped backward. They eased through the line of Simese hunters, the other renegade Jafn. *They* were transfixed, all of them. Not even the king moved.

A little distance off Arok's men halted. Their dromaz mounts were here, tossing their heads and mumbling, lifting their pads in relays from the ground.

'Here's our chance,' muttered Khursp. 'Chaiord? We depart now? *Look at the sky.*'

Blue was congealing to curded vanilla. Although the cloud column had not spread the upper air seemed to have turned deadly pale in fear of it.

With caution, and moving curiously slowly, they mounted.

The dromazi were evidently only too eager to be off. All around others of their kind were worrying at their tethers. Several had not been carefully secured and were pulling free. The horses too were now tugging and pawing the snow, raving their maned heads. None of them made any vocal sound. As if they did not dare.

A trance was on everything human. Arok felt himself mount up and his limbs and hands move to direct the dromaz as if through gelid, turgid liquid. His eyes seemed not to focus, or rather as if each eye saw something different. Before he could behold what came out of the thorn trees he had succeeded in turning the dromaz away. His five warriors galloped with him.

Yet the galloping also was – slow. Time had altered. Each second lasted a minute. It was like a dream.

The Simese king, a man who seldom offered all his thoughts, stood with his mouth ajar. The Padgish warriors, along with the remaining Jafn, gazed fixedly at the thorn thicket. White clouds made of snow-smoke parted. Some element – but which: light? wind? cold? – passed through, and so through the group of static men. Their skins cramped, their blood sizzled with frost. Not one did not feel it. None cursed, called or cried out. They had already perceived that, as the unidentified element went by the dead pig, the animal had turned to solid ice. Its bones were faintly to be glimpsed, set there in the iceberg of its meat.

But the *element* had brushed by, through and onward, travelling at great speed away from them. They were released.

Among the men of Padgish, one now silently fell dead. The remainder, Padgish and Jafn, revived in stages. Two or three wept, the tears freezing to their faces. Their feet seemed dead blocks of stone. Hands bore ominous white patches, a disfigurement of frostbite seldom now ever seen except in the very old or young who had spent days and nights lost on the waste.

The king closed his mouth. The teeth were knives. His lungs tingled full of frost.

In the thicket the clouds were thinning. The other pig that had gone in there abruptly trotted out again, a terrifying white-eyed swine made of dense crystal – that shattered in front of the men into tiny fragments, like a dropped goblet.

Much distance off Arok could know nothing of this. Nevertheless he was aware of it. It was like another figment of the nightmare that pursued the six of them, as they and the dromazi rushed so dawdlingly away towards the south. And Arok thought of the Jafn left behind. *God forgive me.*

Overhead the curded sky darkened. The sun was eclipsed by cumulus, and a lizard's tongue of lightning darted through it. These lightnings had a shape, hard and at odds with themselves. The Jafn had not anywhere seen lightnings quite of this type before.

Then the piece of the nightmare that pursued began to catch up.

Elbar turned his head.

'Chaiord – the clouds are chasing us.'

Arok did not deny this. 'We'll outrun them.'

He kicked the dromaz but the dromaz took no notice. It was anyway galloping as fast as it could. A second was a minute, a minute was the third of an hour.

Arok seemed now to behold all the spent moments scattering around them in gem-like bits – as if someone had dropped an enormous cup of cloudy crystal.

'Oh, Chaiord – Arok – look behind us,' rasped Khursp.

Arok did not want to turn. But he, and the others, even as they ran looked back. As almost every myth of any people on earth instructed you must *not*.

There it was. The fact.

The fact streamed from the direction of Padgish and the royal hunting park, out of the north. It was *weather* – it was an element.

'Great Heart of God,' Arok breathed.

They ran so tardily but this that followed was so very swift. Its time and theirs were quite unlike, and yet they were able to exist inside the selfsame dimension.

The impression Arok took was of a flying spear, even the one he had flung into the badger-pig. The centre was a darkness, but all about was a *whiteness*. Clouds boiled and funnelled, but more than anything the mass had a gliding motion. He and his men though strong and coordinated were ungainly. The pursuer, despite the crazy idea it had been quiescent, maybe even unactual, for centuries, was graceful and certain. The swiftness of it rent the mind. Only something unhuman and utterly extrinsic beyond race, superstition or dream could move and *be* like *this*.

'Khursp – all of you – ride on. I'll remain. If it wants I'll meet it.'

'*Chaiord—*'

'*Go, you bastard son of a bastard son.*'

You did not call any Jafn man a bastard, let alone his father. It had been a reason for blood-feuds that had lasted generations. Arok had just assumed that he and his no longer had generations. Doubtless *he* had only three seconds, though of course for him now they would last three whole minutes.

Khursp did not argue. Cheerfully glum as a skull he grinned and saluted.

They fled away, the five Jafn. Arok reined in and coaxed the dromaz to turn about. It obeyed, sapped of all energy.

Like that then he faced what sped towards him.

Overhead now, all around, the cryogenic cloud of ice-spume roiled. Man and animal were enveloped in a seething cauldron of freezingness. The dromaz had a beard of icicles. Face coated and eyes glazed by rime, the Chaiord of the Jafn Holas watched this spear fly in.

It hit the target. It was there. It was motionless.

About two shield-lengths off a figure stood on nothing, between sky and ground.

Another man? Never. It only looked like one.

Arok stared at the snow-pale face, the snow-white, silk-like clothing, the hair, eyes and brows that were jet black, the wicked mouth.

The Chaiord tried to speak. 'Believe I respect you. I can't bow down; I can't – move. Why do you follow me?'

The thing laughed, fluidly and attractively.

Next it spoke in a voice that was beautiful, like that of some high mage or bard. But the unkind lips scarcely altered.

'Why do I follow you? Because you killed my beast.'

In Arok's brain something seemed to snap.

The apparition was not ugly; its teeth did not seem to be pointed. Despite that, 'Tirthen,' said Arok. He remembered how he had offered for bad weather, facetious, unheard-of deed. And then – the inadvertent blood sacrifice of the hunted pig.

Then his intelligence and ethnicity rebelled. Only *God* existed. All else were demons and sprites. What then was *this*?

'I beg your pardon, Lord Tirthen,' said Arok in stuttering Simese, 'for killing your pig without properly dedicating it to you. Everything here in Simisey obviously is yours.'

'No.' The mesmeric voice had no surface or depth. But the word it seemed to say transparently repeated in Arok's ears in a sort of tinnitus. 'Everything,' clarified the Winter god, 'everything on earth is mine. Every hill and mountain, every valley, plain, river and sea. And every living thing, plant, beast or man. All mine. Five centuries' worth of mine. And five centuries to come. And then five more, and on. For ever.' The words piled up, stone on stone.

Arok's brain began to congeal. His blood was already frozen he imagined, dark uncut garnets tight-packed under his skin.

There was no point in praying to anything, or begging for any respite. He was betrayed by a Power he had believed in, that did not exist. There was only this to pray to, and you could not pray to this.

'Where were you going?' asked Tirthen.

'My – garth,' mouthed Arok. The answer meant nothing to him.

'I shall go there instead.'

Arok shuddered. Like a drunkard he enunciated with strict emphasis, 'I'm dead.'

When he said this the dromaz on which he still sat began slowly to go down, collapsing like a huge boned cushion into the snow, that had itself frozen by now to a sheet of steel.

A screen clicked shut across consciousness. There was no space for resistance, anger, panic or regret. He had always hoped to die in battle. This was like uncontrolled sleep. And he had reckoned death would be like that. Vaguely, as all slipped from him, he remembered Nirri with apology, for he should have thought of her properly, and next of his sons. But he could not, though he remembered who, remember *what* they were. Titles – wife, son – were meaningless. How stingy death was. It cheated. He had not died as he should.

Nirri raised her head. She had been sewing with her women in the improvised chamber. Now the wool lay flaccid on her lap.

Something had passed from her. What had it been?

She did not know. For a brief while she wondered if she had felt the first threat of her approaching death. She had supposed herself healthy, but anyone might be mistaken. She was troubled by the notion mostly in a practical way. If she was soon due to become ill and die, many aspects of the garth would need to be organized. Her husband was absent and might not come back, otherwise there would have been less to bother her. On the other hand the mystic and exclusive spell that trapped the upper room must be addressed.

Though she sat abruptly motionless, her face full of inner thought, her girls let her be. They liked her. She was kind and pleasant and brave, and knew what she was about. So what, she had been a fishwife. She was also Holas and had borne the Chaiord two sons. If one was lost the other was being polished up into a hero by a mighty wise-woman.

Nirri put the needle once more into the cloth. As she did so it caught the light of the candles and glittered. The glitter was strangely like a tear falling. She regarded the single new stitch. It was the Olchibe and Gech who wove their writing into cloth, yet now this stitch seemed to have become writing of another sort that she could understand. And in it Nirri read the death, not of herself but of Arok.

The woollen cloth slid to the floor as she rose straight up from the chair.

'Nirri-lady, what is it?'

Whether she would have replied she never did know, for at that instant knocking thundered against the House door.

The men grouped on the yard. Behind them bulked the monstrous animals they had ridden, which none in the garth had ever seen before. Were they tall deformed sheep? Khursp was the first to step forward. 'Let us in – in the name of God.'

At the gate of the garth below there had been a similar procedure. The watchman had known them, despite their mounts. A gathering of urgent weather brought lancing snow on pelting wind. Let in, up through the garth the men had travelled, and from the dwellings people came out to see though by now the daylight was blotted up. Malted lights behind membrane-shuttered windows patterned the path, at once familiar and alien.

Khursp entered the hall of the Holas House, under the horizontal sword of peacetime.

In fireglint, faces lifted.

Khursp thought, *Where's the wise-women and the werloka? Hiding probably.* He scanned the faces. *How few of us anywhere. We are done*, he thought. And cast the thought from him like a broken blade.

'Where is Arok's queen?' said Khursp.

Behind him the others who had outraced the ice-devil from the north stayed in abject and desperate union. On the yard outside the dromazi lurched, pulling their pads from the fresh snow, snuffling, too big and too unknown to be approached. Men and women and children gathered.

'*Where is Nirri?*'

'Here I am.'

There she was. A plain woman, not young, lovely in her courage. But Khursp had only once looked at her before and seen such agony in her eyes. That had been after Dayadin was taken. Incongruous, the glory of her hair gushing about her; only its sleek vitality gave him the answering courage to announce what he knew.

'He—' Khursp began, wanting poetry, dry of it.

She said, coolly, considerately, smiling slightly to help him, 'The Chaiord is dead?'

Khursp sank on his knees before her.

Nirri recalled how Arok had done this when she had persuaded him to come to this land of his death.

Elbar thrust nearer, intruding.

'A Hell thing is after us. It's some Winter demon of the corrupt people here. Summon the werloka, lady – maybe he—'

The others pressed in.

'No werloka can help. This is some crappish ungod – rubbish from a midden but dangerous—'

'We must close up the garth.'

The last man murmured in metaphysical sorrow, 'The sky is full of murder.'

Despite everything the day before, the excessive snow-gale they had tried to outrun had caged them. The six men and the demigod, and the total god Curjai, had taken refuge in a sort of tunnel through a cliff. Curjai had melted the way in with a bolt of heat. Inside he lit a fire on the floor of the ice-cave. He did not even call the fire; he never did. Curjai entered and the fire was there waving its flames. He had aged: all of them saw this in the firelight. About eighteen he seemed to be now. Although they had become used to his maturing, never had it come on quite this fast. They considered why – if so powerful and a god of fire – Curjai could not combat a bit of severe weather. Surely he had often done so at Padgish. Curjai glanced at them. He said, as if he had heard the doubt in their heads as maybe he had, 'We must wait. Something very strong is out there running amok.' He did not sound afraid, only practical, like a father who said, 'Don't play with that snake, lads. It will bite.'

Beyond the mile-long cave the tempest belled. Slabs of snow the size of villages that had clasped the heights for decades chipped off and detonated on the valley floors. Booming ice-spouts spat back into the whirlwind.

The cave thrummed. Slender cryotites flew from the rock-roof and squalled in the fire.

Men swore and dusted ice off themselves. The animals had been picketed further in. They could, between the gusts, be heard stamping sluggishly.

'I never knew a storm this savage,' someone remarked.

'It isn't just a storm,' said Curjai. He was lightly offhand. From somewhere, nowhere, he had produced red wine rich with spices that glimmered in a pot on the fire.

The assembly waited for the next comment.

Curjai said, 'It's only Tirthen rampaging about. He's got a flea in his ear.'

Some of the Simese made gestures against uncanny malice.

Curjai looked at Fenzi.

Fenzi said, 'That's your Winter god.'

Curjai said quietly, for Fenzi alone, 'He isn't like Attajos. He was never active before. Things are waking up.' He seemed not to mind this, yet had dropped his tone not to upset the others.

Beyond the cave a grisly bang betokened what might be the top of an entire mountain plunging down. The tunnel quaked.

'We're safe here,' said Curjai generally. 'It isn't us he wants.'

'Who then?' said Fenzi.

Curjai did not reply directly. Another man said, 'Pity the poor creatures whoever they are.'

And Curjai amended, 'Truly. But if Winter's in a mood it – he – senses his time is coming to an end.'

None of them understood this. Even Fenzi did not. This world *was* Winter, the earth a globe of ice. Curjai himself looked slightly puzzled the moment he had said it. One did not often see him discomposed.

That would change. A figure with a dog entered through the mouth of the cave.

All of them gaped at it – and at the dog. Curjai too gaped.

'Oh,' *she* said.

That was all.

She was clad in radiance and luminously pale, stately though so young. The dog was *blue*. But she, and the dog, stood there. And all she said was *Oh*.

But it was worse than that.

Curjai stared at her and then – he *blushed*.

In the name of Attajos his sire, he, this god Curjai, for one monumental heartbeat was an adolescent.

He had got up.

The blue dog wagged its blue tail but was demonstrably too well trained to leave the girl and pounce at him.

'Ruxendra?' asked Curjai.

In this alone they all heard the vocal crack of breaking boy-hood.

The woman said, 'Something went by overhead. It was a deity, or so I believe. A nasty *little* deity, yet grown colossal.' She had matured also, Ruxendra. She was now about sixteen or seventeen. Her stint in Hell had apparently enabled her to become more adult.

Her eyes were large, stretched to take in the image of Curjai.

And he had conquered his confusion.

'Tirthen,' he told her.

Ruxendra looked down. Rather prissily she walked on into the cave. 'There is a man with a riding-animal some miles up the slope. He's frosted over. I think this god Tirthen froze him as he passed. But he should not have died.'

'How do you know?'

'How can one *not* know such things,' snapped Ruxendra.

A wealth of honest post-human anger lay behind the remark. But also a new-found non-human knowledge. Neither he nor she now, luckily, used any language either Simese or Jafn could understand.

Curjai glanced at the others.

In Simese he said, 'Wait here.'

The blue dog led the way back out of the tunnel.

The tempest had shifted. Even the snow-cladding left on the heights only trembled. The sky was washed. The stars peered.

When he got near Curjai could see the dromaz was dead. It had been turned to ice as well. He felt pity for it and an instant's mortal ire at the waste.

The man lay beside the beast. He was white-haired so Curjai knew him for a Jafn. And then for Arok.

How was he here? He must have evaded the court of the king.

'He has died before his hour,' pronounced the girl.

Curjai had abandoned his gaucheness. He could recall holding her in his arms in the blue Hell. For a year they had moved by each other, always on the brink of alchemical sex and emotional love. Then he had left her and so forgotten.

'Why do you say that?'

'I was Magikoy. Such displacing events are readable by various signs. They dislodge other things.'

'Really.'

'A man's fate is decided. But that fate is sometimes improved, or pre-empted. I, for example, died too young myself. As you may dimly remember.'

Miles over to the south a white thunder-sheet of lightning fleered in the sky. That was where Tirthen had taken himself. That way too Arok's garth must lie.

Everything was out of kilter.

Curjai knelt, set his face against the dead man's and called softly in through his mouth: *'Arok. Arok.'*

The body had been dead less than a day. The spirit essence might be reclaimable if it had not journeyed too far off. Any shaman of Simisey could tell you this.

Warmth lit the dead eyes and frost crisped off from Arok's face. Yet nothing replied from the depths within, nor from anywhere around.

'He's gone, Ruxendra.'

'You give up too quickly.' Frowning she also knelt on the snow and began some sort of – perhaps improvised – ritual.

Curjai watched, pleased with the way her arms lifted and her hands gestured, and the flow of her dark hair. The blue dog scratched itself. Curjai thought it was one of the jatchas from Lionwolf's Hell, in fact Lionwolf's own hound. Curjai was

189

returning into his more ordinary state, that of self-knowledge and godness. Inevitably he moved apart, enjoying, compassionate, but no longer fully committed.

She though, Ruxendra, laboured away at the corpse, moaning Rukarian in her appealing voice, conjuring abilities from her previous if unfinished training as a mage.

The dead man jerked his head away without warning. It seemed he did not want to hear.

Then Ruxendra was inexorable. She went mad, dancing about, singing and clapping her hands, garlanding the cadaver with energies.

Finally Arok sat up. He put his hands to his head as if he had drunk too much or slept too long, and was unsure what he must do, let alone if he could do it.

'Rise!' cried imperious Ruxendra. 'You are safely back in the world. I have brought you intact to your interrupted life. Fear nothing.' She squinted at Curjai. He was fascinated. Did she become cross-eyed always at such moments? 'What did you say his name was?'

'Arok.' Curjai shrugged.

'Who calls me?' said Arok. 'Who are you? Where have I been?' He stood, not entirely steady but at once reaching for his knife. 'Where are . . . men?'

Across the night sky another purge of thunder and flap of light raised the horizon's roof.

'I must – go *there*,' said Arok. 'My – a woman's there. A son.' He too did not sound committed, only alarmingly duty bound.

'You see,' said Ruxendra, 'he had things to do.'

That elemental force which had been channelled into Tirthen had gained the Holasan-garth. The zones of time were out. Chronology had been dismissed. This would not save anyone.

Up on its platform the garth had walls and gates but was ringed too by a hedge of something else. This was a combination defence, including human self-belief, but having too some of the same unusual matter as Tirthen himself.

Yet it was far more flimsy. He flicked it and the protective aura split.

Along the winding lanes of the garth the thing Tirthen roared. For those who heard he was like more of the freak storm wind that already beat the vicinity, and streaming white. As he went by huge caps of snow formed on the houses. The shuttered window-places were shuttered again by ice. Anything stranded in the path of his advance turned instantly to solid crystal death.

But most of the people here were either clamped to their hearths or had gone up to the House.

Just before he got to the House Tirthen altered. He became again what could be taken for a man. He was vain, too. His male beauty was awesome and his garments kingly. Despite only recently becoming self-aware some piece of him, or it, must have been studying the human microbes that were his victims. He – it – had made them die under Winter's lash, the Ice Age that was its personality, realm and *soul*. But it had also seen how they adapted and so survived, and their world of flora and fauna with them. Their success in that balanced maybe their eternal transience, and kept his or its rancour at bay. But not now. This being, now male and passing itself off as a god, foresaw the future and took affront.

For amusement or contrariety too, Tirthen toned down his attributes, the bludgeons of freezing. What fun was there in knocking on a door or heart that immediately broke or ceased to beat? He was learning the dreadful sport of gods.

In the yard outside the House, the Jafn gawked at him far more avidly than at the Padgish dromazi. Children with round eyes stared; maidens caught their breath, not completely from fright.

Every dromaz however, arbiter of taste, shat and averted its head.

Tirthen blew gently on the House door.

Above, the peace sword of the Jafn gave a tinny whine. A mark ran up the blade, but that was all. Not everyone saw. The door undid.

In real time what was this moment? It was precisely two

191

seconds after the last of Arok's warriors, returning, had exclaimed, *The sky is full of murder.*

Tirthen knew what had been said. He knew much of what he
did not witness, all languages. Presumably he was now a true
god. How else did they form save from the demanding worship,
terror and pleading of mortals, sacrifice, circumstance, and their
own sheer egomaniacal bloody-mindedness?

'The sky is full of murder.'

'No,' said Tirthen, 'murder is here.'

Godly eyes absorbed the Jafn hall. Hunting birds on rafters,
a dog or two, a quartet of old lions, both genders ruffed, lying
growling under a bench. Human components consisted of such
ordinary models as already met with. A woman with some
little authority or other, men of the expected castes, fighters or
decrepit or too young. But then—

Winter Tirthen picked up the glow of something that came
down a ladder-stair and entered the room at its other end.

Did he recall? He had not been then as now he was, yet in an
obscure if definite way this and he had met, face to face, hand to
hand, fury to fury, once or twice before.

On those occasions he had had no face or hand, *only* the fury.
She had changed a little, but nothing to his changes. Would *she*
recollect *him*?

Across a crowded room two strangers who have met and
hated and striven but incredibly mislaid both the name and the
appearance of the other stand briefly at a loss: Tirthen and
Saphay.

Whatever else the disguise she had till now mostly worn here
fell off her like a carelessly pinned cloak. The looks of an elderly
hag-witch curled round her feet and faded.

Tensed like near-snapping bowstrings, the Holas in and out
of the hall took in this pale girl adorned with saffron tresses and
a royal gown.

Tirthen spoke.

Such a beautiful voice. Among so many gods his was among
the best, or *the* best. He must have been training it away from its
original coarse accent of screaming winds and grating glaciers.

'I see you have arrived ahead of me.'

Yyrot? she asked herself. Was this Yyrot, Winter's Lover, in his most gorgeous guise, with some fresh charisma never before put on? *Yyrot* . . .

Saphay glared. Flame moved in her yellow hair. She raised one hand and it was the paw of a golden lioness.

'*Ah.*' Tirthen had identified her. He inclined his head.

And she in turn knew him, even to his adopted name, and put out her fire. For she had fought with this one previously and bested him – or at least beaten him off. She thought of ice pyramids, and the icy waste she had struggled through lashed by winds. She thought of the fleet of icebergs sent against her people of the Vormland, and how she had smashed them – but through that the Vormland fleet too was wrecked, and her people lamented and abhorred her and cast her out, and now as she vaguely guessed her name among them was a dirty word; several dirty words.

Tirthen was the cold heart of this continent and, she perceived, of the whole earth. Tirthen *was* Winter.

The joyhall and garth were full of vulnerable humans. And above, Athluan her husband, whom she had searched for so long, lay sleeping in her flame, not yet ready to be woken.

'Greetings, sir,' said Saphay to Tirthen. 'Will you not sit down . . .' and with the court irony of Ru Karismi she added, 'by the fire?'

Winter of the World sat by the fire. And the fire now and then cowered. Saphay sat across from Tirthen, and when she glanced into the fire it bloomed up in showers of sparks and heat. Sitting there and seeing that she had come also to an unheralded knowledge of herself and her present vocation. She became – *happy*. But this distracted and she put it aside like a small appealing animal she loved. In a while, my darling, soon. When I have dealt with *him*.

'What is it you desire?' she asked him.

'I have no desires. I need none.'

'Then you're content.'

'That concept can mean nothing to me.'

'Your visit to us therefore is because . . . ?'

He met her dark eyes with his dark eyes. In this one aspect they did share something. Each seemed to notice it. They were both astonishingly callow as yet at their own business; he, such a terrible entity as he was, more than she.

'Patently I am here for a purpose,' said Tirthen.

'Which is – if I may again inquire?' She thought how she had spoken like this to kings in her city, even her own father. Especially him. One learned to be wary.

'Do forgive me,' said he, robotically perhaps mimicking her courtier-speak, 'but I must put you away in a cupboard.'

Aghast, Saphay lost her sense of self and her knack of fawning.

'*Cupboard?*'

'A figure of speech.'

Insane. They did not really *speak* anyway, they uttered some language of gods.

In the shadows at the hall's perimeter, outside in the snow, confronted by what they assumed to be this super-gler, the Holas waited.

Tirthen stood up again. The hearth fire went ashen. The fire *froze*.

Saphay did not attempt to rescue it. She rose too. A glimmer of her power went visibly fluttering through her, like birds that flew inside her bones.

'Saphay,' said Tirthen. 'Such a pretty name.'

That was all he said.

Even all those who could not talk the tongue of gods picked this up. Yet none of them fathomed it and nor did she, the goddess by the iced fire.

She did feel something like a delicate frost on every inch of her body. She felt that, and then it melted from her. And Winter stepped aside out of some non-existent door which shut after him. He left only everything else behind him.

None of them moved. None spoke. No dog barked or whim-

pered, not a hawk stirred a feather. Long ago the lions had
ceased to growl.

Conversely there came a deep soft sound. It reminded a few
of the noise of heavy fur or velvet drawn over a smooth surface.
That was all.

Every person and creature in the garth heard it, and at the
same level, and the tiniest child or infant, the littlest rodent for-
aging in the stores, the hard-of-hearing, *did* hear. Outside, they
stared upward. Inside the hall they stared inward at a mental
picture telepathically conveyed.

Next day they left the cave-tunnel. No trace of the uncanny
snowstorm lingered. The Simese went about looking for it,
checking each height and inch of sky in case a bit of it still
lurked there. Even Fenzi did this. Ruxendra sat in the cave,
playing with the blue dog's ears. Curjai had been rather keenly
aware of this. The night before he had introduced her to the
party as Ruxen-Ushayis. This was a Simese adaptation but
emphasized that he thought she must still stay incognito. Fenzi
had bowed low to her. Ruxen-Ushayis accepted that as her due.
Obviously she was neither impressed nor startled by Fenzi's
appearance. In Hell there had been all types of man. Curjai she
glanced at only rarely.

That Curjai had aged another year or two rather suddenly
was not lost on him either.

He rehearsed their time in the Otherland. Had she come after
him here because she loved him? Or, more disturbing thought,
had his attraction to her, forgotten by him though it might have
been, summoned her?

Now anyhow there were other matters to concern him.

Arok had lain all night on his back in the tunnel. He spoke to
no one and never moved. But he was not asleep. Curjai, who no
longer needed sleep unless he wanted it as a luxury, sat by and
often looked across at Arok. They – Curjai would not blame the
girl for all of it – had returned Arok into his body. Whether he
had been slain before some Fatefully ordained hour Curjai was

uncertain. Nor was he certain either that was really a good enough reason for dragging the life-essence back over the threshold. Untimely death must often happen. Hell had been full of plenty who seemed bewildered and regretful out of all proportion to their method of dying or loss of earthly friends and possessions. Probably you got over it, adjusted and if necessary rejoined the world hurriedly to tidy up anything left undone. Arok for sure did not seem relieved let alone glad to be here again, while his initial muffled urgency over home and family seemed done.

Near sunrise the distant lightnings also disappeared. Only the ripple of the low fire lit the cave. The remainder of the people, even the goddess Ruxen and the dog, were slumbering. Curjai had approached and crouched down near to Arok.

'You can't sleep, Chaiord.'

'All Jafn spurn sleep.'

Curjai took in Jafn Fenzi, who did seem to be asleep.

'Yes, Chaiord, forgive me, I remember now. You equate sleep with death, don't you?' That was blunt enough. Any response? None Curjai could either see or detect. He murmured quietly, 'I apologize that we woke you, sir.'

Arok failed to say, But I told you I was not asleep. He grasped the point and answered dully, 'Yes, you woke me. She did.'

'What—' How absurd. Curjai, who recollected all and everything of the outer life, was attempting to question this survivor. Refusing to hold off he continued, 'Do you have a memory of where you went, where you came back from?'

'None.' Arok's eyes gazed only up into the roof of the cave. The firelight ran over them in wavelets. He had not blinked, Curjai noted, not once in many minutes. Perhaps not since he had come to out there in the snow.

'When you – recovered, what did you think had happened to you?'

'I know what happened. One of your local gler ungods struck me, turned me to ice. Death. I didn't want to go. It was wrong.'

'And so, you're not displeased to have woken up?'

'What's pleased?' said the dead-live man. 'What's not pleased?'

'Dawn's coming. Then we'll move. Get to the garth, and you'll see your wife and son. Do you remember you said that? That you must do that?'

'Then I'll do that, I'll see them.'

Curjai leaned near to Arok's face and blew very lightly on him, a sparkling, clean and warming breath of healing, the sort only gods might give. Arok did not bat an eyelid or lash. He lay there.

'Pardon us, if we did you a disservice.'

'What is a disservice?' asked Arok. 'What is a service?'

In the name of Attajos, Curjai thought with crucial dismay, *he's left most of himself behind.*

Curjai had never reckoned gods might be embarrassed or depressed. He was both. He recaptured uncomfortably his own distress at his own childhood death. But that end had led to all beginnings. Maybe gods actively disliked rubbing their own noses in human horrors. That could explain a lot.

'Would you prefer . . .' Curjai hesitated. The sentiment felt blasphemous, but blasphemy against humanity not deity. 'Would you prefer to be dead?'

Idly said Arok, 'What's dead? What's not dead? Prefer . . . What's prefer?'

Once the day fully started, and since the weather was average enough to travel, Fenzi took the Chaiord up on his dromaz. Arok moved stiffly yet not ungainly. He made no protest, no comment, offered neither thanks nor any token of authority. Fenzi's face was unreadable. Sombrec, Fenzi's lover, was giving the pair a wide berth.

Then Ruxen refused to mount Curjai's dromaz. She poised on the snow combing her silky locks with a scented comb evolved from thin air, while the Hell-dog galumphed about after non-existent snow hares. 'I shall journey in my own way.'

Curjai could have done the same, but seldom did when in the company of ordinary men. An oblique modesty. Only his mother Riadis, or the shamans, had seen him regularly de- or re-materialize. He knew in himself his time with Lionwolf had made him less Simese. He found a Rukarian mode in speech, in manner, perhaps even Jafn. It seemed to Curjai he was quite unlike himself by now, even as he had been in Hell. The least he could do therefore was ally himself to humans when with them.

The group rode off, the dromazi loping in their ground-devouring strides, while the confounded girl and the hound popped out like dawn stars.

They reached the Holasan-garth inside the day, about an hour before sunfall. The weather had been elaborately helpful, not a wisp of wind or flake of snow, sky like a well-scrubbed plate.

Presently there was a height and the line of riders drew up there, looking over to the south-east.

'Well,' said one of the men, 'why are we waiting?'

Curjai, alerted, saw Fenzi's mask of face had reformed to blank astonishment.

'What is it, Fenzi?'

'God knows, I do not.'

'A Jafn riddle?' Sombrec joked with unwise sarcasm.

'*No riddle.*' Fenzi swung from the saddle leaving the resouled and soulless Arok sitting, *his* eyes unblinking, face unchanging. 'It was there,' said Fenzi. '*There.*'

They stared where he pointed.

Snow-plain soared and sank. Far away uplands hung ghostly in the last milky sunlight. Closer to hand were hills large and small, some very round, like upturned bowls made of chalk.

Nowhere was there any signature of mankind.

'It's gone,' said Fenzi.

'Storms can confuse a landscape. Could you have mistaken the—'

'No,' said Fenzi. 'Chaiord,' he said, not looking round, 'you know I speak a fact. The Holasan-garth was over there.'

Arok remarked, 'Yes. Just there. Where there is.'

Curjai stared with the rest. It seemed to him irregular fur-rows and runnels showed in the plain that might be the leftovers of short fields of dormant crops, and across from them a low mound that might have been an orchard of some sort. But mostly Jafn kept their agriculture within the garth walls. It was not much of a clue. One of the smaller of the bowl hills did rise just beyond. It shone with the colourless sinking sun. But also . . . how curious . . . from some kind of light trapped deep inside.

FOUR

Guri grew up two years in every one. This was just like his adopted nephew Lionwolf, on the first excursion to earth.

At ten Guri was a man of about twenty. Leopard-skin yellow of complexion, blue-black of hair, tall and mathematically flawless in build, he was a peerless exemplar of his race. Needless to say his strength and stamina too were matchless. He could run in enormous leaps mile on mile – rather as he had when in his previous earthly 'spirit' form. He could also inevitably fly. He could raise colossal weights, accurately fire ten or more arrows from a specially made male bow, to bring down ten deer together, and stroll up the sides of rocks, trees, and buildings.

He had been Lionwolf's inadvertent apprentice. Watching the fabulous brat had taught Guri his trade of deitility and now he did not miss a trick.

Despite that, this second beginning had not been very auspicious.

His mother, Yedki, had abandoned him as soon after labour as she could walk.

They had all reasoned with her, most significantly her Crax. Yedki would not listen. 'I was deceived,' she said. 'I never asked for *this*.'

'Yet you have it. See, you've borne a hero—'

'Befuck it,' said Yedki, packed a cloth with her effects and went away on a young female mammoth. Either she perished in the wastes or found another sluhtin. The Crax, who thereafter could not find her in any occult fashion, possibly did not try very hard.

Ennuat was the one who reared the child, feeding him the mixed milk of two mammoth cows and also of her elder sister, who had herself just given birth to a normal kiddling. Guri thrived. Not that any named him Guri. He was known as Gthesput. At the start the name muddled then amused him. Then he grew used to it. When he was about twelve – or six – he incorporated Guri into the name. *Guri*thesput.

By then his fame was automatically waxing, and with it an additionally bizarre story. Ennuat was the virgin coven member. The tale went Guri was therefore the result of a virgin birth. This seemed less disgraceful than what Guri knew as the reality: that he had fathered himself. Therefore he did not deny the tale. As for Ennuat, she would look so forbidding when anyone mentioned it, soon no one did.

When he was sixteen, that was eight, Guri left the sluhtin and went to visit the sluht-city of Sham. A crowd of adoring young warriors rode with him, all of them on fine mammoths.

Approaching the city they were met on the road by a caravan of y'Gech.

Though racial 'cousins' some rivalry and caution did exist between y'Gech and y'Chibe. Seeing twenty mounted Chibe warriors advancing along the road, which was Shamish-built and a paved one, the caravan ushered its own fighting men to the front and right across the way.

As Guri and his company drew level the caravan's Gech witch ran out too. She had green and black hair and shook a rattle made of crocodile bones and small brass bells. Imperiously she pointed with one long finger at the ground. The Chibe warriors must dismount.

Only Gurithesput did so, amicably enough.

'Hail, magical woman. What's up?'

She was young, but with old, flat, venomous eyes. Perhaps she had lived among crocodiles and other swamp oddities too great a while.

'You shall not go by. You mean ill to Sham. I can *smell* it on you.'

The Chibe men snarled and the mammoths snorted. No one liked to be insulted over his smell. They had got themselves up in their best, too, for the visit.

But Guri only grinned. He was a god, acknowledged it, felt still renewed and young enough, not to mention wild enough, to *revel* in it. Along with the other perks of godism he smelled excessively good, he knew, at all times.

'Are you sure, Magica? Why don't you come and sniff me? Then you might change your mind.'

The Chibe chuckled. One of the mammoths put up its trunk and bellowed in a bold paraphrase of the male erection.

Magica stamped her boot. Stalks of greenish fire burst from the paving and made a low crinkling barrier between the warrior Chibe and the Gech caravan.

Guri looked at it. 'When a man likes a girl,' he said, 'it takes more than a fence to keep him away.' And with that he walked right through the fire, which at his touch went out.

He towered over the witch and now, if she had doubted, very likely she sussed a hint of his enticing personal aroma. Then he kneeled on the road before her and kissed the boot which had stamped. Instantly the kiss-shape appeared on it, made of white silver.

Guri got up again.

The witch's eyes were no longer flat or venomous. They were full of tears. For a moment Guri triumphed, and then he felt sorry. He had not meant to humiliate her. He had always had, and had now, vast honour for sterling mageias of most sorts, and always for the Crarrowin and Cruin.

'I'm sorry,' said Gurithesput. 'I went too far.'

'No,' whispered the witch, 'I see what you must be.'

'A god,' Guri risked admitting.

'There are no such. But yes. A g— a g—' A proper sound atheist, she could not even get it out.

'I am Guri,' said Guri, to help.

'Whatever your name or nature,' she said, throwing back her

head to meet his eyes full on with her weeping ones, 'you will bring shame and death among us, and on mighty and glorious Sham you will bring down ruin. This prime city will be trampled to a cake of mud, because of you and your – *godishness*.'

Guri went sallow. His eyes flickered as if he might faint. He was convinced she was not cursing him. She had sensed – *smelled* – on him some awful flavour of forecast events. Dumbly he thought back over his past, so far in these people's future. Yes, by the time of his first life, Sham had been nothing, a heap of dirt with one lone wreck of a gate. And the glory of Chibe was reduced to scattered war packs whose sluhtins crouched always under a weight of unvoiced nonentity. As for the country of Gech it had been a borderless ramble – tiny villages amid the ice swamps, wanderers and wise-women who served others, such as Jafn barbarians. The coven-name *Cruin* had been forgotten.

He steadied himself and said to the witch, 'Can't it be averted? You tell me. I will be guided by you.'

'Perhaps,' she said, averting instead her gaze. She put her hand on his and a shiver went through her. 'I can counsel you.'

At which Guri gave up, for he saw she fancied him as most women did, and wanted him for that, the more important axis of people and land forgone or lessened by desire. Women. But that was unfair, his sixteen-year-old acuity told him: men were just as bad in such matters.

Exactly as the elderly might feel young inside their bodies, the young might sometimes feel, inside their own youthful hides, ancient, tired and nearly historical. The Chibe detailed in their woven songs, and in some of the carved or written graffiti found on stones or walls, that the recurring birth–death–birth cycle of reincarnation was the reason. Not everyone every time lived to a ripe old age. Thus old age, when experienced, was the *less* familiar state. But the first stages of life, childhood and youth, might be repeated thousands of times. The young, even children, could well feel old and worn therefore.

Now Guri, young externally, fully felt his entirely remembered earlier life. Plus his timeless yet eternal-seeming sojourn in Hell. Regret and anxiety battled inside him with a dire scepticism. His fate was cast. He was to be a god, and to bring misery and down-fall. That was often the way of the gods. Why should he be the one charming exception?

The witch let the caravan go on along the road. They had another witch in tow. Guri's witch – she never gave him her name; he only ever called her by the nickname of Magica – stayed with Guri.

The nineteen other Chibe warriors looked at her, unsure. They were gratified Guri had picked up such a girl, but nervous, and so acted up like pillocks all the rest of the way to Sham.

Once in the city, however, the sights saw to it they pulled themselves together. Sham impressed. Though sometimes called the 'sluht-city' it did not resemble any sort of sluhtin. They craned to see towering metallic gates, the towering towers, the arenas and long winding markets, full also of darkish basement areas where myriad displays of goods glittered like stars. Saurians waddled by in harness, their claws gilded; tree-wolves with dyed pelts fought in yards packed by spectators. Exquisite whores posed on terraces, baring one perfect breast or depilated leg, their furs otherwise so thick the cold caused them no trouble. There were high metal-sheathed doors in Sham in those days, bronze inlaid with silver, iron with copper, tin with pyrite, all in complex patterns. But behind a door that was of fossil-wood the witch led Guri to her chamber. She lived normally outside the city. When she was there this room was always hers, kept for her empty and clean.

Gurithesput had already had plenty of women in the sluhtin, aside from Yedki, his own mother before she was. The leader of the community had encouraged this. He and many more believed Guri would gift them a pack of healthy half-hero sons; the fiction that Guri was a hero not a non-existent god still held there. But from the numerous couchings no baby was conceived. The leader, a terse man named Har Jup, then instructed women who had already borne children to lie with Guri. Guri would accept only those who were widowed, or free Crarrow, and will-ing. He did not mean to offend husbands or insult wives.

Nevertheless plenty of candidates arrived and he lay with them. Again, not one took.

Gurithesput had realized swiftly. He was to be like Lionwolf in this too. His body was able and potent. His seed was not.

Magica screamed four or five times in ecstasy at the climax of their unions. The psychic force of her orgasms blazed in the room for hours after, so they rarely needed lamps or brazier.

Guri himself predicted he might fall in love with her and grew terrified. Witch though she was, she was mortal and already some years his senior. Physically at least.

Unsensibly a night came when he told her where he had come from, that was his other life up to twenty-eight, then the ghost-life, association with Lionwolf, the wars and horrors, and the punishment in Hell – all, all of it. She listened as if in a trance. He hoped in the morning, after he had indulged in unneeded sleep, she might have thought he lied. But her eyes, once so flat and eldritch, had become while she heard him out young and absorbent as a kiddle's. When he turned over on the morning pallet she was long gone.

Now and then she had gone off before on her own errands. This time she did not come back.

Later he went to search for her through the city. She was nowhere to be found.

The Chibe men, who always tried to rally round Guri given a chance, kept attaching themselves to him. Finally they carried him off to drink in a beer-basement. He was a hero, that was all; there were no gods. Drink up, Gurithesput! they cried. Heroes were allowed to go soppy on a woman. Even to be abandoned by said woman, although obviously any woman who did that was mentally deficient. Heroes could get drunk as well. Only gods found anything like that very difficult.

Guri could not rid himself of the correct idea that Magica had buckled under the burden of his autobiography. He visualized her hanged in her own hair. Or walking willingly into a croco-dile pit.

The clash had begun inside him between godhead and an

inherent learned mortalness. And too between inner agedness and inner adolescence.

He recalled how Lionwolf had struggled with all this hopelessly. You could not live this double – triple – *multiple* life. Nor, being now immortal, could you avoid it.

He never saw her again, Magica. Probably he could have scried her, located her. Like the Crax of Yedki's coven maybe he did not try very hard.

Two more years went by. During these Har Jup died. The election of a new sluhtin leader selected Gurithesput inevitably. Equally inevitable was Guri's refusal.

Until then he had remained mostly in the sluhtin. He was invaluable to them in everything save the business of siring babies. They forgave that, indeed stayed optimistic things would change. They must recall, in actual years he was only ten.

For himself, Guri knew, he had been in hiding. He had not even revisited Sham. He could not bear to, loaded as it had become, in hindsight worse than at the time, with her prophecy.

At home he hunted and performed the other masculine chores, along with the men and his own inadvertent gang of admirers. He oversaw their weddings, and the fast acquisition of their children.

He spent many days and nights, sometimes months of them, alone out on the snow wastes, in the forests of ice. He even trekked to the sea shore and beheld the extended vista of ice-beach, and the thread of black liquid water miles beyond.

Gurithesput was alone anyway.

Guri preferred aloneness.

The former ghost-life had prepared him.

But after the election when he put aside the leadership, and heard his gang ranting, and women wailing as if at a death, Guri determined to go away for good.

He was bound to Ol y'Chibe – to *Olchibe*. He would serve them as best he could, but the terms of his employment must become more broad.

Partly he had resisted branching out in the world, recapturing the image of Lionwolf bounding to begin the Jafn drama of vengeance and kingship which had culminated in Ru Karismi and the White Death. Only intermittently did Guri think of the *other* Lionwolf, the god who had subdued death, and transformed Hell to a heaven. Guri did not trust this memoir. He himself had not yet reached any equilibrium between gods and humanity. He shied off from putting such success on any other.

But Guri branched out nevertheless at last.

He left the sluhtin, riding one of the male mammoths. The females were the law among the herds and he did not want to worry the animals as he had had to the men and women.

They rode down into what would be, hundreds of years on, the southernmost Marginal Land.

Sluhtins and individual sluhts received him. Ranging bands, not yet much committed to war with anyone else, welcomed him into their camps.

He tried to learn their intrinsic ways, which were not like the ways of his people in the future, aside from everyday basics. The whole paradigm was different. It was not only their theology but their worldly aims. They moved inside a measured and established ethos, their goals straightforward. They wanted survival and security, status to the limited high points of their own clan-group, pleasure and happiness where able, re-creation of what was known and enjoyed, where able. They moved like breathing through life and into death and out again to life. He had seen that even a hero among them was useful only inside such spheres.

Guri assumed that what had altered them centuries on was their fall. When, prior to his first life, the Rukar invaded Olchibe and Gech and smashed their universe on earth – and therefore, worse, also in their Elsewhere. Crawling up from the cold mud they had substituted, for the theft of faith in self, a faith in the Great Gods who would assist them to their aim of revenge.

And she, his witch, had smelled on Guri that he was responsible.

'The future is in my past.'

And was the fate of his nation, which had made him Guri in that future-past of his, now in *his* hand?

Guri overlooked one salient fact.

In his mortal past he had never wondered what the Great Gods were. They were, that was it. In his day, rather like the God of the barbaric Jafn, they were formless yet omnipresent. One did not portray them even mentally as they were undelineable, and anyway visible in all other things.

Roaming about hero Guri came to be revered. It was unavoidable. All he was and the abilities he demonstrated, often without thinking, showed him off.

Then other adventures happened.

A cluster of huts among pillars of frozen trees and a child throwing a fit. Guri steps forward, what else, and touches the child, which relaxes, revives and is never sick again. A shore village, and a man gored by a horned shark. Guri steps forward . . . A mammoth dying with her calf trapped inside her. Guri steps . . . An illness from bad meat. Guri . . .

There had been more minor events like this in his own sluhtin. But there they had just accepted it. A Crarrow, a *coven*, had reared him. He had picked up some skill.

But now, oh, now. Guri, Guri, Guri. Gurithesput. Star Dog Lit Among the Nights. That was what the composite name meant, if woven in cloth or scratched on a wall.

She had been able to stammer it out, or nearly, his witch on the road. G-g-god. God. Guri the god.

Like the subtlest whiff of incense-smoke or burning honey from a Crarrow spell-fire, the odour of sanctity floats around the confined world of y'Chibe and y'Gech, under that low horizon.

A day comes, the region not so far from glorious Sham. Two war bands of the Chibe are about to be engaged in battle. But Guri, who had loved battle with the best of them, has learned in his Hell that what is done is always paid for. He wants to forestall the killing.

Guri . . . steps forward.

Between the two onracing packs of mammoths and men he stands on the snow and only breathes out once.

Not fifteen feet apart both battalions lose their speed. Without being harmed, not skidding or toppling, without even a hint of being jerked back or muscular whiplash, all ceases. They are slowed inside some other space, and come to rest on their own gentle as feathers.

Amazed, the men sit their beasts among the skull banners. But the beasts are much ahead of their riders. One by one, and several together, the white mammoths kneel to Guri, and on their backs the warriors goggle, so shaken by surprise and so *un*shaken physically that they are silent in life as death would have made them.

Guri smiles. He has about him that irresistible sweetness Lionwolf had eventually reached in Hell. Sweetness and calm sadness and antique wisdom in a young face of countless years. He has made peace.

g-g-god . . .

g-g-God . . .

Great Gods, what has Guri done?

FIVE

The pair of sentries pacing round outside the palace had met on their nocturnal hourly circuit for a mutual swig of wine. Something had been going on in Kol Cataar for several months. No one was completely ignorant of it. You felt it in the air. After the sky fell, or rather the meteorological ice-lid on the city gave way, any doubt was banished. Despite that few grasped, let alone guessed, the real substance of events. And the sentries had only been doubled after all.

'I heard he was gone,' said one of the sentries.

'So did I. None saw him leave. Do you reckon it can be true?'

'It's unthinkable. The king's son. Unless it's some secretive mission entrustable only to Prince Sallusdon.'

'But where would he go? There's none of us left. The population of the Ruk was creamed off by the Death. Just the whey left now, steads and little towns like Kandexa – and most of *them* have come *here*.'

'It can't be true then. Sallus must still be in the palace. Did you hear about the whore?'

'Which one?'

'Some woman. They say she carried a big bellyful for thirteen months and then gave birth to a pig.'

'Some wondrous father then.'

'Some mother.'

They laughed very low. They were under the windows to the back of the regal house. Below lay a courtyard, frankly a parody of the courts at Ru Karismi. Two trees made of silver-wire had been roughly fashioned. Queen Tireh would walk here and the

210

two infant princesses played ball. Above in the King Paramount's apartments the first family would currently be sleeping.

'Somebody said a Magikoy had come to the city,' the second sentry muttered. 'That is, apart from the two ladies we already have.'

'I heard that rumour too. But he was old, they said. He must have died like our other mage gentleman.'

'What's that noise?'

Gossip sloughed, each man turned towards the court a combat-machine, all senses alert.

From the unleavened night a slight filmy motion stole up to them.

Being careful to tilt a wall lamp downwards, the first sentry angled its beam on to the paving.

'It's a snake—'

'Snakes – scores of them—'

Both men snatched out their swords. This sound was masculine and positive, the sound and movement below feyly feral.

Long, slender, quivering, questing skeins wriggled and crept and slipped ever onward—

'Are they chazes?'

'Never. Too thin – and see, they have spikes – is it spikes – gods – gods – see, look, they're growing other snakes out of their own bodies all the time—'

Eyes wide with fear the men kept up their battle stance a cupful of moments more. Then the shaking light picked out the other snakes, which were now pouring in like spilled water over the nearest roof.

One sentry shouted, then the second. They must wake the house.

A rumple of other sounds now, and out of these the striking of flame and kindling of lamps indoors. Whole windows flowed up suddenly molten behind shutters of wood and glass. The hind face of the palace flung light across the courtyard, the fake trees, walls, accessory buildings which in their turn were also flaring up.

And so Bhorth's men were the first to see that it was not

snakes which had cascaded in over the house and up from the ground, but creepers, black as oil with a sheen of emeraid, and here and there a red, red bud.

Bhorth had not been sleeping, nor was he occupied with his wife. He had been padding quietly up and down like the sentries, though his route lay indoors, through his study, along a gallery with a rough library in it, along corridors, down a stair and back into the study. He had taken up this practice about a year ago on odd nights when sleep failed him. He found it courted slumber better than poring over some unwanted book. He thought too of his former Rukarian estates where he could have prowled nightlong, unchallenged by any and unsettling none. But he had never *been* insomniac then, save through choice with a woman. All this too made him feel old. Oldness had slunk in on him in these years of disappointment, compromise and platitude at Kol Cataar. Before there had been a while when he thought the black witch who left her seed in him, and so prevented his death, had made him invulnerable and splendid for ever. But of course once the seed was expelled, Sallusdon conceived and borne, the sublime insulation leaked away. Bhorth had no designated purpose after this, or only that of the average man, to strive uselessly and reassure falsely, to get fat and sour and feeble. He had tried hard not to mind it. Much as he had seen others do. It was foolish to grow bitter at the inevitable. Yet his short span of believing he could outwit the common fate gave reality an extra vicious bite.

And then Sallusdon went away. He had not explained, or his explanation had been so abnormal as to be inexplicable. My son—

My son.

Bhorth blamed the strange girl Azula. Her shaved patchwork hair and tawny skin. What was she? Did the young man desire her? Sallus had seemed sure Azula was his sibling, which made a romp unlawful. Had that been the cause?

Her fault anyway. Sullen and draggled, following Sallus about, some commoner's chick—

I am unfair. I can't know his going is due to her. And what are commoners? My subjects and people, of whom I am the guardian. Am I one more filthy Vuldir to judge them nothing, traduce and discount them? We are all men.

The other thing lay under all this like a leaden chain, slowly weighting the rest, even the sorrow of Bhorth's missing son, down into a black hole beneath the palace.

A black hole that was a walled-up storeroom.

Bhorth had reached his study for the fifth time that night. He was not yet weary enough to go to bed. By the glim of the wax-furred candle he pawed at some papers on a table. They were written accounts of various failures and mishaps in the city. The paper was knobbly and badly made and the inks either too black or too watery.

Some vellum had been brought from Ru Karismi but had been eaten by rats in the chest.

There was a slight quirky movement of one of the lamps outside. Sentries were passing—

Then came shouting, a descant for two voices. 'Help here! In the name of the kings!'

It was a ritual call, once used even in war.

Bhorth snatched up his swordbelt and buckled it on as he sprang from the room.

In an awful way he knew he was glad to be interrupted, as if boredom and depression were worse than active danger.

Not for a moment did he think this alarm anything less than significant.

Nor for a moment did he, most curiously, connect it to the underlying pull of the leaden chain.

On a terrace of the king's house most of the palace people had gathered. From windows others stretched to see.

But all over the city they crowded out. The streets were full of doors flung wide, lights lit, footsteps, cries.

By now only an hour stood between them and sunrise. The night sky was fraying. The stars ebbed, less as if dying than concealing themselves, the better to spy on everything else.

There was a change in the air. It was *warm*. Some had experienced thaws. These often portended lethal shifts in the general snow-crust, or a flood as undetected frozen waterways threw off restraint, slurrying up to make mess.

In this case the snow and ice had somehow *ebbed* away, like the stars, making themselves invisible, intangible.

Along the avenues of ice-brick, in plots among the houses *earth* had appeared.

The ground there was *black*. It was a compost of firm moist mud, usually about three yards lower than any previous surface. From it stubble seemed to have grown. Grass? Additional botanic things were rising. The formation of an ice oasis, so the Kol Cataarians labelled the change. Some hot spring, dormant for a century, must have been unlocked in the underlay of the city. Would the buildings be safe?

Perhaps they would. Nothing so far had cracked or collapsed. The packed snow around and under their bases had not given way, with the result each edifice now looked nine to eighteen feet higher than road or pavement or courtyard. In parts the surrounding areas went down even further. Porticoes, doorways and steps were stranded more than the height of a man above street level, leaving occupants marooned in or outside. Meanwhile floral sprays rose with sorcerous rapidity. It was just possible to watch the grass growing. Creepers, no longer mistaken for giant worms or hydra-bodied serpents, sprawled limberly up walls and over the plaques of stone paving that had stayed intact. Ancient trees, ribbed birches and the candle-branches of rhododendrons, had shed plates of ice. The blond or black cradles of their boughs thrust through naked as skeletons. Such a marvel had never been seen save in some dwarf form within a hothouse. Oases, as most knew, could begin and perish in months or days. What then would become of all this roused life, woken in the hours before dawn?

Drenched with sights and scents, wet wood, budding plants,

blossoms, incipient gourds, soil, rot, minerals, the people of the city named for a risen phoenix did not know if they were enthused or afraid.

Wagons were being rumbled along the vine-seething roadways, and planks thudded against the elevated houses so those trapped inside could jump or climb down, and those outside clamber back in.

In paddocks lashdeer pranced over pads of grass.

As the sky grew ever more threadbare, going up rather as the city had seemed to, they began to see the enclosed fields beyond. What was lifting there out of long pockets in the ice? A smoking-tower, its fume-plume still glowing in the last darkness, had itself let go a sheath of ice. At its foot a round pool gleamed back the reflection.

The palace terrace by now was definitely a good thirty feet above the surrounding complex.

Bhorth peered over, himself stranded too high to jump, like so many others.

The snow-cladding of the foundations held here too. But nevertheless he was well aware the underpalace, basement labyrinth of stores and cubbies and one walled-up room, was now *above* ground. Even as he eyed it, barrels began to roll out of some gap.

He and his court watched them bumbling off along the avenue.

Everything will give way, thought Bhorth, with a resigned anguish. He had stopped being able to reason, considered in absolutes, gave up.

He had done this, the evil insane god Vashdran. Any moment the demonic creature would also erupt from confinement, perhaps bearing the chewed bones of the Magician Thryfe in his lion-wolf jaws.

Across the terrace Bhorth saw his queen. Behind her a nurse held one of the little girls, but Tireh had the other, the more frightened one. Tireh was white with shock and wore her bedgown slung over by a fur. She spoke to the child calmly. 'Ssh,

dumpling. Don't be daunted. Look at that pretty flower growing there. Isn't that a lovely thing?'

Bhorth thought how Tireh had been when she knew their son
had left them. White like this, staunch like this, saying to Bhorth,
'He had no choice. How could it hurt me so if he had had a
choice? He was never ours. Didn't we know that? Surely we did.'

The sun lifted into a misty sky.

With the dawn the hugeness of change flashed on every gaze.
Though they had been monitoring what went on for at least an
hour a collective cry sounded.

Pinkly golden the light described the wonder of it, the *comedy*
of it, the abstraction. Marooned doorways and buildings on
stalks of snow, the river of roses along Rose Walk, the glinting of
leaves. Over the city walls the runnels and ditches of the fields
were getting tall with parchment-coloured quills of grain.

In the distance, the mist from which the sun had dashed out
seemed to form a secondary wall. This circled round the city and
its agricultural land. To the west the mist grew wan; it was like
a frost of milk left behind on the rim of a glass.

Directly above however the sky was blue.

Bhorth's more timid daughter stared up and gave a wail.

Tireh said, 'It's only birds, my baby.'

Hundreds of white-kadi, swarming in from the western sea,
ribboned over the dome of the sky and away into the misty ring
beyond.

'Does it end over there?' Bhorth mumbled. 'Or are we shut in
again by another bloody spell?'

'For a little while,' said a quiet voice. 'These things . . . take
time. If they're to prosper.'

Bhorth moved his head round, slowly. He saw an adult Lionwolf, looking nearly exactly as Bhorth had seen him last, on
the plain under Ru Karismi, stationed there at his elbow like a
favourite courtier. Like a shadow made of light.

As he progressed Thryfe felt only well-being and energy. The
god's healing of him had been thorough and he felt himself

abused by it. It reminded him bizarrely of the boyhood beatings by his father. Not so perverse an analogy either; punishment had helped drive him towards recognition of his own powers, typified perhaps by the eagles which had then come to aid him. To what would the pitiless kindness of Lionwolf propel him?

They had emerged from the labyrinth by mundanely walking down the opened corridor. A narrow door was undone and in the chamber it led to some barrels, probably of beer, had crashed over into the wall, knocking loose the stones. If nothing else had occurred the outer layer of ice-brick and established snow would have cemented the wall together. But thaw had happened on an intense scale. The barrels had rolled through and on down the road outside, which was patched with black soil and had plants uncurling from it.

The god had caused the thaw. Tritely, a sun god; thaws would be his métier.

Thryfe then glanced about at Vashdran, and found he had translocated elsewhere.

People were all over the road.

Once out of the palace confine Thryfe noted how the levels of the city had dropped, and jasmine was knitting shawls along the roofs, while steps and doorways hung up in air looking silly and macabre.

He felt incorrigibly young and did not welcome or like it. Thryfe had struggled to become old before his time. Only with Jemhara had he been prepared to relax from himself his grip. But Jemhara— He did not know what had become of her, trusted no other to tell him. It seemed to him she lived, yet was dead.

He had not allowed himself to grieve. And he could not hope. While to die had not been unreasonable for him, to cling or to lament were both useless, and contemptible.

Despite all these feelings, or because of them, he got through the crowds unnoticed, and went out beyond the city.

Here he saw the fields of dormant grain all metamorphosed into vibrancy. A lemon grove had shed an avalanche of ice like melting window-panes. Little bitter-green fruits gemmed the boughs.

Where there had been an ice barricade round Kol Cataar now there was another fortification, this of thick mist. It left a wide crater overhead with *Summer* sky in it. The sun was warm, so warm he thought he could not stand it, and that none of the Kol Cataarians would be able to, so adapted were they all to five hundred years of utter cold. The smell of growing stuff was overwhelming to the point of nausea. He went past apple trees, black humps with the fruit nestling against the ground, acid green like the unripe lemons.

Pools appeared, each time startling him. Their mirrorings leapt off the earth, where shattered bits of sky seemed to have dropped.

He considered if he could get through the obstructing mist. Outside, the Winter would lie, familiar enemy reassuring as a friend of long-standing.

The last stage of his short journey – it had taken less than an hour – drew him across a wheatfield. Chunks of ice still stuck here, with the wheat speared through them arrested in mid-arrival, fossilized and white as salt. The mist curtained the edge of the field.

Seen close to the mist was, as it had already seemed to be, opaque and concrete.

The sense of warning stabbed suddenly in Thryfe.

Why should that surprise him? It would be an act of imbecility to thrust through the mist and out into the true world. Or maybe it was even impassable, might attack him, throttle, or dissolve his flesh. Not that this particularly mattered, but such a force would need to be reported on. Most men did not want to die.

Thryfe spoke one word to the mist.

It was a word to dismember granite.

The mist did not react.

He tried another, actually three words, a persuasive phrase to do with the seducing of immoveable blockades that were partially sentient.

From the mist, not a quiver.

The magician said then words one might offer to a reluctant

or damaged Magikoy oculum, a request to be shown what lay within or on the other side.

Without hesitation now an oval portal formed. It appeared to rest in the mist-wall, and so displayed the depth of it, which seemed to go on otherwise unbroken for a quarter-mile. Down the long, horizontal chimney Thryfe beheld the world he knew, clear indeed as if projected through a seeing-glass. The picture was for a moment featureless, and then something slid out of its whiteness, blind black as the whiteness was blind white.

A wolf prowled there on the outer perimeter of the mist. It was a black wolf, of the type Thryfe had known in his youth, one of the tribe which had torn his mother in shreds.

The disgusting associated horror of the image was sufficiently apt he recoiled, but his mage-educated brain read the sight in another way. Here *was* the enemy personified. The enemy of the sun god in Kol Cataar, and of himself too, and of *every living thing*.

Winter lurked and prowled along the verges of the wall, scenting their lives and the psychic cunning that kept it out. Ice Age Winter was the wolf, jealous and angry that the sun had risen, and might rise for ever now, and so forever end five pleasure-filled centuries of merciless hunting.

Giving off a sparkle like needles, the mirror-aperture closed.

Two white hares fled through the tassels of frozen wheat, towards the tastier crops nearer the city.

Curjai had led the others down on to the plain. Now they were ranged on their dromazi below the chalk-white hill which, perhaps, had been the Holasan-garth. It was about the proper height. Fenzi had pointed this out. Even Arok agreed, although in his new, deadly-dull tones. At least he did not say, Curjai thought, 'What is the Holasan-garth?'

Otherwise Ruxendra had not joined them. Women were of course always unreliable.

The sun was long down.

Stars and three quarter-moons hung from the sky. The light was serene, and ineffectual.

Nevertheless something still shone from inside the hill. Against the surrounding sobriety it soberly burned.

'If it's the garth they've lighted the lamps.'

'It's locked in ice.'

Curjai nodded at the egg-smooth shape. He smelled the fires inside, man-made. His nod now opened fire from air like the wing of a crimson butterfly, the kind he had only seen in Lion-wolf's Hell.

The fire settled on the ice-hill, ribbed it like the stem of a precious goblet. And died.

So determined?

The god of fire, son of a god of fire, glanced across at the zombie Arok seated there on the dromaz.

'Who would be in your garth, Chaiord? Your wife and son. Who else?'

'Wives,' said Arok, 'sons—' He was off again.

'Attajos!' Curjai cursed, taking in vain the name of his father.

Flame lanced directly from the eyes of Curjai and struck the side of the hill.

For a second all of it changed to liquid cinnabar.

Then again warmth and luminescence died.

The men stood, or sat their beasts. Above, the minimalism of the night sky watched with little cold eyes under the arched eyebrows of quarter-moons.

'Has he returned?'

Saphay reined in her exasperation. 'No. That one sends cold and dark, not fire.'

'Was it fire?'

'He is Tirthen. He's *Winter*. Stand back.'

Nirri stood back.

The hag-goddess had become very young and glamorous, and seemed angrily fascinated by the flares of orange and blood-scarlet that had just now erupted outside. Outside anyway had an altered meaning. For with the departure of the Winter god the entire garth had been sealed in a hive of ice. Those inside exercised on the whole Jafn stoicism. Saphay of course had lost her temper.

'My son,' whispered Nirri now.

None heard, or if they did thought her remark only inevitable.

She had gone up to see him instants after the god-thing – Tirthen? – had evaporated.

Nirri had climbed the ladder-stair to the room, and he lay there undisturbed, cupped still in the fireball the goddess had constructed.

Nirri had crept close. He had suddenly aged – her son was now some sixteen years. Had the influx of the god galvanized the process? Or had it merely come gradually, and she been too afraid, too intimidated before to look close and see? The web of unconsciousness contained him: that had not changed. A piercing sorrow assailed Nirri at this outrageous precis of his childhood. Then she saw the other thing. The fire the goddess had wrought for him – was *frozen*.

'Like the hearth fire below.'

No other fires had congealed in the same way. Only the hearth in the hall, and this one. She stared.

How strange to see these curling flames all knotted up and motionless.

And Athluan trapped within the chrysalis.

She had turned her back to it and gone straight down again to hall and seen them all to be, even the goddess, trapped too in the ice-hive that now shelled the garth.

It arced high over the walls. Its whiteness was so virginal even the smoke-smear of torches and lamplight below made it bloom. Nirri thought of being imprisoned inside a great white tooth, the tooth of a giant whale maybe.

Time passed. She had no idea how much. And then came the external flares of scarlet.

Saphay ran forward, out on the yard.

Her disgraceful beauty – the Winter god had also been like that if in quite another mode – disgusted and distressed.

Khursp and Elbar, and the few others who came back with tidings of Arok's death, crouched in the lee of the House wall, glaring and showing their teeth like dogs. They did not know what Saphay was, had not asked or been told, and did not like her. At Khursp's grunt they rose and went to stand by their queen.

Nirri found the people of the garth drew off from Saphay and came to Nirri herself, marshalling around and behind her. It was a move of defence, but also reminded her, yes even the warriors, of chicks huddling under the wings of the mother hen. This hurt her too. She could not protect them. But she stood her useless ground as if she might.

For Saphay some other revelation was at hand. She had, when face to face with Winter here, realized profoundly and for the first what she was. She was a goddess of day. She had function and title. At once she had visualized light beginning on the sky's edge, and that out of it was birthed the blazing sun. This poetic allusion had moved Saphay, and went on doing so. It consolidated her emotions. Rarely if ever before had she known her place in the scheme of anything. Now she did.

'Someone is outside with the ability of fire,' she announced.

And only then she experienced the aura of the presence out beyond the hive of ice.

My son—

It is Nameless – it is Lionwolf—

While in harmony, *My son*, thought Nirri too, thinking of Athluan.

But more than miles away another woman thought those words in her own tongue, that of the Simese. Her thought was louder and more frantic. It cut the night like a razor.

And both Saphay and Nirri heard it in the hollow of their inner ears, and believed it had a bearing only on themselves.

He had bided his time, the king in Padgish. He was measured, patrolling the brief limits of his brain, a villain of little importance and no remembered name, until this moment.

Had he loved her, the tan-haired Riadis? Doubtful. But her unusualness had appealed to his lust, and besides he took many wives from hill clans aristocracy, a procedure meant to shore up his power and wealth. The first child she bore, that crippled lump which thankfully died in its early years, he had never reckoned was his. What, he to sire an abomination? Never. In any case he had not properly touched her for months. The king suspected her personal shaman, Korch, to be the culprit. *Her* tale, that she got it from the fire, he accepted because at that hour he had not wanted to take on a feud with her kin. Really she should have been exterminated at once. But he waited. And in the end lost interest. Then a sickness decimated the herds of her kindred and their influence began to wane. He kept the news from her, and watched with half an eye as they faded.

That too was the year she came to him and said the fire had been at her again. The *fire*! He thought he would let her swell up and bear the thing, for it was unlawful to kill a pregnant or breast-feeding mother, and the king stuck to the codes of his kingdom. The child was certainly from the same source, Korch, and would turn out another malformed cretin. He would then bring Riadis to trial for treasonable unfaithfulness and have her burned – another custom if a rather old-fashioned one. The monster would be simple enough to smother.

But then she birthed it. Not only was it a perfect male but it grew with supernatural speed. At a couple of months it was like a two-year infant. And though by then the boy had been weaned, the numinous stories that already surrounded him, and so her, made the king keep his hand off.

So they all went on. And the legend grew. That Escurjai, as Riadis had named both her sons, was himself a god. The king did not think that, however. He did see the magic acts the child, then the youth, put on, and relays of other miracles – healings, weather adjustments. The king put all that down to the boy's real father, who must be schooling him on the sly. Shamans naturally could perform feats of magic, create fire, doctor the sick, and sometimes chase off storms. The king's slow brain could not encompass the sublime. He was a fool. And being one he did not believe in gods, only paying them lip-service. He paid that to Curjai as well. And Curjai, supposedly so divinely wise, failed to read the king's subterfuge. Both the king and Curjai himself never reasoned that the clearest eye can see through clean glass, but seldom through a pathless mire.

All the while, as the god rapidly grew up, the king was nice to him and waited. With the arrival of the foreign barbarians who claimed to hail from some unknown continent, a chink of possibility showed itself. When the king allowed a small party to seek the foreign garth Curjai went with them. Let Curjai's shaman magic meet the outland hostility of these savages. Very likely they would slaughter him, at least take him prisoner against Arok's return.

And as that happened, the king would erase Riadis from his life. By now she enraged him, sweeping about, no longer young, and with her garish hair and reputation as the fire god's concubine. Well, let her see what the fire god thought of her burned alive.

The king did not quite have the gall to bring her to trial, not in the end. He went another way to work. In this his priest mages assisted him. They had their own gripe with Riadis's hubris and did not value Curjai much, for the converse reason. They *did* believe in gods, and those gods should only be accessible to such as themselves. One walking about and there for everyone in the brown skin of a boy would not do.

She was weaving in the Simese way, the handloom balanced on her knees as she moved the shuttle through the warp. The cloth was the colour of fire. In the rhythm of her weaving Riadis was at peace.

Nearby the tiger had been sleeping on a rug. Curjai had reared it and it was a credit to its species. Now it woke with a wide yawn.

Presently Riadis heard it growl.

'Hush, baba. He'll be here soon.' She meant Curjai and hoped that she was correct. She drew the weft to completion. Her hands fell loose on the loom. She had herself no fears for her unearthly son. What could harm him? But she felt his absence. Altogether there was a strange note of separation in the afternoon. She could not explain it. She recalled the deep stillness that had clasped about her rooms that day Korch had shown her Curjai in a piece of mirror, riding a chariot through another world. Today the king was off hunting in the royal park; most of the foreign men had gone with him. Through her windows the sky was darkly white and nothing seemed to move.

The tiger growled again. It got up from the rug and back across the tiles, shaking its paws as it went as if to rid them of something sticky. Its charcoal-blue eyes were fixed on the brazier of coals.

Riadis said, 'Haven't you seen a flame before, baba?'

But she too cast a look at the brazier.

Something was in it she had not noticed, there at the bottom. It seemed, rather than a coal, to be a round blackish stone, and now cracks were appearing in it, filtering green. Intrigued, Riadis watched.

The tiger yowled. It ran about there yowling, by the upright of the bedchamber door.

She would have to get up and go and see what was the matter with it. There was a sort of comfort in this, the tiger conniving, becoming a baby for her.

Eyes still attracted by the curious fracturing stone Riadis was rising, just about to turn her head, when the nucleus of the fire exploded.

It was magecraft. A gout of atomic incandescence broke upward and outward in a wave. The wave engulfed Riadis before she could even cry aloud. She was instantly dissolved in the inferno. For a few feet around furnishings singed, and the small loom itself caught alight, fire-tinged cloth clothed in fire. Yet almost at once the incendiary was burning out. Pale cinders floated through the room and settled like powder. Nothing was much disordered. A brief black tarry mark was on the tiles with some charred sticks – the loom – beside it. An odour like newly forged steel clung to the air.

Riadis, who had just been totally thaumaturgically incinerated, and was dead, did not know this.

But someone held her, smiling down at her. This was a man of extraordinary attractions, very dark of skin and hair and golden-eyed.

'Attajos,' she said. Her voice was a girl's again.

The god smiled on. Dislodged, the memory of burning arrived and prompted her. Her soul asked, *Was it you?*

'No. But now, in the most appealing way,' said Attajos, 'it will be.'

As he bore her off over a hazy country she was not yet able quite to see, Riadis gazed back only once. Some frenzied part of her sang the name of her son. But even so soon the longing for him was heartlessly leaving her. Her fierce thought was left adrift to echo above Simisey.

Below she did not see either a figure sprinting. It was the shaman Korch. Poisoned by the king he had quickly sped here. He had been here often enough to know the way by heart.

Back in the everyday world of viciousness and violence, the tiger cub struggled to its paws against the far bedroom wall. It had been blown through the doorway and on twenty paces by the fire's ignition, but was not hurt. Together with rearing it on milk and broth, Curjai had also given it a sip of his blood. Disappointingly though so far he had not realized who it was, or had been, and so not named it correctly. He called the tiger affectionately *Catty*. But the tiger was a lot more than that. Ahead of its years it was already nearly full-grown, building up with the same celerity Curjai displayed.

A window screened by membrane had torn at the blast.

'Catty', who was not, threw himself at the rent and squirmed through, dropping down into a tiny snow-garden of iced mimosas.

In the palace and the town no abnormal sound gave warning of anything. Only the odd stillness of all things showed any indication now of further events.

The tiger trotted beneath the walls, through gateways, along narrow side-slips under tall royal blocks. He reached a colonnade of the huge iron-tree pillars. This was the direction the king of limited mind would travel, on his return.

Catty lay down to wait.

His animal consciousness did not comprehend or therefore need to analyse the awful snowstorm which next took place. Catty knew it was Winter, now in the person of the god Tirthen roused by unthinking recognition and sacrifice, but also by the moronic evil of recent murder on the doorstep. *Human* sacrifice. Catty could have told you, had you asked and he been equipped to answer, that Winter had only put on the form and idea of Tirthen in the same way someone without one, going out, put on the nearest fur cloak in his size. Winter was up for it, and Tirthen just happened to fit.

It was some hours before the king's hunt did return.

They had been smitten by horrors, and one of the warriors was dead. None of them cared either that all of the barbarians survived and some had made off. Did any of the Simese even recall?

The king had left his horse and walked slowly up the colonnade, leaning on two servants. It was doubtful too if *he* even recalled his queen had been executed while he was out.

Catty emerged like a loyal and concerned hound from behind a column. Actually Catty had *been* a hound in his former existence. He had been an eyeless jatcha in the blue Hell, not to mention a female. Atjosa, Curjai had named her/him there. But more than a Hell hound Catty was plainly a Drajjerchach-Chachadraj, one more spawn of all the cat–dog matings of the surreal. And now he was a nearly full-grown tiger.

When Catty sprang the servants were knocked spinning. They tried to rally and others came running at the screams. But Catty had completed his task by then. The king's face and throat were off and out and neatly sprinkled on the snow in bite-sized chunks, and Catty-Atjosa was over another wall and away.

It came to him like something breaking in his own body, or in the night.

Curjai knew he had experienced a blow so large that it meant the death of another. And his initial thought was for Lionwolf—

And then he knew it was not Lionwolf, as how could it be,

and anyway, brother and beloved though Lionwolf was, only one familial tie would perish in this shock, like the cutting of the umbilical cord.

He stood in silence and the roar of severance bored through him. Riadis was dead.

Perhaps as appalling as the rest, he understood too she had died some days and nights before this juncture when he felt it. Being what he was – being not a human man – should he not have known before? Even some men did that . . . An unintelligent and wooden aspect of his own self had somehow shut awareness from him until now, when he paused baffled by the hill.

On this cue the fire came, the combustion which had slain his mother. He held it within him one endless split second, then smashed it against the slope of ice.

About him men gaped in terror as Curjai fell headlong to the earth, and something like a lightning crashed into the hill that was the garth.

There was a boom like that of a berg giving way into the open sea.

As the ice gave, showering off like glass, loud yells and shrieks were audible from the far side.

A colossal archway penetrated the hill. Inside you could see the garth's outer walls and gate, then the jumbled mass of houses and the upper eminence of the big House. People were rushing to and fro. Dromazi were in there too, charging along the tracks—

Curjai had got up. 'It's well, Sombrec. Let me be. Where's Arok?'

'He – ah, there he is. Look. He hasn't moved.'

Curjai shot a look at Arok the zombie. No, he had not moved. *Un*moved by all of it.

Curjai took in Fenzi standing by the dromaz that Arok sat on. Fenzi also seemed relatively unmoved. Or rather, more concerned with something he could see in the distance – where nothing was.

But there was a ribbon of pearly golden light, anyone could

spot that now, spilling down from the high House, and something walked in the middle of the light that had hair like a young torch flame.

My mother is dead.

I am an immortal, and my mother is dead.

People were coming out of the garth and there was excited interchange of questions and replies.

When Curjai looked up again a woman with saffron hair was there beside him.

He did not know who she was, and perhaps he might have done for he had known Lionwolf.

She in turn did not know Curjai at all. And yet she had mistaken him for someone else not hours before.

Neither spoke to the other.

All around the flurry of everything else, the human calling and hurrying, the rain of slivers of ice still evacuating the entrance, the pandemonium of the dromazi, and Fenzi turning abruptly, walking off over the plain. In the midst of it Curjai and Saphay remained unspeaking side by side. Both their heads were bowed. Fire god and day goddess, their tears dropped molten on the white ground. Lambent inside their glowing ice-hill of woe, all other things left them strictly alone.

Zeth Zezeth saw none of that. He was observing from some other vantage the stupid girl from Ru Karismi, cavorting in the night sky with her hideous mongrel.

He would have both of them.

He would bend them to the right shape, maybe simply snap the dog in half and throw it away. Her too, probably, her too.

Back along an ormolu avenue, with fiery vines making a pergola in which blue beetles of rage devoured little pink flies, Zth regarded his other catch, the witch Jemhara. She was quietly seated, reading a book he had permitted to form for her. The esoteric knowledge in it, copies of such essays penned on earth but ethereally distended, might scorch out her brain. But so far she had managed to cope with it. Remarkable for a mortal, even a

Magikoy. She would be far more use than the other one, the girl Ruxa or whatever her name was.

Zth raised a goblet of orichalc and drank a liquid that lighted the avenue.

He unwittingly drank because men, who had made him in their image, had done it first.

For that reason too the drink made him – could it be? – just slightly drunk.

But now he was benign. He was actively enjoying his fury. Pink blood dripped from the vines.

Mentally he reviewed his plans. Jemhara would be sent to destroy Lionwolf. The Ruxa girl would also be sent to destroy Lionwolf. And then he himself would leisurely descend again and destroy Lionwolf, and destroy the bitch-doy Saphay, and the other useless article, that damned whale. Destroy all of it, blast the whole curse-fucked world, and sit laughing in glory on the blackened clinker.

His own god-mind unmind was turning to gold, fusing his thoughts there like marvellous jewels, so he could go round and about admiring them. He basked in himself, in proposed restitution and reprisal.

Along the avenue Jemhara intermittently watched him over the rim of the great gilded scroll. Time did not truly exist here, but nevertheless she was aware Zth used up a vast amount of it in the same way as now. Nor had he as yet made her carry out any of his plots. His wondrousness tugged at her frighteningly. Yet she could see through the fissures in it to glimpses of indecipherable anomalies. Occasionally he called her close. He might award her dainty and overwhelming caresses – a finger brushing her shoulders, the tip of his tongue against her hair. These seemed enough to kill her. Often he spoke of possessing her entirely – and that he must not for then she *would* die of it. Or that he might anyway, an ultimate punishment and reward. Some aspect of this, even wrapped in delirious fear as it was, had begun to ring a bell of recollection. The note of the bell was not quite as it had been, which made it hard for her to be sure which act or person from her past it evoked.

She lowered her eyes for now he was looking round.

Perhaps he had seen her gaze on him. It was inevitable she would stare at him. How could she not? He would expect it.

Something anyway distracted him.

In the riot of the vines the pink flies had grown bored with victimization. They were setting about the beetles, ripping them apart. Blue iridescent segments clinked on the path.

Zth disliked that. Blue was the sigil of his wrath. Nothing could get the better of it.

He went away. Through trees of a sort, water of a sort, a kind of sunset—

His world grew honeyed once more, fusing to gold like his mind.

Jemhara laid the scroll aside. She had instead a vision before her of an elderly man sitting on a luxurious bed. He was holding out his twig-like claws urgent to receive her body. His old gnarled voice, no longer much that of a King Paramount, quavered to her. 'Jemhara, Jemhara, if only I could enter you – I long to, my darling, I *dream* of mounting you – once I was strong, if only I'd seen you then – is there not some potion you know of, you cunning minx, so I can stand up like a man—'

King Sallusdon in Ru Karismi. The wreckage of whom, for the sake of heirdom, Bhorth had remembered in the name of his immaculate son.

How the old king had begged her for the ability of male erection. All the rest she gave him was never quite enough. For it was really his youth he wanted back. Rather than whine for potency and orgasm he warbled to be young again. She had had to give in. How glad Vuldir was. Jemhara could now poison the senile fool and leave no trace. And that she had done.

But why think of dead King Sallusdon now?

Bhorth spoke, his tones level.

'What will you have then? Everything I suppose. The city. My apologies it's not a finer one for you to trample, not as succulent as Sofora and Kandexa were, let alone the capital. But there. I don't expect you'll worry, will you? You are a sun god I believe. Did Thryfe say that? The gods know who said what. You'll fry us or demolish us. Too much to hope you'll let any live. You and your armies never did. Not even women, or children above eleven years. Or was it twelve? Not even a cat or dog, or a bird.'

Lionwolf stayed quietly, listening in a polite, somewhat detached manner.

He looks sad, Bhorth irrationally thought. *No, it's a look of disdain. Or neither. Why would he bother? Whatever he is, he is here.*

'Yes, I am here,' Lionwolf said.

And he can read thoughts. As inevitably he must.

Lionwolf smiled.

They had come in through the crowd on the terrace, none of whom had seemed to see Lionwolf at all, but then none of them had seemed to see Bhorth either. Fat, solid, scowling Bhorth, their king.

This room was a small vacant chamber off the hall, which had wine and water jugs standing on a table. A child's toy, a fish made of wool, had been dropped on the floor.

Lionwolf bent suddenly and picked up the fish. And the grace – the *power* of this insignificant movement dried Bhorth's mouth so that he felt he would choke.

'A fish,' said Lionwolf, gently. He placed it out on the air as if on a surface, and at once the woollen toy began to swim along, wiggling its tail and the two little fins.

Bhorth's eyes bulged.

He's a child! But there was something so appealing in the sight of the inanimate toy happily splashing along in mid-air that moisture came back into his mouth, and a type of animal joy flooded him.

Lionwolf said, 'I don't hurt things now, Bhorth. Where is my need?'

'Did you *need* before?'

'Yes. I was partly human before.'

Bhorth found he took a step backward.

The fish dived abruptly by and into a jug of water. There it went on cavorting.

'What do you want?' Bhorth asked again.

'Everything. And that, Bhorth, is the spark of humanness still in me.'

Bhorth sat down heavily. He looked at his boots. Water from the jug was being slopped out on the floor. There it turned to – were they diamonds? Yes, yes. Why ask?

Lionwolf was sitting beside the king. Bhorth had not seen him approach. He had not *approached*. Manifested.

Bhorth had the insane urge to laugh.

Lionwolf laughed then. And Bhorth began to laugh.

'I want nothing from you, Bhorth. I want *nothing*. Nothing and everything. Look.'

Through the laughter Bhorth looked and saw a flowering vine had come up from the floor. Red grapes swung bursting on the vine, their juice dripping, and there were tiny turquoise beetles and little insects with wide rosy wings, but these were made of gems and gauze.

Lionwolf got up and Bhorth got up, and Lionwolf put his arms about Bhorth. Then Bhorth wept. Trained to creeds of man-liness, and in himself a man of wilful self-control, he had not shed tears for what seemed decades. They all spilled now, like the jewelry water and the juice of the grapes. He wept for the cities and for the world, and for the going away of his hero son who once, only a moment of years before, had been a child and the snake bit him and Bhorth sucked out the venom and his son Sallus lived, and now Lionwolf sucked the venom out of the bite in Bhorth's soul which had been all the past, and Bhorth too would live.

When the god let him go Bhorth balanced on the surface of the air as the toy fish had done. He felt warm and new, and his belt was sagging because he had grown fit and lean again in his own stocky way.

Lionwolf was no longer there.

So Bhorth went to the water jug and took out the now inanimate wet wool fish and laid it on a bench to dry. Since it was better to be kind, where you could.

But out at the border of the fruiting fields of Kol Cataar, the

Magician Thryfe saw a figure tower up in the wall of mist. For a second he believed the black Winter wolf had gained entry. Then he saw properly what walked towards him out of the shadowy door.

'Greetings and well met, Highness Thryfe.'

The Gargolem was as it had been always. Beast-headed, maned and fanged, its body that of a human male yet above the height of the tallest man.

'Gargo,' Thryfe found he said.

It spoke like a man too, as ever. And was always addressed in turn.

'You are here for the king,' said the Gargolem.

'It seems so. And you?'

'I am here,' stated the Gargolem, as some of the gods had recently done. But it turned its head towards the city. 'This place shall be raised up.'

The grain, even in these minutes, had itself lifted higher. The blossoming trees were opening narrow wings of foliage. Among these cascades of growth the unmistakable metallic forms of lesser gargolems were appearing, brought into being presumably by the Gargolem.

'Will you attend the palace?' the Gargolem now inquired.

Thryfe acquiesced. Former habit, Magikoy conditioning, encased him. He could not avoid it; to avoid it would not be excusable. Aside from that, what else was there for him to do?

And as he stepped forward towards the city, the Gargolem said, as so long ago it would have done in the City of the Kings, 'I will send word then. Proceed.'

The hordes of living fish that fluttered to his mouth seemed to want to tempt Brightshade. *Can't you see how tasty we are?* they seemed to tweet.

Brightshade however did not often rouse himself to eat them.

It was unappreciative of him, and a dull guilt at slighting their edible charms began to pervade his synapses. Sometimes he even did consume large unwanted mouthfuls, so as not to insult and upset them. Pity and empathy had come belatedly to the whale, and he had got them wrong. But there. Conceivably it was a start.

He was cruising mostly along the sea-bottom by then. Randomly, he had thought, he had drifted about through the oceans under the ice floes. When he supposed he must breach he did it always with intense caution. He did not want to meet Zth again out ranting in the bright air.

But it was on such a mission of breaching that Brightshade emerged into the cold sunshine, and saw he lay adjacent to a vast plate of land. It was the sword-like South Continent, its western side, and he had anchored below the tubby portion of the hilt. North, south and west therefore the landmass stretched. Extravagantly gigantic though the whale was, even he was not quite as big. In size contest the sea did not count. It was fluid. But the *land* resembled another Brightshade.

For some reason he was reassured by this.

He coasted to and fro a while, admiring the icy shores. Ice-forests scintillantly embroidered the snow.

Had Brightshade missed the sight of land? Formerly it had often brought him many delights, such as fisher-fleet and village wrecking. But here no trace of human habitation remained.

With immense delicacy Brightshade flapped his tail. A spray of lucid liquid hurtled shorewards. Some trees snapped like splinters. *There.* Empathy did not catch him out this time either. He grinned and turned his horned face, and the lesser continent of his vegetable-clad back, to the sun.

And in that comfy second he felt the twitch of another's attention scrape against his own insides. It was the regard of Zeth – unmistakable. In fact, a random regard, although Brightshade in his abrupt terror did not guess this. Zeth had only thought of Brightshade – *that damned whale* – and in the most abstract fashion. Which was enough.

Down to the ocean floor Brightshade plummeted, displacing gallons, tons of liquid sea that gushed back over the shore. Most of the artistic forest broke. Whole leagues of coastal ice split off and went careering skyward, next landward, coming to rest on far-off hills.

In another submarine trench the leviathan cowered.

Can anything live like this? Some must. Some will not.

Crushed again by Zth's implacable and bullying eminence, Brightshade's persona veered at last towards rebellion. How lucky that he had after all a thread of elastic woven in his clunking iron psyche.

He was enabled suddenly to see it was not necessary to lie in a trench all the remainder of his immortal life.

A curious mental *shape*-picture entered his thoughts. He saw a tiny whale swimming around in a water jug.

Somewhere deep in his throat, Brightshade *laughed*.

He *could* laugh. He was a god.

And gods who laugh do not spend eternity in hiding.

Thought-*shapes* abounded now, a high tide of ideas.

There were others who had great powers, surely Brightshade could sense them, and besides some of them had defeated him here and there. Now he could accept they were his equals, and one, one he had hated above all things – *that* one was greater. Certainly they had been enemies, Brightshade and his half-brother Lionwolf. But Zeth was enemy to both.

Smiling, and he was a god, he could smile too, Brightshade eased upward through black water to grey to vinegar green. He fixed his physical sight once more on the land, and with his sight his inner vision. And saw the burning *shape* of the one he sought.

Sea god, however, the whale could not travel over land, only through the waters about and beneath. No doubt there might be an underland route, but this would bring destruction to everything around when finally he rose. And that seemingly would not be the best reintroduction to Lionwolf.

Brightshade pondered. Then he knew. Gods have so many talents.

Inch by inch, mile by mile, like a vast vapour, a sky-wide cloud, the etheric insubstantial *in-ness* of Brightshade slipped from the landmass of his flesh. When all of it was free, only a slender rope of nacreous light connected whale body and astral body. But the rope also was elastic. It could extend – for ever.

Like that then the projected soul of Brightshade now hurried to meet his kin. To meet him for the first, for they never had *met*. Not even when Lionwolf had stridden over the whale's back or, darkly perceived, been tossed into infinity – or only Hell – from the height of Brightshade's skull.

Parked by the shore the huge whale physique was not insensible. It kept alert, on guard. It calculated everything. And when more fish sported near it, it ate a few of them courteously, killing them as quickly and gently as it could.

Ninth Intervolumen

Does the leaf remember
The tree which gave it flight?
Does the star recall
Which fire woke its light?

Love Song: Ruk Kar Is

Sea filled the floor of the night.

Each one of them must travel it.

Their own intent and flawless darkness was or would be pinned by starlight on the black backdrop of heaven and earth, among the silver-creaming of the liquid waves.

The Children of Chillel.

Her magnetism pulled them surely on and in.

At first they had had to walk over the land, those countries of Simisey and Vormland, the Kelpish and Fazion isles, the coasts and inner reaches of the continent shaped like a sword: Gech, Olchibe, Jafn. All of them gained the sea. Some were alone and some in groups. There were more of them too than any who locally witnessed their number ever estimated. All were male but one. And every male participated in the journey – but one.

Elsewhere Dayadin, son of Chillel, Arok and Nirri, stayed moored with his half-sister Brinnajni. But here, on the sea floor of night, Azula, daughter of Chillel and Beebit, sat with her half-brother Sallus who was the son of a king.

They had ridden in a sleekar drawn by lashdeer. It was Sallus's property, though he had not before often used it. A small example of luggage and provisions was in the chariot.

Azula stood behind Sallus, who drove the team. When occasionally he glanced back to check on how she was, Azula was always mute and expressionless; her cloak and short hair

streaming back from the racing speed were all that demonstrated she was not a statue.

When they paused to eat or sleep they spoke very little. He
let her sleep the most. She seemed to feed on sleep more hun-
grily than on food. Did she dream then of her human mother?

Her hair was growing back swiftly and she had rinsed it in
black dye before they left Kol Cataar. Now it seemed only one
colour. It was just her skin and eyes that might attract comment.

A couple of tiny, terrible villages appeared and vanished. One
was clearly a nest of partly demented robbers, who rushed or
hobbled at them waving their arms, shouting the fake over-wel-
come of a spurious host. Oaths and dooms were heaped on them
as they sped away. In other spots they dashed past villages and
steads long abandoned. The bones of animals lay just under the
softer snow, lividly ochre against the whiteness. But as the coast
drew near – the ride had not taken more than four days – a
bigger conglomeration showed, this one not quite mad or ferocious. From here an ice-road led down to the shore.

Sallus haggled for one of the clinker-built black boats, for its
dun sail, oars and fishing lines. He offered only copper coins but
they were the currency of the dead city of Ru Karismi.

Dreadfully, people in the village street shed tears, and came
reverently to touch them. 'Were you from *there*? Is that what
turned you black?' Sallus evaded talk of colour. Carefully lying
he explained he and his sister had been born to steaders outside
the city. The whole family had escaped before the invader came,
or the White Death.

'Where are you heading on the cold hard sea?'

'A mage put it on us to make the voyage,' Sallus said. 'I had
to promise my father we would. Seek the coast of Kraagparia, he
told me.'

Then the villagers made old religious signs of the Rukarian
pious. They moved away from Sallus and Azula as if they were
sorry for them but no longer wished to be in their vicinity. The
boat they got for only twice its reasonable price. He suspected
the copper coins would not be spent but kept as heirlooms.

But they must go farther than the hem of Kraagparia.

They must go down to the very tip of the blade of the sword – and further. South-east to south, following the shores, further than any apparently had been. And further still. South-east to south and next south to east. *There.* If *there* existed. And the boat – was not so strong.

It would be a voyage of months, conceivably of years.

Who knew anyway after such a journey, whether travelling in hope or denial, if it were possible ever to arrive?

Fenzi, son of Chillel, a fisherman and his woman, met four half-brothers, the two Kelps, the Faz and the Vorm, in the middle of the northern sea.

They and he had simply set out overland on the coastal ice of the north-west continent. He might even have met them there, had he reached it more quickly. The four had taken a fishing boat from the village they called respectively Kelfazvor, Fazkelvor or Vorkelfaz. Fenzi, fisher's son, had knocked one together on wooded land above the shore.

A storm blew up one night, one of those nights floored by the black and silver sea. Amid the lightning flares and tall waves the two small boats were steered into each other's vicinity.

Five men now, they roped their craft together. Greetings were cool. Oneness did not really provide a sense of finding or family. Only Chillel the magnet had true relevance.

To the islanders Fenzi was landlocked Jafn, and they to him were thieving reivers. It was inevitable they join forces, but not especially to be celebrated.

Fenzi then sat alone on his Jafn-built boat, tied to the others by cord and symbolism.

He thought about his father and mother to whom he had not said farewell. But he and they had not been like Arok and Nirri with their Dayadin. Fenzi's parents were always slightly bemused by him, and after Dayadin was lost, apologetic.

Fenzi thought of Sombrec too. He had not bidden him any goodbye either.

Fenzi thought of himself. During his ultra-short childhood

and adolescence he had been quite a sunny boy, sure and sometimes psychic. In fact he had not changed so much until that
gallop back to the garth, until the hill of ice, until Arok returned
dead from death. Until the Pull became everything.

They knew where they went now, the five Chillelings.

Once the storm subsided they steered by the stars for the far
south-east.

Obviously something was there, some land or other, despite
elder beliefs that nothing was. The other continent at the world's
top to which Arok, and Saphay, had sailed them those few years
before, that too had been a place unknown, non-existent until
they anchored there.

Azula watched her brother sleeping. She kept her hand guid-
ingly and lightly upon the tiller, as he had shown her how to.
The chaze snake had coiled about Sallus's waist, its head resting
on his chest above the heart.

I hate her, Azula thought. She meant the goddess Chillel, her
other mother. *Why should I want to go to her when I hate her? I don't
want to. I could slip over the side into all that black water, and go to
Beebit-Ma instead. I hate Chillel.*

'I hate her,' said Brinnajni.

She lay on her back, her red hair spread across the pillows.
Her brother Dayadin lay against her, one arm about her waist as
the snake had coiled about Sallus, and Dayadin's head too rested
on Brinnajni's breast. During the past months brother and sister
had become lovers. It carried for them no faintest stigma, though
among the Jafn it was reckoned a sin, and amongst the hill shep-
herds where Brinnajni had begun her life, a crime that merited
terminal stoning.

'Who do you hate?' Dayadin murmured. He raised his face to
look at hers. Her eyes were shut. He kissed her lips and asked
them, '*Who?*'

'Who do you think, beloved?'

But Dayadin did not know.

In the deerskin that hung across the door, the hovor Hilth blithered quietly, playing with the drape as it sometimes did. The black sheep, which had by now grown as large as a cow, was outside the hut, nibbling grass which had bloomed out of the snow near the wall.

Brinnajni – Burning Flame – had built this crochety home with a couple of muttered supernatural instructions. Trees cracked in ice, ice-brick skirled. Up it went, in they went. The bed had been brought from longitudes off, some furnishing left to rot in a fine house somewhere. Now dressed with fur and cushions it was a couch fit to conjure with. And they had.

'Who do you *need* to hate, Brinna?'

'My mother.'

He looked long at her, then, without a word, rolled over to his back. At last he did say, 'Are you *able* to hate Chillel?'

'Yes. Trust me. Quite able.'

They lay side by side in silence. Slowly his hand stole out to discover hers. Their hands clasped, became one.

'I love you, little brother.'

'And I you.'

'I was old before I was young, Dayad. She sloughed and left me. I had to make my own way. My darling sheep was more mother to me than *Chillel*. As for a father – well. Old before young, your Brinna. Now I'm young with you. You grew up nearly if not quite as fast as I. Dayad—'

'I'm here.'

'*Stay* here. We are too strong for her.'

'She is nothing to me.'

Unthinkable, thus unthought, the slightest doubt assailed him when he made her this automatic vow. He accepted instantly however it was *not* Chillel who meant anything. It was Nirri, Arok.

' . . . Nothing,' he said again, mild with truthfulness.

Guriyuve the Chilleling from Olchibe – son also to Ipeyek the Gech, and the Crarrow Hevonhib – had put out long since on the more south-easterly seas, travelling from the Marginal Land of the sword continent. *He* had said farewell to his mother. Ipeyek the father, though made leader, had a year before wandered away from Olchibe back to the Urrowiy, his nomadic people of the Great Uaarb.

Hevonhib, now the nubile and child-bearing member of her coven, was already teeming with another man's kiddle. She looked at Guriyuve with only a formal regret. She, who had been so proud to get him. 'You were named for a dead warrior. He wished his name to live on among our sluhts. Your name has also come to include that of the sluhtin's priest and leader of most renown, Peb Yuve.'

Guriyuve replied, 'Yuve is like a Rukar name. Does it result from one of their gods known as Yuvis?'

Although offended Hevonhib did not show it. The Crarrowin ruled lots of the sluhtins by now, and here the same. Her coven too was the chief one.

'How do you know a Rukar name?'

'I can't say, Mother. Sometimes I know things.'

'Then know this: we keep enduring enmity with the Rukar. Time out of mind they ruined us and destroyed the glory of Sham, that great city better than all. Also the Lionwolf came from their blood who caused much harm.'

Guriyuve thought uneasily that his mother sounded more portentous when she was with child. No doubt she had been that way too when carrying him. He said, 'I'm sorry the ghost warrior Guri will lose his name here. Before I leave shall I give it up? Then you can gift it again to your next one, which is also a boy.'

'I know it's a boy,' said Hevonhib sternly. She was Crarrow. Crarrow knew these things. She knew too the father of this second son had not been pre-prepared by the astonishing seed of Chillel. The man was not very strong, nor would the child be strong. Fast-grown Guriyuve of course was perfectly stalwart.

But Hevonhib had foreseen and was resigned. She gave him an amulet of the Crarrowin he would not need, a flat greenish stone with a circle carved in it.

Guriyuve thanked her and departed.

He rode one of the female mammoths he had grown up with. The other three, always till now companions both to her and to him, stood mourning at the exit of the caves.

Parting was usually cruel. But Guriyuve felt much more regret about leaving the mammoths than over the authoritative women.

His mount, Sjindi, bore him eastward, callously delighted he had chosen her. When they reached the variable coastal ice fields that fringed the sea Guriyuve led Sjindi far out on to the ice. Before them, not five dawnshadow-lengths off, jet-black fluid ocean rolled.

Guriyuve scrutinized the surrounding ice. It was about a quarter-mile thick.

He whistled then on a single note. Turning slowly round sunwise, that is east to south to west to north, he kept on whistling. The ice without demur neatly split away, leaving him and his mammoth on an irregular platter, fifteen to seventeen feet in width and some twenty-five feet long.

This ice-raft floated forward and out into the open sea, bearing the hero and his mount with it. *Her* only comment was a solitary triumphant trumpeting.

It seemed Guriyuve could do such things, a kind of magecraft. But all of the Children of Chillel could do sorcerous things, and had talents in magic. It was apparently a question if they recognized their own cunning in this way, or felt it ethical to use it, as to whether they became wizards.

Guriyuve's voyage was definitely the fastest by any account. He positively *flew* around the coastline and then due south. Either there had come a mighty wind to blow the raft, or somehow he called or invented one. Or he had a sail of some magnitude the Crarrowin had spelled, or the amulet spelled. Or the wild gulls, the white-kadi and the inky sea-ravens of the outer rocks, flocked in to fan the raft along. Or it was the horned sharks that surfaced and towed it. These tales abound. Whatever it was, he beat the record, and reached the south-east ocean before his siblings.

247

The route thereafter is charted. But whether fact or fiction none will be sure.

Two months beyond the leave-taking of his human mother, Guriyuve sailed the raft across a deep blue partial strait, a sinking indigo dusk at his back, three full moons glaring in his face.

Huge islands loomed around. They burned like phosphorus in the moonfire. The surf thrashed about their aprons of ice. And tiny icebergs like ivory pins dizzied along.

Until out of the very eyes of the three moons another country rose, isle or continent, but it was not like any similar place.

Resembling spun white sugar the meshes and webs that walled it, architecture or strange vegetation. Guriyuve could not tell. And beyond these twists and twittens was a darkness even the moonshine did not clean. Sjindi, who had been dozing, her legs folded under her like a cat, got up again. Guriyuve looked and saw why. The ice-raft was melting under them. Already the long belly-tresses of the mammoth were salty wet and her feet were awash, as his boots were also. Two hundred yards from the alien shore perhaps they could only drown.

During the prolonged journey the dye grew out of her hair. It was not now two colours but three. When she hacked off the black-tinged ends *still* it was three. For on her right side it was once more black, and on the left side pale brown. But through both the black and the brown threaded strands of silky white.

Beebit's death, the lightning storm, had bequeathed her something else then beside a bone.

Azula remembered Aglin, the mageia from Kandexa. Aglin had tried to befriend Azula after her bereavement, but soon enough all Aglin's concern was directed towards the Magikoy woman Jemhara.

Azula had not said goodbye to Aglin.

Sometimes she held the snake in her arms, rubbing her cheek on its incised smoothness.

Sometimes she stood on her hands, made a hoop of her back,

248

folded herself up like a blanket for a box. Things her mother had done.

The lines Sallus set caught fish, but not regularly. Their provisions they rationed, as with the water. When ice passed them and the sea was still, Sallus would swim over and cut slices for the water-skin. It had all sorts of tastes, this brew, brackish or fishy, yet also perfumed, redolent of heated gardens.

Both of them, the young woman and the young man, surrounded by the immensity of ocean, seemed to grow further off from each other.

They had kept a calendar of days. They were very particular over always making the scratches along the rail, the planking, at length the mast. To start with they had often counted up the days, twenty, forty, seventy. But then they stopped counting.

The chaze seemed content. It fed on fish and never strayed into danger, curling by or about them to sleep. They slept together too, for warmth under the fur. But there was no likelihood these two persons would become sexual partners. They had joined so utterly and dissimilarly, their loneliness was amplified. They were like certain small pieces of frozen land that went by, linked by some causeway or wiry isthmus, and pushed by it also ever apart.

Bad weather occasionally took place.

They and the slim boat survived it all, the lash of hail and outpourings of snow on the sea. Sea-life such as big horned whales surfaced miles off. Cloudy sunsets and dawns would drift away or towards them like cities of basalt and gold. Once lightning writhed and fought overhead, seeming to fill the water with blue-white serpents. They watched it. Azula was not even reminded of the strikes at Kandexa. Her mother's death was growing into her, becoming indigenous. It was beyond memory, ever present in some plaintive, unfigured way.

They met no others of their kind.

Above moons came and went in their random sickles, globes, solos, duets and triads.

Sallus and Azula's was one of the lengthiest voyages of the Chillings. Yet winds did propel them, and something other thrust the boat on too, so it went skimming and darting about the continent, and upwards and around and over and down and along, until they entered a sort of timeless inevitability. Which was that of reaching their insistent and mostly unwanted goal.

For did even Sallus *want* to reach Chillel? He was only magnetized, while a feeling of betraying and dishonour, bred by his upbringing among Rukarian refugees, became always stronger in the back of his brain.

It was an hour after sunrise that they came among a clump of islands, and to the ragged outline of the biggest island or small landmass.

All night a splatter of weird stars had lamped their way. The stars were disturbing for they were in the shape of a crescent moon. 'Ddir,' remarked Sallus the Rukarian.

Azula, also partly Rukarian, had omitted to hear of this god. But she only said, 'Yes?' in her lovely, lonely voice.

The afterglow of dawn still flushed the east dim yellow under blue. It was a fine morning. And despite that the stars in the crescent shape were only just now fading overhead. And . . . it was warm.

Though they had missed the thaw at Kol Cataar, they had been told about episodes of *Summer*.

This must be one.

As more light filled the seascape fish rose like opening flowers. Sallus caught them easily, even with his hands.

'They're bemused – touch, it's warm, the water.'

She trailed her fingers among the swimming fish who, fearlessly unaware of the danger of Sallus's lines and grip, nibbled at Azula's skin. She withdrew her hand with a startled laugh.

She said, 'Like water heated for a bath then cooled.'

Even the curious volutes and kinks of snow that shut in the large island looked *warm*. A warm white, twined with dabbles of warm shiny icicles.

A haze hung over the land. There was a scent in the air, again a kind of perfume, indeterminate.

Sallus gave his attention to the boat. Azula took in the sail. They rowed for shore.

Ice fields lay, as was normal, against the littoral. But there were areas where the sea gushed like a liquid river straight forward to the coast. This itself was dense with layers of ancient permafrost, impacted snow and ice and glassy striated rime.

They landed the boat in one such cove and dragged it in up the cryonic beach. The walls of twisted ice ahead ran irregularly. Mostly, if not always, they came right down to the ice fields, or the open bays. This stretch of beach here was at least four times as broad as the length of the boat.

Slipping and sliding on the polished surface rime, they hefted their last provisions, and Sallus the snake, and began to make towards the fretwork 'wall'.

Several entrances were visible in moments. Sallus chose one and they entered by it.

Was it an ice-wood? Or some cave system largely demolished by weather?

Inside the 'wall' the whiteness now was like lacework or clever tatting. It was sharply beautiful. The sun flittered through, luminous then blinding; the snow seemed sculpted. The 'wall' was full of forms and faces.

Gradually the warmness became spasmodic. In spots it cuddled, in others it was shut away and the ordinary cold hit like knives against their bodies.

'What's that sound, Sallus?'

'Yes, I hear it too. I don't know.'

They paused to listen.

'Is it music?'

'Perhaps.' The snake lay heavy and supportive over his shoulders. These were fearsome sounds, he thought dispassionately.

'I dislike it,' she said.

Flutes maybe, he thought, piping. They fluctuated in little frills and skitters.

The voice of the sea was ebbing away.

Into a region of crimped ice-pillars they walked, then of ice-pillars that seemed to have been clotted into ringlets.

The flute sounds did not stop and now there began to be an

unnerving odour. Sallus was reminded of the roast acid tang of bronze beaten on an anvil.

One more series of openings appeared. These were exits. The structure of lace-caves ended here.

He and she stepped out. The chaze lifted its head.

It must still be broad daylight. They had got through the enclosure in less than a pair of hours. Yet beyond lay dusk.

No sun was to be seen. Smoke hung over everything, in which the metallic smell eddied in gusts. Something must burn somewhere.

Again, as on the slippery shore, they moved carefully and slowly. Last pillars and pylons of the 'wall' phantasmally rose in front of them like bergs in a sea fret.

If it had been music or not, the fluting was gone. Now there was a low hissing. It was like a snake's, and the chaze, which had the faculty of hearing or had gained it, rippled round his neck, undoing its jaws, sipping the air uneasily with a black tongue. Ahead a light shone blearily in the smoke.

The hissing serpent revealed itself.

Before them the snow had broken. Far below a chasm wormed away through the mist. Gaps too undid the murk.

A fluid river bubbled in the channel, sending up a cloud-like fog. In colour the river was like mercury. It had a doleful satiny sheen, lit up from within.

'Don't breathe it.' He pulled her back and they went aside into the thicker fog.

'What is it?'

'I don't know, Azula. A million swords might have melted there.'

'Will it kill us?'

'No. We have a special strength from *her*.'

Azula spat on the smoky ground.

The chaze had burrowed its head inside Sallus's shirt. He drew them both away. Eventually the curve of the land guided them out of the smog and away from the metal river. It was day again here, but a sombre one, the sky overcast with steep banks of cumulus.

'This place is a Hell,' Azula said. 'This bitch lives in a *Hell*.'
'No.'

'*Yes*. She was a whore – oh, so was my mother, but my mother did it professionally, properly. This – this prak, she just did it to ruin men – and women too—'

'It seems she did it to keep them alive. Don't you know yet, every man, and your mother, survived the Death because Chillel had lain with them? Didn't your mother *love* Chillel?'

Azula began to weep. Her tears, horribly, had the same gleam and sheen as the antipathetic river. 'More than me,' she whispered.

'If she had,' he retorted, 'you wouldn't love Beebit as you do.'

After a while Azula wiped off her tears with her three-shade hair. She said, 'Who told you about Chillel? Him – the king?'

'My own mother told me, Tireh. What do you think *she* felt birthing the baby of my father and another woman? Tireh told me about Chillel, and that she was a goddess. She did it in secret. She wouldn't say how she herself knew. Had Bhorth told her? Perhaps she'd only heard stories. My father never did tell me, or not exactly. Maybe he expected I would simply know, as birds know how to fly. Come on. There's a way through this country. Why stand chatting?'

He stalked ahead. The snake did not glance at her.

Azula had the sullen urge to stall, to be left behind, but the territory scared her and presently she trotted after him.

They went by another parallel channel soon. The steam and fog here were localized and sulphurous. The 'river' was a brazen stream, like laval piss. Heat rose and huge cracks in the bank betokened collapse. They hurried on. A steamy smoky swamp began. Dead trees, stripped of both ice and cryogenic foliage, poked like dead black hands from whitish mud. They trod with care the frozen tracks of stone and coal that veined it.

Night fell. To Sallus it seemed some hours too early.

There were no moons, no stars. The sky itself gave off a watered luminosity.

By then they were just through the swamp, and over a final

brook of what seemed liquid vitreous smelling of marzipan and bile.

The air was clear at last. With clarity and cleanness warmness came again.

A big amorphous animal passed quite closely in front of them, undetailed in limited light.

But 'A saurian,' he said. 'Such as there are in the far north at home.'

It paid them no attention.

When it was gone they stared into the formless glimmered dark beyond. What lay ahead was most unsure.

The passage through the dark also went on for some time. Worse than a lack of moons or stars they seemed to have entered a confine, and there light had not yet been invented. The vague sourceless luminosity confused rather than illustrated.

And although they trod again so carefully, there *was* apparently nothing here to blunder into or stumble on. The area was empty not only of true light but of all true elements. Any external sound had died. When they spoke to each other, briefly, in monosyllables, their repressed voices had no expression, were almost without gender.

Eventually they reached a high hedge of what seemed to be fossilized wood. Perhaps millennia-old trees made arcs and arches of carbon.

They went through one of a selection of narrow breaks.

At once everything changed.

It was easy to see. Though no moon was up the night was encrusted by stars, some a piercing citrine or aquamarine, or like watered wine.

Azula had been told religious legends by Beebit when they were young together. 'Is it Paradise?' she asked now. But she did not sound either glad or overawed. If this were heaven it was Chillel's personal and private one. Beebit would not be here.

Sallus said nothing.

They had come out on the brink of a wide plain that curved into shallow valleys and low hills.

Black pelt covered the land. It must be verdure, grasses and trees completely free of ice. Hollows and rounded slopes were powdered by starlight. In the grass that bladed from the ground in front of them, turrets of pale flowers were spread.

The warmth was constant now, and the curious scent had become an unmixed perfume of hothouse blooms, salad and fruit. The eerie piping notes were sounding all about. A bird flew across the stars. It was followed by others. These creatures were what made the piping.

But for all that which returned or began again here, another thing, till then perpetual, was gone. The impulse towards the magnet of Chillel had ended.

Sallus felt this with a bewildered uncertainty. Of course the tug on him *must* end here. He had reached the source. Nevertheless it was as if he had been stranded. He knew the self-angry dismay of the swimmer who had struck out confidently and now found himself too many miles from shore, the mirage he had meant to gain having vanished.

Azula would not feel this.

She had never wished to find Chillel.

Sallus saw her eyes were fixed far off. 'Look,' she said, 'there where that big hill goes up.'

He looked. The hill, the tallest of the vista, lay over beyond what seemed to be groves. The hill appeared to be burning at its top with a fresh and paler light.

'A moon's rising. Two maybe.'

'It isn't the east.'

Nor was it. Despite differences, some of the star formations above were the same as those he had encountered when they sailed over into southern waters. Was this, he wondered, the large stellar cluster that had copied the form of a crescent moon, and which they had seen before they beached here? That was the rogue creation of a god. Therefore it might move eccentrically.

They watched the hilltop. The white glow did not increase or fail. Nothing scaled the height.

Sallus started to think he could see a funnel or chimney which rose from the hill's apex. It must be the centre of the light. But there was so much darkness in this country, so much that was not ice or snow. His eyes might be misled.

More birds fanned over.

He too disliked the noises they made. That twittering and fluting was almost like a melody—

'*Something comes.*'

At her whisper Sallus shook himself back into alertness. He drew his knife and would have set Azula behind him but she would not obey, and had a little dagger clutched in her hand.

Ten men appeared from the nearest of the groves of trees. They were running forward, and hard to make out in the unusual dark, being themselves darker.

He knew them at once. That went without saying. They were his kind – his and Azula's elite kind – get of the goddess.

In an instant they arrived, positioned in the long grass.

None of them said a word.

Sallus said, 'My name is Sallusdon, son of Bhorth. My people are Rukarian.'

The leader of the group, if so he was, nodded. 'I'm Guriyuve, son of Ipeyek. My people are Olchibe and Urrowiy.'

Sallusdon said stonily, 'Does that make us sworn enemies?'

'Not here. Who's she?'

'Our sister, yours and mine.'

'She isn't the proper black.'

Sallus smiled. He put his hand on Azula's shoulder. 'But much better-looking than the rest of us, wouldn't you say?'

Guriyuve stared at Azula. The other nine men, all brothers too and from all the lands of the former continent that was a sword, either stared at her or glanced off.

Azula said, 'I am better than you men in other ways. I am solely *woman-born*.'

'She had no father,' Sallus explained. 'Her mother conceived directly from the goddess.'

'The seed was uninterrupted. I am the stronger. If any doubts, he can fight me now or, if he wants, *try* to cutch me.' Then she leapt straight up and whirled right over in a double somersault, landing on her hands. Like that she strutted up and down, both her legs held up together as if pinned to one another and the sky.

A couple of the others chuckled, applauding.

Then Azula lowered her legs, leisurely, effortless, and with no interval of readjustment stood confronting them. Her tawny skin showed colour in the cheeks. Her eyes were bright.

Sallus was astounded and delighted by her. She had woken up at the right time.

He added graciously to Guriyuve, 'Also I fear you'd have to take me on too, if any of you tried any of that with my sister.'

The snake had roused itself and was running along his arm to Azula's shoulder. The chaze was showing as well who was with whom.

'What's your name, woman?' said Guriyuve.

'Azulamni, daughter of Azulamni-Beebit. My land is Ruk Kar Is.'

'What's up there on that hill?' asked Sallus.

'None of us is sure. We have our camp over there. Better come with us. This country is unsafe.'

More than fifty men sat together on the ground. They were all armed, dressed in the various styles of their native cultures. They did not seem oppressed by the strange heat of the night save in random ways.

Sometimes they talked. Now one would say this, now another would say it or something very like it. They were in agreement, and could each understand exactly what every man there said though the languages were several and the dialects diverse. A band of brothers, now and then they would put a hand on another man's shoulder, to concur or chide – even jokingly to cuff him.

Only Fenzi stood outside the fellowship now, morose and bereft, two states that a year before had been virtually alien to him.

It was not that he could not also fathom the languages, or

make himself clear. It was not that he did not grasp their mutual if contrastingly seen predicament. Nor was it that he was particularly unwelcomed, though none of them, despite the chaffing camaraderie established, was really keen to be friends with any other.

At the beginning he too had been relieved he had arrived, and suspicious of both region and company. But slowly, going about on this night plain with them, or seated in their untidy circle around their frail pale camp fire, Fenzi had learned, he believed, his difference.

For these other men, heroes or minor gods, whatever they were supposed to be, were somehow sure of their *human* station. They had had their mortal fathers and mothers, and come to their awareness of their second goddess-mother as had he. Yet in Fenzi's case there was the dilemma of Arok and of Dayadin. At the time he lived through it Fenzi had not beheld this. Or not done so in any form that encroached on his own ego. But leaving the Jafn Holas in that precipitate hour – Arok dead yet *not* dead, the garth clutched by ice and then broken into – Fenzi saw the facts as they were. They were these: Arok the Chaiord had, in the most elusive manner, represented a father to him, and perhaps Nirri a mother. Though they had been too careful or too fastidious to adopt Fenzi, son of a fisherman, in some hidden corner of Fenzi's heart he had taken the place of lost Dayadin, not only warrior but prince, not only favourite but family. It was not that he valued status much. It was – love. And this loving son had watched his father dragged back from death a soulless husk. Then stridden away towards the other pole of familial love, which was not familial and not love at all, Chillel. His physical father and mother he had not even searched out in the garth. He had not said goodbye. His identity, which he had never before examined, was lost as surely as Dayadin.

I did not even leave Sombrec, my friend, with any grace.

Perturbed, Fenzi moved around the edges of the circle.

Even the patchwork-coloured young woman was seated with them, next to the other newcomer, a Rukar king's son it seemed. Guriyuve the Olchibe, who had told the story of his own advent here, sat listening with the others to Sallus now telling of his voyage. The mammoth Guriyuve had brought had been tethered nearby, munching turf under a black-leafed ilex tree. The Olchibe, after his ice-raft sank, had pulled the animal through the sea to the coast. He had conveniently been able to swim himself, though never before knowing how. Many had complementary tales of swimming abilities, knacks of long-distance running or skirmishing never taught or tried before.

Sallus's story bored Fenzi although the rest seemed involved.

All of it bored Fenzi. The plain that was like a night garden bored, the over-pouring night in which only fleeting twilights indicated morning or evening, and where no sun or moon ever got up. The mythic quality of it was anathema to him, a sort of drudgery. He wished, without words or a single thought to picture it, that he had stayed at the garth. He could have served Arok the best he could. He could have remained himself.

But she. This demoness-goddess they called Chillel, or sweetly sometimes of all things *Winsome*, or by another name he did not quite catch or that maybe they never quite correctly pronounced. *She*, by whatever name, had forced him to her. He had already two mothers, both forsaken. What did he want with *Chillel*?

'She has enslaved us,' he said to the circle.

None of them registered his words. They were intent on Sallus and his yarn.

Only the girl passed her eyes over Fenzi in an odd glance – black, hazel. She was solely female-born it seemed. No father then to answer to.

Turning, Fenzi gazed off across the night. On the hill the chimney or tower had cancelled its intermittent halo. You could not swear it existed.

Fenzi considered going off that way.

Not one of the others, despite the tales *they* would soon produce of the spirits or sprites that menaced them here, was inclined to act.

Fenzi decided he *would* go.

'Farewell,' he bitterly said.

No one heard him. Even the patchwork girl did not.

As he set out, loping through melanic grasses, he pondered if he would meet demons. But obviously he must. He felt no fear, no reserve. He could smell fruit and leaves and an indescribable wild fragrance. The accountancy of his mind did not add up.

How long would it take to cross the plain, surmount the hill, confront the shadowy tower? He did not care. He was already well into his stride, running less towards than away.

'If we sleep, even if some keep watch,' said the Faz-born named Three-Hundred-Eyes, 'a beast will prowl the edges of the camp. If any of us out venture, to hunt the deer-animals that wander there, come it may, this beast, and fasten on someone. That is, despite the deer that take it could.'

Three-Hundred-Eyes had been called this in his own language, for the timeless Faz practice of digging out the optics of dead enemies and fixing them in glass as jewelry. He was not the Fazion who had travelled first to the north-west continent. Three-Hundred-Eyes until recently had stayed home in the islands.

Like all of them he spoke in his own tongue. And all of them knew what he said, as he knew all they said too.

If Threehe had noticed Fenzi turn and go away he did not seem to. He looked at Sallus.

'Like beardless lions these beasts are. Great cats, black as we. With pallid gaze.'

'Liopards,' said another of them, a Chilleling from the Ruk's eastern villages.

'Is what, liopard?' asked the Faz.

'I don't know,' said the Rukarian. 'They're in old ballads.'

All of them puzzled an instant over the word. It had a resonance of *catness*, that was all.

'But you say the beast – or beasts – come and drag men away?' said Sallus. He wanted it clear.

'Yes,' said Threehe. He did not wear any of the monstrous jewelry he had been named for, at least, Sallus thought. What would it have been like to spot what looked like dead Rukarian eyes staring at you, here?

One or two more of them talked about the 'beasts' now.

Beyond the circle and the dim fire little rustlings of the flexive living leaves and grass added descriptive menace.

Perhaps they were all mad; perhaps any who came here went mad.

'Don't you hunt and kill them, then?' asked the girl, out of nowhere. Her voice was interrogatory, even brusque. 'You take the deer, but the liopards take *you*?'

'They're sorcerous,' said another of the Chillelings. He spoke to her contemptuously. He was also Olchibe and she a woman from the Ruk, and besides not properly coloured in. Had she been pure black like himself and his brothers, like their mother indeed, he might have been more polite. Or if she had been yellow and a Crarrow, of course.

But Azula performed her trick. From a sitting position she rose fluently to stand before them on one hand. It was certainly attention-grabbing.

'So are *we* sorcerous,' announced Azula. 'Or are *you* only cowards?'

They stirred scowling, and Sallus too between amusement and concern.

But Azula simply spun herself into the air, effortlessly hooked a bough above her, swung on to it and crouched there.

She peered down at them, making in her throat a kind of lion-ish growling. Her eyes glittered from the fire, opal, agate.

Many among the Chillelings sprang up.

And from out of the dark rim of night beyond the firelight, Azula's growl was replied to in a lower and more fearful register.

They were behind him, several of them from the sounds.

As he ran images burst in Fenzi's mind.

When first he had arrived in this night country, he had thought the men's mutterings of beasts might even be apocryphal or analogous to the dark, and the dark mystery of Chillel. But soon a time came when he woke violently from the deep sleep of a sleep night and saw with his own eyes a jet-black creature, lean, cat-like, and untenuous, pulling a fellow sleeper backward from the fire.

Fenzi had tried to rise and go to assist the man, who had not apparently woken even with the fangs of the animal fastened in his clothes and hair. Yet he could not move. His brain jolted and raged but his body lay inert. A cold sweat broke out on his skin and he felt sick to death. In this horrible trance he, and all the others gathered there, watched as the chosen victim was drawn away into the night.

When finally he had been able Fenzi staggered up. He reached the place beyond the fire and tried to see among the trees. He called to the rest to help him. None did so. Instead a few crawled off and vomited. In a while so did he. After, he fell down nearby and lost consciousness. In the morning it was not discussed, and he would have reckoned it a fever and some fever dream but for the marks on the turf and the small fact of a man's being missing.

At his questions they grumbled that they had warned him. They would not even calculate how many of their brothers had been removed in this same way.

Fenzi searched about for bones. He found nothing.

Some night periods later he was taken hunting with six other men. They brought down a deer from a wild herd. Even these deer were not quite like any he had met before. The night deer were very dark, almost black, the better for camouflage probably.

Then, while they were bleeding their kill before the return to camp, two of the black cat-beasts came slinking down the hillside. They were plainly in sight, and Fenzi gave a shout. His knife was already in his grip and painted with hot blood. Yet once more the awful, insulting horror of paralysis enveloped him, and all of them. Their eyes could move, their hearts still leadenly beat, thoughts leapt in panic in their skulls. But they could not operate hand or limb. Like thinking statues they must stand and await their choosing by the beasts.

Now he saw them close, Fenzi examined them with a type of irrational and petrified need to find them entirely supernatural. But they were not.

One padded right up to him. It lifted on its hind legs and put one heavy forepaw on his left shoulder. It sniffed him briefly, its eyes of ghostly flame dripping their gleam into his. He had thought he was to be that night's choice, and his senses flickered out. It was less terror than nausea. He counted himself dead anyway. As he fell miles down inside the confine of his own stone-struck body, he felt the sinuous rasp of *its* body glide against him and away.

When he came to he was sprawled in the grass with four others. This time he managed not to puke. Two of them did. And two were gone, of course. None of the survivors had seen, as they never did, where the great cats had dragged them.

They called their goddess-mother Chillel. All of them had learned this name, either told it or somehow finding it within their own brains. Now another name surfaced among them.

Fenzi heard it uttered over and over in his mind.

Vangui . . . Vangui . . .

What did the name represent? Was it the secret and absolute name of Chillel? It had, unlike all other names, no *meaning* in any language Fenzi knew, or had discovered he could speak.

Vangui . . .

It was a dark name, a melanic name, shaded like the grasses and groves and hills of the island. It was an *angry* name with blade-like edges. A hungry name that hunted for its sons, hypnotized, selected, seized and abducted them. A name that devoured.

Was it that he gambled now the demon cats would not pursue him if he ran *towards* the unholy, part-amorphous tower on the hill?

If it had been that, he miscalculated.

Really Fenzi had most likely only decided, on some obscure

level of inner reasoning, that he would seek his inevitable fate rather than be *picked out* by it.

Autonomy however would not be allowed.

Once only he glanced back.

He was by then approaching the higher ground, the tree-lathered base of the larger hill where the tower was, or sometimes was. Tonight he could not see it, and no moonglow burned there. When he looked over his shoulder the stars were eager enough to show what followed.

How they pelted on. They poured over the starry nightscape like spilled silvery oil.

Surely by now they should have reached him, brought him down, if only by causing the paralysis that they – or she – inspired. Maybe it was their entertainment, to hunt like this with delay, cat with mouse.

There were nine of them tonight.

Nine, and all focused, fur and fang and talon, on him.

An honour?

Fenzi ran.

Twelfth Volume

NIGHT'S PLEASURES

'Who passes?'
'I am you.'
'*I* am here.'
'*I* am here and you are *there*.'
'Are you my shadow?'
'You are mine.'
'*What* are you then?'
'What *you* are.'
'Begone.'
'I am gone.'
'He is gone. But where then am *I*?'

Apparently unanswerable riddle, found in various forms:
Most lands of most continents

ONE

At the top of the stair the Gargolem stood, looking down towards the city of Kol Cataar.

How many years had passed? Less now than two. Everywhere time was working differently as, in the worlds beyond the world, it seemed it always did.

Two mortal years had even so watched the re-creation of this city into a version of the burnished jewelled metropolis of Ru Karismi. Under the instruction of the Gargolem, the lesser golems had performed the task with the efficiency and speed of elegant ants.

It was sunrise. The sun flashed and was suddenly in the eastern window of the sky. The new and now impressive urban heights winked ruby and diamond from the tinted parasols and domes of mansions, palaces. The thousand steps of the rebuilt marble stair flooded with a vainglorious blush. The thousand statues, diagonally set, flaunted the dawn like rose-quartz not figures of steel.

Daybreak coursed and filled the lower city and gradually the streeted slopes. Other objects of metal shone. There was no waterway. The frozen necklace of the River Palest did not exist in Kol Cataar. Nor did any occult Insularia, warren of the almighty Magikoy, tunnel under the river and the thoroughfares. Only three Magikoy survived. They did not require – or merit – an Insularia. But the Great Markets, even the temple-town of the Ruk's neglected gods, lay, with the endless threading weave of boulevards, squares and alleys, spread like a map for many miles. High barriers enclosed the complex. As before they were broken only by tall gates, Southgate, Northgate. The night's torches were being doused there as along the winding roads.

But one other thing was in Kol Cataar the Phoenix. And in her forerunner this had not existed.

Although the sun was up clouds were massing from the east. Light snow was driving in torn ribbons across the face of morning.

As the snow slanted in over the city it altered. White feathers changed to transparent beads. Then it was *rain* falling on Kol Cataar. Rain, unknown as such for five centuries. And the rain libated upon the orchards and the gardens, the parks and lawns, catering for the thirsts of cedars blue with needles, oaks and tamarinds with leaves of bronze and rinds of wooden bark. Into the goblets of drinking peach trees and aloes, apple groves and clinging grapevines and roses, the crystalline breakage of the tender rain plashed down. Pots and jars, tubs and big barrels stood waiting on every terrace, by every wall, at every public corner. Had you never tasted rain? Cool and sweet, far better than reconstituted ice. Better than wine. Seven thousand households would serve rain tonight in cups of clay, pewter, gold and glass. Children erupted from the differing prisons of artisan apprenticings and scholar schools, to splash and roister in puddles like ponds. Women washed their long hair over balconies.

Thryfe trod up the slippery stair in the rain, not pausing to breathe though he had climbed the entire thousand treads without hesitation.

There was no longer any hint of a limp. His left hand flexed with ordinary strength as he wiped rain from his eagle's eyes. 'Good morning, Gargo.'

Bhorth, King Paramount, waited on his balcony, looking at Thryfe.

The balcony jutted from the King's Hall of Kol Cataar, out over the glittering three-mile-deep abyss of sunlit rain and city.

For a moment Thryfe was caught by an eerie flinch of déjà vu.

But this often happened, for the new city was deliberately so like Ru Karismi, and Bhorth was the last of the kings.

Thryfe anyway was always now at odds with himself. The god's healing and revitalization of him left a strange dichotomy. Young and strong and fit as ten years before, Thryfe's body contained the bitter and dissatisfied mind of an older and more damaged man. Was Bhorth too in this state? The god had touched him also. Yet straight and vital Bhorth carried the mind and heart of a man who had lost his son. *And I*, thought Thryfe, *lost everything*. But he struck the thought off at once.

'The augurs that were taken, Bhorth, have reshaped their aspect.'

I choose similar words. He had recalled the former time this one reminded him of. Not déjà vu, only memory. It had been when first he warned them of the advent of the Lionwolf.

Bhorth did *not* remember. He said, 'In what way?'

'Your son is alive. This is now sure. But *where* he is is indecipherable.'

'Then – it *is* death.'

'No. I have said. He lives.'

'So our wretched priests tell us we all continue to do, after dying.'

Thryfe felt the familiar impatience.

He had, delivering that first warning, foresensed the death of the Ruk, and of her kings and people. But Bhorth survived and the population of Kol Cataar had decidedly risen from the ashes. The recurrent influxes of Rukarians from all over the south, east and west disproved previous prophecy. The nation had seemed to re-emerge from beneath the very snows.

Thryfe chided himself as recently he often had to do.

Be kind to him. All that remained was duty. Besides Bhorth was a good king. And unhappy.

'Sallusdon your son may return to you, Bhorth. But for now some other bond has claimed him.'

'He's trapped?'

'Perhaps. Perhaps willingly.'

'Is it the girl?'

'Azulamni? No. There's a hint of her presence somewhere in his life, that's all. You know, Bhorth, don't you, when the gods meddle in human affairs, these lacunas appear. Sometimes even they are physical. The problem of where Sallus is seems like that, a physical place, some inaccessible and unknown crag or island, maybe.'

'Chillel,' said Bhorth. 'She has him.'

'A goddess then. You have some hope from that. She was, I think you said, only very nice to you.'

Bhorth nodded at the irony. 'Yes. Extravagantly nice. And saved my hide into the bargain. What goddess is she, do you guess, Thryfe, eh? If *he's* the sun.'

The peculiar conversation was quite normal. Hundreds of persons must consider in this way, now deities wandered over the world in full view.

'You told me she was black, like your son.'

'Black as night. Stunning as the moon.'

Both men glanced again down the terraces of the city to where, in Ru Karismi, the River Palest would have shown, the entry to the Insularia under its ice.

'Night then,' said Thryfe.

'There are a collection of gods of night in our temple-town,' said Bhorth bleakly, 'and have been for centuries. Why does night need another one?'

And they laughed quietly, angrily, these two elderly and impaired men, there on the glittering balcony in the warm sunshine and the smell of flowers, and their unlined, healthy skins.

Beyond the phoenix city, the fields and orchards had piece by piece extended. Banks of fog attended their outer limits, reaction to the warmth and chemical shifts of permafrost and soil. No wolves were seen here now, though in patches among the trees and vine-stocks sometimes a votive or shrine might have been put up. Most featured the Rukarian gods of agriculture. One or two had a small clumsy stone effigy that did depict a black dog or wolf. Winter had departed from the area, but blind instinct must have dictated a little insurance.

Where the hot-spring weather ended, outside the fog, icicles formed long skinny stalagmites growing a hundred feet or more from the ground.

After the stalagmite fence the Ice Age recommenced.

This plain of wind-riven white bore no sign of anything unusual. Here snow, when it fell, *snowed*.

From a distance out there nothing was visible of Kol Cataar. Even at sunrise or set no single ornament glinted on her heights. But as Thryfe had noted, this had not prevented thousands of refugees from seeking, discovering and entering the city.

The phenomenon of the phoenix Spring was equated wrongly but handily with those abrupt oases of heat and flora that now and then happened in the southern continent. All oases vanished in a period of time short or long. But as longer periods might last up to fifty years, the tales reported, better make hay while the sun shone. A man could be dead in much less.

The heat was not really intense. It would have killed them if it had been after such adaptation to cold. The plants, the grains and flowers too, had needed only the faintest tepidness to bring them on.

Oddly, the heat sometimes caused one curious mirage or hallucination, to the east of the foggy perimeters.

There a stone, tall as a man, appeared. It would seem to have been erected in a stand of sorry wheat that had tried to grow but, just too far outside the limit, had frozen in upright black bars. The statue looked real enough, and rough-hewn enough, a male figure of fierce and regal bearing. The face was the most finely carved, with even a short beard carefully delineated. But parts of all the rest of it, including forehead and hands, had not been fully excavated from the pitted native granite.

A sourceless cruel blue glow sometimes played about the statue when the sky was overcast. Then it looked ominous. But at other moments it was not uncheerful, and certainly the most interesting of the votary objects kept outside the city.

Then again the statue would disappear as regularly as it showed up.

Some had even gone out to visit it and witnessed its melting away in the air in front of them.

None had ever had physical contact with the stone.

A child who had strayed into the black wheat had told her mother that once she saw a young man standing there also. He had been studying the statue. The mother, aware of all the travellers who presently flocked to Kol Cataar in their wagons and slees, took no notice until the child insisted on description. 'His hair was *red* – it was red as the red glass windows in the king's high palace. His eyes were red too, inside. But then he smiled at me and his eyes were dark blue like—' at which point the recital ended in a shriek. Mother had slapped child.

'Sew up your tongue! Don't tell lies! Don't ever speak of *him*.' For though they had, almost none of them, this time seen him, or even ever seen him in the past, the legend persisted of the demonic invader Vashdran, who had nearly brought history to an end.

Vashdran . . . Lionwolf . . . Nameless . . .

As he walks over the world the god memorizes himself, all he has been, all he must become, and those intersections where Before and To Be mingle.

When formerly dead in Hell, some of his first life had gone with him to help him make, from the material of his psyche, the country and cities there. But aspects from his future had also followed him, for in the kingdoms and republics of the fore and afterlife time existed/exists exotically or not at all.

So, for example, the mendicant priests from the original Kol Cataar had gone around in Hell, one of them singing too, if not as well as he would on earth.

Hell had *been* Lionwolf, and he his Hell. The King of Hell, also Lionwolf, was a being hewn of mobile if obdurate stone. And now at the border of the place of Lionwolf's third rebirth, the Hell King was an idol in the frozen wheat.

Lionwolf had indeed studied his statue, or granite alter-ego.

The addition of the beard – something *grown* – had beguiled Lionwolf. In Hell the stone King was hairless. The beard represented, rather firmly, the idea of age and wisdom, a mature and noble god less hard of heart than of fist, sinew and resolve. To Lionwolf he seemed far kinder than the smooth-shaven monarch who had smitten him with agony and dragons.

Did Vashdran recollect later the girl child who had ambled up to him that day? Yes.

She had glimpsed the scarlet crescent that lit his pupils from some angles, but was not afraid. When blue-eyed he smiled, she smiled too and he saw *his* smile sink into her. She would live now to be extremely ancient, without illness and frequently lucky. A shame her mother would hit her – he foresaw it like a tiny blotch on the snow. But such problems would become rare.

He loved to bless them. He loved to heal them. He loved it with such a savage and barely containable delight that he knew he must curb it in himself. It was not his task to refashion all humanity to perfection, as the army of gargolems had done with the city of Kol Cataar. Mortals grew another way. He tried to leave them alone, but occasionally – this indulgence.

When the child had darted off Lionwolf walked on.

That too was somewhat like the controlling of love. He could fly, levitate, dis- and re-integrate, simply *be* elsewhere. And so, he walked.

At first the boundary of fog, where it thickened, had been impassable to men – even to a mage like Thryfe. Now any could go in and out for the warmth of the magical Spring had consolidated itself and was secure. Once Lionwolf had walked beyond the loosened barrier, however, he might have expected to see no other except some approaching refugee.

Yet about three miles further along the plain he passed someone neither approaching nor going from the city.

It was Tirthen, the black wolf.

Lionwolf spared Tirthen a glance, without actually looking at him.

Dismissed, this lurid personification of Winter, Tirthen caught

Lionwolf by the shoulder. Save it was not obviously the catching of a shoulder by a hand, not even quite a shoulder.

'And?' said Lionwolf.

Tirthen *walked* by him. He was handsome as before, clad now in black wolfskin that matched his wolf-black hair, and icy mail.

'I slept too long,' said Tirthen. 'I missed *your* waking.'

'But, well,' said Lionwolf.

'I met your mother once,' said Tirthen. 'Or twice. Among icebergs we fought. The second meeting was more civil.' The golden god said nothing. The cold god said, 'Perhaps Saphay and I will grow fond of one another. She's a juicy piece.'

'She is not,' said Lionwolf, 'exactly my mother.'

Even Tirthen, who seemed to have learned his dialogue hanging as icicles on the eaves of taverns, was shocked.

'She conceived and bore you.'

'She conceived and bore me. Next Wasfa did so. A while ago Jemhara also conceived and bore me, despite your artistic attempts to prevent it.'

'Three mothers. I shall visit each of them. Compare succulence.'

Winter had lost much of his grandeur and his compelling in the snare of human-like impersonation. It was a complicated role to learn, that. Harder than bad dialogue. Yyrot had fallen in such a trap, but was not unhappy. But then Yyrot had given up his more strident side centuries ago.

Lionwolf anyway seemed unconcerned. They walked swiftly. Five or seven miles skidded by about them at each step.

Tirthen began to murmur in his beautiful voice.

After all, something up his wolfy sleeve?

'Ice twilight,' murmured Tirthen, 'twice light. Ice twilight . . . twice light.'

'A riddle.'

'There are others. Who passes, asks the wolf. The wolf answers, I am you that passes. No, says the wolf, you are my shadow. Your shadow, says the wolf, is me.'

'There's another shadow and another wolf,' said the other god. He sounded wholly like a man, Lionwolf, and in his tone was the identical intelligent impatience of his third father, Thryfe the magician.

'Your first daddy, Zethzez.'

'The Sun Wolf,' said Lionwolf.

'He is not greater than I. So much is self-evident. Is he greater than you?'

Lionwolf halted suddenly.

Ridiculous. Borne by his own supernatural speed Tirthen had steamed on over the horizon like a comet, and was gone. Then had to hurry back in an explosion of disturbed snow.

'It gives you pause,' tried Tirthen. Trying it seemed to cover his overshot.

Lionwolf smiled.

Even Winter personified could not help but produce in him a strand of compassion and care.

Besides you could just see some vestige of Yyrot in Tirthen now. Yyrot had left his job in the Rukar pantheon in order to spend more time with his family. Ddir, the other member of Zth's trio, had done this ages before in order to spend more time with his stars. Debris, fall-out from Yyrot's resignation, had partly enabled Tirthen no doubt to be coined. But Tirth was a god of Simisey initially. There was, if Lionwolf could detect it, a racial memento of Curjai to him.

'We'll be friends, you and I,' said Lionwolf, smiling still. Tirthen writhed under the smile's glory. It hurt him, it pierced his icy marble with golden veins. 'Lalt and Tilan,' said Lionwolf, flirtatious. They were the Simese heroes Curjai had told him of. He batted Tirthen gently across the cheek. He did not do more.

Tirthen might have thawed. Instead he vanished.

There was only pleasure in the god Lionwolf. All he kept with him was affection. Though his love and healing could be witty, cynical, potentially caustic, they were ambient. He loved his enemies too. To those who might hate him he was only too pleased to do good. He existed in light. He no longer cast any shadow at all.

On he walked. Places of the earth were passed. From his footsteps vines grew and streams of liquid water sprang. The dying revived at the distant whisper of his breath. The living prospered.

At last a night came when he dreamed of his first father, Zeth Zezeth.

By then Lionwolf was far from the Ruk. He had gone up into the southern mountains that divided the continent. Kraagparia had been across the border and in his first incarnation Lionwolf had entered it. The awful horror which had preceded the entering no longer troubled him, though it burned itself into his id and there lived with him, in harmony, but such things were only possible to gods.

Kraagparia conversely did not appear to be there now. Those people had learned long before the irrelevance of concrete blockades, the immovable shutness of flimsy things. Or, they were only serenely hiding.

In the dream Lionwolf, a god of love, unearthed sheer venom from the cellar of his essence. Everything that has life after all will cast a shadow. A sun more than most. A burned sun more even than most.

The dream.

Zth drives his chariot through the gaps between the stars, which are golden too, azure and amber and mauve.

Lionwolf flies towards him through the airless outer environment of space. Up here are the gateways, or so they say, to afterlives and astral planes and a medley of fascinating alternate venues.

A moon crests the black hills of the interstellarium.

Seen clear of the dark reflection of the earth, the moon is permanently full, round and blissfully white as the rounded bud of a white rose. A second moon pursues the first. Then comes another from around another space-hill. But two more rise next. *Five* moons?

Lionwolf to a large extent ignores this achievement.

He flies on, wingless and profound, straight against the meteor of Zth's chariot.

The team of blue wolves leap from the traces.

Lionwolf is in the vehicle.

He grabs and manhandles – godhandles – Zth, who struggles molten as a torch, evasive though grasped.

'Let go of me,' snarls Zth. 'Do you want death? *What* do you want?'

'*He I have hold of,*' answers Lionwolf. 'And I have hold of *you.*'

'I shall punish you.' Zth speaking like sparks. '*Then* let us see how you will be. To me you can do nothing.'

'I will kill you.'

'How?' Zth relaxes. They poise in the chariot in space, clinging together like surprised lovers. '*How* will *you* kill *me*?'

'I trapped you in my shadow. Only to *kill* you should be easy.' Lionwolf is aware that both Zth and he repeat phrases already spoken. Yet even repeated the words are not what they were. Lionwolf says with a hate so velvet it puts the scratchy rasp of love to shame: 'Your death is mine. I own it. It is all for me now.'

A light has begun, even as they have striven, even as they have become quiescent in each other's incorrigible clasp.

Where the five – six? – white moons ascended in round plates, the solar frenzy comes as a disc so white it is a rainbow, and from its circle a billion spears, daggers, swords stick out, which are the rays it has extruded to rend and rip the fabric of the void. And the void too flames. All space is scarlet, scarlet and blue. Aureoled in the inferno the miniature ball of the earth so far down seems destined for cremation. But the earth only flushes mildly along one narrow curve. This boiling terror then is an old sun, an elderly, bitter old sun in a shallow sheath of healthy splendid fire.

Lionwolf hefts his father, his only true father and finally his only true hate, from the chariot.

He holds him out over the rising disc of rainbows, knives and blades.

'Look, Dadda,' says Lionwolf. '*Look, Dadda.* Yours.'

And hurls him down into the heart of the sun.

Sham, city of Ol y'Chibe and y'Gech, in the years of its magnificence has acquired a single temple. The building, built of obsidian and plated with brass, gold and polished coal, dominates a rise. It is reached by a road of black slate on which, over and over, the name of the god is inscribed in patterns.

Sometimes the god drops by, and is without exception terrified by his temple.

He lurks in disguise on the thoroughfare, squinting at pilgrims, lines of priests and fine animals brought for sacrifice, mumbling and cursing under his breath.

On countless occasions the god has been arrested for blasphemy, chucked into prison or prepared for slaughter by Shamish gladiators or giant crocs. Of course he always miraculously disappears before he can confront and so hurt them. Ah! they exclaim, it was the Great God himself, testing us.

The disguised god, an age-loaded beggar, a ragged stripling, even a fat priest, has plucked up his courage and actually gone inside the imposing fane. Here he has gaped groaning amid the stew of incense and chanting.

Once he allowed himself to get drunk. Allowed, since a god needed to permit his ethereal cells to process alcohol in a human manner. Staggering and shouting he had charged about the enclosure, scattering acolytes and worshippers, tumbling over two sacred goats kept to provide milk offerings, ending in the silver font. Somewhere in the mayhem he had shed his disguise. He had not meant to. He was identified instantly. Ah! Now the Great God was displeased.

Three hundred people threw themselves on their faces. Many voided bladders and bowels as they did so, the two goats included.

Gurithesput, Great God of Ol y'Chibe and y'Gech, sat in the font. He knew by now it was hopeless to explain, let alone try to dissuade them. He had tried before.

Oh, he had tried and tried.

Yet these lands, which had rejected all chance of any god coming between them and their untrammelled faith in their own ability to live, die and reincarnate, had taken to this deity with gusto. Not only rumours but evidence of his swift gain of adulthood, his gift of healing, his just peacemaking, his magicianship and – decidedly – his ethnic purity, wooed and won his fellow countrymen. Seldom are any believers more fanatical than converts. What has changed our mind, convinced not others but *us*, must be of superior quality. Ego triumphs over logic. Perhaps too they had been a little lonely, having only themselves ever to rely on.

At least he had now ensured their warlike ways were channelled. They went into contests and the games in the Sham stadia, most of which were 'friendly' bouts. Feuds among neighbouring sluhtins now hesitated to start. If started, discussion generally settled them.

This must be a virtue.

Disarming them, Guri did feel some pride. His appalling punishment in his own Hells had been his judgement on himself for his days of warriorism, the tortures, rapes and executions he had performed so righteously. A racist then, he had never fully thought other races had sensibilities. Had not credited they felt horrible pain exactly as a man or woman of his own kind did. Hell had cured him. He did not want his nation to stray on to that same path which had spawned himself and his brothers. This being so he also attempted to open the eyes of y'Chibe and y'Gech to other societies. But in this country of the past, few examples of such other peoples came their way.

Guri had therefore searched about the continent, roaming even as far as the outer isles that would, in the future, become the Vormland and the habitats of Fazions and Kelps. He found that at this date these peoples too were ignorantly insular. They also viewed Guri, even acting human, with total fright. The Jafn race along the north-east coast of the continent were primal too. If not reduced to gibbering by Guri's black hair and yellow complexion, they treated him as an object of curiosity, a sort of silly vrix. For the Jafn were even then riddled by such sprites and devils. The odd thing was God-Guri could not see these spirits. He would have expected to, for in his future they had been real enough in their own subreal way. Once a ghost he had been able to spot them if he let himself. He suspected now the Jafn must gradually have *made* them real inadvertently from belief, the constant repetition of superstitious avoidance or night-fear horror stories told during the many nights they refused to sleep. The schizophrenic gods of the Rukar had evolved like that, surely. Faith was a dangerous weapon.

And the Rukar were the final mystery. For nowhere could Guri unearth or unsnow any trace of them.

The southern north and west that had been their wide territory had nobody there. The southern east had only the tribal louts with mottled skin, who worshipped wooden gods, like Ranjal in Guri's future, or volcanoes that puffed out smoke.

Thus Guri brought no introductory human offers home to Olchibe. The examples he had seen would have gone mad or died of alarm, which could hardly have recommended them.

He did, where Olchibe had some inkling of another area through trade or accident, tell tales of such cultures. His nation sat marvelling, loving every word of what they acclaimed as imaginative fantasy.

When the temple went up in Sham it bothered Guri too for another reason than his hike to godhood.

He had been elsewhere on his journeys, sometimes riding his mammoth. Though leisurely, he thought he had taken months, no more. Mostly he had not indulged in riding. He could spin as he would from here to there or anywhere in seconds, or, if dawdling, hours.

On returning to Sham his immediate shock had been nightmarish. Such a work as the temple, unaided by god-power, or the weird sorcerous-mechanical power the later Rukar would come to have, must have needed several years.

Soon he knew, questing disguisedly about the streets, the temple had been erected at vast speed and the cost of a few thousand lives, in one and a half decades.

Guri had not grown older, naturally. His divine aggregate seemed fixed at about twenty-five, twenty-eight. But where had fifteen years gone then? He went to look at the mammoth. He read the signs. It was old now and must retire. The mammoth might have been his calendar, but willing and stoical in the way of its kind, it had not complained. It had still fluidly knelt and risen, galloped and preened; still threatened over-feisty wild elephant or lurking fleer-wolves mewling in the wastes. Now he praised it and saw that it went to be a pampered stud. And Guri found himself alone. He could not however shake the thought that, at the beginning of his short journeying about, the mammoth had *not* been old at all.

Static amid mortality and mortal time Guri grew mithered. He was powerless at least in this. Despite his regression to the past he could not retrace what now had been let slip. Some laws still applied. If not to him, certainly to the forward propulsion of the earth.

He did manage to squeeze from time one backview of the temple's building. It was about five years in when he reached it. But the scene was like a picture painted on a rickety wall. It faded and wobbled, could not be entered.

Sometime after this, Guri fell in a sort of love with a priestess of his own order.

Until then, after leaving his sluhtin, he had been abstinent. Sex had become an itch he scratched in private, quickly and without much interest. His godness had not enhanced masturbation either.

The attraction to his own Olchibe priestess was classic both in its mythic precedents and ordinary inevitability.

Guri tried to hold off. But why hold off? He would not harm her. It was about then he recalled Lionwolf in similar circumstances. Lionwolf had not harmed. Nor had he sired a single child. Guri had only sired his own self.

Tactfully Guri sought the priestess in one more guise as a mortal. But he was a good-looking specimen now he had to admit.

The girl had been a Crarrow. The priestesses were generally picked from the covens. She was combing her long raven locks when she saw Guri standing outside in the courtyard, with a pitcher of greenish wine.

'How did you get in?' she asked coldly. No men were allowed in the precinct.

'I saw you in the temple,' said Guri, exquisite in the braid-paint-skull haute couture of ancient Ol y'Chibe. 'I climbed the wall.'

'I saw you, too,' lied the girl. He had not been there, was only here.

He gave her a fig he had woken from the ice. It was like a small brown-purple animal, and she stroked and toyed with it until she nearly drove him out of his mind.

She was fourteen, a virgin, and once they had joined on the slender bed the priestess girl said to him, 'You are the Great God, Gurithesput.'

'*Shush*,' he chittered, breaking out in a thick sweat which, being what he now was, was delicious as wine and honey. 'He'll smite me! Great God hear amen.'

The girl giggled. 'No, I foresaw,' she said – her name meant Kitten. 'You are God.'

'Ah? No, no. You're mistaken.'

'You have lived and died and lived,' she murmured, 'you have lain with mermaids, you are uncle to the sun.'

He realized then their coupling had brought on a trance, and sincerely she had sussed him. He possessed her again hoping to quash the visions. She slept, and he left her. Next night he was eagerly back.

She knelt down on the floor, touched the stone with her forehead, got up and jumped into his arms.

To be the mistress of a god was only a treat to her; nothing onerous or scaring.

Kitten did not become pregnant. This disappointed her, he knew. Then one evening Gurithesput entered her cell and Kitten lay asleep on her bed, cold as ice and dead.

He did not examine her. He had been tentative and subtle, unleashing his need only when sure she was able to withstand him. She had been so happy. Her body was unscathed, outwardly, inwardly. Yet – he must have murdered her, his lovely girl.

Had Magica died too? Up there in the Gech swamps, dying abruptly from the delayed sting of the paranormal. Had they *all* died before their time, the ones he had lain with in the sluhtin? Some had, he knew – was that his fault?

It was soon after this, after they had buried Kitten with innocent ceremony and written on the basalt above her grave the pattern of God, that Guri got drunk that time and ran amok in his temple, finishing up in the wet font, with a carpet of terror-shat people all around.

In that awful moment he faced responsibility like a white-hot brand.

'All is well,' boomed the Great God, shaking off his drunk. 'I have tested you. You are not wanting. I am yours now. I am your Great God. Trust in me, trust and obey what I have taught you. Not feared of me, are you? *No.* You needn't fear your God, your old Olchibe God. I like you all finely, and you me. Listen to me, you call out for me. Call by my name, which is—'

Three hundred voices quavered: *'Great God.'*

'Amen,' said Guri, and slid away and through a crack in the incense. He would still haunt the temple, the road, and grumble, but the fight was out of him.

Mostly, now, in a cupboard of darkness he sat alone, and let their prayers ring and tremble like a far-off outer sea. He unbraided his hair. He had spoken to them like kiddlings, like *his* kiddles. They were all the children now he could ever have.

A month after her death he left the bough of a fig tree on Kitten's grave. It rooted, but then froze to vitreous. Those who saw it made a fuss. Then they forgot. But Guri thought on and on about Lionwolf, the very first one he had ever promised special protection of a non-mortal type. He had done it with phrases inadvertently resurrected at Sham. *Uncle to the sun,* she had said. Olchibe Uncle Guri.

It was a day of pale air. You looked at this air and gauged from it the closed veil of the cold. This was a day in aspic.

Lionwolf walked down from a tall mountain, possibly one of the complicated chain that separated the southern Ruk from Kraagparia, or not.

He walked as nothing human could, his position sometimes horizontal and his head on a parallel with the plain below.

Where he reached the summit's foot an ice lake opened. Someone else sat on a mound in the middle of it, about a mile away. He seemed to be fishing through a hole in the ice.

Lionwolf was curious, perhaps. He had retained certain everyday emotions and some whims, though they were often of the more animal variety. He sped out on to the lake, skated towards the seated fisher. He spoke without delay.

'Caught anything tasty, Uncle?'

Guri looked up. His doleful expression morphed to one of embarrassed relief. 'No. I can make them swim up, but then I take pity and let them go. The fishing line's just for convention.'

Lionwolf sat down beside him.

They peered into the hole, which was suddenly blocked by the faces of some twenty or thirty fish, wriggling to leap up and touch the gods.

Lionwolf blessed them, breathing a golden sigh into the hole. The fish themselves goldened. They dropped back, and for a while both gods watched them shining under the ice as they frisked about.

'They'll live for years now, immune to all peril,' said Lionwolf. 'I must stop doing this.'

'Is that what you do here?'

'Too much. But – it's a wonderful feeling. You pass a sick man on a village street and let what you are enfold him. He – alters. A bird falls dead out of the sky. In my footstep. It shakes itself and flies off like a firework.'

'You intellectualize too much,' grunted Guri. He could hear his own Rukarian phraseology. 'It's your corrupt Rukar blood. Even now.' He drew out the line. One extra fish came up with it, not hooked but clinging on, waggling at Lionwolf.

'Oh, very well.'

Golden, the fish plunged back with a silent, noisy wail of ecstasy.

'Well, I've healed a bit, but I've not done anything kind,' said

Guri. 'Maybe that will balance yours.' He stared at the ice hole as it closed. And told Lionwolf of Kitten.

Lionwolf listened without comment, then turning began to braid Guri's hair, threading into it as he deftly did so tiny beast skulls and Olchibe beads conjured from nowhere.

Guri let this soothe him. Lionwolf had always had a gentle side. He was complete now, so fully masculine at last the female element too had found its parameters.

'Did that . . .' Guri paused. 'Have you ever had a similar mishap?'

'Diddled a girl and found it killed her? Not last time I was here. They all lived. I doubt I changed them. This time, well. I haven't had the urge.' The god smiled. Guri felt the smile soak into him, warm weather. Above them a hole had appeared in the paleness very like the hole Guri had made in the ice. Blue sky filled it. 'Rather,' amended Lionwolf, 'I've had the urge, but for only one.'

'The black woman.'

'Chillel Winsome Toiyhin.'

'Is that her name now? Ask her to pardon me. I said *woman*. Goddess.'

'She won't take offence, Guri. But I don't see her. Except in my mind and in the little independent brain that dwells in my loins.' Casually he added, 'Chillel is her dispassionate name, the crescent moon that is a physician and a whore. Winsome is her wife-mother name, the moon at full. Now she's the warrior moon, celibate, the thinnest crescent before darkness. Vangui is that name, but Vangui too has her other self, Toiyhin, the moon's shadow, like a bird.' Lionwolf shrugged. One of the fish, the last one probably, was still glimmering busily about under the ice. It gave off an inaudible merry squeaking. Lionwolf said, 'I inadvertently filled the new Ruk capital with golden rats.'

This made Guri laugh. His hairdressing was established. He felt better. He would either have to make do sexually with memory, or find a goddess he could get on with. And Kitten – she was safe now, and would be born again.

He shifted his thinking to other matters.

'I exist in the past,' he said. 'My temple's at Sham. Sham's a glorious city in these – in those days. How is it then I meet you?'

'You and I, our sort, we can go in and out of time. When we want we find doors. Did you think you'd meet me?'

'Nothing was further from me.'

'Nor I. But it's good.'

'Yes, Lion. *Good*.'

They spent the day in the plain under the mountains, which might have been in Lionwolf's present era or Guri's past time, or in neither, instead an extension of that intriguing 'tween world Guri had accessed in his former living ghost-life.

They ran and flew. They hunted deer – phantoms – which waited in an ice-jungle for them but reacted in a non-uncanny way and did not glow gold. Two mammoths met them also, were duly mounted and ridden. One was Guri's older mount from the Hells, the mature female. He scrubbed her tusks and fed her black juicy grass that flailed from the snow when Lionwolf spat on it. Evening came and the tired earth sun, or its facsimile, rolled off over the edge of daylight in a welter of crimson. Chil-lel-Winsome-Vangui-Toiyhin's night encompassed the sky with black silk and platinum stars. Only three moons rose, a full moon bracketed by two crescents. Did she send a message to her lover? Or was Ddir playing about again? The first crescent moon did look suspiciously like a cunningly arranged cluster of stars.

They made camp, and in the Olchibe way to content Guri the fire was kindled in a small pot.

'Do we eat?'

'Let's eat. Tonight, Uncle, we'll be human.'

Venison steaks were to hand at once, jars of wine and spirit. A full-blown cherry tree exploded out of the ice and rained fruit on them. As they had long ago they made illusory naked girls gyrate in the fire-pot. When it proved too reduced a stage they installed a Jafn camp fire and the illusions danced there.

'I like that one. She's Olchibe.'

'I like *that* one. And look, she isn't black.'

Guri tried to muscle off his own xenophobia. He had never much fancied any un-Olchibe women, even, Great God Guri forgive himself amen, the ones he once took by force. But it clawed at him to think of them, and he had paid expensively for his crimes. He tried to like another dancer.

Disconcerting himself slightly he saw she was quite a hefty female, with uncouth billows of dark hair. She kept drawing his eye. He could not fathom it. 'Is she one of *your* inventions?'

'That one? She seems familiar.'

The dancer with rowdy hair flaunted and winked at them, then vanished with a sharp crack. Out of the camp fire whirled a tangled twig. It must have broken off the cherry tree.

The moons swung over.

The gods lay on furs and bundled grass. The mammoths chewed calmly nearby. Guri told Lionwolf stories. Lionwolf told Guri stories.

'Shall we sleep?'

'Let's sleep. Tonight we're human.'

'Does it sadden you, Lion – does it make you afraid . . . it used to, I remember that, being a god.'

'Everything alive, if it can think, may be afraid of itself. No, I left my fear in Hell. I left my *self* there. Now I'm no-self. Self-less, Guri, as I was Nameless, once.'

'But you – love.'

'I *am* love. Fire and warmth and hope and health and love.'

'Then how—' Guri faltered.

Lionwolf provided the question. 'Then how do I love the ones I truly love?'

'You and I, Lion,' said Guri in a little voice. 'That boy-god in Hell – what was his name? Escurjai – Saphay your mother – and *she* – your black goddess? Or should we just be jealous now, lumped in with all things, loved equal, no one worse, or better?'

Lionwolf laughed. The stars flashed, looking earthward to bask in the properties of the laughter.

'I'm no longer a man, Guri, but yet I am a man, still.'

'Ah? A word game.'

'Who passes,' said Lionwolf, 'it's yourself. No, I am here and you are there. Yet *I* am *there*, you *here*. If you leave me I shall have left myself.' The fire crackled. No one danced in it now. It was like a flake of the sun mislaid in midnight. 'All of us, all things, are one. The material which made us is the same, even if each of us is fashioned in unlike ways. The snow is the moon and the moon is the sky and the dark is the day, and the day the dark. You are Lionwolf, Lionwolf is Guri. A man dying a million miles from us is you, and myself, and we are him. A woman giving birth below the mountains is Chillel, and Chillel is Lionwolf and Lionwolf is the woman giving birth. All equal, Guri. Equal. But this equality is in every instance unique.' Lionwolf raised his right hand into the moonlight. 'There is my present lover, Guri. My crude and basic born and man-made instrument of wankery. But I am Chillel. My hand – is Chillel. And when I find her again as she is, all things will be there in her. I shall love her best, and all things therefore best. When I kiss her mouth, I shall kiss every lover, every friend, the lips of the earth and the sky, of space and of eternity. But Uncle, as you know, any worker or soldier or king who lies tonight with his own lover does the same. As so does he or she.'

The trees murmured, tilting stars in their branches. Leaves had eased from the ice. By sunrise they would be withered but for now they softly sang. The phantom mammoths snuggled, and observed the night wind blow, like dreams, along the plain.

Back where the mountains, Kraag's barrier or not, braced the sky, another shadow had shown itself. It seemed to have been cast by some colossal, otherwise invisible planet far overhead. Enormous and semi-transparent, the shadow had eclipsed most of the mountain range.

Now and then a huge lamp, or *two* huge lamps, gleamed from the front sides of it. Eyes?

Brightshade's released astral body lies on the bony breast of the crags, waiting for morning to draw near his brother.

This is partly reticence and proportionate unease, plus egoism. Yet he has picked up something of Lionwolf's monologue.

Brightshade, musing on its *shapes*, is puzzled, yet grows rather less reticent, uneasy and solipsistic.

He too scans the stars and the moons, and every so often a peculiar and to him minute figure, crunching about in the top-snow of the plain. Is this another tree that has not only woken up but begun to walk? Or is it an oversized badger? That it is able to be noticed at all on such a night implies some freakishness in its make-up. For even if all things are one, the fashioning of *this* one thing is *unlike*. Unrecognized, another goddess not remotely resembling Chillel is stamping cheerily southward. *She* has her eye on Guri, from whom she expects, as usual, absolutely *nothing*.

TWO

Five panthers entered the Chilleling camp. Two ran straight at Guriyuve, leaping over other men to reach him. Two bounded at Sallus. The hideous trance had overcome each of them already. But somehow both Guriyuve and Sallus put up a brief fight before they too slumped down and the white teeth closed on them.

Azula alone, up in a tree, did not experience this paralysis. She stared terrified from her bough, involuntarily twitching to throw herself over on to one at least of the cats. But a pair of icy, luminous eyes now held hers. The fifth creature had climbed half up the trunk towards her. Its mask was opaque fur, only the eyes and paler patch of nose to be seen, and then the silvery slit of its undone mouth. The rumble of threat was so low she seemed to hear it sounding in her arteries.

The fifth cat kept her in place by this irresistible method until the other four had dragged their captives from sight.

Then it made a kind of grin at her. Like a segment falling from the night it was gone.

Azula tumbled down the tree. Only her double-jointedness saved her from injury.

The other men were reviving, groaning, some crawling or staggering aside and spewing violently.

She stood screaming at them – Hurry, hurry, we must go after. Somewhere in the trees she heard Guriyuve's mammoth trumpeting. Its outcry seemed as redundant as her own. For none paid any attention. The ones who heard her turned from her in a combination of contempt and shame. Go after? What point?

Draw near the liopards, the beasts of night, and the abysmal trance would drop on them again. Helpless they were and would stay so. There was nothing to be done.

Azula abused them, shouting, kicking at them.

Her own former trance, brought on by Beebit's death, had evaporated in this hellish country. After her mother Sallus was the only one who had ever genuinely and compulsively seemed to care about her. He was her true sibling. They had travelled far together, albeit silently, in spirit as much as in the physical world.

She bent suddenly and lifted the chaze snake from where it lay among the tree roots. It had been coiled up with Sallus, somehow sloughed or thrown clear as he was seized.

It hung a moment like a dead rope on her arms, then quickened and curled about her, its head and ticking tongue against her throat.

'You and I then, brother,' said Azula to the chaze.

Fast as any liopard the girl sprang out of the camp, through the trees and up the rising ground beyond.

She was unused to running over such terrain.

The turf and flowery grasses impeded her. They felt more precarious than the most slippery or crumbling snow. Sinews spread from trees into the ground; unseen rocks and stones were obstacles she jumped high to miss.

She thought she might see the mammoth running as she was. There was no sign of it.

The liopards and their prisoners had vanished. Vague tracks bruised out in undergrowth seemed to indicate their progress. But other animals moved in the night: sombre deer, a clan of which she noted gazing at her from a wood; lizard-things as large as dogs. These too might have created the tracks.

Yet Azula had seen the higher hill where a tower seemed to be, and how it had been weirdly lit as if by a small internal moon. She guessed the liopards went there. Chillel the bitch goddess was *there*. And the cats were *her* beasts. Besides, in a story, the hero must always go to such a tower, the tower of a god, even if he was a man and a warrior – even if he was a she, and a woman acrobat. Beebit had told her such a tale, Azula thought. And in it there had been three towers. The echo came to her as she ran. A tower of the sun that glowed gold, a tower of ice with crops in it, and one of cloud in the sky. Yet there was another tower too; that one caught fire and burned.

And then there was this tower, which shone silver.

Now it did not shine.

The lamp was out.

Obverse of a beacon then, the blind spot seemed to signal: This way, *this*.

A band of groves, loose-linked as crowds of persons holding out their hands to each other, spread across her route. About to dash forward between the low branches Azula halted.

There was more to the trees than boughs and black foliage. Emerging from the blackness flowed another blackness featuring three gleaming dabs of light and next a slit of light that growled.

Beebit's daughter did not draw her knife.

She danced on the spot, twirling over into a cartwheel that bowled her directly at the liopard. With a snort it flung itself aside, hunching down into a snarling heap. The chaze, which until now had effortlessly coiled her, let go and sought the closest burrow. Azula did not realize.

'Here, puss! Hey, puss! Not scaredy are you?'

Azula's voice was shrill with fear sublimated to anger.

She spun at it again and the great cat pleated itself away, raking the air with its claws. It missed her, and she came at it again and again. Over and over the manoeuvre was repeated. Every time the claws were seconds too late.

'You're only a big stupid *kitchen* cat! Can't catch a *mouse*! Have to hunt *humans*! Poor *thing*!'

Springing from cartwheel to handstand Azula slapped the liopard across the muzzle with her left foot and next her right hand, and reeled off once more.

What happened then almost robbed her of her perfect balance.

Rocking home on her heels she stared at the liopard, which

292

slowly rolled over on its back and lay limp-pawed and quies-cent, looking at her sideways from quicksilver eyes. The growling had altered to a throbbing purr.

A trick?

It was the beast of the bitch. Probably it could reason, even if only to a limited extent. Azula would neither approach it nor flee, nor would she stay put. She shot up one of the low trees and the chaze shoved itself out from the roots and rushed rippling after.

Again Azula glared down into the mask of the fifth panther. The snake looked over the branch too.

Chillel's beast rose, shook itself, padded to the tree and there rubbed itself, flanks and back and face, releasing from its pelt a feral scent of grass, meat, fur and the tenebral.

Then it lay purring under the tree, singing them a lullaby, *smiling* up at the girl and the serpent with half-shut, mercury eyes.

Fenzi had reached the tower hill inside two hours.

He had been *shepherded* by the nine cats that followed him. Never had they accosted or attacked, nor did the trance over-come him; plainly he raced towards the pen intended for his keep.

Only when he gained the slope of that ultimate hill did he see the sheen of renewed light. Against this the tower was evident. It looked blacker than the dark but not as tall as he had reckoned. The architecture was not unique. Also the glamour of brilliance was behind it not inside. There were no windows he could rec-ognize.

In the past now and then he had run as fast and for more impressive distances, but tonight he was exhausted.

He had ceased to be afraid of the liopards.

Everything, if he considered it – he did not – had given up its sensible meaning. There was no rationality here. And his own seemed to have been destroyed.

He stopped about thirty strides below the summit. He

breathed, breathed and waited for equilibrium, but though his lungs became glutted and less demanding, his mind was not appeased.

Chillel.

He thought of his mortal mother, the fisher's wife, and how he had employed her as children do, caring, careless. *This* one above him in the tower, if she was, was unusable.

Knowing nothing directly of the liaison of the Lionwolf with Chillel, even so Fenzi, now a man, felt the *otherness* of the female being. Darkness, moon, kindred, alien. Woman.

Below him down the hill the nine cats too had ended their race. They were seated watching him. No doubt if he tried to leave they would prevent it.

Simply walking now Fenzi went on towards the hilltop and the tower.

Borne backward across the scroll of night, too warm, entirely dislocated, Sallus son of Bhorth, Guriyuve son of Ipeyek, were unable to thrust off the sickening stupor the beasts invoked. Momentum was illness. Night was Hell. Living was dying. Almost anything tortured for too long resists through non-resistance. *Yes I will* becomes the wall of adamant.

At some boundary torture finished nevertheless.

Fangs withdrew their scalpels, precipitation ceased. The stink of carnivorous respiration was replaced by the fragrant moisture of landscape free of snow, which was naturally no less inimical.

All light was blotted out. The stars, which speed had coalesced in streamers of radium overhead, were now extinguished. At first the total dark was welcome. That did not last.

Nausea slunk away. More comfortable, the two men must regain awareness. They did so. Then utter rage and panic filled the space. Each man clamped them in mental fetters.

'We are in the tower.' Guriyuve, coldly.

Coldly Sallus: 'This is another dimension.'

'Rukar philosophy.'

'Perhaps. But this isn't the world. It's beyond it – or inside it, some psychic cabinet we've been thrown in.'

They got up after that and felt around the angles and openings of the prison. Although it had seemed lightless, now they thought they could see somewhat. Barriers of apparent stone contained them. These climbed up and up to a vault of nothingness. But three wide archways gave on other stone containments, and these in turn each had three fresh wide archways leading to similar areas, also with archways, also leading on.

'A maze,' said Sallus.

'We must stay together.'

They had already searched their clothing for any means to make flame. Sallus had possessed a flint, but it was missing. Guriyuve said, 'A Crarrow birthed me. She could call fire out of her belly. Would the knack had passed to me.'

Deliberately they vacated the first area where they had been sloughed by the cats.

In a while Guriyuve remarked, 'I can still smell her animals.'

'You're right. We've been drawn after them by their scent. Why not? Where they've gone we can go. There may be a way out. Yet it may not be any physical way.'

'We have powers,' said Guriyuve dully. 'Even your sister-girl said that.'

'Your sister-girl too. Azula.'

'So. Very well.'

They stood in the vaguely visible stony unness.

Sallus said, 'My powers aren't tested. I grew up quickly. I killed a snake and it returned to life and stayed with me. Everything was quite easy. I never questioned until this thing came on me, this *impulse* to be here. And then I only obeyed her geas.'

'More Rukar words.'

'You know quite well what they mean. If I can pick the meat off the bones of *your* Olchibe hooting, you can tell what *I* say.'

'Shall we try what we can do?' said Guriyuve.

'She – this Chillel – she's reduced us to little boys, as our mothers never did.'

'She makes all men fools. Even her lovers. The demon

Lionwolf she turned into a clown. My father Ipeyek was a nomad. He *travelled* to be rid of her. When she got close to him again in his mind through me, he deserted me and travelled back alone to the Uaarb.'

'My father wasn't like that. He forgot her by staying put. Yet – he remembered her too. Yes, if I'm honest. He'd look at me, and think back to her. I can see it now. My real mother could see it *then.'*

'But we're men,' said Guriyuve.

Both of them put one hand on the nearest wall.

There was no need to discuss this.

Jointly they let the rage and panic off the leash and sent them headlong in every direction.

The prison roared. Huge cracks and splinterings resounded. Chunks of masonry burst outward. From above a torrent of stones and stanchions plunged down. But the debris was insubstantial as smoke, and the falling stuff like a deluge of dark feathers.

When the dust settled they stood untouched in the middle of a vast open hall, like that of a king, but a king greater than the monarchs of dead Ru Karismi.

Overhead the roof had become non-existent. The stars blazed. With an almost musical choreography, nine round white lamps of differing sizes circled and partnered and abandoned and crossed each other.

'Are they moons?'

Which of them asked this aloud? Both believed the other asked.

Then from a long way off up the hall they beheld a woman, moving neither quickly nor slowly towards them. Limned by the moon-lamps she was slender and quite tall, clad in a colourless garment, with black hair budding and lustrous as a plant of the outer garden, heavily drifting out behind her to the ground. Her face they could not properly see. Even as she drew nearer, they could not see it. Was she veiled or masked? It did not seem she was. But everything else was exactly visible now, everything but for her face. She was black as they. She was Chillel. Chillel moved towards them. Chillel – and they could not see her face.

Azula dreamed she had slithered down the tree in the groves, the chaze looped about her shoulders.

In the dream this seemed quite a canny move.

When she reached the liopard that lay calmly by the foot of the trunk, she stretched out her arm and the panther started running its head against her hand and wrist. She knew it was called a panther at this point.

The feel of its pelt was like the shorter and more wiry grass, yet with a lushness woven in the coat that surprised her. The snake did not try to escape. Eventually the cat got up and she and it trotted, a sort of *dog* trot, towards the hill with the tower. Azula saw the glow had come up again behind the tower. It reminded her of the big cat's eyes.

Just then she woke up.

Azula learned she, the chaze round her neck, was dog-trotting with the panther over the turf towards the tower.

A liquid splash of fright went off inside her, covering her insides, heart, viscera and brain with abject dread. But next that washed away like water tipped from a bowl. She thought, *It's too late now.*

Gaining the tower's foot Fenzi paused, looking it over, up and down. Before he did this however he glanced back again. The panther cats were no longer to be seen.

As he perused the tower structure, its ponderous yet oddly familiar stonework, he heard a terrible noise from deep inside it. Fenzi had had second-hand experience of reiver fights along the Jafn shore, and first-hand of mishaps of the voyage with Arok to the new continent. He had been there during the pig-hunt and its aftermath, Winter the godforce hunting them. Fenzi knew a cry of agony when he heard one.

Was he startled? No. Or startled only by the inevitability of this doomed quest's conclusion.

Death was in the tower. Vangui the rending she-wolf, the moon's cruellest, thinnest quarter: a claw.

After the ghastly cry there was an interval, less than a minute. Then other cries were heard. They varied in loudness and in tone, even in intensity. Yet all were comparable in that they were grunts, howls and screams of shock and intolerable pain.

Fenzi was sure every cry was voiced by a different man – none was not male. He found he had started to count them, somehow also including the number of those uttered before his count began. Every one went through him like a blade. When he had, or thought he had, counted over seventy cries, he pounded up the last of the slope and in at a tall slot he discovered in the stones. It was unlike a doorway, reminding him more, if he had considered it, of an enormous keyhole.

Inside stretched a space, roofless. High in the vault of it nine minor moons made patterns, passing, repassing.

Fenzi felt like a child. How old was he after all? Three – five – seven – nine?

He had known himself an adult man. Now this was cut from him. The urge to curl up tight on the stone floor was very insistent. He drew his sword.

Then Vangui entered the space from another chamber or another world.

How fearsome she was.

She had clad herself, over her physical blackness, in white mail, and a dark cloak trailed from her to the ground. Her head was shaven. Fenzi could not see her face. Instead there was a gleaming mottled redness, the kind of marks that might show on the moon's face during an eclipse – which he had never witnessed but been told of, or somehow divined. In her narrow hand too was a sword of whitest steel.

No use to battle with her. She was more powerful than a god; she was his source, the First Mother. And what man could slay his mother? Damn her then, this seef bitch from the guts of a rotten moon. Let her have him. He threw down his sword. When it hit the stony floor it shattered. Symbols, when very trite, often wound the worst.

Through him life beat in a flood, bearing his true parents, bearing Arok and Nirri, bearing Sombrec the lover, and even the tiger baby he had given to Curjai – and then blankness, more horrible than the trance the great cats cast, for he was not helpless, could move and operate his body, and yet was powerless as a man whose every bone had been ground to mist.

They saw her, most of them and all of them essentially, in a dissimilar form. To Guriyuve and Sallus for example, standing together, she had appeared rather the same. Yet her colourless dress was of a differentiated style for each, her unseen face was, for each, *unseen* in an unlike way. Fenzi saw her as a warrior goddess, hairless and defeminized. Among the rest of the Children of Chillel, she was visualized as seventy or eighty – more, more – other beings.

Some even watched a dual creature approach, partly masculine and partly female. Some gazed on a giantess, or a monster from their own personal set of myths – Fenzi was not alone among the Jafn-raised to compare her to a vampire. Two of the Chillelings from the Faz calculated her a shark-woman, but in either instance a *different* shark. Several Rukarians saw her in the image of one of their plethora of gods, the malign side always . . . To some she entered that desert of space as a panther that walked upright, with a woman's breasts and genitals flaring silver, as did her teeth, eyes and talons.

That was a constant, however. The talons.

The number of the Chillelings had never been certain. Somewhere between thirty and one hundred men? One was absent, of course – Dayadin, born son of Arok. And two were daughters – Brinnajni, Azula – and neither of these currently in the tower, and one not now to *be* in the tower. But all the men had either entered there, or been dragged there, or would enter or be dragged in. And time naturally in the fastness of a god, as in the otherworlds, had slight meaning.

She steals towards them individually and all, with the tread of dawning night upon an isolated island. Though already in the dark, *her* dark is final.

Even where two or four had grouped together, as had Sallus and Guriyuve, she draws close and then no other is by, no other exists. The whole earth is only himself and her.

She is not Chillel. But nor is she Winsome either in name or type. She is Vangui. They all grow aware that she is Vangui, and those who had guessed achieve a second depth of understanding that she is Vangui. Vangui of the Claw.

When she is very near the musk of the animal or creature she appears to be, or the perfume of the woman she appears to be, smothering and killing invades their nostrils, then despite the fact they are not paralysed their feet seem to have grown into the floor of the tower. Their arms lie leaden. If their hearts beat it is only like drums. If their eyes can see, and they can, it is only like mirrors.

Vangui regards them with her own black-silver gaze. No mercy or love in it, no family feeling. Not motherly. Never kind.

The right hand of the woman, the right forepaw of the beast, even if it is an armless serpent or a shark, springs back, a living thing in itself – and tears forward.

Four talons that seem made of iridium score the son who stands before them. They score as if he is quite naked, making nothing of any garb – leather, cloth, metal. They score inward and down from just beneath the left pectoral to the lowest root of the ribcage. They score to the skeleton, so through the torn blackness and spurt of fiery blood the human ivory is for one split-torn second clearly revealed.

And he screams. In all of the thirty or eighty or a hundred or more voices. Screams in agony, in affront, in horror, in misery. And the night captures each cry and stores it, files it carefully, hangs it like a jewel upon the air.

As she steps across the last inches of turf and enters the slot-like door to the tower, Azula begins to think she is under a spell. She feels no alarm or distrust. That must prove she has been duped. But what can she do? The panther has brought her and the chaze has companioned her. But now she is alone in a vast empty hall, and above her nine white globes dance together and faintly chime.

Azula supposes she will die here. Whatever comes at her she will loathe. And still she can experience her prospective loathing – that's good. Thank the gods. And if she dies anyway, if there is a Paradise, her ma will be there—

Something is gliding over the distance towards her.

Azula focuses on it. A woman? *Death.*

Chin up, brace the spine, take breath and meet death eye to eye. Azulamni is only a little girl a few years old, but when did that ever matter?

And I hate you, you goddess of rubbish.

Hate you.

THREE

Brightshade had descended from the mountains. As his non-bright shadow cascaded outward over the plain, wildlife fled to every compass point. Men, where the semi-ectoplasmic entity had passed by, took it mostly for a reflected cloud. The occasional magio had grimaced and fired off incantations. But anything non-human knew and ran.

One other thing there had been on the plain, not animal, not human, but this was gone.

Guri too, and the mammoths, had left the region by then. Lionwolf was sitting under an upright fan of ice sculpted at sunrise by the wind.

Brightshade's shade filled the world.

'What nostalgia,' said Lionwolf, looking about. 'How well I remember all those impressive filth hills and jingle-jangle bone forests decorated with corpses on your back. Some have been jettisoned. Never mind, Brighty. You've garnered several new ones. I especially like the artistic fortress of broken ships' masts. Besides, when I *walked* over you I never saw *inside* your guts. You have a fine collection there, too. Let me see – is that a whole shore village which you've swallowed? You must have sent a wave to throw it adrift.'

Brightshade loomed. He regarded the *shapes* of Lionwolf's friendly sarcasm, and picked up the regret with which Lionwolf also judged the wanton slaughter such a 'collection' involved.

'Forgive me,' *shaped* Brightshade. 'Brother – forgive.'

'It's done. No doubt I can't persuade you to give it up.'

'I will,' sprayed the *shapes*, inaudible but deafening, 'do any-thing! Only forgive what I have done to *you*.'

'To me? I have forgiven it. You helped me. Didn't you know? Death and Hell were my anvil.'

Tears rained from the stained-glass palace windows of the leviathan's eyes.

Reaching the snow they sizzled, leaving oval slushy places, each about the size of a shed.

'He persecutes and harries me,' *shaped* the whale. His agility with language had been got from multifarious meetings. Per-haps its dramatic tone was inevitable. Most of the ones he had heard using words were dying in terror because of *him*. 'Save me from the father – save me, brother! I will be your slave. I will serve you. There is none but you.'

A particularly valid tear splashed out an oval the size of a cot-tage. They were not corporeal, the tears, yet had the force of sincerity. Until this moment Brightshade had been partly acting, to win Lionwolf's favour. But suddenly the script overwhelmed him. Now he wept like a sea.

Lionwolf began to speak soothingly to Brightshade in a kind of melodious gibberish. It was rather as mothers spoke to infants. Brinnajni, Lionwolf's daughter, had done something like this before, when she lulled the whale asleep and rescued Dayad from his stomach. Lionwolf could see the scar this rescue had fixed even on Brightshade's astral body. If the whale had ever grasped how he was robbed was unclear. But the chastisements of their father, Zth, were also plain enough.

Only too well did Lionwolf recall his own anguish of fear in pre-infancy when he had been threatened by Zeth Zezeth.

With his phrases and voice, Lionwolf reassured his half-brother. The plain beamed about them. It was, perhaps, the one lying just below the southern mountains. They were therefore in Kraagparia, Brightshade and he. What was real was unreal, what was unreal, real.

'Forget your awe and fear of Zeth,' said Lionwolf at last. The *shapes* of these words swam deep into the consciousness of the whale. 'His day is done. His power is going out. *I* am the power now,' said Lionwolf, without modesty, arrogance, amazement or unease. 'Trust *me*, brother. He can never hurt you again. If he draws near you, say my name to him.'

'*Lionwolf*,' whisper-*shaped* the whale. It was a sigh like a sea wind far inshore.

'And call to me,' said Lionwolf. 'Then watch the old dad *run*.'

Miles off over hills of ground and time, Guri heard his nephew's laughter behind him and the more oceanic mirth of the whale. Guri scowled, guessing, knowing, all that went on. That bloody whale had impaled him – *twice*. Forgive? *He* would thump the thing when next he met it. Or not. Maybe not. But then anyway Guri saw Sham again before him down a sort of swirling tunnel. Sham by night and goldworked with ten thousand torches. And it had grown bigger, and the temple of Gurithesput had grown *much* bigger. And Guri galloped forward, his scowl now like thunder at seeing this urban sprawl.

Jemhara had been left to her own devices for a long while. At least so it seemed. She had tried to reckon up the days, but as there was never really any night here, only a brief flicker of evening which seemed to occur as and when it wanted to, her estimate varied.

The god ignored her as a rule. This she had become used to. Also that *having* ignored her for what seemed several months, he would abruptly seek her. He always manifested from the golden air. Or out of a tree. Something like that. At first she believed that was simply what he did, a habit, a foible. Then she began to suspect he did it to discompose or thrill her.

Why should he think that necessary? He was Zeth Zezeth.

She asked herself if she attempted to make sense of her own incarceration here, his prize or experiment, by inventing flaws in his psychology.

Yet the Magikoy training she had inadvertently attained insisted to her Zth was no longer quite himself. That is, not what he had been in mythology or temple-lore. He had gone downhill.

His constant boastful references to destroying her in the sexual act, and how he *would* not; his diatribes against the Rukarian state, mankind in general, other gods – Yyrot, Ddir, the one he called a *doy*, Saphay – and so on. These were like the rantings of the angry and enfeebled, unable to lash out with anything but temper and tongue.

As for the main anathema, Lionwolf, Zth now seldom mentioned him coherently. Nor did Zth command Jemhara to any of the unspecified tasks of vengeance he had suggested. Of this she was glad. Yet she drew a conclusion.

Her instinct had already compared her celestial jailer to the aged King Sallusdon.

Those wasted limbs, wilted loins, crass, conceited and unfunctional *mortal* brain – to make such a comparison was risky, surely. Zth could read her mind if he wished. But, he did not . . .

Here he was now, extracting himself from an orichalc column.

Jemhara obeised herself.

'Ah, get up, get up.'

It *was* Sallusdon! That foolish and inappropriate glee at her gestures of slavishness.

And his golden gaze on her was like that of a man not merely unintelligent but – *senile*?

They strolled in gardens of iridescent leaves.

Zth recently seemed to like to see things that approximated earthly fauna, preferably killing each other. And so the glades were frenzied with sapphire wasps seizing ruby spiders, or vice versa, and cobalt wolves with auburn cats in their jaws. It was illusory but unneedful and sickening.

Was this too his own vitriol having to be performed by others?

'What will you do for me, Jema?'

'All and anything, supernal lord.'

'Yes. You do love me so, do you not, my Jema?'

'Lord, more than all and everything, what else?'

And off he went then on a rant. And after the rant he gave an outline of what he might do with and to her. The one he always gave.

When he brushed her lips with his finger a shiver of impossible bliss consumed her. She allowed herself to collapse at his feet. He enjoyed this.

He enjoyed – *this.*

And he credited her fawning lies.

Later once, just once, Jemhara bit the inside of her mouth to prevent a yawn.

When he buzzed away she sat motionless. The blink of twilight disrupted the sky. It seemed to her that it lingered many seconds more than previously.

That he could read her thoughts was still feasible. Jemhara cared less that he should finish her than that he might make her harm others, particularly Thryfe. She had forged her own plans for suicide in whatever format seemed workable, should that finally happen. It would go against her life-wish which was very strong, even here. It would not be easy, but it would be done. Vuldir had used her as his puppet to be rid of Sallusdon. If any will, human or superhuman, used her now it would find her *useless.*

Dusk returned. And a dusk it was. It went on for an hour, she thought. At the time Jemhara bathed her eyes and heart in its grey-blue sweetness. There were even groups of stars, and one quarter-moon, more slender than the white curve of a baby's nail.

She sat in his garden, and watched the raucous leaves calm to ashes.

Somewhere a bird sang. Jemhara had never heard such a thing. Even the caged birds of Ru Karismi had not had songs. It was exquisite. She fell asleep.

Being what now she was, sleeping she was entirely aware of her journey out of the Sun Wolf's confine, down or out towards the earth.

She went along a path, a milky way here and there pasted with small stars. The larger stars were aeons off, greater than worlds.

Unlatching a door, she stepped into the room of a mansion. She was in a mage's towery. She had reached Kol Cataar, and the house of Thryfe.

When she saw him, dream-projection that she was, all of her seemed to fissure like crystal at a blow. It was a blow of love.

The magician wore lighter clothing – the climate had grown warmer here. He had posted himself before an oculum, and this thaumaturgic instrument was itself new-minted, and had a few innovations Jemhara had never heard of, let alone seen before.

She could see too he was strong, this husband of her soul, not as when last she looked at him, either in the flesh or through her psychic eye. Jemhara read him as the god could not read *her*. Thryfe's wretched deprivation of her, and how the other god, Vashdran, had healed him of illness but not of grief. He had wanted to keep his grief, it seemed. But he was himself.

'Good evening, my love,' she said.

Yet Thryfe, awake and in the world, Magikoy though he might be, did not hear.

Jemhara found herself close enough to embrace him. She did this, leaning her head on his shoulder while her hair poured over him.

Curiously at that moment she felt his ring again on her finger. It was not there, of course. *Oh, it is truly inside me then, inside my finger, safe about the bone.*

She wanted to tell him this, explain.

He knew and saw and felt nothing of her.

But in the oculum, which a minute before had been blind, a picture was painted.

Jemhara watched with Thryfe as something black tore apart something pale under a tree daggered with ice.

Futile as a nightmare, the magic mirror was showing him the horror of his mother's death. Naturally, the mirror seemed to say, he had always feared to have Jemhara taken from him too. Thus, losing her, he could only accept the theft, and that the thief would be death. It had been bound to happen.

The vision muddied and was gone. Now a world hung there. Jemhara did not know what this was, this greenish-bluish globe panelled over with white. Thryfe had come to know, for he had been shown the sight before by this oculum. The earth looked back at him like the pupil-less iris of an eye. The pupil instead might be the black of space that stretched about it.

As one looked, some of the whiteness went from the iris. Thawed lands and seas flowered out in green and blue.

He had not decoded what the apparition of the earth said. Only that, with the coming of another sun god, things might be freed from the ice. In itself that was a dangerous prophecy. The change would be vast and violent and might cause the end of the world.

Presently the earth dissolved in the glass. On the dark background Jemhara stood in the oculum.

Thryfe caught his breath. Jemhara also.

The portrait was exact, even to the gown of tissue given her by Zth.

'Good evening, my love,' said the Jemhara in the mirror.

Thryfe waited unspeaking, like iron.

The Jemhara who held him shed sudden tears. In the oculum, that Jemhara too shed tears.

Thryfe said woodenly, 'Don't cry. Why are you crying? Is death – so harsh?'

'*I am not dead.*' Both Jemharas spoke together. Their crying stopped. 'I am here in the room with you. But you refuse to see me.'

Inside his iron case she felt him, the Jemhara who held him, turn to rock. 'You are nowhere. *Oculum*. Cancel this false image. Do it. Or I shall smash the glass.'

The external Jemhara let her lover go.

The internal Jemhara in the mirror, like the earth – dissolved.

She positioned herself in a corner. She watched Thryfe as he investigated the oculum, with a jinan summoned to assist. Nothing was found wrong with the mechanism.

Then Thryfe paced the chamber a couple of circuits. She was afraid he would pass through her and drew back to avoid the possibility. Even the jinan had not seemed to pick up any indication of her at all.

'She's dead,' Thryfe said aloud, at last. 'I know this with my intellect but not with my mind. I must school myself. I must let her rest. All I have is this unwanted house, this unwanted and unmerited honour given me by a demoralized king. This unwanted work – gods help me – my duty of care among mankind. And I care *nothing* for any of them. Did I ever? I doubt I did. I degrade my training. I am dross. And he, that shining demon, has ensured I shall survive and live long to know my worthlessness and my just punishment so well deserved. She's *dead*, Thryfe, your Jemhara. One day you'll join her in oblivion. Pray for that to whatever rootless spirit will listen. Till then, *this*.' He went from the room. After which, so did she.

The stubborn shards of ice had been hacked away from the garth, like the carapace.

Daybreak had hacked off the residue of night.

The settlement had a damaged look, though it was almost intact. Something in its persona perhaps had been vandalized.

In the Holas House Arok the Chaiord had sat down, or been organized into sitting, in his carved chair. His face seemed drawn and elderly. He had aged by thirty years they said, his people, loitering about the lean lanes, or in the House yard. His warriors did not know what to do with or for him.

Nirri tended to him in a collected manner. She had the women mull beer with ginger stalks from the hothouse, and then served him this in the bronze flagon kept for him that only he, or his favourites or son, could drink from. The true favourite had gone, of course, Fenzi, lost Dayad's stand-in. Some had seen him merely stride off over the snow. Others muttered that it had been his phantom anyway, he was already dead; as Arok was. The other son of Arok's body they said nothing of. They knew the Saffi-goddess witch-hag had done something, made some mad sorcery. They had no mages to counteract her mischief. The wise-women had refused to come out of their house. As for the werloka, he was cunning at drinking and gambling, but not worth much at anything else.

'How are you, sir?' asked Nirri of Arok, in the most civil and accommodating way. Her eyes, some said, looked more sunken than Arok's own.

Arok said in a low crust of a voice, 'Don't bother me with how I am.' And he drank a mouthful of the hot beer and put it from him.

Those warriors who had been with Arok at Padgish had informed Nirri of all the circumstances. The Winter god she had seen herself. She had not faltered. Only her eyes – sunken.

Upstairs something burned and froze at the same moment.

No one dared go to see. Once Arok had come in neither had Nirri.

Outside the garth still the handsome foreign prince Curjai lingered with the blonde witch-woman. Let *them* go off together for all the good they did now.

The werloka stumped from the Holasan-garth, leaning on his staff, ignoring all those who ignored him. His grizzled mane was uncombed and the tousled tatty wolfskin he wore to keep him warm he also slept in. He knew their opinion of him in the garth, as in the village from which, back on the other continent, he had been ousted by a talentless numbskull. Despite all that the werloka had confidence in his own ability.

Although the ice had been shattered and the garth seemed full of walking dead, not to mention glers saying they were gods, something else irritated on the perimeter of sight and hearing. It was just over there, beyond the fields of dormant crops. It needed seeing to. The werloka knew that none other here, for whatever reason, was remotely capable of that. He hoisted himself along. He was unsure if *he* was. He meant to try.

Half an hour on from leaving the garth he crested a slope and saw what he had come to face.

He halted, and leered at it.

Winter sat on the adjoining hill in a carven chair, not unlike the Chaiord's. Doubtless he had glimpsed it in the House and now inadvertently copied. While Winter was eternal and presently universal, Tirthen-as-Winter was a rather untried god.

To the werloka however Winter-Tirthen was only one more gler.

'Be off, you!' shouted the werloka, and went at once into an unshaven rampaging jig, flexing his staff. This had been effective, sometimes, in evicting malignant Jafn sprites. Bewitcheried lights littered the vicinity.

Tirthen looked down his long, chiselled nose.

He had been already in many places in his adopted guise. Back to Simisey to bluster and remind those who tended his altars; across the ocean to Kol Cataar where they did not know his name but, drawn by the crisp of heat, he had been a wolf and snarled and new altars had risen. He had also circled this insignificant dunghill, patrolling the hull of ice that kept it in. When the ice was breached he was offended. He was a jealous god made in the image of man, beautiful, envious and insecure.

It would be a minor deed to freeze this cavorting idiot with the wolfskin and staff. But Tirthen had made that fatal error when, an elemental, he had assumed human characteristics. The greater gods went the other way about, human to deity. Childhood normally works best by coming first.

'Oh, desist,' said Tirthen, foppishly. 'Do you fail to know who I am?'

His words filmed the werloka with ice.

But the grumpy old warlock was not overcome. Inside his slovenly muddle something burned.

'Gler you are. I *name* you gler. Begone. Bugger off!'

Tirthen rose. But the werloka had by now entered an orgy of contrasuggestiveness. The atmosphere turned scintillant purple as he whirled and exorcised.

Tirthen started to come down from his hill.

The ice-domes at Kol Cataar and here, the attacking icebergs out at sea, the storm of hail and lightning in Kandexa, the splitting glaciers beyond Kol Cataar, all those and other epic stratagems had been due to Winter's jealous and instinctive murderousness. Ignite a flame, he would blow it out. Mindless then, and without either personality or outer form, he-it had laboured to prevent the renewal of the fire. But the fire had returned. Winter had lost the game, though irrelevant moves would continue for centuries. A new order began. Only in little things now could this fiend find triumph.

From the hill a giant black wolf launched itself. Icicles fringed its coat. Its teeth were like the broken edges of some gate to death.

With a howl the werloka flung down his staff. He did not himself wear wolfskin for nothing. In his youth he had been borjiy, a berserker, and his inner guide animal, savage and hot, was also *wolf*.

His bundle of body toppled off. He pummelled out of it. A grey old wolf with a hoary snout parted its jaws on yellow fangs. The werloka hurled himself in turn to meet the god. As he went he roared the blood-joy of the borjiy, and meeting the substance of Tirth plunged in his claws with the boiling glory of berserk fury.

The goddess Ruxendra, flying across the snow towards the garth, discovered she must haul her hound back. He was eager to join the fight below. Crossly she bit his ear. 'Leave it, Star-Dog. They're not worth it.'

While for a mile around the young morning went deep red, as if laved in blood.

FOUR

During the night, and she had not been, was not now, quite sure which night that was following her return to the earthly plane, Ruxendra had seen some of her shrines. She had had a sensation of being tugged many ways at once. To begin with this panicked her. But then she learned she could move in several directions and *be* in them, and yet also stay together all in one place. It was, she concluded, what the liquid sea must experience, or even the driven snow.

This had happened because people were regularly praying to her, and making her offerings. Ruxendra wafted through the air of a small fane in Kol Cataar's new temple-town. Her shrine here was entrancing, gold and pink. Women were hanging little trinkets there. The statue was like her – but not like. *They have made my hair too light.* It seemed she was a dawn goddess, and one of the very, very few Rukarian female deities. Even so, like other Ruk gods, she had two sides. One was lively, valiant and caring, tearing through the ramparts of cold night. The other side was *dead*. How frightful! A dead dawn. This side, a lesser image, looked grey and had been veiled.

Ruxendra was both flattered and upset. She wondered how they had known she died, or how they knew her Hell-coined dawn name.

But soon she was in the ruin of Ru Karismi, and drawn to another shrine, a poor little one near the river. It was made of loose stones and set out of the way of the winds. One of the stones was her actual memorial from the burial Morsonesta of the defunct Insularia. Someone had dared that forbidden and previously impenetrable region and dug up the marker. She spotted a similar plaque far off over the ruin, that of Flazis, another Magikoy who like herself had perished of the White Death. What god was *he* supposed to be then? A god of mending broken bones, it seemed. But his shrine was neglected. Hers had been kept up. A fresh rose lay on it, turning black from frost. How had a rose grown outside a hothouse in this ravaged pile? Vashdran – Lionwolf, she thought. He must have passed by.

Although she was no longer enraged at Lionwolf, she did not like to recall their last encounter.

No one was about in Ru Karismi that she could see. Steel prongs of freezing weather searched it like heartless surgical fingers. She felt the reverse of nostalgia; a dread of remaining.

Another shrine showed up at a miniature village, far into the north-east sliver of land known as the Spear. That was in Jafn territory.

She was confused by this. The Jafn did not worship gods, only, barbarically, one God. How then did they come to claim her?

But in Hell there had been men from many countries, not all of them ever identified. And the shrine she now saw was less to a goddess than to a sprite. It had food offerings. From certain accessory items there, a lamp, a piece of glass fixed to reflect the sky, she assumed they took her as a spirit of radiance.

Eventually Ruxendra seemed to find herself and be in such a lot of areas she lost track of them. A compendium of altars, vessels, votives, demonstrated her as dawn or first light. In a handful of these ideas she was even fierce, a scarlet gull: Dawn Red-Winged. This was the memory of her time as a vengeance in Hell, a fifteen-year-old at her most militant. Yet there was another shrine in the Marginal Land beyond the Ruk, where she had been depicted as a goddess of love.

The far-flung mosaic of her consciousness flew back together.

She had by then also dodged the fighting wolves, and lugging her hound with her landed inside the Holasan-garth at the House door.

She had anticipated she would find Curjai again. But he was

not there. Instead a Rukarian princess sat on an upturned bucket by the doorway.

Saphay. Ruxendra had never seen her, but knew her. Gods knew things.

With stilted Rukarian etiquette Ruxendra gave the female bow needed if still they had both been ordinarily alive. With matching starchiness Saphay inclined her head.

Ruxendra was aching with the wish to recover Curjai. Saphay was gurning with recollections of a dead beloved whom, even though reborn, she must either wait for – Athluan – or could never meet – Lionwolf.

As if just in off the avenue Ruxendra fastidiously complained, 'There is a vile wolfish minor god brawling up the slope with a stupid man who has changed into a wolf. They're biting slices from each other. They nearly splashed my dress. And my dog here, well, I had to pull him away.'

Saphay said, 'Males.' That was all. It summed up male gods, male witches and male dogs. It contained great condemnation.

'Oh, naturally.'

A frightful bang, as if thunder had cleavered open the sky, shook everything. Snow gushed off the House roof and crashed around them, missing *them* completely but swamping other things. The clouds above burned up blister-red, then faded back to paleness.

The rest of the garth had gone to earth.

No one, nothing non-supernal, was to be seen.

'My former companion,' began Ruxendra, 'a young foreign prince—'

'He has left,' said Saphay. 'Some awful act happened. He said they had killed his mother . . . Something in him reminded me of my own—' She stopped. She said, 'I doubt though if *he* would notice if *I* were killed. But then he knows I can never be killed. It is,' she said falteringly, 'very hard on a mother. To lose – in whatever manner – her only—' and stopped again. Stopped as if struck dead as she never could be, now or ever.

The dog, who had sat peaceably through all this, even the

cosmic bang and crashing snow, raised his nose and let forth a long, dismal howl.

Instantly every other dog, but also every cat and lion and hawk of the garth, began a complementary wail.

Saphay rose. She clapped her hands angrily. *'Be quiet!'*

With an impatient violence she clutched her mantle round her, and omitting another word glided off, not walking but slightly levitating, towards the distant slopes beyond the garth.

Ruxendra watched her a moment then leapt airward. The dog, silenced with the rest, pounced after her. Knowing where the town-city of Padgish was merely because she wished to know Ruxendra blew towards it. Escurjai must be – was – there. Ruxendra had matured. She was done with waiting. And her lover had been hurt.

Saphay however ascended the hills and soon found herself about six feet clear of the earth, above the bizarre statue of a gnarled old wolf. It seemed made of snow, glazed very dark. It was the remnant of the werewolf werloka.

Out of a tall snow-drift something turned and was Tirthen.

'You are like Zth,' blurted Saphay.

In her voice was the purest horror and allergy and anger, but also some other element. She stared at the god, his raven hair and eyes and coldness, and contrasted him to the laval Zeth fiery in the womb of the ocean.

'And you,' said Tirthen. 'Whom do you resemble?'

'They are my people, over there.' She found she had de-levitated. Her feet were on the ground.

'That muck-heap? That anthill?'

'Once before you damaged the humans in my care—'

'Your care. You care nothing for them.' A flare lit in her mind. He read it apparently. 'Very well. *One* you care for. A child – or no, a man now. I remember. You sealed him in fire. But *I* sealed him in ice. What is he? He does not count.'

'You can't harm him. I've made him immortal.'

'But you have not made him a god.'

Saphay became flame and lioness.

Tirthen became silver and giant wolf.

316

They slammed together like two doors kept apart for centuries and now breaking free of restraints.

As god-flesh clashed on god-flesh the whole surrounding landscape gave a groan. But it was not like any note of pain.

The cloud-bloated sky darkened to untimely night. A transparent image writhed on it. It copied the long-lost vision of the mage coal, thrown skyward years before, a lioness and a wolf locked in battle, but a battle which was foreplay.

Saphay did not know what she did.

Her brain and nerves were full of the past conflict among the icebergs, raw energy flailing from her. Through this thrust other sensations. She smote ice, she whirled and sank among it, and there was a jewel of fire, not in ocean now but in the crux of her body. The coldness was weight and heat. It scorched the length and depth of her.

Realigned with the human aspect of her divinity the day goddess found herself clinging to a god of Winter and unlight. In a pyramid of frozen glass they were coupling, breast to breast and mouth to mouth. And as he struck through into her core he was not cold at all and she grappled him closer, until they might become one single thing that galloped on the spot, atoms splitting everywhere about it in rainbow radiation.

Breakage sped every which way.

A noiseless shrieking made the vicinity into a crystal bell that presently disintegrated on three rocking buffets of noiselessness.

The dark sky drooped. Clouds seemed likely to fall off its surface. Snow skulked down.

At the garth nothing moved. Live creatures kept motionless. Some enormous miracle of happening had shaken all to bits – yet nothing came down.

But in the upper room of the Holas House—

This too produced no sound effect.

A kind of tingling slap, only one, inside every skull.

Nirri was the first to stir in hall. Going from her mute and disjointed husband and the host of women, children, warriors, beasts, she stumbled up the ladder and off into the bedchamber.

No shred of fire or ice lingered.

317

Her second son, Athluan, a white-haired Jafn man of about thirty years, sat on the Chaiord's bed. Grey-eyed he looked at her, his most recent mother. His face was already modelled in low sorrow familiar and controlled. 'There, lady, he said. "It's over now."

'I was dreaming of my father.'

'Do you still dream?' she asked, curious.

The fire of her hair looked suddenly incongruous to him against her blackness, and his own. Why did he think that?

'I'm human remember, Brinna. By two-thirds.'

'Perhaps I dream,' she said. 'But I don't ever recall. And besides I won't have it you're human, not remotely.' She grinned her wonderful clown's grin.

Encouraged Dayad said, 'In the dream – Arok was sick. He had become – spoiled.'

'Arok . . .' she said.

For a benighted moment he assumed she had either forgotten the name of his father like one more irrelevant dream, or worse pretended to.

He frowned and sat up. 'My dream might be a true one. Among the Jafn we—'

'Oh, the Jafn.'

'Among the Jafn dreams have value. They can show us things. Arok had grown old before his hour. He was like – he was like the dead.'

'Possibly he has died,' she remarked.

She combed her hair and the glorious scent of it disabled his irritation. But the hair of his mother, Nirri, also had a beautiful smell when washed and combed.

'Brinnajni, if I said I must go home—'

'*Where?*'

'My home—'

'You *are* at home. Your home is with me. *I* am your home.'

'To my father's garth then. Does that pedantically content you?'

'No.'

'Brinna—'

'You will go nowhere but where I am. You're mine.'

'Come with me, then.'

'*There*? To such a little place?'

He left their bed; he walked to the doorway of their house and looked out into the nameless snow waste. It was night and a double of moons was rising, both halves, as if they were one moon snapped apart.

'I was stolen from Arok and Nirri as a child by reivers. Next I was borne away towards another land, another continent. My father and my mother loved me dear.'

'But *I* love you, Dayad. And I saved you from the belly of a monster. Is such a love not enough for you? It should be worth all and any love else.'

He thought, *She argues like a woman now, only a woman. I did this for you, and this. Therefore you are my property. No god argues that way. Does she?*

Dayad said, 'I never and could never forget what you have done for me.'

She too had risen. She furled about herself some garment magicked from nothing. The black sheep had come in and leaned against her, but unusually Brinnajni did not seem aware of the sheep, which otherwise she called 'sister'.

'Your words sound like farewell. Ah but pay heed, Dayadin, you don't know how to find them, your father, your mother. Do you guess even where we are, you and I?'

'I can find them. I have no doubt of it. I've always been there with them, some piece of me.'

'And I thinking you were always and only with me.'

He would not answer that. He said, 'If I or any think of another very often, though separated by miles of sea and land, we live in the same country with him. So it is. He sired me. She bore me. They are my parents.'

'And you are no longer a child.'

'No and I never was, or only for a moment. Nor you, Brinna. We grew too fast. Let's not squabble like children now.'

'So you will leave me.' Her voice was pale as ice.

'Just for a while.'

'Why limit yourself to a *while*? Go then. Go away. What shall I care? Human? Yes, so you are. Not *her* blood, one little third. But I am all god – Chillel's, *his. Siring, bearing* – such trivial nonsense. I may hate *she – he* – but they made me as I am.'

'Then understand, those humans I love have made me what *I* am.'

'And I have only loved you. What has *that* made you? Faithless fool. Go away.'

Outside, clothed for a journey and standing in the snow, Dayadin saw the hovor sprite Hilth bustle from a hilltop and flicker towards him.

When Hilth burled foamily around him, he was lifted off his feet. The hovor too had become more vital, and full grown, in this unmapped wintry retreat of theirs.

At first Dayad took Hilth's antics as a game, trying to cheer him. Then he saw they were moving with purpose and swiftly, sometimes skimming the snow, more often whirling high above it.

The sad severed moons moved too, now flying with them and now at an angle away.

Hilth was carrying Dayadin where he had said he wanted to go.

Perversely doubt assailed Dayadin. All this change had happened so abruptly. Then he looked back – back in some inexplicable manner since already they had travelled in every direction, east and west, north and south. But he could have seen Brinnajni distantly, if she had allowed it. Therefore it appeared she would not. He was bitterly sorry then. Yet he would be sorry whatever course he chose, for choose he had had to. The pull Chillel had exerted on all his brothers, like that of a mother planet, had not touched Dayadin. He knew nothing of it, and if Brinnajni did she said nothing. It was the dream which compelled him, the memory of his past that, until now, had seemed shut behind a screen of ice.

When his boots again contacted the ground, Dayadin sensed

he was once more properly in the world. He could not recollect passaging over any ocean, but he knew nevertheless he had reached the second continent, the landmass Saphay had been intent on gaining. Arok then presumably had also reached it.

Cliffy heights soared up. On their terraces ice-forest masked itself in the strange white-blackness of moonset.

Acres behind there was the pulse of the sea.

He feared it a minute, though it was too removed to be heard let alone seen, for Brightshade lurked somewhere in the oceans. However Dayad might plot a course from it. The Holasan-garth would lie inland.

Dayad ran over the plain, strode up the mountains. Though only one-third god, still he had capacities few men could call on. Hilth billowed along with him. Sometimes Dayad spoke to Hilth, as in the old days. Hilth had always conceptually understood Dayad, others seldom or not at all.

The moons were down. Another rose. This moon was full and gave off a fluctuating carnelian glare that menacingly surged with black.

Hilth poured over Dayadin, trying to bear him away backward. The bloodshot moon was rushing towards them out of a rip in the night.

Struggling with Hilth, Dayad was thrown on the hard rime of a plateau. The moon resolved. It struck him just below the heart. He felt his flesh peeled open to the ribs in four long runnels. He could not even cry out. Blood spurted. The spurl of moon – all flame and pitch and claws – curdled, condensing to a crescent. It faded as consciousness went from his eyes.

The hovor collapsed behind him, spattered too with Dayadin's own blood.

The dark was empty. Emptiness whistled over the plateau, poking out the stars as if with a stick.

It would be dawn in less than an hour.

And I hate you – hate you – cesspit – forecutch – trech—
   Azula blinks. She had not thought she could do that; her eyes

had felt as if fixed by glue. The blink seems to last longer than usual, and when her lids go up again there is in front of her the object of her dedicated hatred. The goddess Chillel now called Vangui.

But this is not Vangui.

The goddess, five or six feet away, is tall for a woman but not astonishingly so. Made ostensibly of black satin with hair of trellised skeins of crimped black silk, she wears a simple dress. It looks like undyed wool. But her exquisiteness is such the rustic garment itself appears wonderful draping her.

And now she bends forward a little, just a very little, gazing into Azula's face.

To be impervious to the loveliness of Chillel, either man or woman would need to be, as the ancient poem had it, part dead in flesh and soul. Even her aroma, which is not any perfume only *herself*, is delicious, and . . . kind.

She is *kind*. Her heavenly eyes are *kind*. Are holy. 'Azulamni,' says Chillel.

The name grows ethereal and gleams on the dark.

But Azula grips herself in barbed wire and rasps, 'Slay me then. Be quick about it. You've murdered my brother or destroyed him in some other way. I'd destroy *you* if I could and I can't. *Vangui*,' says Azula, getting out the name like a curse.

'I am not Vangui now. I am Toiyhin.'

Azula falters at the new name. It is from a language she has never either heard of or subconsciously thought was in the world. She *has* heard of a profound mad race known as the Kraag. Is it a name of theirs? Azula has a notion that *toiyhin* means *dove*.

The goddess is *not* a dove. She is a panther. She has claws.

No claws, no pelt are visible. Her hands are perfect as is the rest of her, with clean oval nails of an organically pastel shade most beautiful against her blackness.

The inside of her mouth too is rosy, and her teeth are white, but only like the teeth of a woman.

Azula remembers how Beebit spoke of this, and reverently of the vulva of the goddess too, like a rose-heart—

'Shall I tell you a story?' asks Chillel who is Toiyhin, in the marvellous voice of a mother. Azula says nothing. She becomes sensitive to the space they are in, and that it has altered. The hall is now more like the great hall of a Rukarian palace, which she had heard described. In fact it is much larger than the one at Kol Cataar. There is a central fireplace where a low fire smoulders. All around are benches and chairs, where men are seated. It seems there has been a feast or dinner. The remains of luxurious foods and an ongoing largesse of drink indicate this.

The men are black. Azula thinks lucidly they are her half-brothers, all those she has met and others too. They are dressed in their travellers' clothes but are well groomed. Their faces are variable, some stern and some quite frivolous. Some look tired, some antagonistic. Some are very angry but it is an anger they are used to and do not mean to detonate. None of these men is injured or ill. None is bleeding. None has been slain. Unless, she thinks, the girl borne solely of two women, they are ghosts.

Try as she might she cannot single out Sallus among them.

Then the goddess speaks and Azula can only concentrate on her. Her soft voice fills the hall, as clear as a moon chime.

'I am your life. If you will live through me, you will live. If you will not live through me you will live, but I will not be alive in you.'

The hair crawls on Azula's scalp.

Toiyhin continues: 'From nothing I was made – from night and snow. I am the vessel of what made me, who are three gods, or one god that has three persons. For this, and to be this, I was created and am. But also I have been made the vessel for renewal and further creation, both to receive and to release. I have joined with gods and with men and I have formed sons and daughters who are gods, or so close to gods that in the end only gods will tell the difference, by which time, who knows, my children may have become gods greater than such gods as I am or he is, the Lionwolf. Once,' says Toiyhin, 'it was *Summer* in the world. The sun dropped down into the sea one night, and never ascended any more. Only the phantom of the sun ascended, and gave no heat. Winter slunk into the world. But now there is another sun and he will rise, is rising, over the world. The door is undone and open wide. All things are suspended in the gateway of the dawn.'

The unfinished story finishes then apparently. Toiyhin who is Chillel ceases to speak.

Azula says in a child's tone, '*This* isn't a story.'

'You, my children, are the story,' says Toiyhin, but now she is only Chillel. 'Hate or love me, I have scarred all of you just as your birth-mother did, but I have not left a tiny scar upon your bellies from the birthing-cord, but torn you open to the bone. You are marked with the power of eternity. Hate or love me you will live through me, and I through you, to time's ending.'

'I'm not *scarred*,' says Azula defiantly.

Chillel puts out her hand and gently brushes back the three-colour hair of Beebit's daughter, acorn-brown, crow-black and the strands that have gone white. Chillel gazes into the hazel eye of Azula and into Azula's ink-dark eye. 'No?'

Azula is afraid then. The fear is not like the terror of before. This fear is only human, or perhaps only godlike.

'*Those aren't my scars.*'

'No, Azulamni. Your scars lie within you. They must reach your surface. Listen, I will tell you your true name.'

Chillel leans forward. Her own exceptional tresses brush Azula's cheek. How uncanny. They feel only like silky ordinary hair. Chillel whispers.

Azula alone hears her true name. Her eyes widen. She knows it. She is cut through to the quick of herself, not by pain but by understanding.

Chillel kisses her lightly on the forehead.

The kiss seems unique, and burns pleasantly, a moon-kiss, then flutters off her and away – a moth, a moth that was a kiss, fluttering away.

Everything else is gone too, the hall and the half-brothers and the goddess-mother. There is only the outer hill covered in warm night grass, and here she sits. There is no tower at all. Azula feels first after the bone of her human mother, kept for safety in an inner pocket. It is where it should be. Then she feels for the chaze, and it too is where it should be, round her neck, twitching consolingly. She says to it, 'I'll tell you my true name,' and whispers the name against the snake's head, about where she has always reckoned it hides an ear.

As Curjai walked back to the city of Padgish, he aged. All the dregs of adolescence were sloughed.

He had nearly always been in his first and mortal life an optimist, affectionate, expecting and meaning well. When he had thought he learned these values were misplaced, he was broken up like the mirror in which he had witnessed fatal reality. Later, when he died in that first existence he learned also ultimate horror and despair.

Next was Hell. And Hell cheered him because it gave him instead a complete body that would do all he wanted it to, and a gamut of mythic warrior codes, along with comrades, and one especial companion, Lionwolf. So then much of the benign philosophy returned. In Hell mostly Curjai had prospered.

Reborn thereafter to earth, a god now, his happiness had known no bounds. Even lacking Lionwolf, he had no doubt of their reunion to come. Once more Curjai anticipated only good, for himself, for all those he loved. Even for those he only liked or tolerated, such as his earthbound non-father the king. Why should any try to harm Curjai? He was invulnerable. Why should he not do magnificent things for all others – and why should they not accordingly be glad?

But the mirror had again been broken.

The facts of his mother's death were entirely revealed to him.

He walked, still disclaiming more flamboyant locomotion. Yet he covered miles in seconds. And in his development of self it was rather the same.

The current self however was acrid. He tasted this acrimony and aged another fifty years.

It did not affect his outward looks. A young and singularly attractive male he reached the exterior parks and plains of

Padgish, with the invisible ageing nailed to him like a banner to a post.

Here it was that Catty came running to meet him.

Catty had washed his face and front fur in the snow to remove the blood stains of regicide. Despite that Curjai was instantly aware of what had gone on.

'What have you done!' he shouted.

The countryside shook. Piles of ice from adjacent hills tumbled with a hissing roar.

Catty stood his ground. He had been a she-dog Hell hound and was now a Drajjerchachish male tiger. Once fed the ichor of Curjai, he did not fear him.

Curjai calmed. He had wished to extract death himself but Catty had done it.

Perhaps this was better.

Curjai foresaw another thing in that moment. He was unlikely to be a violent god of retribution.

Humbly he went to Catty and they leapt into each other's arms, wrestling friendly on the snow while the epilogue of the started avalanches dropped in valleys.

'I must still go there,' he told the tiger when they had wrestled enough.

He knew Riadis was now far away in another world, but terrible memories were flushing through him. She had always been despised in the capital after she had borne a cripple. When he was born again as a hero and divine, she had been praised yet still shunned as a freak. Riadis had not cared. She was proud, and only wanted Curjai to flourish. And he—

And I neglected her. A gift of flame, a snatch of words, a necklace or coronet of jewels – 'How long will this diadem last?' 'As long as love lasts.' 'Love,' she said, in play. 'Does that then last?'

Living hearts are warm as flame. That was what I said.

But *dead* hearts were not cold.

He and Catty flew the final miles to Padgish.

Curjai had exhibited few of his abilities so blatantly.

On the streets below horses reared and dromazi cast their riders. Mages pelted from their esoteric houses. Women shrieked.

Curjai shifted his focus and appeared suddenly in the tree-pillared royal hall, his white tiger at his side.

There were mages here too. They grouped, looking at him askance, unsure for once of their mediocre and cliquish talents.

They had not yet decided on a replacement king. Theoretically it should have been Curjai, son of the king, and by now in looks at least the most mature of his heirs. Besides he was the son of the god Attajos, *via* the king. Some advances were made to Curjai of this type. Warriors and statesmen and nobles crowded about the hall. Curjai recollected his first childhood, when he was a boy of intelligence and heart without functioning limbs or 'human' attributes.

Only eventually did he speak. By then the hall was bursting with people and all of them trying to appease him. Incense sickened the air. And now too evening was also arriving, the hour of lamplighting, and everywhere flittered hurrying tapers.

'My father is the god of fire,' said Curjai. He did not think he believed it quite, not now. But they did, at least by lip-service. 'He has passed the importance of fire to me. Now it is under my jurisdiction.'

He looked about.

One by one the fresh-lit torches, the limpid candles failed.

A sort of gasp winged through the chamber. It was like something going away.

'I take back from you the gift of fire,' said Curjai. Tears sprang into his eyes. He *grieved* for them, he saw, even as he spent on them his curse. He could have razed the city. Yet was this any more lenient?

'Any flame you conjure here, for light or heat, to cook, to comfort yourselves, any flame will die. As my mother died from your lack of honour. And as your scavenger king died from the claws of my cat.'

A hush, multiple, imploring, descended.

Dozen by score the lights went on going out.

Beneath their feet the warm floor turned to ice.

As the night swept in it found the palace thick with shadows. The capital sank to turbidness all through. Though they struck their flints again and again, though their mages and shamans again and again drew up the magic sparks, each glint of fire immediately died.

No torches burned now along the streets. The lamps of houses were void. Coldness entered and strolled with the dark in the rooms and thoroughfares. A faint moaning and weeping lifted. The stars stared down. A single moon, a crescent like a cat's claw, gained the zenith in a kind of mockery.

Like a city sacked, ruined by war and plague, Padgish a necropolis, with ghouls and ghosts wandering about sobbing and praying, striking flints on walls, watching the bright seeds shrivel, one by one.

Ruxendra found Curjai seated in the hunting-park some ten or so nights later, with Catty lolling at his side. Catty had caught a deer and, having vainly tempted Curjai to eat some of it – daintily bringing him a severed leg or haunch in his tigery jaws – was enjoying a solitary supper.

The blue dog bounded to join in. The tiger and the Hell hound had a brief tussle, cleverly recognized each other from their recent astral past, and began to dine *à deux*.

'Animals can be so disgusting, don't you find?' said Ruxendra primly, inappropriate with emotion at finding him.

'Human men and women are animals,' said Curjai, not glancing at any of them.

'And we are no longer human.'

Curjai rose and strode away along the slope.

He had been so difficult to find.

Ruxendra sped after him. 'Curjai!'

'What is it?'

'Do you remember me?'

'You? Yes. You wished to slaughter Lionwolf and failed. You forced Arok back from death and did him harm. You are a travesty.'

She baulked. Recovered. 'It is you who have made a mistake.

Now you blame me for an invented error. My brothers were like that. But I could always get round them.'

'I am not your brother.'

'I'm glad of it. In society, where once I was brought up, incest is frowned on.'

At her own words Ruxendra coloured. But she was a goddess now. She blushed like a dawn.

Curjai did not see this, did not look. She was irrelevant to him. All things were.

He stared towards the capital, obscured now by ice-woods and elevations. 'I robbed them of their fires.'

'They killed your mother. Why shouldn't you punish them? They hurt you – you might have rained fire *on* them and well served.'

He turned to her, perplexed. She bristled there, furious for him. She had no tact. She was like Catty. She would have ripped off the king's face to pay him out, then brought Curjai dinner, probably cooked in some Rukarish way – useless and ill-fitted gestures. But motivated by love of him, he tiredly thought. Like her bold claim that he was not her brother, so might be loved by her in carnal ways.

'You know what they did then.'

'Of course,' she said, with a slight impatience.

'They will die,' he said. 'And not all of them are guilty. Their children, their beasts. I had no call to punish *them*.'

Ruxendra went to him and put her hand lightly on his arm. 'Look there.'

This different side of her took him by surprise. She was also capable of gentleness, sense, and magery. He recalled that now. He looked where she pointed.

In the snow a picture blossomed.

Curjai beheld droves of people, all those in Padgish, leaving the metropolis. Leaving the lean, well-paved streets and central wide boulevard, the tree-trunk pillars and high roofs and windows with patterns of coloured crystal. He saw the dromazi and the horses and the dogs going with them, and cats on leashes or in baskets, and birds in cages or on wrists. And with them too, huge and upright glowing shadows on the unlit shadows of the dark, the great god Obac Tramaz, with his dromaz head and fine black eyes, and his small elegant blonde mouse wife Vedis – for there were plenty of her kind too concealed in the furnishings and provisions packed on the carts.

These two gods were involved and nurturing. They attended and presided over the exodus as the people did with their loved pets. And though the citizens of Padgish did not see the giant presences that moved among them, perhaps they felt some strength from them.

'*There* are the gods,' said Curjai.

'The old order. They are the past.'

'Then the past – has been more kind.'

He noticed among the persons passing out through the black gates two of Arok's Jafn. One of the men held a child caringly in his arms. Humanity also could express kindness.

What have I done? Can I undo it?

He knew he could not. He had passed sentence, and it was not in him to revoke his bane; he would be *unable* to take it from them until for him too the anguish calmed.

Ruxendra began to speak in a haughty superior way of new duties and acts among gods, then stopped. Instead, with a quiet firmness she said, 'I will send them a fair dawn, your people. A benign omen for tomorrow.'

Her own reversal of tactic pleased her. She was pleased to have spoken more softly – he did not need abrasion. If he was to love her he must learn he might trust her, even though he was a man, a hero, a god.

And she imagined painting in extra tints on the sky and for a moment, making her jump, a fan of diluted cerise rouged the midnight east. There was no sun there. It was a false dawn, and next went out like her blush.

Curjai had not even seen it, she thought, though numbers of those fleeing Padgish had craned over their shoulders in fright. One must be more careful.

Back along the park Catty and Star-Dog exchanged two or three buffets and then lay down for a snooze.

330

How could she woo Curjai? How awkward he was. Alas, in her past in the ordinary world, outside her training she had only had to deal with fairly petty troubles, until the very end, by which time she was dying, then dead, unable to take notes.

'Curjai?'

But he did not hear. He was reciting, barely aloud, the Simese lay of Tilan and Lalt. The two heroes met and were united, kindred and beloved. Tilan and Lalt; Curjai and Lionwolf. That then was the only one who could comfort him.

Ruxendra-Ushah forgot how his voice had cracked before when he spoke to her, and their alchemical if non-physical and never verbal congress in Hell.

She summoned her pride, and went away.

She did this as a woman not a god, and so had only reached the slope beyond the wood when from nowhere Curjai stood in front of her on the snow.

Ruxendra managed not to start, nor to click her tongue with disapproval.

He had left off reciting.

He held out to her his hand.

'Walk with me,' he said.

She gave him her hand.

How warm and strong he is, she thought.

How cool and serene she is, thought he.

God and goddess, they began a stately perambulation, as if both were in their mortal nineties, erudite, and had done all things over endlessly.

Beyond the height of the deserted capital neither Obac Tramaz nor Vedis paid heed. Old gods indeed, *centuries* old they were, but ancient adults do not always spurn young lovers. Some see such love like a lighted torch that illuminates the future. Kiss then the more when the fire fails. Kiss the more when the lamps go out. Kiss tomorrow awake – who else will bother to do it but love?

Somewhere among the snows Curjai and Ruxendra embrace. Fire and morning; heat and light. And in the mournful procession now a hundred miles from Padgish, the brands shine up without being kindled, and in their cages, thinking daybreak has come, all the cage birds call.

He had been looking at the agony for some time.

It was a long way off now, across hills and seas and continents.

As it sailed further from him so he came closer to himself, and finally he knew he was Dayadin, son of Arok, and that he lay on his back on the hard snow.

Maybe a quarter of an hour after this he went up a stair in his brain and looked out of his eyes. He beheld Hilth the hovor cavorting in a small home-grown blizzard. Poor Hilth. Obviously he had been badly frightened. Now he rushed to Dayadin and forced upon him the only type of adoring hug a wind spirit could offer.

Once he had dug himself out of the resultant snow-drift, Dayad soothed Hilth down like a testy hawk.

Dayad felt by now only the thinnest resonance of any wound. But putting his hand over the left side of his ribs he saw instantly an image in his mind of what had been done to him. Four scars, scored spitefully deep, embroidered his diaphragm. On his blackness they were white as the bones they had, however briefly, exposed. But the healing it seemed had been almost as swift as the mutilation.

Who had done this, and why?

He thought it had been Brinnajni. She had marked him from female rancour, the way some Jafn girl might scratch the face of a man who spurned her. And a god naturally must always exceed.

Dayadin believed it was a latent fury that made vitality burn through him from the scars.

He got up and, with Hilth flapping round him, began to continue his advance inland. Soon he felt much better. The advance grew up into a sprint. The white world dashed by. Either he was again flying now or as near as made no difference. Delighted, the hovor kept pace. And for the first occasion ever Dayad thought

332

he glimpsed the face of Hilth, fey yet almost man-like, coming in and out of the moving air.

There was a volcano in the end, far over to the north and east, puffing up a cloud on the lightening sky.

Here below a wolf made of rock and ice posed in mid-leap. Presently ahead a habitat appeared. There were walls and gates up on a platform, and a high house with a cracked sword horizontal over the lintel.

It was the Holasan-garth, rebuilt in another country.

Dayad the Star Hawk dropped to earth nearby. Fallen slabs of ice lay about strangely on the platform's terrace.

Through a sort of psychometry he knew at once all about Tirthen's ice-dome and its shattering. He knew of yellow-haired Saphay, and her departure.

Dayad had got up over the wall of the original garth those handful of years back, when he was a child and chasing his father to the battle. Hilth had assisted then, and insisted on helping now. If there were sentries, they did not see.

The Jafn Holas identified Dayad instantly. Mystically in their minds he had been growing to manhood as fast as he had done in fact.

They advanced on him; greetings and cries, cheering on the seething lanes, impeding him. He did not want to be churlish. Yes, yes, here I am. You knew I would come back? Of course you knew. He wanted them to make less noise. What would Nirri think? And Arok, his father—

Then they recounted the tale of what had happened to Arok. The dream had been true. Oh, he had realized it was. He had left Brinna for that, though he had seemed to love her more than all things, and now he did not love her at all. The people in the lanes beat on him like seas. So much sorrow, so much hope.

These people, this place, Arok and Nirri, they must fill up the gaping cavity where sexual love – first love – had been.

He reached the yard of the House. It was full of long-necked hump-backed beasts. He gaped at these, and a man of about twenty-nine years came out of the door.

Then the hush fell.

The crowd offered no explanation. It seemed caught in some conspiracy which excluded Dayadin and the man equally. But whether a conspiracy of unease or compliance it was impossible to be sure.

Dayadin looked solidly at the man. He was strong and well made, unmistakably Jafn with light eyes and white hair. He had an air to him too. Dayadin, if he had not been told Arok still lived in body, would have reckoned this man some usurper Chaiord.

'Who are you?' Dayad spoke loftily. He found himself envious and wrong-footed and shrugged the feeling off for he could not know if his reaction was a true one.

The white-haired man said simply, 'Your brother, Dayadin. My name is Athluan.'

At once the clamour bubbled out again.

'Second born, but older now than you are, Dayadin.'

'A mageia did it. She fancied him older.'

It was Athluan who raised a quietening hand. The crowd duly quietened.

Dayadin said flatly, 'Greeting, Athluan. If you are brother to me, then where's our father?'

Athluan stepped to one side. 'Go in and see.'

Dayadin had forgotten Hilth. But Hilth had led the way, then hung himself up like a shirt just inside the door.

To cross the threshold.

So easy? It was done.

The joyhall was like the dream again. He had recalled it so often, he saw, he seemed to have robbed it of reality. And anyway that hall had not been here, had not been now. The confusion of return, massive as abduction, rocked Dayadin. For a moment he faltered, not knowing where he was or quite who. Perhaps when she had struck him on the snow with her claws he had died, and all this was some mirage of the Other Place.

He glanced at the beams, and the skeleton crew of striped hawks gathered there, at the dogs and the old lions in House collars. Women poised at the hearth and two or three at a loom. The warriors, fully armed, were banded in silence. All was silent finally. It was like a house of the dead where only statues of the deceased, faithfully carved and painted, displayed what had been done in life. Dayad even noted a man in a corner with a tawny skin and beaded hair, not Olchibe but some other race indigenous here as were the animals in the yard. But this man too was a statue.

And Nirri was standing in the firelit shadows.

How much older she had grown, yet how queenly. Of course, her statue showed her at her best, the age on her put in for gravitas. She stared at him unmoving as a statue must.

He saw the gems of water spilling from her eyes.

She wept. She lived. She was not, even if all the rest were proved to be, a dream.

With a clutch of the heart that was almost terror he acknowledged she would have known him if he had returned in the shape of a bear or as a vrix. She would have known him probably from a single knucklebone or crinkled hair. And he had thought *her* a statue.

He reached her with uncanny swiftness. She only smiled. He held her in his arms and not a word was said between them, there in the silence of the joyhall.

And then she did speak. 'There he is, there he is, your father. Go to him, Dayadin.'

So then he let her go and turned his eyes to the wooden chair where Arok the Chaiord sat.

One of the wise-women had left her house and run panting up the garth. Now she appeared by Dayadin and mumbled again the story of Arok's misadventure. 'We could do nothing. He died and was brought back – but his soul was caught among the stones.'

'I see that, lady,' said Dayad.

He did. He crossed between the other statue people and the fire, and stood in front of Arok.

'Father,' said Dayadin humbly, 'here I am.'

Arok said nothing. Then he dully said, 'Who? Where? What does it matter?'

Dayadin beheld the source of statues and dream-state.

He put his left hand four-fingered on the four scars under his clothing. He only knew to do it. A throb of power shot into his arm and through his spine.

He thought *Not Brinna – She – it was Chillel—*

'Father,' said Dayadin, 'come back to me.'

Arok muttered. Then vaguely he said, 'No, son. You stay there and guard your mother and the women.'

In Arok's floating, bloating brain a kind of upheaval occurred without warning. Huge blocks seemed to loosen and move this way and that, crunching over each other.

He was fighting in the snow.

No, that was not what he was doing. Someone, some Vormish enemy, had bashed him on the head. The blow had sponged him with unlikely gentleness. He had turned over and gone down and men on foot ran across him, and a reiver fish-horse jumped to clear his body.

Now I finish.

He could not move, yet he could still see.

What he saw was his son, Dayadin, dashing over the vista.

Illusion: Dayadin was no longer a child but a grown man, a warrior.

I shan't live to see that then. That's what it means. I lived through the White Death, but Chillel's purpose is accomplished. I am redundant and can die.

Arok remembered what his son had said. *Come back to me.*

Nirri was for ever remarking that Dayadin nearly always got his own way . . .

Arok floundered. He had to reach his son.

'God – God—' Screaming deep-voiced like a stag, Arok burst upward – out of Hell or out of Heaven, out of coma, through every obstacle of flesh and spirit, from snow and blood and earth and stone and smoke and winter and time – and landed in his own body in his own garth in the new continent, with his chair crashing over and the world spinning, and seized Dayadin in his arms – 'My *God* – you *live* – you're *alive*—'

'Yes, Father,' said Dayadin modestly, holding him close. 'And so are you.'

'And so – am I.'

FIVE

When twilight lingered longer than two hours, eight or nine moons came up.

They were very slender and gave slight brilliance. Nevertheless luminous shadows were cast in the gardens and groves of Zeth Zezeth's flaming world. And in these shadows now and then, tiny cool fires glittered like watching eyes.

Jemhara felt the dusk empowered her. She trusted her magical instincts. Though never Magikoy, yet her abilities were sometimes phenomenal. Looking back she had viewed them with bittersweet awe. They were the fruits of her life. Yet here in this part-death she surely kept their essence; perhaps, though unordered, they were much stronger.

She contemplated her knack of shape-changing to a slim black hare.

But she could not attempt that in Zth's province.

Instead Jemhara put out her finger and squirled open a miniature window in the crepuscule. She had learned, or guided herself to, *this* knack only a short while before, after her melancholy dream of Thryfe.

Through the portal she beheld the earth. None could mistake it was the earth, snowbound and itself turning from the sun of day.

Out of the earth-sky a gilded spear flashed down.

It was the god himself, Zth.

What was he doing?

Curious, Jemhara observed him skittering along a frozen shore. Something vast basked against the plates of ice, between the ice fields and the moving ocean. Jemhara was reminded of a seal that sunned itself. But this creature was so large she could not make out what it was, only its mass, the citadel of a many-spurred horn—

Then, something horrifying.

It was like a bomb of the disappearing sunset that exploded back into the world. All was brightly lighted to a stark nothing-ness. And then darkness mopped everything up.

Through the dark, which was too rapid for the natural end of day, fireballs bangled about and arching rays slashed the upper air. This did not go on for long.

Things settled.

Yet the sparkly little atomy that had been and was the god was bounding away and away, hemming the darkness and the shore like a lunatic mending.

The creature she had thought like a seal seemed eliminated.

From a continent's distance a grinding noise started in the substrata of the sea . . .

Jemhara smoothed over the pane of dusk. The eyehole was no more. She was glad she had seen nothing else, for surely the ranting little maleficent deity had caused some cataclysm, some strike that had no excuse, and so was unforgivable.

Soon he would rush back into his own domain. The stench of his evil would be on him, enthralling as sunshine.

Best prepare herself.

She thought of the wicked bitch who had abused her in girl-hood, and of others, of so many others. They processed before her mind's eye. Vuldir, Sallusdon the king . . .

Only of Thryfe she could not think, for to entertain his memory even for a second in such foul company was – *unthink-able*.

Smoothing closed also all the cracks and ravines within her own mind. Smoothing, smoothing, Jemhara summoned a foun-tain from the dusk, glittery with the tiny shadow-stars, and bathed there.

She experienced lightness and happiness as she did so. Next she enhanced the garments the god-thing had given her, and

339

fashioned jewels from moon litter. As she arrayed herself, most other elements were discarded. Even the lightness, the happiness. How could they stay?

Spangled and honed, Jemhara stole about the gardens. She was waiting, all prepared, as only once before.

I am inside the ice. Again.

The girl, no longer a girl, the woman of twenty-six or seven years, lay coiled among her covers and gazed up into the tapering pyramid of glassy freezingness.

The familiarity of it might have angered her. But she did not feel anger. At least, she was angry only with herself and that in a makeshift way.

Really it was pointless to lament over her deflowerment by Zth in the cold core of the sea, of her later imprisonment by fate – presumably – in the pyramid from which her Jafn husband had released her. Nor was it valid to complain of Yyrot's worrying triangular bergs, stuffed with wheat and corn that died and went black.

Tirthen would also logically make use of such uninspired retreats.

Saphay threw off the voluminous covers of fur and silk. They vanished.

She stood up naked and lovely and shook her hair.

Tirthen was seated across from her, naked too, his attractions heart-stopping.

'I shall leave this *den*,' said Saphay. 'Now.'

'Why?' asked the economic Tirthen, languidly.

He was *not* like Zth. Less worshipped and therefore less formed and fuddled by mortal expectation, Tirth managed to maintain a vibrant, primitive forcefulness, a sort of genuine animal magnetism.

As he rose, in each proper sense of the word, Saphay's resolve dwindled.

But she said, 'I can dismiss your powers. I am not your prisoner.'

'Dismiss me then. Like the last time. Such enjoyable dismissal. Let us be each other's prisoner.' After all, a hint of Padgish courtier-speak.

Saphay broke open the side of the pyramid with a look. Indeed it did not have the resistance of the dome at the garth, or such resistance had been deemed superfluous. Probably the latter.

Tirthen approached her in one step and drew her against him. The side of the pyramid sealed shut.

'I refuse this,' said Saphay as she wound her arms about him. Down among the rehabilitated furs and cushions they sank. A minor external snowstorm veiled the iceberg.

I have been so long alone, she thought excusingly.

What Winter thought goes unrecorded. Maybe little – he was an element. Yet, beyond the pyramid intermittent leaves split their chrysalids, a runnel of muscular water pushed from the ground. And the storm was feeble, more sleet than snow.

Zth walked through his garden and it became again the heat of the day.

He was full of himself, the god. He had done something momentous out in the world, and was warmed by his own ability. It had reminded him of his past when he had visited the limited sphere of the Ruk, lording it over mankind; his glory days. But why should he not regain all that? Everything he required would be given him.

Zth had lost the coherent idea of the Lionwolf, and that the Lionwolf must be destroyed. Or that this had proved always impossible.

Zth was in denial, which he discovered to be both ennobling and restorative.

When he saw Jemhara, his acolyte and chosen victim, sitting in a shining shade, only the most amiable memories stirred of inter-species congress.

Had he forgotten who she was, what she had done, what she had borne and birthed?

Jemhara got up and came to him. She knelt on the path and obeised herself, her hair sweeping up the petals of fallen flowers.

Sportive, for the hundredth time, 'How tempting you are, Jema. You must go away or I can't be answerable.' He sounded quite elderly.

Jemhara spread her body out at his feet.

'Don't send me away. How I love you, lord. Let me stay.'

Zth paused. He felt, conversely, very young and polished. If he had her, he would kill her. But did that matter dreadfully? She had served her purpose . . . surely she had. He did not need the help of a woman anyway. That had only been his game. He was Zeth Zezeth. All *she* could ever be was a toy. And of course she loved him more than her paltry little life. It would be a kindness to oblige her.

And look now, she was raising herself like a serpent, flexible and velvety, pleading with her wondrously depthful eyes. How enchanting her scent. It was natural to her, he had noticed before. Fragrant, and so clean, so clear – like the inner waters of the earth itself.

'Let me die for you,' he thought she said.

Something stabbed in Zth's inner awareness. He had a sight of subsea blue and a girl with lemon hair, and of how possessing her had robbed him of an intrinsic facet of his power. But that could not have happened, or if it ever had he had repaired from it. They were only bits of clay, these mortals, they never lasted even when one was careful.

'Then you shall,' he said. 'Die for me, that is.'

As he lifted her up Jemhara's eyes were brimmed with triumph. Presumably he did not see that either or misinterpreted it as well.

Then all the marvellousness of this sexual contact drowned her. Within the tidal wave of supernal ravishment only the slightest fragment of her actual self survived, swept round and round in the maelstrom. It was such a minuscule crumb. Even she could barely know it.

There had been nothing like this when she lay with wretched King Sallusdon, allowing him to enter her and use her as he wanted, while inside her vagina she had previously inserted a rare thaumaturgic pessary. To its venom she, having taken the antidote, was immune. But Sallusdon, King Paramount, was poisoned.

All her life, shallowly lived or profoundly, seemed to have tended to these two paired deeds, the regicide of a king, and now this deicide.

Zth would not exactly die, it was true. Nevertheless some essential aspect of him was about to be corrupted, corroded and *ruined*.

Yet how could that be?

Jemhara's flawless core harboured no poison now. What earthly poison anyway could harm Zth?

Somewhere among fields of light, illimitable conclusion raced towards the woman and the god.

Another sound that had no sound rang through the air and the unworldly soil. The sunflower sky tore end to end. A sort of matt bleeding soaked out there, dimming everything.

Zth started back. It was far too late. He had spent himself against the woman's womb, and she herself, all of her, burned up and flowed and separated to a sequined pollen. Nothing was left of her, nothing left of beautiful Jemhara, no particle or tint, for even the pollen was fading now, sucked down by the thirsty fake of Zth's landscape.

And Zth was hopping, springing, dancing a fever-dance of wizening and withering, twisting as he did so in an invisible but hungry furnace. He was becoming a locust, a grasshopper. Brown and brittle like burned grass, like a single grass-stalk pulled from a hearth, *charred*, his radiance flaking from him.

She had come to understand her own ultimate weapon as he had come to forgetfulness. For Jemhara had borne the Lionwolf. She had carried him inside her a year and more and brought him forth fully a god. It was not a poison this time in her loins, but an extraordinary panacea, inimical to such a creature as Zth, as pure fire must be to impure gold.

Zth the locust sizzles away over the ups and downs of his private terrain. A greasy unwholesome smoulder is rising from his passing, and all the while the private sky above is growing more sallow.

Saphay had also contained a damaging power for him when they coupled, but she, having a purpose even if unrevealed to her, survived the union.

Jemhara's purpose, however, is fulfilled, and she has not survived. Jemhara, whose blood had held the scent of clear water, whose eyes had held a depth in which eternity might be seen, had served clarity and eternity, and was dead. Jemhara is dead. Is dead.

Tenth Intervolumen

Since Today is weary and would like to sleep,
kiss Tomorrow awake.

Found on the wall of a hill-brothel:
Simisey

The city was like a baby: it kept getting bigger, and the noise it made too got louder and more demandingly urgent. Whether you loved this kiddle or not, sometimes you were daunted. Great God Guri certainly was.

How many decades had elapsed by now? He had heedlessly not properly made a note. And he detected errors too in the priestly or mercantile reckoning of Sham itself. Probably it was around ninety or a hundred years since they built the temple to him. There was a slab of fossil coal in the holy sanctum that pronounced it much longer, but then there was a woven cloth behind the altar that counted it at only six decades.

Time, to Sham, was adaptable.

He had wondered, time-traveller that he had become, if he was to blame for that too.

Even so the bough he had left on Kitten's little tomb, though it had changed to adamant, had somehow also grown. It was currently a big gnarled tree, with no leaves but stony purplish fruits. When they fell they made a clank. Remembering how she had played with the first fig made him sorrowful.

Why had she died? Surely all the others had not subsequently died simply through coupling with him?

Sham gave him a headache anyway with its row. Not that it was a real headache, yet it ached.

That morning he was standing by the fig tree looking at the tomb, and he wore the disguise of an elderly gladiator-master. When a woman approached and spoke to him *sotto voce* he took it for the usual thing. Despite his various disguised and often

347

nasty appearances, women were still attracted. He always resisted now, frightened of causing them hurt.

This one though, he thought, half glancing round at her, it would not be a vast sacrifice to forgo.

'Ah?' said Gurithesput unhelpfully.

'Bow me,' said the woman, very low. '*Give* me.'

'Be off, you harlot,' grumbled Guri. And from nowhere a bolt of energy swiped him. On this occasion it did not floor him, he was a god, but he staggered nevertheless.

Guri flung round. He knew who it must be, and a nearly welcome irritation spurred him on.

'What in Hell are you at here, you old blather?'

As long ago, she grinned. 'Old not now. All me young. God I, like Gurithesput.'

'All right, very well. You're young, young as a fine morning. What do you want?' And reluctantly an inner voice said to him, *You should be nicer. She assisted you once.*

'Nothing,' said Ranjal, goddess of wood. '*Give.*'

'Great fucking God me amen,' cursed Guri, and threw a handful of nothing before her. To his astonishment it instantly became a heap of vulgar gold trinkets, ribbons and sweetmeats.

Ranjal, who always insisted on nothing and nothing but, stamped upon and squashed the pile to silt, and glowered at him.

Guri stood there. 'Well. So you see. I got it wrong. I'm not much of a bloody god I can tell you, old lady.'

'Learn better be,' said Ranjal.

'If I could.' He turned away and gazed gloomily at the fig tree.

Ranjal spoke again, very low still. 'Who you think make on grave-spot tree to grow?'

'I,' he said dully.

'*I.*'

'*You*? Why would you . . . ? It's a girl I had and she died – you never—'

'See you sad, I. Ranjal sorry. Make the tree. I goddess of wood, remember you. Tree to remind you dying is lying. Can tell you where,' wheedled Ranjal, 'your Kitten born back—'

'*Don't*. Don't tell me.'

'Not trust self you now? What fool is he, Gurithesput. She not die of *you*. Just die. Some do. Die young. *You* her make happy so she go glad and easy.'

'Do you say the truth?'

'Why fib?'

'You might. What do you care what makes me grieve?'

Ranjal said, 'Before, I tell you. Ranjal-Narnifa I, and you make it for me that I become god.'

'I never meant to,' he said sheepishly.

'Who care? Is done.'

'Then it's done. What do you want now?'

'*Nothing*,' said Ranjal, abruptly and startlingly with a sort of witty female slyness that was alarmingly unmistakable.

She was interested in him, it seemed. In the romantic way. And now he fully looked at her—

Her badger hair was brushed and scented and had been made quite magnificent. Young indeed, the mottled effect of her skin, fawn and pale, was glossy and healthy, if odd. Her eyes sparkled. Her teeth were no longer wooden: somewhere she had bothered to redesign them white and clean in a fresh pink mouth. Though big she was . . . buxom rather than hefty. Her very large round breasts pushed invitingly at the woollen cloak she seemed to wear. And her hands, though many-fingered, were cunningly shaped and graceful, and unnervingly suddenly suggested all sorts of erotic extra-fingered possibilities—

Guri stepped back and the fig tree slammed him across the shoulders and head.

A fig dropped with the usual clank.

To his total dismay, Guri had found himself vastly aroused. He had just recollected, too, the dancer he saw in the fire on the plain with Lionwolf. It had been this one. It had been Ranjal goddess of wood.

'With me now, come. We sport a bit.'

'No, no,' said Guri and nearly groaned at the pain which shot through his balls at the evasion.

'*Give* me,' said Ranjal.

Great God amen.

'Not – here—' stuttered Guri, sweating his enticing sweat and seeing her nostrils widen appreciatively. She too he must admit smelled glorious—

She rested one finger of the many on his chest.

The temple rocked. A sort of earthquake dislodged on all sides showers of gilding, brass votaries, plates of coal, scores of stone figs.

The responsive noise of screams and alarmed shouts and running feet was audible all around.

'Stay yourself, girl,' grunted Guri, 'not *here*. We'll bring the whole building down.' Both she and he smirked, a youth and damsel nearly caught out in the fruit shed.

He put out his hands and gripped her. Oh, she felt like the Rukar Paradise. 'This way.'

It seemed to Gurithesput, Dog Star Lit Among the Nights, that he was aiming to spirit them back to that plain where he and Lionwolf had played at being human. It might have seemed like that to Ranjal too, for she had stalked Guri there. For sure, it was a plain, but if he or she had looked they were *north* of the mountains, and not therefore even non-physically in mutable, generous Kraagparia.

Guri did not guess this. He had tried to avoid causing damage. Now all he could think of was sex. Most of a mortal century, and the gods knew how much supernatural time, he had kept abstinent.

Down among the white blankets of the snows they hurled themselves. Warm as new-baked bread they found each other. Oh the touching and caressive grabbing, oh the thighs and breasts and loins and mouths and apertures and nooks, and oh the waves of lovesome lust that sent the top-snow itself into incessant javelinesque ejaculations.

An avalanche or two slipped slowly down the higher slopes. Brief hurricanoes whipped and whirled.

As frenzy subsided a sigh-like wind combed over all, optimistically tidying.

'I shan't be faithful,' said Guri staunchly. He felt he owed her the non-promise.

Ranjal, who herself was apparently rather more than in their past, remarked, grinning her white teeth, 'Not want faithful. Want nothing, I.'

'Was it a good nothing I gave you?'

'Give again. I see.'

After a while the combing wind gives up and leaves.

The cold plain, warmed in curious ways, takes a tally. What has the cold plain received? The bawdy upheaval has scattered both electrical and man-made tokens widespread. For example shards of treasure from the temple, transported here inadvertently in the lovers' stampede to get cracking. Among other things slivers of ornaments and filaments of wood and stone – including several stone figs. There are coals, chips off the ancient fossil blocks that Sham, the city called None Greater, uses for screens and panels, doors and roads. There are too traces of less concrete items. Shreds of spells and prayers, woven or carven, or simply made nearly actual by verbal repetition, flit and roll and settle all about for thousands of miles. A random sprinkle of such stuff comes down as far away as the continent's eastern hilt – Jafn country. But whole clusters thud and tinkle home across the nearer plain. While hitting the distant mountain range, now south, the odd spatter infiltrates a cave or two.

The god-charged artefacts and elements surely mean nothing in the broader scheme of history?

Guri has already been about this plain of the past, searching for the Rukar civilization. During his first life in the future, the Ruk had been mighty. Up there had stood Ru Karismi, capital of kings. And from this land called Ruk Kar Is had ridden the Rukarian destroyers of Guri's own people, who had mashed Sham to a mudhill. But in the past which is now, he has found no clue to them.

When eventually they have partaken of enough, the two gods see evening is curtaining the world.

By then everything else has settled, been absorbed. If they

had in their delirium ever noticed the disturbance, now no evidence confronts them. All is well.

Guri was relieved and sorry to see Ranjal depart. She flew off over the dusk in her old broomstick mode. It was most unlike the luscious companion of the day. She had her own people to attend to. And he, he supposed, would go back to Sham.

Idly he bent and retrieved a piece of dark coal from the snow. Surely, not a memento?

Otherwise he did cast one last look at the plain, yet failed still to recognize it.

They had united in the Ruk's heart, about two miles from the height which would, in less now than twenty years, wear Ru Karismi for its crown.

If Guri felt any buzzing beneath his boots he took it for a slight subsidence in the permafrost.

It was however the vibration of a hibernating civilization roused by divine sexnastics – and waking up.

Two centuries of Winter, as they named the Ice Age, had driven these people below. The story of the earth, and of themselves prior to that retreat, became wrapped in the fog of drastic climatic change.

Some code of conduct they managed to keep.

This told them they had been, so should continue to be, couth and educated, a nation of hierarchies.

Soldiers, hunters, land-workers gave respect to scholars and esoterics. Above these were kings, and above all the gods. For unlike the continent's northern Chibe and Gech, the Rukarians were spiritually less confident.

The undercity which they constructed against the arrival of the cold did not lie underground in quite that sense. A mountain supported their largest urban development, and in the mountain were adjacent mines. Into these they tunnelled, using up battalions of their soldiery and slaves. Here then were erected housing, thoroughfares, bridges, and vast rock chambers due to become markets, temples and palaces.

As the ice established, they went to ground. Above, the original metropolis collapsed and vanished. Its wide upland river turned to ice more than a mile in depth. The surrounding region rose higher as the snows built it up. The mountain no longer looked like a mountain, only a hill perhaps. The rest all lay beneath.

In this warren then the people of the Ruk lived on. Or died on. The Winter was unkind and they were slow to adapt. Because of that they started to elect three kings together, one the Paramount King, but with two others Accessorate. Should the King Paramount perish, as he often did, a replacement was to hand.

They had some magic. Their scholars had already learned some. Incarcerated in the sub-mountain they practised more, and a selection among them with the most talent perfected certain aspects of utilitarian sorcery. The making of fire from air without the need to strike it was, unamazingly, one of the first developed skills.

Meanwhile their attitude altered to their gods.

The Rukarians ceased to like them at all, again through lack of self-confidence blaming the gods for the ice and snow, yet still of course fearing them, fearing them more. And so the number of the gods was doubled and redoubled to cover all potential of calamity, and besides each god came to have two sides, the benign and the malignant. The second was sure proof of human blame and fear, the first of nervous human hope.

Adaptation progressed also as decades went by. It had to, or every creature not only in the undercity but in the world must have died.

Into this static equation then fell the levinbolt from the adjoining plain.

Gurithesput and Ranjal's bit of 'sport' galvanized the central Ruk. An unseen rain of unhuman enlightenment penetrated the shortened mountain.

From being a weakling among the surviving nations, the Rukarians grew over a space only of three or four years into a special race, their genes gold-veined with shining strengths. Not all were affected, naturally. But where the bounty landed it heightened in perhaps predictable ways. Among the ascetic scholarhood strains of spiritual and thaumaturgic genius were sown, and came to flower. From this the order of the Magikoy was born. Among the kings and their military strata a warlike and grasping tendency pushed up. And from that was born the will to conquer and to steal.

As the maguses called forth their servant genies, and constructed their robot golems and scrying oculums, the Ruk emerged from cover and built a modern capital on the banks of the frozen river. Tall, vital and aglow now with powers both mental and automatic, they looked about. Then they clothed the land with towns and steads, farms and industries. Later the laziness of pride would level much of that, but such an hour was not yet. Soon instead a brazen face of war turned north, and east. The fascist Ruk had remembered there were inferior peoples out there, some of them quite wealthy.

The Jafn they had problems with. They were fighters and anyway their area was energized in its own wild way. What had fallen in their country had caused the Jafn make-believe to come alive: sprites, wind demons, vampire seefs and sihpps – a diabolic host of *things* – had channelled Jafn belief to one unimpeachable God. They were also toughened in more ordinary form. They proved difficult to subdue, and though the Ruk might spar with them for years, treaties would result, tricks would be resorted to. Jafn was not lightly digested and so the brazen face glanced elsewhere for more available bounty.

It was in that era the Magikoy moved their headquarters into the abandoned undercity. They titled it the Insularia. Here they maintained their secretive cells of personal command and austere service to others. But here too, at some unexplained persuasion of the militant warrior nobility, they commenced study of a sorcerous armament.

Deep in the chasms once employed for survival, the maguses of Ru Karismi constructed their deterrent. Long after the subduing of north and east, the arrest of Jafn development, the despoil of Chibe and Gech symbolized in the sack of Sham, that thaumaturgic weaponry lay in the heart of Ruk Kar Is.

It lay there until launched, centuries after, against the Lion-wolf and his thousands-strong Gullahammer-legion. The White Death of the weapons would decimate all the peoples of the continent, not excluding those of the Ruk. And it would itself sack Ru Karismi, changing that crown upon the height to a rubble, littered with sugars of broken coloured glass.

He had taught them peace.

He had meant only for the very best.

He did not want them to incur the ego-wrath Hell he endured after his deeds in battle.

Guri, Gurithesput. The once and future god of Olchibe.

The strange thing that had already occurred to him was made more clear when for a longer while he kept outside the limits not only of Sham, but Sham's present time frame. By his own estimation he had been there all told seven months, or a little more. It was true, aside from his earlier excursions, he had indulged absences with his mistress Ranjal, or even to sleep, which he did not need. Also he roamed about the city's outer areas, its slums, the swamp beyond. But presently Guri consistently saw that time seemed to jump away, even when he thought he had been watching and aware of its passage. For example, a plant in a hot-house would have put on sudden fruits – or shed them – in what he took for a single night or, worse, a couple of hours. He next noticed an extra house for the priests built on to the temple. One morning it had simply *been* there, and weathered too, the product at least of half a year.

Sham had rulers of sorts, a group of elders, priest-kings. Guri did not pay them much attention providing they obeyed his holy tenets; the concept of kings had been and stayed remote for Guri. Yet he manifested in the city one midday and found himself in the midst of an elaborate funeral for two very elderly rulers – whom he had seen, both of them, hale and youngish only that morning. He had been close, too, out in the swamp looking at crocodiles. He had sensed nothing speeded up or odd. Yet some fifty years had evaporated.

It made him dizzy, and uneasy. He fought to understand it and why it happened. He wanted to discuss the anomaly with Lionwolf, but did not want to slip off to some otherwhere to find him in case another time zone flooded away while he was gone.

It seemed something was *editing* Guri's era at Sham, and now forcing all onward at breakneck speed.

Was he himself the culprit? Was an inevitable boredom in his residency now making him slapdash and over-hurried?

But he did not even know where time was taking him, where he was heading.

Guri felt fate tug at him like a worrying dog.

And then.

It was high noon and Guri was wandering a bazaar, disguised as a fat young merchant with a gaze for the girls.

Abruptly the sky *blinked*.

There was no other way to describe it. A vast eyelid flicking down over the eye of the sky with its iris of bright sun, a moment of nullity. Then up the lid went again and everything was as before.

A quaver of consternation spread over the market, rumbled through the whole city. On all sides animals howled and lowed and screeched. People who had turned to each other in fear, wondering what had happened to their vision or minds, now realized with added terror they were not alone: the effect had been common to all the city – perhaps to the world.

As for Guri, his memory only plunged him back-forward in time to that last battle below Ru Karismi. Everywhere then the rush and tumult of human warfare – and next a glimmer like softest lightning – a *sound* that quenched even the roar of the Gullahammer – a thunder that passed to silence. And the silence *white* – and white *was*, white whiter than whitest snow, white beyond whiteness, *black*, the night that cancels all days.

The White Death, end of that first world. End of that first true faith.

Although the blink of the sky over Sham was not really like

that, yet it was precisely similar. It was, he knew, the same horror, even if in a different shape.

While the crowd collected itself, laughed the event off or hurried to the temple, and some frightened bells and brass pots and gongs were beaten, Guri fled behind a wall and vanished. He blew northward, knowing also exactly where to go.

There had been legends here and there in his former life. In Gech certainly, and among the vainglorious Rukar with their clever maguses and myth of magical super-weapons.

High up he crossed the swamplands, and sped into the northern wilderness beyond. He saw villages and settlements. The region was sparsely but not emptily populated. The beehive dwellings however wore the look of tombs, and nothing moved.

How long now had passed? Minutes? Guri checked the sun's position. But the sun too seemed stuck where he had seen it from the bazaar.

Then he beheld some dead animals far down among ice-net willows, and an ape high in a mangrove much nearer, but also dead.

A wind was blowing out at Guri from the north.

To start he had not assessed it. He had taken it for the rush of air against him as he flew. But soon it was very strong. Then liquid rivers of boulders gushed past him. Some even smote him, doing nothing to him – a couple shattered on his godish hide – but they were big. Many crashed down to the ground, broke, and then he saw they had been larger than he calculated.

A pack of wolves was running far beneath, howling like the dogs in Sham.

Guri, in an instinctive and maybe petty gesture, cast a lasso of protection about them. They streamed away into the ice-jungle not knowing they would be saved.

Trees had snapped; they lay dying.

The cold was savage now, no longer like cold, more like scalding.

A rock chunk the size of a small moon, dressed with wrecked

shrubberies and jagged caves, slammed by. It had been the top of a mountain.

So Guri beheld the mountains of the north. They seemed to be in a cauldron of hurricanes, boiling there like vegetables, white and brown.

Then the wind stopped. It did not drop or sink away. It was the effect of a lung that had exhausted its contents.

Anything other than a god would have been dashed headlong to the earth. All about him Guri witnessed such dashings – mountainsides, slain birds.

And by now the mountains were a ghastly sight, all chipped and cracked like old crockery, with all the wrong angles to them, the balance of centuries dislodged.

He knew that despite this there would be a vast plateau still extant, held up high among them like a table-surface. Prehistoric this table-plateau, but now polished and laid for death.

Snow was falling when he got near. It fell straight as pins from brown sky to white land.

Had any lived here before? Perhaps. In the later time when Guri had first been born, the nomadic Urrowiy had migrated back and forth only over that tableland. *Ask the snow what it is*, sang the Urrowiy to their children, as the dog-teams of the future moved, and the bones of ancestors grumbled in their lacquer caskets,

> *Ask ice, wind, sea and sky,*
> *Ask also the whale, the crait, the bear and the wolf,*
> *Ask wisely, not one will not tell you name and self . . .*
> *But what am I?*

They had come to know, it seemed, if nowhere else but in their lullabies. The meaning of the little song was now revealed in awesome horror. For what it really told was of the great white silent voice which had spoken on the plateau. And which had said: Go ask the snow and the ice, the wind, sea and sky what has been done to them. Go ask the beasts and they will show you they are dead. And I, mightier than all, what am I? *I am the Death. I am the causer of this.*

What fell on the plateau in the north mountains was a bitter, beady little snow, harder than flints. It would never melt or fundamentally alter. It would become the inimical ice-sand of the north desert called the Great Uaarb.

Guri did not go all the extra distance to look.

He turned back to Sham, closing his sight against the rumpus and shambles in between.

By the hour he returned over the outer swamps, time *had* passed. The sun was setting. It was blisteringly cold and snowing here too, flakes and feathers, nothing abnormal, and nothing lay dead – or no more than usual. The breath of the calcined Uaarb had not reached the city.

But some nights and days had gone by, so much was evident now he had detected time's trickery.

Guri sat atop the Copper Gate, watching the ordinary sun go down. He knew the Magikoy from the Ruk must have journeyed through this country, perhaps even gone through Sham itself, unseen by his supernal perceptions. Naturally they too had been incinerated in the north mountains when their experiment took place. Conceivably they had become part of the falling bitter little snow.

Others of their kind would nevertheless have picked up the pith of the event, its 'success', through their oculums. They would anyway have guessed it was a dangerous mission. Why else send any of their genius magicians so safely far from the Ruk?

Guri racked his brains. He was trying to find the after-image of Rukar Magikoy in Chibe or Gech terrain. But he could not. And backward time here in the past was always murky. He did not strive very long. He had learned some while before that endeavour was not always rewarding.

The weather improved. Sham bloomed.

There was no plague, no striding ruin. In the nearby surround of country people went about their lives. Only now and then news came of a distant storm that had brought sickness on its wings. Finally, spasmodically, a few hundred refugees entered the city. They were from intermediary land, far enough from the mountains to ensure that the scythe had merely glanced over their heads. And though afraid in subtle, deep-rooted ways, their fear went off. Absorbed in Sham they resumed their vocations and trades or took to inventive begging.

He saw one Gech woman from the farther wilderness, who brought her two small sons to his altar in the temple for protection. Guri noted the boys were more scared of this adult god-person than of any remembered tempest. He came down and spoke kindly to them, dressed as a priest. Blessing them he made sure each, mother and kiddles, received cure-alls and long life. Sod bloody Lionwolf and his scruples about healing and benison. Even now Guri suspected his adoptive nephew had transcended too fast and so not grasped the facts of a hard life.

But when Guri tried to extend his help across the whole city he felt his power waver. He too had been curtailed, though by what he did not know. By life itself perhaps, always in cahoots with death.

Five months later confused word began to filter in, this time from the south, of a vast movement of warriors. Most took it for some ferment among the Ol y'Chibe.

Guri went to see.

It was not the Chibe. Although the Chibe had been involved.

Without a doubt his gospel to them of non-violence had impeded their resistance when, with no or minimal warning, the horde of the Rukar coursed down on them.

The Olchibe fought, yes. But guilt attended the skirmishes. To kill was an error. They must indirectly beg the pardon of Great God for any victory; they must atone.

The Rukar had no such scruples. Their gods were gods of smash and grab. Flaying the packs of Ol y'Chibe, they bore on towards the city.

Guri manifested both in his temple and among the sluhtins. He gave priests and people a sermon. He gave the warriors the same sermon while their mammoth cavalry stamped in rhythm.

The Olchibe must resist the Rukar scum. To kill was not always a mistake.

He put on too the appearance of a warrior and led them into battle. Some fights this way were well won. Not all though, for those who followed him had gone over to the manner of peace and compromise. It had been ploughshares for decades by then and the swords were rusty.

The Rukar, in battle, he did not recognize. But he had removed for himself all personality from them. An enemy should never have a soul. Being like the old days of his first life this disturbed him. He too felt yearnings for atonement. Flattened them.

A new myth meanwhile rose among his people. There were *two* Great Gods. One was a god of passivity and tolerance, and one a war-god for conflict, mounted on a roaring mammoth.

Divided in twain Guri marvelled in angst at how the Great God – he – became plural. That peerless totem he had sworn by so often as a man – it was himself, and twice. Like the filthy gods of the Ruk, he also had been made a schizophrenic.

Guri's own sluhtin, where reluctant Yedki had borne and left him, had itself been sacked by the time he reached it. Any Crarrowin he believed must have been slaughtered. Normally they were. Unlike the average woman – or man – they refused to give in and fought on with magic till crushed. He had heard tales of the occasional Crarrow who had used her skill to escape. But mostly they would not desert their sluht.

Almost a year after the sky blink of northern destruction, a quiet night covered Sham.

Observing the dark Guri thought it had outwardly Sham's general night-look. Torches and braziers were blazing on the streets, lamps in windows, and along the frontage of the temple. But he could hear all around a sub-vocal plaint of anxiety like the rustle of rats in the cellars.

It had seemed to him there had been no recent time-slips. He had been consecutively aware of the passing of every day and night here. This was so since the Uaarb was blighted into being. He had used every minute to rally the city, preaching, energizing.

Themselves they had laboured. The outer walls were toughened and built up, the city gates reinforced. Military exercises took place. Crocodiles and the vicious apes had been trained too, to attack a foe as in the arenas. But they were erratic. They often made mincemeat of their tutors instead.

Many declared no force would ever reach Sham. Sham was favoured and invincible. Sham had her God – her *two* Gods. These would protect her.

Guri had considered that aspect. Unbeknownst to the optimists of course he had already seen he could not do it. More to the point he had already seen he had not *done* it. Privy to the future of his first life, he knew that he had not rescued Sham. Even so, he considered options.

To protect the whole city seemed beyond his power. To destroy the enemy wholesale seemed too dangerous. It would require a blasting energy that might rival the Magikoy weaponry and fall-out of some type must be inevitable. It never suggested itself to him that *they* might employ their now newly invented weapons here. The future also demonstrated they had not. Doubtless the Rukar too were initially and sensibly afraid of them and kept them far in reserve.

Knowing the future was the main stumbling block to Guri frankly, and all options broke on the face of it. The events now sweeping in had already happened. Even if he were able, what enormous foundation might he dislodge should he dare try to undo history?

He did not yet know he was to blame for waking the Ruk civilization. He had thus far been spared that.

On this night however, standing on a corner of a narrow street in Sham, Guri beheld the Crax of Yedki's coven wending towards him along the hard-packed snow.

'You are Gurithesput,' she said.

He had been in disguise, that of a gladiator with a skin of drink on his arm to warm him.

He saluted her politely. 'Good eve, Mother.'

She must have been dead surely, twenty or sixty years or

more ago. This was her ghost, her phantom come out from some hell – or hopefully in her case, heaven.

A painful memory struck him of how he once, when dead and damned, had visited his own sluhtin coven, and sent them the black seed of Chillel in the body of Ipeyek, to foster a hero among them.

'You consider the fate of Sham,' said the Crax now.

'Just a little, Mother.'

'Do nothing, Gurithesput. Do *nothing*.'

Shocked. Guri dropped the beer-skin off his arm and glowered at her. '*What?*'

'You know, Star Dog God, that interference is fatal or more likely only useless. Leave it well alone. Yes, you are a god, but you are not in charge of these matters.'

'If not me – then which god rules here? Is it the Rukar trash—'

'None of that. None of you.' The Crax raised her hand, on the wrist of which a bracelet of thin gold shone. She looked healthy for a ghost. 'See.'

A ball of fire rose from her abdomen and floated up to perch as a globe on her palm.

Guri stared. In the fire he saw another globe. This was white, yet faintly stained here and there with a bluish greenishness.

'What is that, Mother?'

The Crax only watched him. She had coins strung in her hair too. She had come out well dressed. Nor did she seem old now he took her in properly, resting his eyes from the fire ball on her face.

'Some things must be,' she said. 'The foul herb must be eaten and the fever endured in order to grow well.'

'I don't understand you, Mother.'

'You yourself have suffered death, horror, salvation and rebirth. A common event. The old sun was the enemy, and then the Winter itself, the time of ice, that was the adversary. But only one other moves you now, moves all of you like bone pieces on a board. Struggle as you may, moved you will be. From the start of it, this One has moved you about. Even your rise to godhead has been *this* One, moving you. And the rest, gods and men, one and all.'

Guri wished he had not put down the beer. He had a very mortal dryness in his throat. Obligingly the skin lifted itself to his mouth and let him swallow a gulp.

'What purpose do I have then, Mother?'

'Your purpose *is* to be moved. It must and will be accomplished. You're not alone, Star Doggy. Your Lionwolf too is a game-piece. Even the night-goddess Chillel-Vangui, even she. And the old gods, they're like children's toys by now. One moves you, moves you *all*.'

Guri said, 'Why have you come to tell me?'

'To save you effort that will only hurt you and others. Poor lad,' she added, with a strange smile, 'I recall how you grew up so fast, and your mother ran away and Ennuat, fussy as a bear, took care of you.'

'I was my own father,' confessed Guri wearily.

'So you were. So are all men, Guri. Now I shall go.'

'Where to, Mother?'

'Ah. Don't you know? I'm a child among the y'Gech now, a boy of seven years who grows in the ordinary slow way.'

'A *boy*—'

'A boy, Guri Lit Among the Nights. My soul's come out this evening in this former physical shape you recall to tell you things. But now I hear my mother singing in the potted firelight. In a month or so she and I will be slaves of the Rukar. I want to be with her now, while I can.'

'Then let me save you – that I can do—'

'Now, my boy, what did I just tell you?'

The fire in the hand of the Crax blew suddenly up into the sky. It drifted off over the roofs of the city, flame with a round core of white and green. And *that* was his adversary, *that* moved him like a piece of bone? Over the temple roof it went and was gone.

When he glanced back so was the Crax.

Tears ran down his face. He rubbed them off with the gladiator's fist. Taking up his beer-skin he slunk to a brothel to

364

pleasure the girls till the sun was reborn. But even in their arms he thought now, *I am being moved like a game-piece*. Even this, then. Even with Ranjal? And somewhere in the busy dark he saw the waking he had caused with Ranjal in the Ruk, though nothing had been further from his thoughts.

A man would have slain himself probably. But that was no solution for a god – nor maybe for a man either, if he must only get up again in another life.

A century after perhaps the Magikoy, or some lesser scholar, rewrote the story of the Ruk. The blasting of the Uaarb, this document insisted, happened in *pre*history. The destruction of Sham too somehow retreated further into the past. Despite that it was happening *now*.

Time must after all have slipped. But he thought not really, the god, starting up from some amorphous otherwhere he had retreated to, as men retreat into drugged unconsciousness.

Scenes:

The big sculpted darkness of Sham against a sea of fire. The walls had given to the south; the siege if such it was had not lasted long. The enemy rode their chariots inside, their deer-drawn sleekars. Banners redder than the fire. A hundred, a thousand faces turning over like broken flowers. A Rukarian man raping a Shamite whore against a burning wall, stabbing her even as he thrust, penis and knife. Tears of blood, vomit of flame. A tower crashing. The roads of coal caught light with perfect logic. Streams of melted snow went running like live boiling rivers. A chest spilling jewels was left by the path, there was so much plunder.

He had seen it all in the legend anyway. In his first human day this tale of the city's sack had been told to all the kiddles at the earliest age. They were educated in it, just as they learned to braid their hair and to say their prayer *Great Gods, amen*.

Guri pelted through Sham. Now he was a warrior, on foot, smiting the foe. Now he was a priest, one of many carrying the treasure of the temple to a place of concealment – which was soon found, of course. The spears went through him, the sword cuts. Sometimes he even fell down out of a sort of unsurprised amazement. There were from him no bouts of bellicose sorcery, no weapon wielded by him that was ahead of its time. He himself did kill, if only with mortal tools. Once, twice, countless tiny times he rescued someone – a woman, a child with a baby in its arms, a little dog, even a wounded crocodile. Even a Rukarian lashdeer trapped in the harness of an upset sleekar. Such small acts did not disturb the huge and wicked scheme of the sack. *Do nothing*, he had been advised. *Something moves you and all things.* There was no choice.

Scenes: The temple, one section of which was exploding under the pressure of fire and oil, shards of bronze and wet silver and coal plummeting to all sides, sparkling. A tangle of limbs, a shattered pillar. One of them a Rukar, a boy – ah, god – God – for a moment his dying eyes, though dark, were like the lost and fearful eyes of Lionwolf that long-ago, far-ahead night as they had marched towards Ru Karismi. 'Sometimes I look back and see the distance I've come,' said Lionwolf, 'or forward, and I see a light as if the earth burned. And sometimes I wonder what choice I have.' And Guri had answered, 'No choice. Your kind – none.' *None, no choice*, he murmured now. *None of us ever, gods or men – none, none, none.*

He breathed on the enemy young man's dying eyes and took his pain, which passed like a black thunder up through the sparks and smoke. *All of us, one way or the other, live for ever. But does that then make this acceptable? Is* for ever *to be only – this?*

Black night went to black day. The sack continued.

Scenes: Scenes.

Guri stood on a high place and looked down and saw already the hideous coffles of slaves, roped, chained, driven through the avenues of sinking or rising fire. Some had been praying to him in his half-wrecked temple. He had not had the gall to manifest. What use was a god who could not help them? All he could promise was life everlasting, but this psychic bandage, at such an hour, was surely contemptible.

Then he saw the mammoth charge.

Naturally there had been several hundreds of them incorporated in the fight. He had watched as they buffeted, kicked and trod the Rukar sleekars and their charioteers to flinders. But now those of the tall pale beasts which survived were masterless. Mourning for their riders and for their own kin, they blundered among the general demolishment, sometimes trumpeting and calling. Sometimes too he had seen that they wept. The curious and awful phenomenon pierced him through; he had witnessed it before in his human existence.

But presently something else blew up at the central point of the city. Guri supposed it was the palace building that as a rule he avoided, the living quarters of the priest-kings. The afternoon sky, which had been cinder-grey, ignited to marigold. How beautiful the colour was. Guri gazed at it affronted, disgusted by the bad taste of its glamour. And then he heard the bellowing of the ourths in concert.

They came like an earth-bound whirlwind through the avenues, dashing all things from their way or trampling them into pulp beneath their feet. They were sombre with soot, bloody, seared by fire. But they pounded on as one single entity, in a rolling harmony, smashing those walls that still stood, those gates that had not gone down, destroying Rukarian and Shamite alike. Their eyes were minuscule dots of sightless light, mad with wrath and terror. Guri also experienced their brains; these were like lava. Dead smoke blew back from their hair, and some bore in their trunks pieces of corpses – a thigh, a whole torso even, entrails roped on tusks – and one had had some curtain topple on its sloping back that stayed caught by golden hooks. But all galloped like the liquid outer sea, a tidal wave, straight through the viscera of dying Sham. Northward they rushed. He saw them hit the ultimate wall, dismantle it, casting aside its last attackers and defenders like twigs from an impeding tree. Out into the swampland the mammoths poured, into the fog of arson that hung there, grew ghostly, vanished. From miles off distant isolate bellows drifted back, and drowned in the lament of the city.

He did not search after the ourths. He let them go.

367

Guri stood on the high place and beheld the greatness of the world razed. And Sham the candle blazed to its end, burned to a stub, faltered, flickered, and went out. The red nights were over, gradually the sable days were cleared. What then remained was not recognizable, only slag and flame-baked mud, from which the living were herded away into the south. No god had saved them. No god would. The past was over. To illuminate the future the fires of vengeance and hatred had instead been lighted. The legend had begun.

Thirteenth Volume

TOWER OF THE MOONS
WITH SILVER HAIR

Both ending and beginning may appear wearing the other's
clothes. Not until they are seen naked can they be known,
and sometimes not even then. Skin too is only a garment.

Magikoy saying: Ruk Kar Is

ONE

Green shoots had expressed themselves from the snow crust in broad swaths. Often there were dips of flushy snow nearby, upholstered by mosses or bristling weeds of some sort. In ice-woods every now and then a sycamore or tamarind might have thrown off a cask of ice. One branch or ten would hold up a spray of chestnut-coloured buds, albino fronds. Dark blue irises sheltered slyly in clusters. Some apples had been let go beneath a tree already reclaimed in solid rime. He ate one of the apples. It was not sweet yet had juice and pith and two black seeds attendant at its core. To him none of this was much of a mystery. But also he came across an upland village where evidently they had been made afraid by such changes. They were entreating Attajos their fire god not to overheat the earth. For what would they do if he did? And in the temple of the ugly Winter god, Tirthen, they grovelled saying *sorry, sorry*, as if it were their fault alone.

Athluan did not interfere. He had learned the lesson long ago of tolerance. He had been *too* tolerant perhaps. But still it was a habit not without credentials.

You could not ignore either the sheer *wonder* of being hale and whole and strong again. Of being adult as remembered. Add to that the fact one was immortal.

At some juncture he would pass through a door in this world, in this continent, and so into wherever it was Tirth had taken his wife.

Athluan by now was not unused to this sort of shift. He had been a ghost and travelled in various climes, before returning to

TANITH LEE

the astral country and so back here. Only the astral phase he did not recall. No doubt that was part of the penalty for his current state.

Another village later had put a different shrine by the track. It caught his eye. It had been erected to a fire god, this one named, so the lettering said, Escur. *He* seemed to be a warrior god yet famous for more kindness than the other one, Attajos, whose son he was. An old woman tended the watch-flame. She called out to Athluan in the native vernacular which he had picked up with unnatural swiftness.

'Yes, lady?'

'Make Escur an offering. He'll grant you warmth and justice and good luck. Only once was he cruel, but that was to his own people after they slew his mother.'

'Which seems quite reasonable.'

'So too, it does. He rides a white tiger he calls Cat, and his partner is a goddess of dawn, Rushais. Thus the altar faces east.'

Athluan had nothing much with him, therefore he pulled off a silver link from his shirt and put it in her hand. The link was quite a fair size now though originally it had not been. His child's clothes which had left him quite naked at one point had cleverly grown up and modified with him in Saphay's fire-spell.

He had taken the woman for a minor priestess. But apparently she had, like the Olchibe, more than one string to her bow. 'You seek Winter Tirthen?'

'I do.'

He thought, *And I am the one believed only in God.*

But she said, 'Over that rise the air sometimes lashes and shines. The weather has been better – or worse. Too warm. The fruit trees bloom and shed their fruit. Something has taken Tirthen's mind off the world.'

Athluan thanked her and went on and looking back five minutes after, as he started up the rise, saw she was no longer by the altar and there was no sign of her on all the open snow. He doubted she could have got to the village that fast.

About twenty paces down the far side of the ridge he saw the shimmer in the air.

372

A single stone stood up from the ground here, like the ones he had seen before on this continent. *They* had been many and very tall, and had given off sheets of emerald light. This was a dwarf of its clan and gave no light at all, but even so he sensed its true nature.

Among the other stones Zth had abused Saphay, and Athluan had demoralized and deflected him. And then the stones had themselves chastised Zth with their energies, hurling him at the sky where he disappeared, and from which he did not return.

Athluan bowed to the stone. He pulled off a second silver link – now only one was left: respect could be expensive. He put the link at the foot of the stone, and went on. Stepping straight into the disturbed air he moved through a semblance of a thin curtain. Then he was on a sea shore.

Out there beyond the shore ice the water was indigo blue.

Lapped by the shallows, an icy pyramid went up, and it was cloudy as scratched vitreous. It reminded him of the occultly shaped berg in which he had discovered her the first time, his bride, yet was not exactly the same.

Besides dusk was settling here, while in the previous landscape it had been morning.

Athluan paused to watch as a single full moon sailed up from what must be the east, out over the liquid sea. The sky was congested, nearly dark as the water.

Down the shelving rock he climbed, and so on to the ice fields, feeling as he did all his restored vitality and ability, young enough, old enough. For him maybe thirty had been the flawless age, and wrenched from him too soon in his former life.

Presumably he would have to scale the pyramid. That had been the plot before.

It would give him no difficulty. This body was ready-made nourished, exercised and flexible.

Yet he hesitated.

Instead of setting off at once he watched the solitary moon.

The sky closed about it, any faint star going out. Cloud foamed over, and one of the sky's mystic firmamental incidents happened.

A single shaft of moonlight speared down, catching the icy pyramid in its ray. The impression then was of a tower, solid at its base and less so above. And directly overhead in the cloud mass the moon still smokily glowed.

Athluan recollected a legend of a Jafn hero, not the famous Kind Heart or more famous Star Black. This man was a warrior of the ranks, but yet he had found in a moon shaft the white platform and garth of a gler that had molested his people the Jafn Klow. Entering the shaft he had met and killed it.

This then was an omen.

Surely even an immortal might receive one?

Before the shaft of brilliance faded Athluan ran along the shore. Reaching the pyramid's base, flaming in the moon, he sprang. He ascended the roughened quartz side with ease, not even really needing the precautionary two knives he pushed in and out and in to aid his purchase.

At the moment he reached the top the moon and cloud altered. A splatter of white-blue stars appeared further over to the south. They described he thought exactly the form of a beast, some sort of lion, but was not certain.

Athluan pressed his face high up to the pyramid's sloping side. It was more clear this high, and in this area it was like a window. He saw.

'Face of God.'

But it was not the face of God, down there in the ice. Nor a woman's face as at the first.

What he beheld was Saphay below, locked in a sexual embrace with a black-haired being. Her delight was unmistakable, as was her unhuman partner's. No mortal might intrude, compete, draw near. No, not even an immortal.

'Enough.'

It was not shouted. There was no need to shout.

One vibrant kick had smashed in the apex of the ice, and he had leapt down the space, thirty shield-lengths, maybe sixty, with the confidence of all he had become. Nor did his body fail him. He landed on his feet without any hurt or hesitation, beside the tumbled couch. They paid no attention, did not seem to see or hear.

The air was spiced and tingling – *musical* – from their pleasure.

He brushed that off him and spoke the one clear stern word.

Saphay opened her eyes. Everything else left her instantly, he noted, except for knowledge and dismay.

She was like any wife in life or story caught out with the neighbouring Chaiord. In the stories the cuckolded husband would then plunge his sword through both their adulterous bodies, cipher for the other betrayed weapon.

Athluan, though he had come armed from the Holasan-garth, did not draw the sword.

Instead he put his hand on the shoulder of the amorous god and with one wrench pulled him free of all contact. It must have been uncomfortable for both parties, even painful. Yet with gods, who could say?

Tirth spun away and as he spun a blizzard enclosed him, in which he stabilized fully clothed, not a hair out of place.

'Unwise,' said Tirth. Another unique word.

'Wise,' answered Athluan.

'In fact not. I shall dispose of you now.'

'She,' said Athluan, 'has made me eternal. You though she's partially defrosted.' He folded his arms. 'Try if you like. I'll wait.'

Tirth came at him then. That was, screaming snow and wind and needles of ice came at him. Athluan stood there immovable. What did this count for? He had been slain by a snow-wind much worse than this, full of lethal animates that tore him in pieces. *This* blast struck Athluan, his body, his face, slapped in at his eyes like bits of glass. But he withstood it, stood it, then ceased to stand for it at all. Shouldering through the mob of the blizzard he reached the entity Tirthen, which still somewhat resembled a handsome man.

In that moment Athluan perceived the god's basic unvalue.

He thought of the lighted stones and Zth, and crashed his fist into Tirthen's face. Winter was catapulted once more across the chamber of the pyramid and, striking the lower wall, flew right through it. Huge ice-works came down. A jagged dark hole with night in it and waspish whitish weather was the result.

Tirth did not return indoors. And above the open triangular chimney of the iceberg surged and grunted, threatening to fall in.

'Now you'll come with me,' said Athluan. He did not glance at her.

Saphay sounded mortified. 'You took too long.'

'Oh? I thought a woman preferred her lover to take his time.'

'Don't play with Jafn lewdness – or Rukarian sophistry. How dare you mumble that to me? All that trek I had to find you – and then you a child – and putting you in the vitalizing fire – and *then* how long I must wait. *Again. Years* I've waited for all this *curse* to be solved. And you, dawdling in the flame, like bread that wouldn't – oh yes, now a lewd pun – *rise*; too lazy to wake up—'

Without turning, Athluan smiled. The theatre of this was not lost on him. He used a voice like a battle-cry. '*Get up.* Now do as I say. I'm sick of your Rukar whinging, woman.'

'*You*—' The fury in her perished.

Outside, her previous precious inamorato flailed and curdled on the night. Useless, all of them. Son, husband, lovers – men.

But she left the couch, which anyway by now was a heap of uneven ice. Once upright on the floor she was immediately washed, dried, brushed, combed and scented with Paradise. Her whiteness had sheathed itself in a suitable gown. Even she was taken by slight confusion, realizing the garment was in the Jafn style.

Although he was not, she sensed Athluan was laughing, there under the play-act of his rage.

A silly smile upturned her lips. She erased it.

'I am ready,' she said softly, behind him.

And she walked behind him too, angered at it, yet tickled and laughing at it also, marvelling and nearly weeping, full of every contradiction that any woman in love might feel and know.

Past the collapsing pyramid, whole storeys of which were

now bursting in the black, moving sea, no trace of the Winter god was to be seen.

Above wretched Ddir, rearranger of stars, had put up a ridiculous effigy of some animal, part lion, part wolf – ah yes. A lionwolf . . .

'Where will we go?' she murmured.

'Where I say.'

'Very well then,' she said. The smile fluttered on her mouth again and she did not resist.

They trod across the sheet of snow, not climbing up the rock, only skirting the ice fields and the sea.

After a mile she said, almost inaudibly, 'I'm cold, Athluan.'

She was, but only because she had allowed it. She did not need to be cold, nor care if she was.

'Soon it will be *Summer*,' he said, perversely perhaps.

'Not for a century at least.'

'Then this is Spring.'

She had never heard that term before, not as such. How clever, she thought, that the barbarian Jafn had language for an interim condition, as Ice Age gave way to ordinary seasons. Though their speech *did* contain more than one language, *was* quite clever . . .

And it was true. Irises inked black-blue through the ice. Nearby a hump of tree had removed its glacial coat, its black leaves unfurling like eager hands.

It occurred to her she might be drawn back to placate the entity of Winter now and then. It was not real infidelity. It would be part of her function to deflect his – its – powers. She mused on this with a strange innocence.

Probably Athluan knew as much too. Would he be incensed?

But she was the goddess of day, and *Summer* day at that.

As she walked, in deep silence, she began to remember her son.

His image had been fused up there on the tapestry of night, but did this mean she would certainly see him again? By now, to see him seemed impossible. So long to wait – you have made me wait – a child, a child in fire growing quick as a plant in sunlight – but he had been a baby, Lionwolf. She had borne him, and then—

Her mind moved suddenly from him and fixed its total attention on her husband, striding before her. All she could see or think was him, and how the cloak swung from his shoulders, his pale hair, the sound of his light breathing.

It was as if she had not seen him before. Now she did. And with that revelation came an overwhelming consciousness of loss. This halted her. It seemed like the sinking of her heart's own sun.

Never before had she felt it, evaluated it, *known* it. Not any other loss, but this loss, *this*: Athluan's death, there in the Klowan-garth so long before. When it had happened she had been only afraid, if rightly so, for herself and her child. Now years, far more, had run away, and the pain reached her blazing, as if one of Ddir's farthest stars fell towards her and crushed her where she stood.

'You died,' she said, staring at the earth. 'You were killed and they brought you home in your chariot, for tradition, and you turned blue in your chair in the hall and decayed, but *you* weren't there and there was no one, no one – and I – and you – Athluan . . .' she sang in lament. And sinking on her knees she began to cry the long-ago widowhood of her youth and her mortality.

Athluan turned then and came back to her. He lifted her up into his arms.

'And now I'm here. Because of you, goddess, I shan't die again either in this world.'

But she only cried, holding on to him, crying, crying.

Behind them both now, above a slope, out of one external half-world and into another perhaps, Jafn warriors waited for Athluan, riding-masks pushed back from faces. Their hawks ruffled their feathers, and the well-trained dogs stood on the snow. The lions that drew the chariots did not make a sound, save when the last whisper of the snow-wind chinked their harness and the beads in their manes.

Athluan thought stilly, *This woman bore the brunt of all our beginning. What has been begun was begun through her alone.*

Her recent adultery meant nothing to him. He too foresaw it might now and then be repeated, in order to defuse the energies of the cold. Another myth, purposeful yet weightless.

In the end, her tears ceased.

She said to him once more, 'Where will we go?'

'Home,' he said, 'to the Klowan-garth.'

'But the Klow—'

'Are gone. Not here, sweetheart. Here they *live*. Give me your hand. I have my own place yet, and you're a goddess. Not till time's ending will we be separated, or suffer. Maybe not even then. Is that the vow you want from me?'

'Yes. Take me home.'

There had never been a home, save there, she thought, in the barbaric and despised Jafn garth. Before that the unloved, unloving, impoverished corner of a palace in Ru Karismi, later a host of spots and spate of journeys, and she on her own, even when she had thought herself among companions. He had told her, they had been meant to love and had no space to accomplish it. As he now dismissed her coming ritual infidelities, so she ignored the immateriality of this re-creation they would go to.

Together they stepped up the slope.

The night undid itself there; paleness and brightness rode through. And then they were all of them gone, gone to their own place, to torchlight and black wine and a lamp that would darken on one side, to the joyhall and the songs and the upper room, and the young lions and the stripy hawks, and the coming of the day, and of Spring.

TWO

Just before the sun had fully set that particular evening, the great whale Brightshade had been basking on some distant shore, this time in his complete regalia of psyche and physical body.

Zeth Zezeth was anticipating returning into his heaven and finding there Jemhara, irresistibly awaiting him. And this now was his final visit to Brightshade. Although, at the hour of performing the visit, Zth did not know how final.

Here was the coast of Kraagparia, the land from which the Kraag had long departed. Only Brightshade was there now. And the dull sun was descending inland, making the snow-hills black and the icy shore rich red.

Having brought himself to it Brightshade too was waiting for Zth. He flexed his massive, comparatively for him small, fore-limbs, tossed the last sun on his horn. In the fishy forests on his back things slithered, twittered.

Brightshade was aware Zth would be arriving. Maybe he had drawn Zth to him to settle the business between them. The whale was no longer afraid.

No, even when the fire-arrow of Zth's advent marked the orange-red dusk.

Zth touched down.

'Well,' said Zth speaking very beautifully, gleaming with malice, 'here you are, as ever. Idle. Did I not give you tasks?'

Brightshade talked in a fine coined voice, an innovation which startled Zth.

'You may take your tasks and chew on them, *Pth*.'

The deliberate mispronunciation of his mighty father's

name's first consonant was extremely insulting. Did the Sun Wolf try to tell himself it had been due to the whale's infancy in words? Or to whalish nerves?

'You rouse yourself to rudeness, you cretinous hulk, do you?' Zth let loose a golden bolt of electric pain. It slashed across Brightshade's body.

Another wonder. Brightshade had himself released a *shape* of thought. It formed instant armour all about him. Though the ice cracked and the sea reared, Brightshade was unharmed. He lay there and looked at his evil parent, and let the *essence* of the armouring *shape* show itself to Zth, freestyle but unmissable. *Lionwolf*, said the *shape*. *Lionwolf my brother, and my loving ally.*

Zth let go his equilibrium. Violence and lights flashed round him. He shrieked his malevolence. Through the tornado of insane rage small phrases sliced. 'So you make up to *him*? So you think he can match *me*? So you think *you* can match me? I will take every fleck of you apart and cast the fragments into noth-ingness.' But despite all that the whale lay there, *smiling*. The missiles bounced off him to hit land or sea or sky.

Only the earth took any damage. An ice-forest above the shore was burning. A real tornado started to brew between water and atmosphere.

High overhead a curious star formation had begun to show a lionish animal, which winked on and off as inflamed cloud raced over it.

'Now I kill you.' Zth, prancing.

'Oh, *Pth, Pth*,' said Brightshade. 'I have only to call my dar-ling brother. Shall I do that? When he comes he will do for you.'

Zth rushed along the frozen beach. He seemed not to grasp his face was in a rictus of fright, let alone that he was running away. To Zth, already much more than three-quarters a deic lunatic, the retreat seemed actually mere boredom at being with his second son.

Zth naturally would murder Brightshade. He would blast him into atoms and seed the clouds with him, and for days and nights it would *snow* whale. But first there was something more pressing . . . what was it? Yes, yes, Zth must punish the coast.

Definitely the Kraag were gone. But other people had here and there moved into the land's interstices. They were fishers or herders, sometimes nomadic like the Urrowiy of the northern North.

Night was now fully present, only one ribbon of non-colour dissolving over the land. Three moons had come up, each some way behind the other. And each only the most transparent crescent. The stars that displayed the legendary Gech lionwolf beast had grown more bright.

Zth Zzth ploughed along the coastline, stitching it to the ocean.

Jemhara, still then alive, was observing through her spyhole in heaven. She had not fully understood what happened next. She had seen only that he let loose some virulent strike that had no excuse, was 'unforgivable'. This act of his now about to take place would decide her on her ultimate action, and she would therefore seduce the god, impair him beyond recovery, and herself die.

What Zth would do, had done, *did*, was to engender a tsunami from the depths of the outer sea.

The landscape had grown warmer by some slight degrees. It was partly 'Spring', no longer all Winter. This made catastrophe simpler. Icebergs sailing beyond the skyline had melted off water into the waves. Currents were eccentric.

Zth summoned the forces of the sea which, since he had been exiled there in ancient myth, he seemed to keep some control over.

The coast began to churn.

Long troughs of liquid and ice were being dredged away to the horizon. Frozen slimes appeared where comatose creatures crawled, revealed unready to the air.

Zth brayed his orders, springing southward from beach to beach. He covered thousands of miles.

By the time he had done his worst, all thought of Brightshade was gone from him. He was assured he had achieved his aim. He then launched himself back towards his own sun-world, where the human woman of great beauty waited, a dagger of destruction in her loins.

Fluid water never left him quite unmoved, not even now he had so often woken it from the frozen state. His passing was like that of a warm creative sun. What else, of course?

Lionwolf had been walking for ever, or for a short intermittent while down the land of Kraagparia, towards its furthest southern tip. Aware of other things, his own metamorphosis was itself still continual. He was, even for himself, like a scroll covered with writing and painted images that unrolled and unrolled finding and showing always more, never coming to an end. But so it must be for all living things, it seemed to him. Their self-discovery merely took them millions of years. But then, he had always grown up fast.

Now he had stopped his stroll high up among mountains and beside a river. He gazed down on the thick rifted ice that culminated centrally in one slender stripe of moving water. Silken worm, it wended eastward to the ice fields and the sea. Lionwolf had stood here physically for an hour or a day observing this.

Gradually the sun began to disappear.

The sun was not yet his; it had not yet begun its transformation. That it gave off more heat was due only to a sort of attraction between them.

Sunset here was strong. Lionwolf examined it. Darkness hung overhead. But below Lionwolf lay an apricot lake of light cupped in a dark blue ice plain, pierced itself by indigo mountains. This alternate country was made only of clouds and afterglow.

Lionwolf turned from the river and climbed further up the mountainside.

Presently the sun, which had sunk, became visible again down in the apricot lake.

He let it sink once more. Then swiftly once more climbed to get above it, and that way watched it sink, for him the second time.

The Winter god had said to him, *Ice twilight, twice light.* Musing as a man would, Lionwolf wondered what this riddle meant. Perhaps it meant only what he had just done and therefore seen, the double sunset.

As the cloud and light had constructed another country so something lay physically beyond the world itself. It was a void that was not a void. There the stars burned and the moons rotated, and the sun was born and died and was born again. He had not yet gone out to the region where these things went on – not yet climbed that high. He knew and had for some while, no longer thinking as a man but as a god, that it would naturally be possible to him to leave the world and travel up beyond the sun, there to look down on it from the spatial void, as he had done minutes before from the mountain.

In that unexpected moment his mind touched Chillel. It had not happened before in this second transcendent earthly life. To touch her was a miracle. Like velvet the surfaces as his thought rubbed itself against the thoughtless beauty of her own. Even for a second, to be lost in her . . .

Southward and south-east, there she was. Vangui the panther with her steely claws, Toiyhin the dove smooth as rain. He gazed in that direction now.

The *sound* interrupted from the other direction, northerly.

It was a huge *soft* bang, like a clap of thunder muffled deep in the sea. But it did not sound and then cease sounding. It went on and on, elongating like something pulled and twisted and growing always harder and more infinite.

Night had covered everything up but for a last scarf of light that had no colour. Three moons had appeared, and over there a weird group of stars that flickered as speeding clouds began to flounder by in herds.

Lionwolf, remote and involved at once, knew what had gone on. Remoteness was shed.

He flung himself right off the mountain into the sky.

Like his father Zth Lionwolf's flight resembled fire, gold and red and sapphire.

*

384

The shoreline shook. It was splitting, exploding. Batches of ice, some big as towns, spiralled high into the air, crashing back and breaking, the shards again shot off, again falling and breaking, becoming eventually powder. The ocean had gushed away to the edge of vision. There it was building a vast wall. Any who looked could see this wall for it fizzled and dazzled, producing some chemistry of its own. It was white water, white as the inland ice. But then it went black.

What had caused this – Zth – was no longer on earth's premises.

But the people who at this time dwelled along the Kraag coastal areas, they had run out to see.

Behind and around them were their homesteads, the sheds and huts, channels of fields, the boats and little ships. Tethered animals called in fear from barns. Children shrieked in terror or excitement.

Some were already fleeing. On the fringed hnowas they had, perhaps, brought from Jafn land, in carts drawn by deer, sheep or goats. Most simply ran, babies and household oddments on their backs. Left behind, the sick and the weak, the old, the lame, the stupefied. No margin for compassion or empathy if you were to survive. Others incredibly dawdled, gaping at the view.

Where the satiny slime plain stretched out to the withdrawn sea, some of a new priesthood still picked between the flapping fish and cast shells. They worshipped the stony bearded god they called the Blue Sun, and now invoked him to normalize the ocean. But the chants faltered and the boy singers sang off-key. Soon even they were hastening away.

The wave was already so high it had blotted out the moons. Even the funny constellation many had noticed, product of Didri Star-Messer, had vanished.

Did any gauge the height of the wave, or the flattening scope it would have when it came in? Tens of miles would be swallowed, or more. Nothing but solid rock could withstand it. Really it was as foolish to flee as to stay put. Escape was not likely.

All this while the night had been growling and quackling as the floes and shore ice broke.

Now abruptly it grew uncannily quiet.

That lasted some forty seconds.

The ears were filled with clotted silence, as if prematurely full of water. Reddish glims threaded the clouds.

A kind of twang, not seeming particularly loud, more like the note of a string snapping, was heard all along the coasts, heard even inland in the hills. Heard as far they later said as Kol Cataar, over the dividing mountains to the west.

Then the black colossus of water turned like cream.

Sourly in it came.

In – in – in—

Curling, feathered with green-red fire along its top – wriggling within as if sea serpents writhed there—

In.

Lionwolf dropped to earth.

At seven hundred different sites they would come to claim he had landed. Seven hundred shrines, and more, would be hewn and erected between the land and the sea. Numbers of future statues would demonstrate the god was an older man, bearded. Others would protest he was young, a youth, a *child* even with long ruby hair. Or he was a male god in the glory of his prime. Or he was the sun's disc fashioned from metal, with rays.

Being himself, Lionwolf landed at every site where he was afterwards depicted. And at uncountable others. He made of his etheric yet earth-linked body, flesh and eternity, a golden cordon that spread along the shore. Endlessly repeated then as if in multitudinous mirrors, a tall image of gold raising its right hand, the hand of the swordsman, the musician, against the influx of the waters.

He was not mild as he stood there on the coast. He was illimitable, a barricade and a fortress against demolition.

Flat, the hand held up against the sea.

'No,' he said. Said almost tenderly, as a father tells an infant not to smash its toy.

No. That was all.

No.

And the mountain of the wave stopped moving.

Off from its top burst plumes of foam and steam. Strands of it curdled and evaporated – whole swags of its molten wetness caved in, each descending with a boom, sending waterspouts high into the stratosphere, where they too hissed and sizzled and became nothing.

An aching warmness flowed along the beaches. The light of the god was sincere as sunrise.

No, he had said.

That was all.

A type of hot erratic rain piddled in over the land. The rain was amazing but not injurious. Women caught it in bowls and buckets but after it was found to be salty, sheer brine. They retained it to flavour the porridge.

No, he said.

Lionwolf was sunrise on the coast, obdurate yet quietly laughing. Some while later too some found their hair had turned golden, or the fleece of the sheep had done it. Or an ulcer that troubled was healed, or love had reinvaded a marriage, or a wanted child was conceived. They had too the healthiest, most glamorous rats that side of the continent.

The sea settled, shivering. It came in couthly like a brisk tide, winding over the slimy floor, reclaiming and sheltering the marine animals. Delicate wavelets ambled up the broken ice, bringing pearls for necklaces and purple weeds that were good for broth. Goldenness had set like the sun. No one could climb high enough that night to see it rise and fall or rise again.

Now it was sometimes day in the garden. A peachy dawn would bring a lucid morning lasting two or three hours. At apparent high noon the sky would flambé and the trees and grass cast no shadows. The deer concealed themselves. The saurians basked shapelessly as scaled bags in the flowers. Then two or three more hours carried the diurnal off down a pink sunset drain. Any actual sun stayed invisible. Doubtless there *was* no sun here. Daylight was a gift the goddess had extended to please or reassure them, or only to accustom them to the outer world they must re-enter.

For over a month by her own reckoning, Azula had watched her half-brothers going off through the park by day or night. Some had even deigned to tell her that they were departing. They meant to go home, they said, or elsewhere. Or they meant to make boats and cross the stretch of eastern sea beyond the island. Another land waited there, the third continent of the earth. It was populated, they seemed to think, but not crowded.

She sensed the ones who went homeward needed the familiarity. Those conversely who sought the unknown country wanted the unknown. Their brief nightmarish liaison with their first mother had enhanced them, and also cut them up. Not only the scars on their ribs then.

But Azula had no physical scars. Those inside her she felt lifting to her surface minute by minute, and more swiftly in dreams. She was not afraid of them. Scars meant healing, like the one that had been on her other mother Beebit's forehead.

Now and then Azula saw Chillel.

She did not know if any of the others ever had, after their ordeal.

Sallus had come to call on Azula only once. By then Azula had made herself a bothy from fallen branches she found among the groves and woods. Probably shelter was unnecessary, but nevertheless she preferred to have it. A fireplace smouldered before the doorway, for Azula knew how to make fire by striking two shards together. Inside was a bed of grass and a store of fruits she had picked from trees also found on her walks. She did not hunt, had never been taught; also the thought of killing the animals repelled her. Being useless at it therefore she did not judge she deserved to eat meat. So far this lack had not impaired her.

Her brother, the prince of Kol Cataar, strode up over the daylit hill and paused, staring at the snake. In a way the chaze had stayed with Azula, and in a way too it had not. One night it had gone out on one of its own hunting forays and in the morning, of which by then there had been seven, Azula saw it had folded itself into a tree. Going closer she discovered this was not quite the case. It was the tree which had twined the snake, throwing a cluster of vine-like arms about it. The chaze rested there in a sort of curving uprightness. Azula had believed it was trapped. Then she saw whenever it wished the snake merely squirmed free, the boughs themselves lifting away to let it go. They would coil back to hold it when it returned. She did not understand what this portended, or if it was relevant in any way. But she went out to explain the situation to Sallus.

'Yes,' he said, when she had spoken. He stroked the snake's triangular head. Its eyes narrowed with bliss, but it did not desert the embrace of the tree. 'I suppose,' Sallus added, 'you're like the chaze.'

'How?' she asked.

'You won't leave this place. Or will you? I came to suggest you might travel back with me.'

'Where?'

'To my father's city. I *must* go back. What else am I for? All this – all this . . . is nothing.'

His face was older and more grave. Azula hoped the sorrow would leave him as he left the isle. She was well aware what had been done to all of them, the young men, the searing and momentary destruction that let in the force of the absolute. All had survived. None seemed glad of it, or felt they had received anything in exchange for their male humiliation, the horror of that severance from the primal mother, worse than birth. It had made any future asset soiled, meaningless.

She did not know what to say, so said mundanely, 'Such a long way.'

'No need to journey as we did. We can walk on water or fly now.' His face expressed disgust at the soiled, meaningless asset of this. He added, scathing, 'Like *their* kind.'

'Chillel's kind.'

'Vangui. And the mad god Vashdran.'

'But can we fly?'

'Or whatever, Azula. This is childish. Will you go with me, even in a boat?'

'I . . .' she hesitated. 'I must wait.'

'For what? For her to rip you to the bone? I thought she didn't need to do that, with you. She's partial to her own sex. She likes her female progeny more than the men. There are human women like that. Or,' he appended leadenly, 'the other way about.'

'No, Sallusdon, it isn't that, not with her—'

'You've changed the tune of your harp, sister. I thought she was nothing. I thought you hated her.'

'I did. Then I didn't hate her.'

'Very well. You'll stay. Farewell, Azulamni, daughter of Beebit.'

Her eyes filled with tears but rather than spill over they swam back into her heart. She said, 'We mustn't part unfriends. After I lost – my ma – you were the *only* friend—'

'You honour me. Thank you. Take care of yourself in this foreign land.' He turned away.

She said, 'I know my real name, Sallus. Shall I trust you with it?'

'She gave it you. Better not to.'

'It wasn't she gave – she revealed it.'

'What worth then the name your *mother* gave you?'

Azula said, 'There is more than one reality.'

'So it seems. Farewell, sister.'

When he had gone down the hill, the chaze hissed faintly from the tree. Azula was sure she detected the syllables of her other second name in the hissing. But she went into her bothy, and sat there and cuddled her mother's bone and cried for Beebit, and for Sallus.

It was near sunset of the short day when Azula came out again, and looking along the sweep of the garden she saw Chillel who was Vangui and Toiyhin moving against a vermilion sky across the grassland, with six of the panthers trotting by her.

Azula put back her hair. She ran up the slope. When she was near Chillel one of the cats sprang away from the goddess and straight to Azula. Azula felt no alarm. The panther threw itself at her feet and flailed about purring. It was the one she had faced up to and it apparently remembered her.

She stroked the cat.

'Goddess,' said Azula, 'what must I do?'

Chillel smiled. There was such sweetness in her smile. She held out her hand. 'Come with me.' You could not deny her. Whatever else she was or might become, at this instant she was only goodness and wonder.

They ran then side by side, keeping effortlessly together, and the panthers with them. The park sped by. The sunset became night.

Azula was uncertain if Chillel spoke to her aloud or only sang to her and told her stories in her mind. Azula learned histories and legends and jokes and games. Azula learned how to hunt and kill painlessly for food, how to find edible herbs and leaves, how to cook and read and speak other languages, and ride several beasts; she learned what lay deep in the sea, and high above the sky, and where the stars were. All was an astonishment, but very simple.

The excursion took the whole night, and they ran together all through it and Azula was never tired. They must have gone all round the island too, for different scenery appeared sometimes. She glimpsed the metallic rivers that guarded the outskirts of the Chilleldom, and also the outer sea. When the dawn returned, they were up again by Azula's bothy, where the snake slept in the clasp of its tree.

Azula sat down on the turf and the single panther stayed with her. It washed itself like the very thing she had mocked it as, a kitchen cat. Once birds ribboned over, fluting their song. The panther gazed, lashing its tail.

The young woman felt only happy. Though learning overflowed in her, it had been given as a loving woman gives knowledge, where she can, to her daughter. The giving had only been extremely fast.

When she looked Chillel was gone, her retinue of cats with her but for the one which remained.

It was not that Azula knew now everything she must do. It was only she knew that she *would* know, and when she did, could do it. She had been gifted also with valid intuition.

Afternoon parasoled the coastal plain that lay at the land's furthest tip. The plain, though shouldered by ice mountains to the north and west, was full of green-gold, full of the stalks of growing ripening wheat.

Four women were dancing in a clearing in among the grain. There was a sort of floor there where the wheat did not grow, kept clear and beaten flat.

The women wore black, and were immediately to be seen. But two had wine-yellow hair and one was fair and one malt-brown. In their hands were four swords that gave off a flash as they smote them together.

Lionwolf stood watching them.

He had reached the southern limits of Kraagparia, and here they were, women of the Kraag, as he had seen them long ago elsewhere during his first life.

In the dance the girl with the darker hair turned her head around completely and looked over at him, even though the rest of her body still faced the other way. Darhana.

When the dance finished, the three blonde girls sat down on the dancing floor. Darhana turned her whole body towards him and walked through the wheat to where he stood.

They had been lovers before. As she had told him, she loved him – and others too. *Faithless*, he said. She had answered faith-*full*.

Now she made an obeisance to him. It was curious. She had never been so reverent as he saw she was, nor last time so happy with him.

'Welcome, Risen Sun,' said Darhana, beaming at him as if he were her beloved and long-lost husband.

He knew now that she lived in this moment as she had in

the former moment of their acquaintance, and both of these moments despite her natural physical death many hundreds of years ago. Since time was also to be manipulated, no doubt it was always possible to venture forward or back, and to leave some essence of oneself to remain sentient there, awaiting a meeting, though the rest of one had moved away.

'Now everything's well with you,' she told him.

'Now everything is or will be well with me, Darhana.'

'Now you are god.'

'Without your kindness,' he said, 'what might have survived of me?'

'All,' she said frankly.

'But my road would have been stonier. Remember fire's called or struck into the world. If none calls it or strikes it with a flint, what then?'

'At last it generates of itself,' she said.

'Why?' he asked her.

She laughed then, and so did he.

It was his flirtatiousness to ask her, for he was the god now and knew. Yet the playfulness and etiquette of his earliest years had not abandoned him. Whether all their cruelty and reckless-ness were entirely gone remained to be proved.

He and she went into the wheat and joined the women sitting there. A sunny wine appeared in vessels of glass and they drank.

They spoke of little matters. Only the unreal was real.

The old sun strolled over a warm and fondant sky and hid behind the mountains.

When the shadows had deepened to bronze, he and the women got up and went southwards through the field of the plain, the great stalks tasselling and rustling as they passed by. Eventually a sea appeared on the horizon, darkest blue, and rest-less in its *Summer* freedom.

An hour after Darhana pointed.

'There is your vessel.'

'I need no ship, Darhana, as you understand.'

'A gift, Lionwolf. A last token of what is not real.'

Narrow and gilded, with one bowed butter sail, the small ship lay at anchor a strong swimmer's distance from the shore.

'How shall I get there?' he inquired, playfully.

'Why, walking on the sea, how else?'

He bent and kissed her, as a husband kisses his beloved wife farewell. 'I love you, Darhana,' he said, 'and all the others you will be. Live beautifully, sweetheart, in your past, and your every present to come.'

But he ran over the blue waves like a boy, laughing again, shaking back his mane, while the fish rose to touch the soles of his boots and get the blessing of his transcendence.

As he could have walked to the island, and to the third continent itself over the ocean, so he could have caused the ship to fly there. He had weighed anchor with a thought. Thereafter the unreal and pretty bark did anything required of it without his even thinking it should. This was one of the finer jests perhaps between the world of men and Lionwolf's abstract realm of gods and marvels: to cross a sea on foot to gain a ship no water-walker would need, and to have it carry him on by its own will. No object was inanimate, even if it must keep still. Lionwolf let *her* sail. She made full speed under the windless sunset.

'Is that you, Uncle, sitting there against the mast?'

This question came about two hours later. By then three full moons were up and the waters were lit like high noon. Even a poor-sighted human must have spotted the hunched, disconsolate figure sitting cross-legged on the deck.

Guri did not answer.

Lionwolf seated himself at Guri's side. There was suddenly a wineskin.

But Guri did not touch it.

They sailed on then for a long while in the silence of vessel and waves.

'Lion,' said Guri in the end, 'I'd thought I paid my dues in Hell.'

'So you did.'

'No, Lion. No. I've paid again since. And because of it – now my debt stinks worse. No man, no god, has a debt can match what I owe. Not even that rabid thing sired you. Not even *Zeth*.'

Lionwolf looked only out at the running waves and the white crystal breaching of the prow.

'Sham,' said Lionwolf.

Guri bowed his head. He was immaculate, braided and adorned like the best of Olchibe, even the authority tattoos on his cheeks that leaders of vandal bands had come to have in recent times. And all this was the mistake of some – not even unconscious – vanity or sense of self-preservation, for Guri had not personally arrayed himself. He had come away from the abyss clad only in rancour and despair. But what he had become now was always beyond automatic disarray. He had forgotten or not known that to look as he *felt* he would have to create it as carefully as, before, he had had to paint his teeth and plait his hair.

'I couldn't help them,' he said in the cool solemn tones of the abyss. 'I tried to make them be fair to each other – and to any others. Put them off war. I'd seen, hadn't I, where war takes you, and what comes after too. *Warriors*. Some god of Gods save me from warriors. But when it was all done, the city all down and bubbling in its own swamp and shit and the fires gone out and the crying *put* out – then I heard them whispering to me, even then. I'd become two Great Gods, Lion, do you see? A God for Peace and a God for Battle. A God for Then and one for To-come. But I'd failed them and they still – *prayed to me – Lion – Lion –* they prayed to *me*.'

'What did they say, Guri?'

Guri wept. He said, 'They were saying it was never my fault. They said I'd help them if I could. But I was a god like men. A god who wanted to be just and valiant but was overthrown. I had done all I could, they said. But I wasn't strong as the stronger powers, not stronger than the evil mad gods of the Ruk. So Olchibe and Gech must keep faith *for* me. They must hold me – both of me – in their hearts, and never forget I had done my best. They heard me sobbing for them, they said, these slaves

driven off under the whip and in chains, women with their kiddles dying – or dead – at their breast, men each with an eye
gouged out to keep them *docile* . . . They valued me, their Great
Gods, who cried over them. And a day would come when they
could fight *for* me. They would make me great again. Lion, even
now, the sound of the waves has got their prayers in it.'

Lionwolf spoke after a gap of several minutes.

'I still hear the unheard sound from Ru Karismi. The *White*
sound.' He waited, then said, 'But it's over.'

'*No*, Lion, no it isn't. In time – it happens again and again, and
Sham happens again and again—'

'No, Guri. Not in the way you mean.'

'But I went *back* to it, and was *born* there.'

'But now you could do neither.'

Guri thought. 'It's so. I can't go back. I tried to. I tried to go
back to before to teach them different things than I taught – and
I couldn't. I can't now. Why, why? Have I done *enough* damage,
ah? Is it only that? I remember in my mortal life, the Great Gods
were only a potent name. No idea of paucity or sadness. No idea
they had been *absent* – when Sham went down.'

And he recalled how long ago he had informed someone, *If
you believe in gods they grow valid and help. Or if you're afraid they
hurt you* . . .

He had then only just become a ghost. He had known so
much, so little.

My people, he thought. But he was calm once more. 'They forgave me,' he said, in calmest desolation. And sat listening to the
forgiving prayers in the running sea as Lionwolf sat listening to
the scream of Ru Karismi.

At length Guri said, 'I was the one woke up the Rukarians. I
rutted with that broomstick goddess. Some ectoplasmic sperm
of mine showered the land with galvanics. They came to and
learned magic. All the Jafn demons and sprites got started too.
There was a rain of sacred coal from the temple at Sham. I only
found one piece of it. One coal. Just one. Just . . .' Guri looked
up. In the moonlight a kind of sheen had begun in the hollow of
the ship. It was richer than the moonglow but not so descriptive.

Maybe it was some sending of his nephew, something healing, kind. Then it faded.

Instead Lionwolf murmured, 'Some might tell you, Guri, that you bear no blame. Even if not meaning to you gave the Rukarians a bright lamp to light their way. If they used it to set fire to things that was their crime, not yours.'

Guri said, 'I met one of the Crarrowin. She said something moves us all. We've had no choice. Is that it, Lion, do you think?'

'Yes,' said Lionwolf.

He took Guri's hand and held it. This was a Jafn custom. But Guri clung on. How good the hand felt, holding him up above the abyss.

'What *is* it, Lion, moving us? The Crax showed me but I didn't grasp it. Do you *know*?'

'No, Guri. Yes, Guri. Guri, listen to me now. You've done only what you must. The past was written. Now you have stepped away and will never return to it. The future *alone* is open and to be made.'

'I'll never set my hand,' he wrung the hand of Lionwolf for emphasis, 'to any other thing. Never, Lion.'

'Ah, but Uncle, you haven't yet been up to see the stars.'

Guri stared at him.

A memory filled Guri's troubled mind of his ghost days long ago. Of how he had longed to leap and touch that stellar silverware – but something had interceded. It had never been achieved. In a wandering wonder he tilted back his head and looked now beyond the strident moons, to the little chips of brilliance that shone behind.

A real, or unreal, wind all at once blew into the sail, which turned itself somewhat.

Two small islands evolved from the waters to the south-east, going by fire-white in their crusts of snow.

'Stay with me, Guri,' said Lionwolf. 'This is almost done now.'

'Is it? That's fine. Fine as gold.' Guri lifted the wineskin. He drank. He said, 'The Rukar stole many of our Olchibe names. They even made a god named Yuvis. That was a name of the Ol y'Chibe. And Peb's name, my leader, Peb Yuve. Here's the coal I picked up on the plain after Ranjal and I . . . then. It seemed familiar. Can you see, it's singed a bit?'

'I can, Uncle.'

'Of course you can. It must have come from Sham. Out of the past.'

THREE

More night than day the island, even now.

Guriyuve, son of Ipeyek and Hevonhib and Chillel, had quit the grassy park, the pale flowers and groves of trees.

Ignoring the rambling deer and occasional slink of saurians, paying no heed to the bat-like birds that flew across the moonlight singing, he had come back to the wooden barrier, carbon and ebony, that edged the goddess's queendom.

Before him unseen, hellish metallic rivers already poisoned the air. Then there would be the lacy ice-caverns and after those the island's end, the sea.

He was the last of the Chillelings to leave, he thought, apart from the Jafn Fenzi. And the bi-colour girl acrobat.

Guriyuve too hated Chillel. Drawn to her like moth to flame he had been burned. Although this had made him greater and more his own, unlocking abilities he had not guessed at, the hate was bound below the cage of his heart as surely as the scars of her claws.

He did not know where he meant to go. He no longer wanted the sluhtins where such as his human mother and her coven ruled. All Olchibe had gone or was going that way. The women, with only dead men or weaklings, had ably taken up the reins. A female mammoth normally led the herd. Why not a woman then to lead Olchibe? If the *men* had not fallen under the spell of the Lionwolf none of this would have happened. It was true, women knew best in some things.

Fenzi had not had such a problem. The depleted Jafn territories were not becoming matriarchies. Rather lawless, and wild lions were rife – an adventure playground. Besides, Fenzi's Chaiord had discovered a new continent, and planted there the Holas sigil of the roaring seal. But Fenzi said the Chaiord's hero son was now with him, Dayadin. There was no place for Fenzi, offspring only of a fisher and his woman. Or so Fenzi seemed to think. Fenzi had added, with shame, that his feelings for his blood kin were long gone. There had been a lover too, but this link had shed its meaning also.

'What will you do then,' Guriyuve had asked, 'seek the next new country over beyond here to the east?' The rest who had not gone home had done that.

But 'All lands are alike,' said Fenzi. He spoke as if therefore all lands were useless, meaningless as any kin, lover or friend.

Neither man had much real interest in the other anyway. They had always all been like that, the Children of Chillel. Though they had tried to band together to attempt resistance of Chillel's sorceries, or to make inroads on the third eastern continent, there was no attraction of like to like. You knew they would cleave to white companions, swear brotherhood with *them*, and be sure even if another black woman might exist to spurn her. She would remind them of their mother. Even their own brothers did that. Yet who could suppose their progeny, even mixed with milk, could be anything but black too? The sublime strain would go on. Eventually there must then arrive a time when some black warrior would form true fellowship with another, or be smitten by a woman with a skin like night. But this was far, far off.

The ourth Sjindi, on whom Guriyuve sat, snorted. He forgot Fenzi and cuffed her light and lovingly, then scratched through her greasy hair. They had grown up together. He was closer to her kind than to his own, whatever his own kind was. She had been brave and steadfast even when he was dragged away to Chillel's tower of agony. Coming back he had met her thundering up to him, so that scores of deer dashed from the grasses, cracking the skies with her trumpetings.

'Shall we ride away on the ice as we did?' he asked her. She snuffled he thought disapprovingly. 'Tell me, where shall we take ourselves?'

Then she tensed through every muscle and bone.

Ahead in the murky gloaming, two figures had appeared.

Otherwise there had been no sign of their approach. Even the mammoth had not sussed them until now.

Sjindi lifted her trunk, but she did not bray.

She held it high in a kind of incongruous greeting – or salute.

'Great Gods witness what I see, amen.'

Guriyuve had heard quite a lot here and there of the Lionwolf, the demon god whose eye-blue standard of a sun had conscripted the flower of Olchibe and Jafn to a mowing.

Had he never heard that an Olchibe man, back then a ghost, had sometimes attended the Lionwolf?

Now one did. Not now a ghost, either.

At the sight of proper yellow skin and hair braided with rodent skulls Guriyuve's heart panged with unexpected nostalgia and gladness. The man had the tattoos of a vandal band's leader.

Guriyuve nevertheless made no salute. He did not tap Sjindi to kneel and let him dismount. He sat and watched the startling travellers as they strode in through the dusk. They were ordinary in their manner, as if they had just come home from hunting perhaps. Did they *know* this benighted region?

The red-haired one, *Lionwolf*, he stopped about forty paces off. The Olchibe warrior plodded on. Reaching Sjindi he rubbed her side. She lowered her trunk at once, and flicked him with a swift but unmistakable caress.

'She's a nice one,' said the man, grinning. 'You should get fine calves from her when you breed her – make sure the male's worthy of her.'

'She wouldn't wear him otherwise, Great One.'

'No, that's a fact. Don't mind me, teaching you your business. I can see you're a son of the goddess's, but you're Olchibe too right enough—' The man had seemed to recall something and then be about to invoke the Gods, but he did not do that. He thinned his lips. 'What's your name?'

'Guriyuve, son of Ipeyek the Gech.'

'Ah?' said the man, softly. His expression was a strange

compound of raw sadness and deep pride. 'You were named for me – for me and, I'll hazard, for my leader, the Great One Peb Yuve.'

'You . . . are Guri?'

'What did they say of me to you?'

'Only the name, and then the other name – the Crax's dead husband.'

Was he lying?

Guri stood back and studied Guriyuve.

He had, Guri, never been able to dight Chillel, nor would he have if he got the chance. She always unnerved, half frightened him, and her effect on Lionwolf had made Guri uneasy – and yet he had known little of her at the time. These memories, if so they were, felt as if pasted on afterwards. None of it counted now in any case. The weird notion obtained however, despite everything, that this man was Guri's own son. And in a way he was. Guri had made certain Ipeyek spent his precious Chillel-seed at Peb's sluhtin. It had been Guri's sole magnificent deed while he suffered in Hell.

The handsome young man, darker than the dark of the isle, looked down at him couthly, polite and attentive.

'And now,' said Guri almost rashly, 'you'll go back to the sluhts, to Olchibe, and be their hero for them – be . . .' he faltered, and then said decidedly, 'a new god for them.'

'There are only the Great Gods. I'm no god. One-third immortal, and *scratchered*. I belong nowhere, Great One.'

'And I'm no leader, not a Great One,' Guri said in a slow, terrible way. 'And the Great Gods don't exist – they never existed. It was an error. Easy to make. Wrong.'

He had affronted his surrogate son. But it would be ridiculous and awful to try to explain *how* Guri knew the Gods were wrong.

Guriyuve did not answer. He frowned. Then he said, 'I shall not go back into Olchibe. It's a country of women now. They can rule without me.'

Guri opened his mouth to protest. Then closed his mouth and lowered his head humbly.

'Yes, Guriyuve son of Ipeyek, you yourself must make up your own mind. Forgive an old man for teaching you your business again.'

Sternly Guriyuve told him, 'You're not old, sir.'

'All the less right then to order you about.'

The mammoth coughed. Her breath smelled of fresh growing grass. 'There, Sjindi,' said Guriyuve.

Guri said, 'Where will you go then, warrior?'

'Across the world. I shall find some place to be.' For the first as he said it, he saw he might credit it.

'May the best always befall and be with you,' said Guri.

He stepped aside.

Guriyuve glanced then just once more at the golden figure of the Lionwolf. Even the dark could not mute him. Even the blackness of Chillel's night had not been able to smother his fires. A demon? No, he did not seem to be a demon. And Guri was his companion, who had denied the real Gods, yet so regretfully.

'May the Great Gods be with you, Guri,' said Guriyuve deliberately.

Guri shrugged and smiled after all. 'Perhaps you're right. Perhaps they exist. Perhaps the wrong one was only – mistaken for them . . .'

The mammoth was turning, her rider easing her away into the belt of swamp and shadow split by seams of boiling brass, platinum, mercury and lead. Mist closed round him, and round the beautiful ourth.

When Lionwolf came up Guri said, 'Do you think it's that? I was *mistaken* for Gods?'

'No, Guri.'

'But *are* there Gods? Surely we – and those Rukar forcutches – surely there is something greater than us?'

'Very probably.' Lionwolf put his arm over Guri's shoulders.

'Is that then what *moves* us about, makes us do these things, is it *that*, Lion? A *God*?'

Lionwolf punched him lightly on the arm. They were the same age in the appearance of their years, his uncle and he.

'Never, Uncle. Do you think a pure and genuine God would stoop so low?'

'Then what does move us?'

Lionwolf himself moved Guri bodily to face him. He clapped a kiss on Guri's forehead. Then put his hand behind Guri's head and gently, firmly, made him bow it to look at the ground where they stood. With his other hand Lionwolf pointed downward, to the earth.

Two travellers came by night to a bothy on a hill.

A distance from the door a white snake shone in the enfolding of a tree, watching them with serious eyes, listening with unusual ears to their footfalls.

Doubtless it had listened also to the young woman's lovely voice that sang in the hut.

Lionwolf, bending to glance in through the door, beheld Azula, Chillel's first daughter, writing on the air with a twig, using her recent education, laughing low as she saw words printed there as if in light. But even Lionwolf could not see them, or did not attempt to do so.

The interior of the shelter had slightly changed.

A flowering vine was trained wall to roof. Flowers and herbs rose in clay vases, blooming in spring water. Many-tinted fruits balanced in a nest of woven grass. There was no meat. Though she had been taught how Azula still elected to kill nothing that had blood in it.

The fire had been brought indoors and blossomed like the flowers in a ring of stones. It scorched nothing, and sent up only the thinnest sweetest smoke. Flat bread was baking in the ashes at its rim. Somewhere she had uncovered or invented grain, something of the sort.

Through firelight and word-light Azula raised her eyes.

For a second her face was sharp with horror.

Then the horror sank away. She knew the Lionwolf, and that he was not as he had been. Chillel had lessoned her in that too.

'Good evening, lord,' said Azula, casual.

Lionwolf smiled. The light of the smile outdid all else.

'Good evening, madam. May we enter your house?'

'Yes, do. Mind the doorway doesn't collapse. It's very flimsy.'

The two traveller gods entered.

A guardian par excellence, the chaze eddied in after them, and stood itself up on a coil of itself, observing them carefully.

Azula poured water from a clay pot – she had made all the vessels herself, baking them on the fire – into a pair of clay cups.

Lionwolf blinked.

The water became the reddest wine, an old Rukarian vintage, both in the cups and in the jar.

'Oh – thank you,' said Azula. 'One of my mothers taught me how to do that. I didn't think to.'

Stately, Lionwolf replied, 'But it is pleasant for a guest to contribute something.'

The night was now pitch-black outside, but gushes of stars, an abundance never seen before even here, were coming out like exquisite prickles on the hide of the sky.

No moons arose. Maybe they would not compete.

The three persons in the hut ate hot bread and a peppery spread of herbs, leaves of lettuce and fronds of graron. Such items were not generally picked wild. The red wine flowed on long after the jar should have emptied. It was potent but nourishing.

The chaze listened while they talked of the distant Southern Continent and Kol Cataar. Azula now began to ask questions about rats and roses and houses cleared of snow standing with their doors high in the air. When Lionwolf offered the snake wine it sipped from his cup.

'And here,' said Azula finally, 'will you seek the tower?' She spoke matter-of-factly.

Lionwolf smiling said, 'How shall I find it?'

A ritual?

Azula clasped her hands about her knees. She put on the storyteller's face – and for the very first time it was possible to see in her her goddess mother. But she had no sound of Chillel. Had she known it, as Lionwolf did, her words resembled a very different message once uttered by the Kraag.

'At the centre of Chillel's park stands the stem of her high tower. It is the Moons' Tower. It was built far back in time, to call up the moons as visitors. And she enters there. Beyond this hill, raise your eyes to the distant heights. Moonlight floats sometimes on the crown of the tower like silver hair.'

Lionwolf got up. He stood over her and gently said, 'Daughter, give me a piece of your fire. Uncle, give me the coal from Sham.'

Azula reacted wondrously. She stretched out her hand and picked a flame from the hearth. She held this up to Lionwolf and only then said in slight surprise, 'I can do that too!'

But he took the flame also in his bare hand. He waited, carrying the light lightly while Guri gaped at him. Guri was the only one apparently determined to fluff his lines.

'What coal, Lion?'

'From the plain below Ru Karismi, where it fell when you . . . talked to Ranjal.'

'But – it's worth nothing – ill-omened thing – no, I won't let you have that.'

'Uncle, once before you did. Do you recall the coal Saphay drew from the Jafn sending-fire and burned in the waste when I was a baby and you had found us? You kept it after and gave it me. But in the White Death it perished with the rest. Guri, the coal is from Sham. It fell in Jafn lands and made magic. This second time it fell with you and your lady on the plain. You found it again. And it holds another of the emblems that I am, lion and wolf. You can't deny it, Uncle. It's come back to close a circle.'

'Which circle?' Guri scurried among his garments as if searching for a flea.

'Oh, some minor matter.'

The phrase struck on something like a coin in Guri's shirt, making it ring. Guri reached in and removed the coal, black and shiny with its only-just-singed youth.

Lionwolf leaned forward and took the coal. He was too quick for Guri's futile gesture of trying to snatch it back.

'Lion—'

Lionwolf was gone.

Outside a river-like ripple shook the night. But it settled in a moment and the stars resumed their chorus.

Another fire crackled now, untended on a slope. Despite not being secured by stones and the tall grass not even cleared aside, it did not abuse its position. It did not stray to eat surrounding vegetation. The fire comprised a solitary coal, and a unique flame. From the heart of it a narrow streamer, not sparks or smoke, curled upward to the sky.

Suddenly aerial lights began to flicker on the ether. They were like the coloured northern lights of Vormland. Presently they had no form.

Then that changed.

A pair of creatures had grown from the random streams of dazzle. One was a big cat, unruffed, less lion than panther, the other a cat of equal size, yet not entirely *cat*. Some who knew might have identified it as an example of that hybrid horde, a chachadraj or drajjerchach – cat-dog, dog-cat. And yet its dog-gishness was far more wolf-like.

Both animals had engaged instantly in a dance of war. One leapt at the other, both leapt, both fell and rolled together over the sky. The stars were snagged in their mouths, in their pelts and in the wolf-cat's mane. They spat or shook the stars out again, wanting only to maul each other.

Uncle Guri, do you see? called the boy's voice from long ago.

From the door of the hut, 'I see,' muttered Guri.

On this occasion Guri was sure, though he was aware the war dance would soon end in congress, he would not be aroused by what went on overhead. He would not now, he thought, *chance* it.

But behind his shoulder the young girl stared with a kind of priestly amazement. He could tell for Azula this ethereal mating would be holy.

There they went, too. The male dog-cat had pinned the female cat-cat to some invisible surface. He was mounting her, holding the back of her neck in his jaws.

As they worked towards their apex, the couple in the sky, Guri felt the urge only to grimace. Well, he was a god now himself. He pondered too that this was nothing to the incendiary madness that must have gone on when he and Ranjal enjoyed their *antics*.

Lionwolf had become utterly *lionwolf*.

In the ice swamps of Gech they would point them out, the marks of wolfish lion-pads in the snow, prints of abnormal size which shone without need of sun or moon. *That* was a lionwolf.

Now in the garden of night the lionwolf had also come to exist.

He was a beast of the size of the largest lion, and he was maned as both male and female lions were, but with the superb exaggerated ruff of a young male. The facial mask was that of a wolf, yet the skin smooth of pelt as was a lion's, though with a wolf's golden eyes, in the pupils of which sequins darted of cobalt and red. The ears were wolvan. The rest of the frame had all the flexibility seen only among cats or serpents. But the structure of the lean pelvis was more like that of a wolf, and the feet of the beast had aspects of both wolf and lion, while the lower legs were clad in hair. The animal's tail was plainly uncanny. It was like a thick club, but composed itself of two elements. The inner cauda was hairy, a wolf's, but about it wove like a liana a *second* tail, which was a lion's and ended in the leonine tuft. Beneath, genitalia were in evidence. These were sheathed after the way of a dog.

The shade of him was nearly white, just as was the vivid image of him in the air. An unanticipated colour maybe. But the mane and ruff were brazen, and the hair of the limbs and tail showed brazen, and the lion tuft of the tail was like bloodied brass.

Over the parkland he raced. From the thickets the deer bolted away, and small lizards fired themselves off like curled balls. He hesitated for none of them as the creatures overhead had spurned the stars. He was intent only on one project.

Ahead the tower rose, with the silvery blown moon static on its top.

In the brain of the god-become-beast was what? Power and lust, intent, culmination. No other thing.

He had gained the upland of the hill when out of some opening in the tower *she* expressed herself.

Chillel had become panther. Though larger than the cats of her retinue, matching in size the male animal that sought her, she was maneless like them and covered like them in a short plush of hair. Yet her colouring too was unusual.

Where his gold and red had gone to snow and brass, her blackness was *blue*. She had spent time in Lionwolf's blue Hell. Perhaps she had been influenced there to this complexion.

She poised on the hill, watching as he rushed towards her. Access to the brain of Chillel had never been available. Either she was too complex, or she lacked all complexity always. Her brain remained therefore obscure and indescribable. Yet in her black eyes which had an emerald sheen on them a sort of tender hunger was, or was imagined.

The lionwolf reached the panther on her hill.

Phallic, the tower went up above them. But it was hollow also, and might symbolize rather the female vaginal canal, contained inside the body of night. The moonglow that anchored over it must then perhaps represent a womb.

Both creatures paused below the tower.

Each sprang.

On earth as in heaven the dance of war commenced. Both fell, locked already by their fangs fastened each in the other's flesh. Blood sprayed, his black, hers crimson. As they rolled over the turf lush plants unfurled instantly from the blood spillage, and the grass grew longer. Sometimes as the two beasts fought and rolled and kicked at each other, the just-grown flowers were snapped off in their mouths. But even these, dropped, grew again. The dual tail of the lionwolf lashed the ground. His weapon had unsheathed. Swarthy and smooth as any bulb, it glittered moisture, touching now and again the paler iris of the she-beast's labia.

The dance and the war abruptly concluded.

Up reared the male and stood over her. He took her by the fur and skin behind her head.

With his teeth clamped in her neck, he mounted her, bestrode her as day topped a world of night, and sheathed the blade of his sex once more, now in the dusk-blue honey of that inner tower.

Above, across heaven, all the lights burst.

On the ground jewelry buds opened wide in petals and penile stalks fiercely pushed and strove like snakes.

The land roared in one prolonged, gargantuan spasm.

They sank together, beast on beast, lowering their heads gently to the turf.

And the sky broke in twain.

To one side, the east and south, it became, in a swift lambent torrent, morning, and a diamond sun flamed in the height. To the west and north the phosphorescent night stood, seeded with stars and now with six quarter-moons strung up like a chain of scythes.

And oh the silence, not that of any quiet day or calm sleepful night. It was the silence of an interval between two vast dramas. The margin between the past and all else that was to be.

Fenzi had hypnotized a deer and slain it without hurting it, as he now knew how to. He was amenable to not causing undue distress. Nevertheless he missed the chase, and even the satisfaction of a quick efficient kill.

When the sky filled with incendiaries he was offended.

Marvels happened too frequently. He had had enough.

And with that to consider, when the cipher of the two doggish cats copulating gave him an erection, Fenzi refused to respond. Tumescence went down as they did. Then he beheld midday and midnight co-existent and total as two pages, up there together in the sky's book.

He sat on the grass beside a grove and looked at this abomination, and felt no hint of future improvement.

Gradually the double face of the sky melded into a twilight, and then into a dawn where the sun and all the over-number of stars and moons became shadows.

Only then did he lope across and stamp out the tiny fire he had noted on an adjacent hillside. Some kind of lone coal was in it, which indifferently he picked up when the fire went out.

Lugging the dead deer he started to walk away.

No other lingered on the island. Only the vicious sorceress-goddess and her filthy cats. Although the woman Azula had stayed.

She was up there in that ill-made bothy, with the wisp of fire-smoke on its roof.

Fenzi thought of the lonely coal left in the forsaken fire.

He too was unused to being alone.

If he took the meat up to the bothy would Azula be impressed? He visualized her dark eye and her hazel eye and the hair and the skin. She had a charming voice, he must admit. He had heard her singing recently.

She loved the goddess.

Well, Vangui was not violent to her own sex.

Fenzi recalled his physical mother, and Nirri. He curtailed that. But then he remembered the little white lionet tiger cub he had delivered to the prince at Padgish. That had been a cat, but it was perfectly all right.

Not wanting to but not wanting either to do otherwise, Fenzi got a more adequate grip on his kill and began to climb towards the girl's hut. Was *Azula* her real name? *Azulamni*? But that was her mortal mother's name. He was most of the way up the hill when her secret name, which no one had ever told him, sang inside his ear. If it made him jump that was only a reaction. He had heard her singing anyway. He was almost at the door before he saw Guri looming there, protective avuncular arms folded, beetle-browed.

Fourteenth Volume

STEALFLAME

Keep something between you and the hot sun.

Advice attributed to the Kraag:
Southlands and South-East Continent

ONE

Azula sees it come, the levinbolt. She bares her teeth and bellows into the core of it.

The levinbolt strikes the earth directly *through* Azula.

At this point she is unaware when the corpse of her mother disintegrates.

Beebit, dead and held in Azula's arms, could not withstand the blow.

For herself, Azula feels nothing epic.

She is conscious of a kind of fizzing in her veins.

Nothing more, really.

Yet now all the lightnings fall on her, singly or in groups, and as each of them blasts through her and is *earthed* and so ruined by her, only her fury makes her drunk with pleasure that this enemy who had murdered her mother is now destroyed.

Then the attack ends and quietness fills everything, and Azula looks about for the bone which is all that remains of Beebit.

Before she sees it, a charismatic man is standing in front of her. Never has she seen anyone like him, although perhaps the Lionwolf is like this in his own different manner – and by now she knows she has met the Lionwolf, though where she is unsure. The Lionwolf has called her in courtesy 'Daughter'. But this other god has long black hair and black eyes and he is Winter, this she sees too, Winter who here at Kandexa has tried to wreck some essential scheme. And she has foiled him.

'How talented you are,' says Winter, who in Simisey is

415

Tirthen. 'You can defeat me. Come then, I shall be your slave, fair maiden. You have no kindred. Let us go away together.'

But Azula can already see how he is disintegrating – not abruptly as did her mother's corpse when lightning struck it – but as a snowstorm may, when the wind blows from the south.

And then she opens her eyes and the swirl of whiteness is only petals shedding from the vine she has twined through her hut.

Outside Guri and Fenzi were cooking the deer meat over a bigger fire they had built, speaking in low voices of hunting and skirmishes, of bows and types of knife, and the best seasoning for particular animals. Men's chat. Azula was not sorry Guri had headed Fenzi out of the bothy. Though a Chilleling Fenzi was not like Sallus, could not remind her of Sallus. She wished he would go away.

The snake had rustled off into the dawn. The prodigies of the night seemed to have made no impression on it.

Azula however believed the creatures mating high in the air had had vast if obscure import. She herself felt some door now stood wide, some barrier had dispersed. Again and again her eyes were drawn to the sky. Clouds difted over and birds, and the light varied. This was not why she stared at it. She was uncertain why she did.

The dream of the lightning at Kandexa had not, curiously, vexed or grieved her. Waking she took up Beebit's bone and stroked it, but then she often did. The dream too was an intimation?

When the meat began to be ready on its spit, Azula grew irritated at it, the al fresco meal, the heady smell and way the men sat there comparing Jafn and Olchibe spices and bows.

She walked from the bothy without a word and trotted off through the park, the grasses brushing her ankles. Neither of the men tried to stay her. Neither spoke.

'It's coming, Ma,' she said to Beebit in her mind, as she jogged along the rim of the land. 'Soon I shall be doing it.' But she did not know what or where, or why, only that it must be, and that Beebit perhaps knew that too, and was watching. A distinct excitement filled Azula. And a slight doubt, which she was sure was only her ignorance, for it would not matter. 'Do you like my other name, Ma? I'll always be Azulamni too. But it's proper that Chillel-Toiyhin-Ma gave me a name as well, I suppose, don't you think so?' Azula's mind sang her second name. Now she ran fast, leaping high above the grass like a young deer, or sometimes turning cartwheels. On their hill the two god-men looked at her. They were no longer comparing bows.

Gold on black, black on gold. They wear their natural colours. They unite as humans would. Only *they* reveal they are gods.

Vashdran the Lionwolf, Toiyhin the Dove.

In *this* reality there is no necessity for one to dominate. The dominance of each is absolute. As is their integral oneness, with themselves and with each other.

Do they even talk to each other? Does the language of eternity now convey all meaning? But do stars converse, suns and moons?

She spoke to her lover in the centre of the day that ruled now the garden of night.

'Remember, beloved, from nothing I was made – I am the vessel of what made me, who are three gods, or one god that has three persons. For this, and to be this, I was created and am.'

'The three gods Ddir, Yyrot, and the other, Zeth.'

But his tone was relaxed and almost teasing.

And the Dove finally answered her own riddle.

'No, beloved. Think only of one god that has three persons. A god firstly born from a mortal, a god secondly dead and alive in Hell, a god thirdly reborn as the sun. It was not who fashioned me, but whose unformed will desired my fashioning. You, my love. Who else?'

Lionwolf held her in his arms. In her face he could find the reply to every question. But in these empyrean moments they discarded godhood. They were only a man and a woman. And if they would never die, neither fully could any man or woman either. Or if at last they *could* die, so might all.

'What will be here tomorrow?' he asked her then.

'What you will have made.'

'Will that be good?'

'Yes,' she answered. 'So very good.'

They smiled at their joke, their pretence of doubt and reassurance. But he at least had been partly human. Maybe, maybe . . . ?

'Kiss me farewell then, wife,' said Lionwolf. 'I must get up and go to fight.'

Chillel kissed him.

And for an instant they were in a Jafn garth, the warriors waiting below, and he had slung on his sword some mageia had protected, and the other House sword stretched upright over the lintel, and his woman stood on tiptoe to embrace him.

'When I return to you,' he said, 'our theatre in this world is over. We will come here, and to such places, but for ourselves we begin elsewhere.'

'I know it.'

'Will we mind, Chillel, becoming what next we become?'

'How should we? For that rebecoming we live. Not even the earth stays still.'

'But you and I,' he said, 'will never part again.'

Regardless of metamorphosis and eternity, they then let go of each other with the same melancholy reluctance mortal lovers demonstrate.

Lionwolf entered his father's private world without show or clamour.

Certainly he had had three fathers. The second was Heppa, a man of little wit and some heart. The third was Thryfe, a Magikoy Master among mages, who had both brain and, ultimately, heart. But the first father was Zeth Zezeth, the god of split personality and heartless discord, the fallen sun.

At once Lionwolf beheld Zth's world was injured.

Amber and fire remained, but they too it seemed had gone mad.

It was a kind of garden, and the trees were burning, and even the grass was tipped with lit fire. Liquid amber light slopped heavily on the surfaces like a wet sick snow. Here and there too molten gums trickled out of the pores of things, turning to a sort of sewage. Zth's heaven reeked of arson and garbage.

Lionwolf selected a path the paving of which bubbled and wriggled. Autumns of flame fell on him as he passed. The dropping amber was tepid.

Zth was deep in where vines bled and lay thrashing on the ground. He seemed to be dancing, circling intently round and round on the spot. Sometimes he let out a caw of delight. 'Yes, yes,' cried Zth, 'they do all I command, for the great whale is my servant, and the woman my slave, and she has gone to act out my instructions, and there are others, many others, and everything proceeds like the clockwork mechanisms of that city where they worship me in fear and love, the Rukarian kings, whom I shall break in small bits, and all of it is mine and only I am the sun and see how I shine – how marvellously I shine!'

Lionwolf halted, looking at the wizened thing that was his father. The god was brownish as an old hothouse locust that had crisped its wings too long in a *Summer* heat, and could no longer fly.

The amber dropped on Zth and he brushed it off, but was smeared in its grease. Brittle brownish hair hung from his scalp. His dried-up face had two eyes in it that were like dull lead and perhaps were mostly blind.

All this had been done to him by Lionwolf, if not in person. Through the bodies of two women the bane had fixed on Zth. Saphay's had robbed him of a segment of his immortal essence, which even when replaced no longer fitted him; Jemhara's had poisoned him with the template of prior supernal birth.

He did not seem to see at all, as he swayed and praised himself, what stood and looked at him, let alone that it was the author of his downfall. But then surely he did not *know* himself downfallen. He was Zeth and he shone, marvellously.

Lionwolf moved forward.

Stasis gripped the garden. The bloody vines stuck to each other and fused. The fire in the grass died in a veil of smoke. Beyond, long hilly fields of flaming grain were shrouded too in a sudden pall.

There came only the drip-drip of the amber. A skeleton of some unreal bird cascaded from the white sky, fragmenting to powder as it came.

Zth glanced up.

Perhaps he did see Lionwolf now, yet improperly.

'Where is the she called Jema?' asked Zth.

'Back there,' said Lionwolf.

'Fetch her here. She should be here, attendant on me.'

Lionwolf said nothing. He had distinguished the traces of the pollen of Jemhara's pearly ashes – they had only been visible even to him since they alone had not caught fire.

'Well,' said Zth, 'if she will not come I shall punish her. Probably she is in terror already and conceals herself.'

'Probably. If so she does it with skill.'

'Meanwhile I shall send you on my mission. *You* shall go to harass and eradicate him for me. I will not sully myself with his death. To kill a god, for now that is what he is, leaves too much debris behind.'

'Not always,' said Lionwolf.

He had come up beside Zth. Zth stopped circling and dancing. He peered at Lionwolf like an old, old man who squints into the sun.

'Who are you?' said Zth, without interest.

'I am myself.'

'No, *I* am myself.'

'You are no longer any self.'

'I am greater than self.'

'You are greater than nothing.'

'Go now,' said Zth tetchily. 'Begone.'

'We are gone,' said Lionwolf.

In that moment Zth screamed aloud. Lionwolf had taken hold of him, and instantly the whole of the personal astral world gave way. It cracked and crumpled and crashed noiselessly in, imploded, evacuated, releasing into gods knew what adjoining regions a trillion atomies, each eager as a swimming sperm.

And it was true both of them, Lionwolf and Zth, were also gone – out into the illimitable environ of space itself.

Of this arena Lionwolf had dreamed. But Zth perhaps never had.

An incredibility occurred.

Zeth Sun Wolf turned his head and burrowed in horror into Lionwolf's chest like a frightened child.

Lionwolf held Zth without effort, and the solar and stellar winds blew back Lionwolf's hair, which was the only fire visibly brought away intact, as he scanned about him.

Some miles below lay the enormous earth.

It was round and white, an astronomic snowball, but for a few watery shadows and veins of vaporous green and turquoise that seemed to come and go, like signs of breathing in a being tranced asleep. Or rather, in hibernation.

The immeasurable mosaic of stars however appeared no closer.

Even so they gleamed and sparkled all about, above, around and beneath.

Just like the dream, six moons were lying on the black velvet of the spatial sky. They were pallid, none so pure as the snowball of the earth. Three were an ancient white like dug-up bone. Two were like dented and qualified nacre. One, currently the farthest off, was bluish. All were pocked and scarred, which gave them an awful loveliness. They were unreal and so quite real; they had suffered, and survived. While, just discernibly, you could see they moved.

But then, then – yet out of the east or not, Lionwolf did not know – three more moons rose up from behind the mask of the earth. And these three moons, also each full, a globe, were like palest beaten gold.

And in this way the phenomenon of the erratic, ever-altering lunar discs seen on earth was revealed. For some hid themselves behind others, or shied away on another orbit – of each other, or some unadvertised magnet. From earth never more than three were ever witnessed together. But nine they were and their mysteries of revelation, at full or half or crescent, were dependent on their procession in space.

Lionwolf gazed at all that, absorbed. Time condensed, unravelled. And he supported the putrid hulk of his father in one arm. Zth saw nothing. He would not look. Or could not look.

Nevertheless in the end, hours later, he spoke.

'I'm cold,' whimpered the god, like any mortal thing. '*Cold, cold.*'

'Hush,' answered Lionwolf quietly. 'Soon you'll be warm enough.'

He looked about sharply then, and called without sound. And from the invisible but unmended tear in space, the entry-exit to Zth's bankrupt heaven, Zth's sun chariot flared out, spitting with smokes and embers, drawn by six wolves that were not indigo now but the shade of rust.

Once the vehicle reached them Lionwolf stepped into it. He roped the reins about his waist as would a Jafn warrior in battle. He kept Zth all the while in his arm, held tight.

Maybe there was an urge to gallop the outer circuit of the world. If so he resisted.

Instead Lionwolf kept the chariot stationary.

Let the moons wheel around, and let the world spin as perhaps it did. Soon the sun too would come from behind the world. For this he would wait.

Did the *sun* encircle the *earth*? That it did Lionwolf, a god, was sure. Conceivably the stalled chariot itself subtly moved to follow the tug of the earth, and so rotated with the earth, *seeming* to stay put, allowing the sun to *seem* to rise in space. Or else the sun did circle the earth, the normal earthly conclusion. The unreal mathematic must therefore have been real.

But the sun's rising was essential.

More time presumably went by.

The living god stood in the chariot supporting the demolished god, and the wolves gnashed their fangs and stamped on airlessness irksomely.

Unfathomed distance underneath, the earth's surface caught three others of the god's soundless calls.

These dipped in through the layers of non-air like arrows.

The first nipped Guri's ear as he sat with Fenzi on the island hillside. A day had gone and a night had gone after it, and now dawn was again considering, prevaricating like a woman, if she would return.

Fenzi slept, for according to him he was due a Jafn sleep night, a custom he insisted on keeping, though now of course sleep was not essential. Besides, he slept more often than he would have done in the garth.

The girl Azula had ages since disappeared on her cartwheeling constitutional over the slopes.

Uncle.

Guri lifted his head, alert as long ago.

Uncle – come see the stars!

Guri shook himself and got up without haste. He scrutinized the horizons where the seeable stars were already fading.

He recalled another night, as it seemed to him now millennia before. He had stared then at the sky, thinking he saw the route there which led into a second world, a world of more importance and validity. He had been infatuated with it, its inspiration and splendour.

And in that pivotal instant he had lifted his ghost arms to fly upward into eternity.

And the cry came from the child in Saphay's womb. *Guri – Uncle Guri –* and he turned his back on what he did not even know but which had seemed to offer him limitless joy, and went to rescue Lionwolf.

In this call now there was no panic and no appeal. However flighty, it was a summons.

Guri shrugged in the familiar way.

Here the stars had been put out, but perhaps up there they went on glittering. And the boy – the man – the god – called him. He was Guri's leader. Guri had better go.

He lifted his arms. He did not need to any more, yet it was a sort of embrace.

He sprang for heaven.

Elsewhere as that happened, Curjai was watching Ruxendra as she walked up a track to a hilltop. A phantasmal flush of yellow was in the east. The dawn would begin soon, and at every dawn Ruxendra climbed this hill. It was her narrow feet which had worn the track in the snow.

She had taken the proliferation of her altars seriously. Sometimes when she had gone to see them she frowned over it, trying he could tell to be virtuous and conscientious, as she had in the school of the Magikoy. But having become a goddess of sunrise plainly she did not grasp her duties, for there seemed to be none; sunrise went on anyway. They debated such matters.

They had other pursuits of course, he and she. The snow house he had constructed, warm enough inside, oversaw their love and its expression. The dog and the tiger oversaw these too. Presently the animals watched Ruxendra on her hill, as Curjai did.

Often he had the sensation she might abruptly leap from the hill and vanish.

This never happened, but his wariness never left him.

He murmured, and the fire bloomed up on the hearth by the door.

Was it natural that they should live like this, like penniless peasants on a Simese hill, who lacked even herds or growing-land, and had nothing to do but hold theosophic debate and make love?

He could not tell if they had even stayed in the world. Very possibly they had expelled themselves into some look-alike domain formed, like house and fire, out of Curjai and Ruxendra's own unusual qualities. Here the dawn might not even be actual. Did it simply show up to remind her of her role – as maybe the fire obeyed him to jog *his* memory?

Curjai now thought of Lionwolf. It was not he did not frequently do so.

Curjai's time in Hell had been both fraught and magnificent, and always free of guilt. He had been at his best. He had become himself there, the best of himself, but who was he now? Even reborn in Padgish, who had he been? A blind fool, he decided. It was that which had allowed his mother to die.

Was he sad? Yes. Was he happy? Yes. The mortal condition had grown stronger in him, he thought, the further from it he went. There was much to be thankful for. And things to do. But when?

We wait, he thought distinctly.

Precisely then Ruxendra turned from the dawn and cried back to him. 'Listen! What's that?'

Curjai heard the call only in that moment. After she had heard it. He came to his feet.

Oh, he knew who it was, what it was. It was the summons of his brother and king.

He bounded up the hill and caught her to him. She laughed, all puzzlement. 'What is it? What?'

'I must go to him.'

Immediately her face fell and her chin grew pointed. She knew who he meant.

She was jealous. Would they never lose such inner sores?

He kissed her, and the dog and cat were cavorting round them convinced some game was about to start.

'If you go,' she said, 'I'll never see you again.'

She had reduced all things to the plane of ordinary mishap; the mundane.

He would not have it from her now. He spoke in other terms.

'Yes, Ruxendra, you will. In the morning, Ruxendra. We'll see each other again in the morning of the New Day.'

And then he was fire. She held fire in her arms unscorched, and then the fire became nothing, only the yellow of the sky to give her any light.

The third recipient of the summons heard it last.

And even as she heard it she felt herself lifted, as though in a vast hand. Up and up, over the park and the groves, higher than the tower of the goddess, into the sky.

She could see to the edges of the island presently, the threaded streams of metal and barriers of dark, and of curlicued ice. In the east the sky was colouring.

Azula was not afraid. A song of her childhood stole into her mind, one Beebit had sung in Azula's earliest days when already she was like a child of seven or eight. In the song it was a twilight time not of evening but before the dawn, and the last stars had gone out leaving only the sheen of the white ice. A woman trekked across the ice waste and she saw the sun begin to come up, wan and yellow at the cold. 'How shall I get any light or heat from that chilly sun?' the woman wept. And the sun saw her, and that she sheltered a baby at her breast. Some cruel steader settlement had cast them out, the woman with her son, to die. But the sun took pity, and from his inmost heart he drew up a greater heat and a greater brightness, just for that one morning alone. And within the glow of the sun's generosity the mother found her way to safety and the baby with her. '*In the ice of twilight – twice the light of the sun – touched the earth like a father's hand,*' Beebit sang. Perhaps she had recalled the song when, her own baby in her womb, she fled over the ice after the Death at Ru Karismi.

'Ice twilight, twice light,' sang Azulamni, lifted through the sky.

Then she looked down and the isle was little as a pinhead.

For a minute she *was* dismayed, but she raised her eyes and gazed only wherever it was she was going. Which was obviously out into the space beyond the earth, where Gurithesput had already gone and Escurjai, and where Lionwolf stood in the chariot, Zeth Zezeth held in his arm.

Around the rim of the world the sun appears.

To begin with the sun is a crescent, but already rays and blades of radiance strike out from it. Rainbows reel across the lens of vision. Only gods can stare directly at this.

And the crescent grows. A half-sun now is visible, like a broken shield of white gold.

Then the sun slips loose and all of it coruscates on the black of space, and the earth and the moons flare as if they were made of burnished glass.

Lionwolf and the chariot and the snarling stamping wolves become burnished too. Strangely Zth does not light up at all. He curls there, a withered dry husk, mewing even now that he is cold, cold.

Guri stands in space to Lionwolf's right. He is in the place of a father, perhaps, as Curjai, positioned to the left, has the brother's place. They have eyes only for the sun. Though it cannot sear or blind them as now they are, yet they are locked in awe of it. The extraordinary stars and moons are like play-things beside this glorious monster.

Can it be this much fire can give only such slight energy to the world? It seems so. The world is frozen.

The sun moves higher – or appears to move higher.

Lionwolf turns and looks back and Azula, who is his daughter only in name, has arrived in the pageant of space, and she is looking not at stars or moons or even at the sun, but solely at him.

'What is your name?' Lionwolf asks her.

Azula says, with a young woman's pride, 'Stealflame.'

'Good. You must stand between the sun and the earth. When the fire breaks you must meet the fire.'

'I know,' says Azulamni who is Stealflame.

It is true she does know, as if she always knew even from her first conscious moment, and perhaps in some way she did. She is quite calm. She contemplates her task and is aware she will complete it. She feels no fear. She is not one-third god but one full half, and her mothers are Chillel, but also Beebit.

Therefore Azula has answered Lionwolf with seriousness as if to reassure him, and for a second this young father who is not grins at her. And then he cracks the reins over the red wolves' spines, and the chariot races for the rising sun.

In his wake two comets fly, Guri and Curjai.

But Stealflame stays where she is, and regards the sun with her inky eye and her tawny eye. And under her feet the earth lies far below.

He had begun, as the chariot rushed forward, to mutter, the old god Zth Zzth. 'Have you seen a woman with a child?' Despite his decrepit state the mutter was quite menacing. Lionwolf did not reply, but demonstrably in Zth's warped unstrung memory someone did, for 'You are lying,' croaked the malign and withered locust. 'Yet I cannot now go past your lie. We shall meet again. *Then* let us see.'

In fact Zth was peering sidelong at Gurithesput, Great Gods of Olchibe, sprinting through space to the right. Zth had met before with Guri. But Zth's cerebral exchange had finished. Another started. 'How will you do it?' If there had been the dregs of venom in his tones before, this time it was robust. 'I shall not see to it.' Though robust, more disjointed. 'Did you not coerce me?' gravelled the husk. 'Do you think a human woman stupidly drowning in her yellow hair could tempt *me*? It was your power – yours, Nameless One. Lacking me, what is there for you? I will have you put out like the blown flame. They all do my bidding. They will destroy you.'

The disc of the sun had grown much larger and was directly in front, on a level with the chariot.

It was as if they rode headlong at a mirror reflecting only magma.

Sheer vast scalding winds blew towards them out of the mirror's mouth, and these were hemmed with flames. A type of roaring came from it too, and howling, like the voices of wolves and lions that were multitudinous and of stupendous size.

The chariot-wolves shied. They tried to veer away. Supernatural as they were neither the rays nor the heat nor the noises could harm them, but all these things had at last made them afraid.

Lionwolf hauled on the reins and brought the uncanny vehicle to a halt. There was no need to ride closer, perhaps had been no need to approach this near. He was intensely drawn towards the disc. He knew it, knew attraction finally was as such immaterial. They had only to wait a while, he and the sun.

He glances at the wolves. They are tearing at their halters and at each other in their automatic desperation to escape. 'Go, then,' he says to them. The traces disintegrate. The creatures dash away, each alone, not a pack, vanishing under cover of the winds and spurts of fire.

Zth lurches in Lionwolf's detention. He screws round his neck and head and gapes at the old sun which is so appallingly brilliant.

'What,' says Zth, stretching out his hand, 'what is that?'

'The sun,' answers Lionwolf without emphasis.

Zth turns back again and stares up at Lionwolf with eyes that are almost no longer to be seen themselves and which, unmistakably, have become almost sightless.

'Warmth,' says Zth. 'Make me warm.'

The Lionwolf looks down into the face of his enemy. His own face is unreadable. There seems nothing behind it, certainly no triumph and no rage.

'Yes, Father,' he replies. 'You shall be warm.'

In his dream the sun had lain below and into it he had hurled the fiend Zeth Zezeth, who had sired and hunted and tortured him and so many others for his sake. But in this waking hour Lionwolf only gathers Zth more firmly in his arms. And the wizened remnant of the god puts up the wires of his arms to clutch Lionwolf, to hold on to him more tightly.

And then Lionwolf leaps upward from the chariot, and as his feet strike it in passing it bursts in bits that, like the wolves, shoot away beyond the moons and stars.

Lionwolf is speeding, himself a star of fire, golden and crimson in an aureole like volcanic corundum, straight, straight as a spear, for the heart of the sun.

On the canvas of space, hammered there like two immovable polished nails, Guri and Curjai can only behold his flight. They must not, perhaps cannot, shift.

Countless distance beyond and beneath, Stealflame is surprised by none of this.

Lionwolf rushing to the target, his burden in his arms, cleaves through corona and photosphere, through bands of smolt-white and melt-pinkened gold, through moments of incandescent lava and gaseous magnesium, spindrift of neon and respiring torrefaction. Eruptive scarlet splinters. Fire becomes fire. Winged with atomic light sun collides with sun.

For an instant, nothing.

Nothing detectable left of the Lionwolf or of Zth. Nothing to distort the sun's mirror or the pitchy mute surround of space.

A tiny hollow sizzle of sound starts up. It is like a gnat. Then like a pot hissing on the hearth.

The hiss grows.

It swells.

An orchestra squalls suddenly in heaven – every instrument of chaos screaming.

And space rips open as the mirror sun explodes.

Curjai does not move. He becomes red fire. Guri, unmoving, becomes white fire.

All the skin of the airless ether is blistering with a hideous beauty. The moons dissolve to whitest silver, and *drip*.

Below and below the globe of the world blushes like blood.

And the blast of the fire gushes out and down – and a single slender object is interposed.

Here is the one called Stealflame. Here she is, extending her arms and screaming back into the screaming torrent of annihilation – almost just as she did on the riven hail-heap at Kandexa, challenging the lightning.

And as the lightning had done so does the laval onrush of the sun. It clashes together in century-wide segments and bolts of *bonfire*, shrieking and spurling, and falls on her.

Stealflame receives it.

Though she is crying out, this is no lament as it was in the past. *This* is triumph, enough for Lionwolf and for all the world.

The screech of fire goes through her again and again, through her and through. With each assault on every side it erupts out of her too, but then dissipates in fading rivers of soft rose-red and a few gigantic handfuls of dying sparks.

Stealflame stays fixed, greeting and grabbing and taking in the fire, all the expended overspill might of a rejuvenating solar disc. Taking and defusing, *earthing* the sun.

What does she feel now, the goddess's child, Beebit's daughter?

Nothing unique. Only enjoyment and a sort of drunken smugness as the destruction of the world reaches out, meets her, and is destroyed by her. By *her*.

This then is her magic.

Stealflame steals the flame, and inch by inch, miles by miles, the vault of space lets go its cacophony of fulmination, its blaze of noise.

In a while through the dark red aftershock, night rises again and fills space with the coolth of black. Over the disc of the sun a black panther of night casts herself down, seizing the flames of it in her jaws, and the fire must bend and bow to accept her.

The moons cease to smoke and steam and run. They too cool and harden to their former shades, bone, silver, milk-gold, slate.

To the left Curjai stands in his fire, and to the right Guri in the centre of a forming planet which is his own.

Slowly, like sighing, the sun achieves equilibrium once more. Until it too is standing up there in blackness, garlanded with its flames that are new as a child's first breath. The sun is clean and very, very bright. It rests on the breast of night, and silence comes back as it always must and will, between one great shout and the next.

Over eastward of the earth the dawn is climbing, and she also is gazing up to watch the sun.

What a sunrise it had been. Had any not been woken and gone out to look? The sky, first nondescript, became splashed all over by vermilion, so rich and total a colour that some grew alarmed at it. Everywhere dogs had yowled, other beasts cried out in their own way. But then the dye was rinsed off, the skies became serene. The ruby light that was like the symptom of a disastrous inferno in heaven drained from the earthly landscape, between hills, along rivers of ice and snow, and from the staring eyes of humanity which had clambered on to roofs or into towers to see.

Even from the closed eyes of those who slept or had taken refuge under blankets it washed away, and left them in peace.

During the succeeding minutes before the sun fully rose several noted an uncharted star, flashing as diamond, going over to the west. In the Ruk they knew Ddir the Artificer had set the star for them. It had the shape of a man, the star. Or some said it was like a lean hunting hound; it was a dog star, which ran before the sun barking with glitter into the morning. In Kol Cataar, when the star returned afterwards at every dawn and sunset, they called it *Firefex*, the Phoenix. In Olchibe they called it *Guri*. Which meant Star Dog. It was, there, as if the name, an ancient one, had only been waiting for a proper subject.

Through that first roast then watered orchid dawn, one *shooting* star plunged to earth. Ddir patently had not made this one, or, if he had, had dropped it. It was like a torch, and threw after it a trail of argent particles on the lightening sky.

As it descended, did the star perceive the world? No doubt it did. It had a vested interest.

Displayed: the Southern Continent, balanced icy on the icy ocean that only grudgingly gave on shadowy liquid green. Islands lay north and west. Further on a second continent reclined, just like the first in its ice if not in shape. Down to the south-east other larger islands spread, and then another continent unfolded its white carpet among the ice floes and open water.

Unallied with any of this, there was now something else.

High up towards the crown of the world's globe, the northern pole housed a fourth, lesser landmass.

Reconnoitred from immensely far aloft, it seemed also more oddly shaped.

It was in the form of a horned whale.

But the shooting star fell on in the way of shooting stars.

Stealflame shot from the etherium rejoicing and wild in her incendiary panoply, her right hand open and her left closed in a fist.

She knew what the landmass was. It had been built from the leviathan Brightshade.

And because Brightshade could now release his astral being whenever he wished and without hindrance do whatever he wanted, his physical body was anchored like his luxurious palace in the ocean, ready always for his return. The body had indeed sequentially become a continent, though of modest proportions. The back of the whale had long been an established ecosystem and now, parked indefinitely, it mutated into a geography and biosphere of swamps and jungle-forest. Now too it was quite cold, but soon would be merely *moderate*. In any context, a surprising term to apply to Brightshade.

Stealflame had saved the world and was skittish. She sang about twice-light.

Below, a tall, dark-green plantation, coated only thinly with rime, invited her.

Into the woods of Brightshade Stealflame descended.

No sooner did her feet touch the ground than she herself was earthed. Stealflame, like the saved sky, regained serenity.

Between the trees the terrain was covered in snow, but through this grass and herbs were protruding. Nearby a baroque assembly of elderly wreckage and skeletons had been grown over by lianas – an arbour. In a valley beyond the woods two broken ships, one with fifty masts, were changing to verdigris.

There were no longer any regional effluvia, no rot or fishy stinks. With the advent of lush fauna Brightshade had become fragrant.

The Children of Chillel knew most things now. Did Stealflame's mental library suggest other past elements of Brightshade-land? Did eyeless monsters still dwell on his back? What lurked in the shrubbery? Nothing nasty stirred. Would it matter if it did?

Using her inner senses Stealflame cast downward instead through the whale's earthworks to see if her step-uncle was in. But only a ticking of sentry mechanisms – lungs, heart, brain and suchlike – could be picked out. Himself was clearly off on a jaunt.

However—

Stealflame glanced up into the higher thicker woods.

A large black animal – no monster; a cow? – was pernicketing its way through the trunks, sometimes pausing to pluck and chew the grasses.

In the end the cow too glanced in Stealflame's direction and stopped in its tracks. It was covered in thick curling wool and was not a cow at all but a gargantuan sheep.

Stealflame stared, and the sheep thoughtfully stared back.

The young woman had not checked her own appearance. Never mediocre now she was arresting. Her solar victory had turned her fawn skin to a deep gold, of all things most like the skin of her unrelated stepfather Lionwolf. Her hair was all purest silver. Only her eyes had not altered, one dark, one light.

The sheep seemed to evaluate this.

The girl wondered how it would react if she began to go towards it up the slope, because if it was here then people were too, surely. Stealflame felt a wish in herself to see some people. She wanted to prove they like the world had stood up to everything, were thriving.

'Where's your master, sheep,' she called encouragingly as she started to advance. She did not levitate so as not to shock the sheep. But the sheep could have told her a thing or two about that. It tried to with an off-hoof bleat. But, 'There, it's only me, your friend,' Stealflame reassured it presumptuously.

'And which friend is that?' said a woman's voice from above.

Stealflame stopped.

In the shade of the frosted pines, eucalypts, flowering palms and pepper trees, she glimpsed a blacker shadow which perhaps held up a fiery torch.

'Greeting, lady,' said Stealflame. 'What place is this?' Although she knew it was Brightshade.

The other seemed to know quite well herself, and that Stealflame did also.

'Mine, and his own,' she said nevertheless.

'Yes, the whale's land,' agreed Stealflame. 'But I meant what people have colonized it?'

'You think there should be people here then?'

Already Stealflame sensed there were, which was more than *thinking* there were. Exactly then, some way off, she heard a faint metallic clink of something, and then a rill of women's laughter. Though expecting it, for some reason it startled her – why was that?

She decided. She began again to climb. The dark woman with the torch seemed more intriguing than threatening.

As she climbed, 'May you tell me your name?' inquired Stealflame, blooming with her own.

She did not expect what came back. It was a sibling name, albeit minted in another tongue.

'I am Brinnajni.'

Stealflame then stopped rock still.

She said, 'You are *Burning* Flame. I am *Steal*flame. That means—'

The dark figure moved out into the daylight under the trees. She was black as black silk. She was black as Chillel. Her torch-fire hair was the copy of Lionwolf's and hung down her back to her ankles.

Oh, said Stealflame's lips, without a sound.

'Yes, yes,' said Brinnajni with ironic impatience. 'I'm *their* child. Whose are *you*?'

'Hers,' said Stealflame, 'and my mother's.'

Brinnajni gawped at her. Something so peerless, *gawping*, could not do anything but enchant. Stealflame gave an involuntary chuckle.

At this Brinnajni's beauty contorted in her clown's grin.

And Stealflame fell in love.

Standing there on Brightshade's continent, looking at her first half-sister, Stealflame gave up herself as lovers must, to reward and rapture or remorse, tyranny, hurt and Hell. No choice. No regrets.

And this Brinnajni saw. Her dagger edge blended to liking, at least to that. And up in the woods the laughter came again, this time male and female mixed.

'I was here before, this whalescape,' Brinnajni announced. 'I came back. The country has improved, I can tell you. I arrived with my other sister there, the sheep. She will be your sister too now. She and I grew up together, with no help from either of our mothers, but you fared otherwise, I think.' Stealflame nodded, ashamed of her luck. Brinnajni said, 'But you and I and our sheep have other sisters too, and some brothers as well. I don't mean the men who went running to Chillel to be clawed by her and remade as little gods. No, these stay here, all of them, and I am queen over them. You shall see.'

Stealflame said, 'But how—'

'Come, Steljeni' – Brinnajni used the version of Stealflame's name she would have been given among the herders where Brinna was born —'surely you must see not all the men who lay with our mother kept her seed intact in them till the last battle? No, they went off with other women and seeded them with it. That way they died in the White Death as mankind are pleased to call it. But the mothers lived, went away as did yours, birthed the children . . . sad tales of *their* beginnings, or gleeful ones. But other tales they are. And how they came to me another story. One day I or they may tell you. Or not.'

Stealflame caught her breath.

Burning Flame seemed gratified. 'Do you see up there, Steljeni, a makeshift house, quite domestic? The whale continent is worth a look. I explore often. When the whale comes home, I must introduce you to him. Can you fly?'

'Yes, sister.'

'I assumed you could. Let's go up then. What,' abruptly Brinnajni added, 'were you doing this morning?'

'The sun.' Modestly Stealflame cast down her eyes. Opening the closed fingers of her left hand she displayed a petite mote of something that would have charred her palm, all her arm to bone, had she not been what she was.

Brinnajni approached. She put her hand on Stealflame's wrist and bent towards the worm of sun.

'From *there*?'

'From there.'

They looked at each other over the stab of stolen sun-fire.

'What a cunning one you are, Azula,' said Brinna, using her sister's other name now.

'I didn't mean to take it. When it was changed and I – did what was needed . . . Later I only found I had.'

'The best thief, not even knowing her own theft.'

'Perhaps I should never have brought such fire to the world.'

Brinnajni put her arm over Azula's shoulders as they climbed, in fact still on foot, the rest of the distance to her shelter. It looked grandiose despite her words, if rather lopsided. Within were tiled floors and the great bed Brinna had shared with Dayadin.

'No, sister, you were clever. A link has been forged, earth with heaven. The earth has wed the sun. Spring's coming, can't you feel it? Spring will last a century. And then we'll be ready for a *Summer*. In the long evenings I expect I will tell you all their stories. Do you *like* stories?'

Where their feet had pressed the soil of Brightshade, anemones were drifting from the snow, dilute saffron like the start of the day. Merciless the black sheep grazed on them. They were mown, champed and swallowed. Impartial and harsh as fate, the sheep went from clump to clump. But on top of the hill the two sisters were laughing bell-like in the bright morning air, Flame with Flame.

If Brinnajni scries, and maybe she is too occupied to do so, what does she see now?

Aside from her own colony, all her hero brothers are scattered over the warming waking world.

On the south-eastern continent they are finding other races, mingling with and becoming heroes for *them*, ruling over them as kings and chiefs. In the depths of these lands antique Kraag cities lie hidden. So the legends have it. But since Kraag philosophy states that what is real is only what is *not*, if ever found conceivably the cities will become non-existent.

Sallus has gone home to the Southern Continent like a sword, to be the heir of a king. Dayadin in the north-west continent is with his own father and mother there, another prince, a Chaiord's son in the Holasan-garth. But Guriyuve – nomadic like his father? – refused the act of home-going. He has undertaken an odyssey across all the seas and lands. This will one day finish in his recursion to Olchibe nevertheless. That must be. For an era will arrive when a brotherhood *will* be sworn among the Children of Chillel, not least by Sallus, then king of the peoples of the Ruk, Dayadin, then High Chaiord of the Jafn nation both in the south and the north-west, and Guriyuve, Great Leader of Leaders of the Olchibe. A fourth king will swear the bond with them in that time, a man named Gunri. He will not be a child of the goddess, not even of the rogue children who are Brinnajni's subjects. But he will be a human of power and courage, lord of the united races of Vorm, Fazion and Kelp. Named for a mythic hero-poet he will be one himself. And before his death at a hundred years of age, when the Black Kings are far older yet still young, he will write something of their history and much of the saga of the Lionwolf.

But if Brinnajni scries this, it is yet to come.

Of all her brothers only Fenzi lingers alone on the island that had been Chillel's.

No other is there now. When he woke up from his short Jafn nap they had all gone, and the terror and splendour of the Spring's first sunrise was over. He had missed it. Even so the park will soon cloud with blossom, the last of the ice barrier will melt, and the liquid metal rivers harden into mines of silver, copper and orichalc.

Fenzi and the animals of the isle will wander among the groves, concerned perhaps by the increasingly fine weather and the blueness of the fluid sea. Fenzi will never take himself 'home'. What in him had been a generous sweetness will modify, through trauma, exile and brooding, to gravity and wisdom. He is to be a mage of unsurpassable knowledge, whose ability will dwarf even the acumen of the Magikoy. And this too is still to come, miles off on the horizon of his immortal life and the centuries of his world.

As for the unburned coal he picked up from the hillside, he will never throw it in any fire. Nor will he throw it away. Most likely in either case, he forgets to.

Yet only a month from the first day of the reborn sun, Fenzi will glimpse Ruxendra Ushais dancing through the dawn sky, with a huge hound bounding at her side. He will put up, like many, a respectful altar to this youthful deity of sunrise. And a while after, next to it, one to her partner the god of fire, who in the Simese mode he will call Escurjos. But to the Lionwolf Sun and to his own mother who is Night, in all his unending days he will never raise a single stone.

Under the carved and painted pillars of the Klow House, and the rafters where the hawks stalked and flared their wings, the Klow sat for their feast. Shaggy dogs patrolled the floor between the benches. The favoured lions in their house-collars posed pragmatically, knowing their warriors would feed them titbits when the food came in. The Chaiord's pair were washing each other's faces in a seemly but maybe greedy manner – licked pelt of a fellow lion being the hors d'oeuvre.

The chamber was full of smoke and noise. Torches winked on jewels. Outside in the garth was the steady note of busy coming and going, and of song. Tonight was a festival of the Klow, the Night of Those Before. From sunfall to rise they would commemorate the ancestry of their clan, its former Chaiords and greatest fighters, mages and heroes, the relatives of the present king, all the remembered dead.

With every toast someone was praised. Among these were the father and worthy brother of the current Chaiord. His other brother Rothger was not mentioned. Rothger, out in the world of men, had brought the Klow to dust. There they no longer existed save in anecdote or curse. And that was Rothger's doing. Yet while he writhed in some hell of the Other Place, all these men and women now present and correct lived on in the personal world of Athluan and his queen. And *he* was an immortal and *she* was a goddess of day. But who those were that made up their court was debatable. Undoubtedly some were the dead who had returned to accompany Athluan, men he had known and trusted, valued women of the House. Others perhaps were even spirits, the very vrixes, corrits and glers of the Jafn earthly plane. Now reformed in a cordial environment they might make well-intentioned comrades, servitors. The House Mage was probably of this sort. Very old in appearance he was hale and virile, and performed eccentric conjurings.

Just now said mage had turned a jug of black wine into a little fat black pig, which pranced about the floor to the disturbance of the dogs.

Saphay was seated at Athluan's side in her royal gown trimmed with silver and belted with garnets. She gazed at the pig wistfully. She was reminded of spells she associated with the brief babyhood of her son, funny things the Olchibe ghost Guri had arranged to make the child giggle.

A toast rang out to Conas, Athluan's honoured brother. Saphay too elevated her goblet. They drank.

She thought, *What if I had borne my son after all to Athluan . . . My son would have been white-haired, grey-eyed. Human. He would have died*, she thought, *when they cast us forth. And so would I.*

Out in the garth there was a more complex noise. Sometimes lifelike events happened here, apparently stage-managed by the composite will to pretend. This however did not sound like an upset.

A ringing knock came on the door.

The Jafn had kept the snowscape, the ice wastes. The vines here only grew, as in the past, in the hothouse or inside the windows of a room. As the door was pushed wide Saphay looked up in human astonishment. The taboos of Let's Pretend were being broken. Outside the yard was full of burgeoning roses.

Athluan's steward hastened forward. 'Chaiord, three travellers seek admittance.'

Saphay saw her husband's eyes were wide.

'Let them come in.'

And into the joyhall three men walked.

Heads shrouded, they had dressed for the Winter, in mantles of heavy fur, clothes and boots of leather. One to the right carried a huge stoppered beer-skin. The man to the left bore a glass bottle stained dark blue, and some weird striped albino dog had padded in at his side. The central figure drew all eyes. He was not the tallest of the three: they were each tall and of a height with the others. And all were strong, muscular and straight, poised as warriors in the interim of some friendly combat. Yet at him all looked first, and back to him again. Across his shoulders was slung the great carcass of a deer, ready-drained of blood.

He spoke, and his quiet voice carried to every corner, pitched like that of the perfect bard.

'The Klow feast tonight, don't you? Please accept my offering of meat for dinner. Fresh slain and kindly killed.'

Athluan had risen. Saphay also had stood up.

'Be welcome,' said Athluan. 'Say your name.'

The hood slipped back from the head of each of the three.

A sort of wordless chorus filled the hall.

Curjai, dark and fine, stood to the left with an exquisite oil of Simisey taken from one of his own altars to anoint the Jafn fire. Guri, tattooed and braided, and the potent drink of Olchibe held by one hand, stood to the right. Lionwolf raised his head the last.

For a second Saphay beheld then the wolf god from under the sea, Zeth Zezeth. For there he was, vested within a shell of gold and scarlet.

But then, across the wide room and the more than a decade of years and more than an always of estrangement, he smiled his smile of love at Saphay. And she could see that, even if Zeth was there in him, Zeth no longer wielded any influence. He had become the tinder. The flame – was *this*.

Lightly hefting off the deer carcass in the doorway, her son walked up the hall.

'Good evening, Mother. Are you well? If beauty means health, never better I'd say.'

She found she had lifted her hands and now he took them. The warmth and actuality of his touch disproved the real and the unreal both. He talked to her in the language of the start, Rukarian, and in the former flirtatious way she had forgotten.

Saphay the lioness stared into his face, his eyes.

'But you are the sun,' she said.

'I am the sun. I am energy, force and light, and so can be anywhere, in any shape I choose. I am this, and other things, and the sun too and for ever, until for ever's done with. Don't be nervous, my dear. The sunlight won't go out if I pay you a visit.' Still holding both her hands, he leaned forward and kissed her cheek.

She whispered, 'I thought even now – I'd never see you again. That would be my one last punishment.'

'But we all make mistakes, Mother. Here I am.' Then he let go just one of her hands and offered the Jafn salute, hand to heart, head unbowed, to Athluan. 'Father. You keep a rare house here. You bade me welcome. *Am* I?'

Athluan said, 'Long ago in the waste of Kraagparia I told you as much. You know it. You are my son, and welcome as long waking.' He moved around the table and embraced Lionwolf as his son. Athluan added, 'And they are welcome too. Your brother there. Even your uncle.'

The deer was taken to be portioned; here it would cook in one minute. The sensationally aromatic oil went on the hearth fire which burned blue and filled with pictures, though any dancing girls in the flames were decently clad. Guri brought the beer-skin which obviously poured on and on, never empty. He was the Star Dog Star and a planet now of morning and evening, but he too could be anywhere else, in the astral 'tween world or on the earth, as Curjai could be also. Beings of energy yet also of flesh. Mortality had taught them one of these conditions, death and rebirth the other. Gods are made by mankind.

That night, or *unnight*, or *real* night, they feasted in the hall of Athluan. Later they told stories, of Olchibe and Simisey and of the Jafn heroes Star Black and Kind Heart.

Later yet Lionwolf would go up another ladder-stair of darkness, and into its heart to his own wife, Chillel. Curjai would seek the couch of *his* wife who was the dawn, and wake her fire with his. And Guri? Guri would chase across the eternity of space, leaping meteorites and nebulas, finding out the distant stars which were not as he had ever supposed them.

But Athluan and Saphay would make love in the stone-wood bed with the lamp turned to its more shady side, and the patterned covers plunging off on the floor.

It was as he was constructing the first of the two altars, the one to Rusa Ushai, that Fenzi was joined by the chaze.

He glanced up and saw it coiled round a shrub, watching him with its cat's eyes.

He was not especially one for cats, let alone snakes.

But he recalled how it had always been with Sallus, a dependable enough man, and then it had been with Azula. Now it seemed it and she had also separated. Like himself, the chaze was on its own.

Fenzi offered it water from the gourd he brought to and from the nearby brook. The snake sipped. When Fenzi had completed the altar to dawn and put a flower and a fruit on it, the chaze went and inspected his work.

After sunfall Fenzi made a fire, obstreperously or couthly striking a flint to get it instead of any sorcery. The chaze positioned itself at the fire's far side and watched him still.

He threw it a piece of the meat he cooked.

The snake ate it.

That was a sleep night. It often was, now. When Fenzi woke at sunrise the next day the chaze lay curled against his back. At noon it brought him a dead rabbit it had hunted.

Fenzi thanked the snake. He knew it would both hear and grasp what he said. Next therefore sometimes he talked to it.

The young man thought how strange it was he had been severed from all he had known and any he had loved, and even from his own earlier self. And now his family was a poisonous white snake with a charcoal ring around its body. But he had taken up gods instead of God, too. What was a snake?

Eventually they were more used to each other. He began to fathom now and then in turn what the snake 'said' to *him*, by its body movements, and symbols it 'drew' in the ashes of the fire. Sometimes it went with him when he walked about, but they were not always together. Fenzi would go off by himself, or the snake would. Once he saw it mate with a long slender lizard. Could offspring be possible? He never learned, nor did the chaze ever tell him. But Fenzi gave the snake the name *Fron*. This, in fisher-Jafn, approximately meant your best team-fellow on a boat. The chaze accepted the name and would, when in the vicinity, come to it when called.

Occasionally too it went up again to the slope where Azula's bothy had been. The shelter had collapsed long ago, but the tree into which the snake insinuated itself had only flourished. Here the snake would lie upright in the embrace of branches.

One evening, put out by the singing birds and a little drunk on some berry liquor he had managed to ferment, Fenzi copied Fron. Wriggling his own way into another larger tree he cautiously wound back the branches to try to make them support him. He fell asleep at this and roused aggrieved, because it really was *not* a sleep night and he had behaved in a totally unJafn way. Then he found his tree had made a cocoon for him and held him firm. Only when he attempted to leave did it mellifluously unwind and let him go.

There had been mystic dreams during the forbidden sleep in the tree. One showed him that he felt the scars on his ribs to be like the strings of a harp, able to make melody. He only recollected these surrealisms gradually. When ten nights later he, and Fron, went back and repeated the procedure, other mystical dreams informed Fenzi's sleep. He discovered after about twenty similar experiences that he began to understand the speech of birds and beasts, and of the trees and plants themselves. It was the initiation of his magicianship, the beginning of the enormous genius of thaumaturgy that would come to him. And it was also the end of his aloneness and his sorrow.

TWO

Meeting a blue sky, a green land. Between the two lay Kol Cataar, the Phoenix city. The magician stared unblinking at the scene. At noon the city had that look it always had, and was intended always to have perhaps. Every wall and tower, every terrace and roof seemed designed as jewelry. But between this luminosity and his mansion, a discrepancy occurred.

He had kept the snows about his southern house. Where the fertile fields and pastures ceased his acres of Winter began. Only three miles further south beyond his house did the frazzle of blowing wheat and corn, dilf and barley blondly resume.

Thryfe's estate had become an island.

'Highness.'

Thryfe turned. Lalath was there, the female Magikoy who retained her own accommodation in the city as he did not.

'Thank you, Lalath.'

She had brought a letter from the king and other impedimenta of the court.

He was aware, with his refurbished instinct for such stuff, that Lalath believed she loved him. He felt regret for her when he remembered this. He would – could – never return even the slightest of her feelings. Being Magikoy she too would know this. She approached him where needful as one did a magus of an august order. Otherwise she never intruded herself. Had there been gods Thryfe would have thanked them for that. He did not want to be cruel.

Yet she turned like a shadow of drooping wings. And when gone she left a remnant of her frustrated desolation in his room.

Aglin was better, he thought. The mageia who had been Jemhara's friend was by now attached to the royal household, a favourite with Queen Tireh and her daughters. Aglin did not seem distrait but she had made a private shrine it was said to her Magikoy tutor, and brought offerings there to Jemhara as if to a goddess. He had not chided her for this though he believed Jema would not have liked it – perhaps she would only have laughed. People sought consolation in various ways. To Thryfe, if she should encounter him, Aglin was scrupulous in forms of respect, but she did not meet his eyes. She blamed him in some oblique manner for the loss of Jemhara. In that she was like Thryfe himself. He did not see what he could have done finally. Yet he would never quite forgive, as Aglin would not, his ultimate incompetence, his inadequacy in the grip of fate.

He vacated the room and climbed the three hundred stairs to the towery.

Some huge old books brought from the former capital rested on stands. He prowled among them, turning a page, reading a few lines, moving to another volume. Outside the windows as below, the distant twinkle of Kol Cataar.

At sunset he must go there. Bhorth had requested it.

And I would rather do anything than go, thought Thryfe with weary wryness. But it was not to be avoided. He was still Magikoy and had been detailed to serve the court of the King Paramount.

Swift as an arrow a bird flew over the casement.

It was of a sort he had not seen before in his life, though his books recorded it from the past. It had a brown body but an orange breast and flicks of azure on its wings. A novel bird of the world's Spring.

How quickly the newborn season raced. Whole forests, jungles, cast off their mail of ice, their foliage expanding to blot out the sky. Weeds and briars pierced the crevices of streets and houses. From the coast came word of splitting ice and high waters that now and then flooded inland. Their ingress was always leisurely and heralded by warnings. The fisher villages and even the small disorderly cities to the north – Thase, the enduring Kandexa – took heed and had no casualties. There was

446

a tale too of a giant wave to the south-east which had been halted and blown away by the god that none of them ever called Vash-dran – Lionwolf. In fact, like the Jafn, they had taken to calling him only *God*. For he was the sun and the sun *was* God at last. The sun had been resurrected out of the cold ocean, or the colder Hell. He rose to nourish the earth.

Thryfe's mind obstinately shifted.

He shut his eyes and thought of her.

To the deluge of pain that struck him what was a tidal wave? He reprimanded himself. He shut himself in the iron of self-control. But nevertheless, he thought on. Of her.

Long ago, not so long ago, when he pursued her to Kandexa, he had believed he could find her and save her, if needed, from whatever had encompassed her. And yet over there in that now glinting city, he had known in conquering rushes of despair that she was lost.

A god had stolen her. Another myth? A true one . . . Whatever it was, he was himself helpless. He had known, he *knew*, he would not see her again in life. And if the condition only of physical life were real, which he dreaded and trusted it was, in the nothing which followed he would not see her either.

Lionwolf – his *son* – had healed Thryfe of all maladies, all damage. Lionwolf, or *God*, had told Thryfe Jemhara lived. And Thryfe had disbelieved him. For he knew she did not. But—
There came another hour.

What had Thryfe been doing in that hour? Did he recall? He did not. For the revelation wiped everything else of it away. The revelation assured him that Jemhara had in some sense lived till then. But now, now in that exact moment she died.

He felt her die. It was so fast. Like a flower that vanished suddenly in sourceless flame. Ashes, pollen, falling. That was all. That was Jemhara. Silvery pollen falling, fading.

And he remembered then the words the god God had said to him. Thryfe had imagined Lionwolf spoke of himself, but saw that he had spoken of her. 'Destiny may sometimes be immovable. The parts we play, gods and men, may be written out for us before we are born. And in that writing we too may have colluded.' The god had meant Jemhara. And now truly the page had closed on her.

Thryfe, having he noted learned nothing after all from the tedious wicked lessons of existence, had been so sure she was already dead. But now she was. Now and for ever she . . . was.

Beyond that hour he had not progressed. He did not want to. Where else was there to go?

He served the court and the people of the city. He performed the tasks, studies and rituals essential to his vocation and his Wardenship. He even slept some spaces of each night. He even noticed special birds that flew, or the name of the Sun God. Or Kol Cataar's twinkling. But he did not leave the hour of Jemhara's dying or the words of her fate. Her fate had become his fate. Her death had become his life.

Over Southgate in the dusk the torches were blazoned. The gate stood wide – they had seen him arriving. He glimpsed the salutes of the guards. He walked through and along the streeted slopes of the city.

He climbed without pausing the thousand-stepped staircase, paying no attention to its statues.

Tonight no Gargolem manifested from an alcove. Although it had come back, it was not often in evidence here.

Other guards saluted him into the marble maw of the palace. Beyond in lamplit air lay the starry halls of the king whose complacence Thryfe had not come to spoil.

Bhorth it was who strode out of the throng to greet him.

He had grown fat again and there was grey finally in his fair hair and creases in his face, even though the God had touched him. He kept the authority of his recent years nevertheless, and his strength, one thought. Bhorth stayed honourable. Besides, he was happy now; all of them were. Sallusdon his son had come home some months ago.

'I am present,' said Thryfe placidly. 'How can I assist?'

'Ah, Magus. Well. Let's go aside into that room there, where the best wine is.'

In the room, elegantly panelled and adorned, the servers brought glass goblets of wine then removed themselves.

Through the doorway king and mage watched the court dancing to music. Tireh the queen was dancing too, with a well-clad old man. The little girl princesses were there. They were growing up. The younger had topaz hair, like the hair of Saphay, Bhorth's niece, mother of God.

'Do you see?' asked Bhorth quietly.

'Yes.' For now the king's black son went dancing by. He did not seem as he had when he returned. Now he looked almost happy too, though in his eyes age waited as it did not even in the eyes of the queen's old courtier.

'Sallus is better,' said Bhorth. 'When first he came back he wasn't like this. The gods – God – knew what had happened to him. He wouldn't and will not say, even to his mother. I mean, to Tireh. We discussed him then, did we not, you and I?'

'Yes, Bhorth.'

'And even the Oculum couldn't show you what he'd suffered.'

'That is so.'

'But now, *now* look at him. The change in him.'

'Very definitely.'

'Guess what it is.'

Thryfe watched the young prince. It did not really require magecraft.

A tall young woman danced with Sallus. Not Azula; she had not returned. This was a more average Rukarian girl, brunette and pale-skinned. She was pliant but not fragile, a little heavy perhaps but well formed. She had gold wound in her hair. Some daughter of high family.

But, 'Not royal,' said Bhorth, surprising him slightly, 'Sallus found her on the street, in a manner of saying. She's from the Ruk east outland, one of the villages there, a farmer family. Worships some goddess made of broomsticks, *Rajel* or something like that, who ruts with a star.'

He gossips now, Thryfe thought. 'And she has revived your son.'

'*Yes.* And his mother. Some women get jealous, don't they,

of their son's choice. But Tireh's only glad to see *him* glad. A fine woman, my queen. As for peasant blood in the royal house, it will build us up. God' – he had got it right this time – 'knows we need it.'

They watched the dancers changing partners and weaving through another measure. How nimbly they did that. Just so they accepted the God, and the gold rats that rambled in the alleys.

'Then what troubles you, Bhorth?'

Bhorth looked away. He stared through a window of the room into the clear and star-tipped night.

'Not myself. Sallus. And this he *has* told me. Of course he can't be like the rest, and it's what he is – how long he may live— None of us know our length of days, especially at his age, but for him, with the blood of the black woman, the goddess, in his veins— He said to me, Mage, he said he may live for ever, at least till those stars go out.'

'And she, his lover, is mortal and will die.'

To Thryfe his own words had the sound of a baleful curse. He grew ice-cold from them, but the king only nodded.

'Just so. Naturally she loves him, but he can't bring himself to confirm it. He won't have her, won't let himself take up with her though anyone can see he rattles with wanting to. Because she will die and he will go on. We'll all die and he will go on. How can he bear it?'

'I don't know, Bhorth.'

I should tell him that twenty-three days and nights of love are better than an existence without it, let alone immortality without.

I can't tell him.

It is not true.

We are better left alone inside our cells of granite.

Something odd took place in the atmosphere of the room. Beyond the door the lights went on glowing. In here a tinsel of frost seemed to form. And from some shadow another server glided out and came to them and filled their goblets from a ewer of wine.

A woman, very graceful, but she retained the shadow. She had a sombre skin. Was she black? No black women were at this court or in this city. None had ever been in these lands but one.

The servant woman murmured.

No one could have caught her words.

Thryfe did so.

'Tell Sallusdon to recall the snake which bit him.'

'Magus,' said Bhorth, 'what is it?'

There was no servant present. The cups had not been refilled. The room was hot and lit by candles.

'Some message has come to you,' said Thryfe flatly, 'or for your son. Was he ever bitten by a snake?'

'Yes, by – yes. Had no one told you? When he was a child. A chaze bit him. He killed it with his own bare hands though he was an infant. I sucked the poison from him. A little while after the snake appeared, alive and well. Did you never see it with him? Biting him I've always believed did the damn reptile good.'

Thryfe said, 'Tell your son to remember that. He must draw his own conclusion.'

'If – you say so, Magus.'

Another more frisky dance had been kindled. The participants whirled along under the latticed golden lamps.

Thryfe spoke from the past. 'Be aware, if I say to you it *is*, then you know I speak the truth.'

Bhorth checked. He did not analyse the reprise but it flew home in his mind. He would tell Sallus.

He tried then to tempt Thryfe out to the feast, where poor Magikoy Lalath stood in her feast dress, lovelorn as any girl. But Thryfe stayed less than ten minutes more. He never would.

In bed that night with Tireh, panting after their extremely rewarding exertion, the king planned how he would reveal the Magikoy message tomorrow to Sallus. He trusted Thryfe. He trusted luck too. How else had they flourished?

Lilting asleep to the lullaby of Tireh's low purring snores, Bhorth asked himself again one never answered question. Why had Chillel chosen him to lie with? All men otherwise had gone to her; so much was evident from some knowledge rooted deep within himself. All men. But he – and one other man of whom Bhorth knew nothing but that fact – were selected by the goddess herself. He did not argue at being chosen. Yet the why of it he never comprehended. He was a king, but at that time a prisoner. The other man, had he been a king too?

It would not suggest itself for many more decades to long-lived Bhorth that perhaps he and that other man, whose name Bhorth would never know to be Arok, had simply been 'chosen' because either Chillel must choose, or there had been no other free to be chosen. Luck had been the factor for both of them. It had had no other reason. Not all things must have singular purpose, even in an era of the miraculous.

But Chillel's message, if such it was, *did* have purpose.

Sallus was informed of it and grew pale in his darkness. Soon he drew the Ranjallan girl aside. He offered her his love, his heirdom, but also his blood to drink. If she gazed at him in revolt or transport none has ever described. Both? But it seems she accepted everything.

Like all his brothers and his sisters he did live for ever, or for *that* for ever, seeing that times change and their geometry with them, and even infinity may be finite. But a white queen they say ruled with him all that while. Her name was from the Ruk royal house: it was Yazmey. But she worshipped Ranjal goddess of wood. And to the consternation of Kol Cataar she refused ever to make her a single offering.

Near dawn there was an urgent hammering on the door of the mansion.

The house of a Magikoy could be concealed, and few but those Magikoy-trained would find it. Only infrequently persons *stumbled* on the spot, locating it by accident where a search would be useless. Thryfe's suburban house was not concealed. It glared from its island of snow among the ripening fields. There was one oddness by the door if any got close: a thriving shrub with fat dark flowers striped over white. A local legend insisted the hand of a woods goddess had been planted there. But as a rule none saw, for none called. Sensibly one left the magus alone.

A jinan appeared before Thryfe.

He had had less than an hour's sleep, but inquired what was wanted.

The jinan explained, by jinanic methods, that three men were below. Yet the jinan was unable to indicate their need or intention.

Thryfe threw on his clothes and went down.

Among the snow-drifts and against the widening arch of pre-dawn sky, one man waited by the cavernous entrance. Another, possibly awkward, stood a short way off, and yet another a dozen feet further along.

From the look of them they were labourers or itinerant farm workers. Plenty such had come to Kol Cataar. Their garments were rough and too thermal for the Spring climate, if not for Thryfe's snow.

'Highness Thryfe,' said the man by the door, and he bowed. In the muffle of his hood a square weather-beaten face was partly visible. He looked shy and in awe but steadfastly determined. He carried something small too, inside a sack in his arms. The other men were more nondescript. The nearer had a fur hood, the farthest off hung a head of shaggy black hair and studied his black nails.

Thryfe said, 'Do you need my help?'

'In a way, Highness.'

Something came to Thryfe. Was this near one actually fawning slyly, making a performance of his own humbleness? Some plot? Absurd. None but a fool threatened the Magikoy.

'Like this it is,' said the suspect labourer. 'We are up the field. Bit of a fire starts. Puts it out. But then this hare runs from the stalks. Think it were a girl, but then no, no girl. But this. And she runs this way, towards your house here, Highness. So and we come to see. But then she's all bemused, like she would be. Go I, gets her gentle and picks her up and brings her.' The man held out the filled sack which now, unnervingly, gave off a sinuous lurch of motion. 'Was all,' said the man in a different, stranger tone, 'I could bring away from there. Out of the ash.'

Thryfe stared down at the sack. And either the man smoothed it off and away, or the substance of it parted.

So he saw.

In the arm of the man sat a jet-black hare, long ears like sable petals folded back, black gem eyes fixed only on Thryfe.

Thryfe could not speak.

He said, even so, 'Out of the fire, you say, the ash.'

'Oh yes, High Father. Out of the fire. All I could bring away. Not quite herself. But all I could bring you. Out of the fire.'

The hare lifted herself, and Thryfe saw something gleam, snagged there in her fur against the breast, like a hollow teardrop. She launched herself forward and he found he gathered and gripped her, gripped her tight. In *his* arms now.

'See, High Father. She likes you. You it was she wanted.'

'What—' Thryfe tried again. 'What is that caught in her pelt?'

'A ring it is, tarnished silver.'

The man in the middle distance said, 'He thinks we'd steal it so why have we not?'

'Now, Uncle. He never does. Excuse my old uncle, sir. He has the feverish Olchibe blood. And that's my brother, over there. He's a boyo and no mistake. Come oversea and the girls won't leave him alone.'

A flash of white teeth from the third man then. And braids sliding out of the Olchibe one's hood. And this one, this one on the doorstep, his blue eyes in the square and wind-burned face, blue as the sky of dawn-dusk was going, and each with a glint of crimson red.

But Thryfe could say nothing, only hold the plush and living body of the little black hare, with his ring he had given her in her human time tangled in her fur.

'She's all I could bring away from the fire,' the first man said again. His voice was like the stillness of the earth. 'She *is* there, I swear to you, Thryfe, her *soul* is there. But never in this life again can she be human. Wait till the next life, Father. Till then, keep her safe. She knows you, if not all she did. Until next time, Highness. Keep her safe.'

And Thryfe stands by his door in the seconds that prologue sunrise, holding the black hare in his arms. And the three men turn and walk away, and their shambling becomes striding, and at the perimeter of the snow, between Winter and Spring, dark and day, each one vanishes. Like a star, like a flame, like a sun.

How long after? Years, half a century. Thryfe the magician is long-lived too and barely changes, and his pet creature the hare, she thrives and lives on too. She *will* live as long as he does. On their last journey neither means to set off alone. There has been enough of that.

This evening, and when it is only the new gods know, Thryfe sits before the magic mirror of the oculum, and he strokes her soft head. She is no pet, of course. Nor is she, as he was told, Jemhara any more. But something within her *is* Jemhara and has persisted. And he loves her, she him. Passionate committed love need not always be sexual, nor pinned between the same species. Love is *love*.

Together then they watch as the oculum sweeps through the continents, conjuring cities as they rise, and garths and sluhtins and all the congress of peoples also rising from the grave of genocide and of the ice. The ice has mainly gone away, retreating to mountains by now. And as the seas have risen from vast waves and meltwater, islands decorate the coasts where once the ice fields clutched them.

Groups of Stones too the oculum has looked at, the tall standing Stones that dot the continents and formerly gave off lapis light and green, and now one and all are only blank grey monoliths leaning up on the air. Silently they form the markers of an active power that grows latent, if hardly lax. Even the Gargolem has obeyed this power. In the end even Winter has had to kneel before it.

Thryfe has known a great while.

Much of mankind knows.

All come to it in diverse ways, often via parochial concepts. But all have solved, or will solve, this ultimate equation.

While on this calm evening Thryfe is to be granted a final definitive vision. It is the profound reply which only the Final

and Profound God can render, and that solely to the psychic and
the mage.

It happens.

The oculum having shown so much, including even the artist-
ically forested continent of Brightshade up by the pole, shimmer-
clouds like abalone. And through the smog someone appears.
Someone – something— What, what is here?

I am here—

She says.

She. Yes, a goddess, of a sort. One of the Gods of the Ultimate
Equation.

Through Thryfe's brain slip all the strategies of the board
game he and humankind, godkind, have been made to play.
What has seemed autonomous has frequently *not* been. What
has seemed to be manipulation – *is*.

And in the mage-mirror these segments float and organize
themselves before him.

The birth of Saphay he sees, and how she has sprung from a
will more potent than any mortal process. The rape of her by Zeth
he sees, and the rape in turn *of* Zeth by Saphay, the robbery of
sunfire. Yet it is *not* by Saphay but by what is *in* her, what has *made*
her for that very deed. In a surge the images chase across the sorcerous screen, each act of the story from opening line to last. Even
Thryfe is there, he and Jemhara, little pieces on the colossal board.

And he beholds the two of them far back, in that previous
mansion when the Ice Age ruled. When time fractured and slid
in panes, staying one and propelling the other onward, the Eagle
and the Hare, so they should fatally meet and so be snared. And
then the timeless gap of their orgasmic first lovemaking, which
preserved them both from the White Death. And he had blamed
her for all that, for snaring him. But neither she nor he had been
guilty. The ice-web of time had saved them for the convenience
of what moved them on the board, before, and since.

And what has moved not only them, but all of them, all and
everything, is this other that now he sees in the mirror. This
Other.

And She speaks again. She speaks.

She is female, the image in the oculum.

Indescribable?

Yes. Or is there the slightest hint in Her of Saphay? Perhaps, perhaps. Why is that inexplicable when Saphay was the firstborn creation, the very first game-piece of all? And in some ways the strongest of them all, perhaps having to be so. The most like her *Mother*.

And is this barely describable She beautiful?

Beautiful and terrible. And compassionate. And without pity.

And *what* is She?

The world, that is who and what She is. She is the *earth*.

Five centuries of Winter smothered and chained Her. Her lovely mantle, Her precious body and locks of fabulous hair. Her lands, Her seas, Her verdure, the life that is Her children, man and beast, all these enslaved, and in the cold forgetting Her. Of course She would rebel and plan Her freedom.

And deep within, as She has broadcast in Her Stones, Her fire still flaming bright. Bright enough at last to cause another sun.

To Thryfe She speaks, and so to the hare, who listens also.

To the whole earth She speaks, She who *is* the earth.

Never believe you have done any of this. Nor have they done it, the pantheon of gods I have made you. Not even he, the Sun. *My* Sun. *My* son. Save only through Me.

None can steal My fire unless I grant its use. For who but I lighted the fire of all things in the world? There is only One igniting Flame. And this belongs neither to men nor to gods. It is Mine, and Mine alone.

No Flame but Mine.

. . . Ended . . .

THE LIONWOLF TRILOGY

GLOSSARY

Balnakalf – Whale foetus: Rukarian

Borjiy – Berserker, fearless fighter: Jafn

Chachadraj – A cat-dog, product of the mating of a cat and a dog (see also **Drajjerchach**): Gech originally

Chaiord – Clan chieftain/king: Jafn

Corrit – Demon-sprite: Jafn

Crait – Type of lammergeyer: Rukarian uplands

Crarrow (pl. **Crarrowin**) – Coven witches of Olchibe and parts of Gech

Crax – Chief witch of **Crarrowin** coven

Cruin – Coven witches of Gech in the time of Sham; by later eras they are more usually called also **Crarrowin**

Cutch – Fuck: Jafn and elsewhere

Dight – To make love, or fuck

Dilf – One of several forms of dormant grain and cereal: general, but found mostly in more fertile areas

Doy – A masturbatory aid used by one unable to find a woman; often applied however to a woman deemed unsatisfactory: Rukarian

Drajjerchach – Dog-cat, product of the mating of a dog and a cat (see also **Chachadraj**): Gech originally

Dromaz (pl. **Dromazi**) – Type of camelid: Simese

Endhlefon – Time period of eleven days: Jafn

Firefex – Phoenix: Rukarian
Fleer-wolves – A kind of wolf-like jackal: general to the Ruk
Forcutcher – Insulting variation, of obscure exact meaning,
  deriving from the word **cutch**

Gargolem – Magically activated metallic non-human servant;
  the greatest of these creatures guarded the kings at Ru
  Karismi prior to the White Death: Rukarian
Gler – Demon-sprite fond of taking on human form: Jafn
Gosand – type of wild goose: Simese
Graron – Rogue leek or garlic, normally a hot-house crop

Hnowa – Riding animal: Jafn
Horsaz (pl. **Horsazin**) – A breed of horse apparently part-bred
  with fish; scaled and acclimated to land and ocean: Fazion,
  Kelp and Vorm
Hovor – Wind-spirit: Jafn

Insularia – Sub-river complex belonging solely to, and solely
  accessible to, the **Magikoy**: Ru Karismi

Jatcha – Hound of Hell, normally only encountered beyond
  life
Jinan/Jinnan – Magically activated house-spirit: Rukarian –
  Magikoy

Kadi – Type of gull general to the Southern Continent
Kiddle/kiddling – Baby or child up to twelve years: an
  Olchibe term which, due to the war, has spread

Lamascep – Sheep of long, thick wool: general to the Ruk
Lashdeer – Fine-bred, highly trained chariot animals used for
  high-speed travel over snow and ice: Rukarian

Mageia/Magio – Female and male witch or lesser mage: rural
  Ruk Kar Is, and elsewhere in the north
Magikoy – Order of magician-scholars, established centuries in

the past; possessed of extraordinary and closely guarded
powers: Ruk Kar Is and elsewhere in the Ruk

Maxamitan Level – Highest level of achievement available to
Magikoy apprentice; the next step is to become a **Magikoy**
Master (NB not all **Magikoy** however are known as
'Masters'): Ruk Kar Is

Morsonesta – Burial ground located in the **Insularia** of the
Magikoy: Ru Karismi

Oculum – **Magikoy** scrying glass, or magic mirror of
incredible scope: Ruk Kar Is

Ourth – Elephant or (especially) mammoth: Olchibe

Prak – Derogatory term for a 'loose' woman; the nearest
equivalent is 'slag': Rukarian, but also found elsewhere

Ruk/Ruk Kar Is – Definition; Ruk Kar Is refers mainly to the
more populated and 'civilized' areas of the Ruk, such as
cities, ports. The term Ruk involves the whole region and
includes the eastern backlands and parts of the Marginal.

Scrat – Type of rat; see also **scratchered**: general to Southern
Continent

Scratchered – Basically, over-used: Jafn in origin

Seef – Demon, type of vampire: Jafn

Sihpp – Similar to **Seef**: Jafn

Slederie – Primitive land-raft drawn by sheep or sometimes
dogs: Ruk and south-east mostly

Slee – Riding ice-carriage: Rukarian

Sleekar – Deer-drawn ice-chariot: Rukarian

Sluhtins – Large city groupings of **sluhts**: Olchibe

Sluhts – Communal tent/cave/hut dwellings: Olchibe

Tibbuk – Room kept for the inhaling of various smokes to do
with scrying and prophecy: shamanic Simese

Towery – Complex of towers connected to each other by
walkways and/or inner passages: **Magikoy**, Ruk Kar Is

Trech – A prostitute who cheats or steals from an honest client: backland Ruk

Vrix – Demon-sprite : Jafn

Werloka – Male witch: Jafn

White Death – The fatal energy blast, and also subsequent plague, that resulted from the unleashing of **Magikoy** weapons against the horde of the Lionwolf: general